Griselda Rella

by

Lee Renwick Steele

Griselda Rella

Cover Art by *The Wild Rose Press, Inc.*

The Wild Rose Press, Inc.
PO Box 708
Adams Basin, NY 14410-0708
Visit us at www.thewildrosepress.com

Publishing History
First Edition, 2023
Trade Paperback ISBN 978-1-5092-4408-9
Digital ISBN 978-1-5092-4409-6

Published in the United States of America

I strode across the dandelion-dotted yard scattering chickens, robins, and fairies in my haste, an open-ended basket swinging from one hand, a pair of clippers clenched in the other, my mind whirling like a storm. No one could replace my father, not for me, not for my family, not for the kingdom.

Reaching the flowers bordering the yard, I threw the basket and clippers on the dirt near the dried-up hyacinths and daffodils. "Stupid bandits," I sobbed, snot dripping from my nose. "Stupid, stupid bandits."

The sun, now one-quarter of its journey through the sky, warmed my face but not my heart. I brushed past the flowering red azaleas and pink rhododendrons, skirted around Isabella's arbor-covered garden bench, angled through the freshly sprouting vegetable and herb gardens, and stumbled my way past the sheds to the fallow field about an arrow's shot from the cottage.

I threw my black-clothed self to the ground and glared back at the cottage. How could my mother marry this man, Lord Rella, not yet two months after my father's death? He was wealthy to be sure, but the man had very little sense—I was sure of it. And he would never be a father to me.

Dedication

To Neil

Prologue

Fairy sight—that was the problem. So mused newly crowned King Benedict as he sat uneasily on his ill-gotten throne.

After poisoning his stepbrother, pretending to grieve over his death, and usurping the throne, Benedict had an annoying dilemma.

The murdered king's infant son.

Of course, he'd claimed that the little prince had died of the same sudden illness that had killed the king. But he knew better. The queen had disappeared with the babe. Whispered rumors abounded.

Somewhere out there was a child with the king's legacy of fairy sight who could grow up to ruin him, to claim the throne.

Fingering the royal scepter in his hands, he pondered.

What to do?

He called for a quill, parchment, and writing desk and began to compose.

Be it known that the recent deaths of the king and the prince, as well as the current poor crop conditions, are the product of the nefarious actions of those with the highly suspicious trait of fairy sight. Therefore, by order of the king, and in order to maintain the peace and prosperity of the kingdom, fairy sight shall henceforth be a crime. Any person suspected of fairy sight shall be apprehended, tried, and if found guilty, executed.

King Benedict scanned the document, knowing all the allegations to be weak and false but necessary to protect his reign and that of his descendants. If he burned all troublesome historical records and blamed all the kingdom's maladies on wicked miscreants with fairy sight, he would have a convenient scapegoat for anything that went amiss. Also, it would reshape his subjects' perceptions regarding the rare gift.

He drummed his fingers on the arm of his throne and decided. Examples would have to be made—immediately.

****

One hundred fifty years later…

Chapter 1

A Perilous Secret

I watched the fairies rise in the air to welcome the sunrise. Nature's winged caretakers spread their arms wide and absorbed the life-giving radiance. Shafts of light crept across the horizon, and a robin called its greeting to the chilly spring morn.

Errant chickens pecked around the yard of my home, Hart Cottage, and a couple of milk cows lowed in the stable. Our dog, Rags, stood watch next to Father's horse, a dark bay with black mane and tail, saddled and grazing near the dwelling door. Otherwise, no one observed me.

I glanced about one more time to ensure that my parents weren't watching, especially Mother. Then I secreted myself near the dark green leaves of our tree-height rhododendron shrubs and stealthily joined the fairies in their morning ritual, albeit with my feet firmly settled on the dew-dampened earth.

As I opened my arms, the sun's warmth filled me like food and drink, but I, unlike the fairies, would be eager for a hearty meal later in the day.

Several seconds passed, my body tingling with a giddy sense of well-being. Then, while concentrating on the feel of sunlight, I exhaled, bringing my palms together. Next, I inhaled deeply, expanding my arms and straining to pull new fairies—any fairies, even just one—into manifestation. The exercise completed, I looked about to see if any points of light containing brand new fairies shimmered in front of me.

Nothing.

No new fairies.

Failure—again.

My shoulders sagged as I watched the tiny, vary-colored sprites disperse to tend trees, shrubs, flowering daffodils, fragrant hyacinths, and freshly plowed soil that would soon sprout with spring plantings.

Everyone knew, whether able to see them or not, that plants needed fairies, along with sun, rain, and good soil, in order to grow healthy and abundant. At least that's what our mythology taught. The problem was that many of this sisterhood of fairies eventually faded back into the light, so new fairies needed to be pulled from the unseen realm regularly, especially in cultivated areas. And no matter how much I strained, I couldn't do it.

The garden pixies closest to me hummed, sending vibrations of life and growth into the swelling rhododendron buds. I examined their activity, trying to determine if they might also be singing but could not tell. Although the winged ones usually expanded their radiance when I was about, now engrossed in their labors, they paid me no mind.

Feeling left out, I breathed in the smell of the dew-dampened earth, tightened my wool cloak around my ankle-length tunic, and moved carefully away from them, an empty feeling spreading in my gut. Yes, I could see fairies, but I didn't fit into their world.

And to make matters worse, since only my father

and I shared the condemned gift of fairy sight, I felt isolated—and threatened—in my own world as well.

In any case, no matter the difficulty, I would have to learn to pull fairies from the unseen. My father depended on it—and so did the kingdom. But how could I continue in the face of these repeated disappointments?

As if to interrupt my melancholy moment, the mare near the cottage door blew out a sputtering breath and shook her head, reins slapping against her neck.

My mother's anxious voice called from the cottage. "Matthew, I can't have it while you are gone. Griselda takes your protection for granted. You must make her stop. I beg you."

I cringed, looked up, and saw my father, Matthew Hart, framed in the doorway of our two-story stone, wood, and plaster home. His brown tunic hung almost to the knees of his black breeches, his travel-worn boots shone with fresh polish, and his cloak draped from his shoulders. A sheathed sword and knife hung from his belt.

In spite of all my caution, I had been caught.

Mother, still wearing her linen nightgown and a thick blonde braid down her back, appeared behind Father, a worried expression stamped on her face. "It grieves me to nag, but Griselda is much too old for such carelessness. It frightens me."

Father, his wavy chestnut hair brushing his shoulders, inclined his head toward his wife and took her hand. "Constance, my dear, I will speak to Griselda."

"Very well," she said, rising to her toes to exchange a quick kiss. "Now, see to it that you return to me swiftly and safely."

While simply chagrined that I'd been caught interacting with fairies, I battled a mounting twinge of guilt at her accusation that I took Father's protection for granted.

No, I didn't.

And even if I did, why shouldn't I?

Mother took Father for granted.

The entire kingdom took Father for granted—though they did not know it.

My father was the mortar that held the kingdom together. All was well. What could possibly go wrong with Father advising the king?

Part of me wanted to argue with Mother, but in Father's presence, I swallowed any retort. Another part of me, a reluctantly generous part, knew that Mother's overprotectiveness was only out of fear for the safety of the two family members with fairy sight—Father and me.

Now, regarding her concern for Father's travel safety, I concurred with Mother completely and fretted along with her whenever he departed. We both knew that Father would be secretly violating the king's law every day of his absence. This always planted fear in my heart, which lasted as long as he was away.

However, I had another reason to lament his departure. Whenever Father traveled, Mother tried to rein me in—as she was doing right now—in a manner that she never did when he was home. She wanted me to be as submissive as my sister, Isabella, a silken blonde replica of my mother, as opposed to my chestnut-haired, green-eyed resemblance to my father. And no matter how hard I tried, and I really did try—

sometimes—I failed.

I attempted—very charitably—to send Mother a look of contrition. In return, she directed an expression of long-suffering across the yard at me and retreated inside, leaving me to stew in her displeasure.

Father, holding the reins in one hand and an oddly shiny, lumpy package in the other, led his horse across the grassy yard toward me, the newly risen sun casting long shadows from them. The squeak of bulging saddlebags heralded the commencement of another long journey. Rags trotted at his side.

An advisor, and sometime tax collector, for the king, Father, like my grandfather and great-grandfathers before him, traveled the realm managing the monarch's affairs and collecting the royal duties. But his real reason for the occupation was to pull fairies from the light into manifestation throughout the cultivated areas of the sovereignty. This ensured healthy, vibrant growth of plants and warded off crop failure, famine, and gods forbid, imps, which I had never seen and hoped never to see. He faithfully performed this vital, though secretive, service for the kingdom year after year.

Unfortunately, interacting with fairies was dangerous, because fairy sight was outlawed in the realm. Even though no one had been executed in my lifetime, many had lost their heads under previous kings. The law still stated:

Any person suspected of fairy sight shall be apprehended, tried, and if found guilty, executed.

The specter of having my father's head chopped off—or mine—chilled me to my bones in spite of the sun's warming rays.

Fortunately, Father did not need to use the obvious

movement and breathing technique for drawing fairies. He could pull fairies from light by single-minded concentration, so there was little chance that he would be discovered. I, on the other hand, had no such skill.

Reaching me, Father put a hand on my shoulder and gave me a stern but gentle look. "Griselda, I must ask you not to join in with the fairies while I am gone."

An obstinate whine crept into my voice. "But I still can't manifest fairies like you can."

"You are trying too hard, my dear, but do not fret, you will learn in time." Then, chin tilted down, mouth in a firm line, his eyes bored into me. "But for now, you need to stop."

I sighed and dropped my head. Joining the morning ritual was such an enjoyable way to start the day. "But only Mother is watching for me. No one else is, and I can try harder to be discreet."

Father shook his head, and his hand squeezed my shoulder affectionately. "Not while I am gone, Griselda."

A robin singing from the apex of Hart Cottage seemed to mock my curbed freedom. I exhaled a theatrical sigh, glancing down and shuffling my shoes in the moist dirt near some aromatic hyacinth blooms, which grew in a row in front of the rhododendrons, interspersed with the daffodils and soon-to-bloom tulip buds. "It's just so hard to be different."

When I looked back up, Father's face wore his frustratingly familiar shuttered look, and I knew that he was withholding secrets from me—again. But then, after hesitating, his expression opened. And he said something unexpected and most welcome. "When I return, we will have a long talk—perhaps an overdue talk—about our gift, how to use it, and why only we—"

I gasped. "Oh—why not now? Can you not tell me something now?"

He looked across the yard, past Hart Cottage Lane, and down Castle Road. I followed his gaze to see a couple of riders coming our way.

Father looked from the riders to me and shook his head. "There is not enough time. So for now, obey your mother."

Vexed about the delay of the long-desired talk, I fumed. "I will try to obey Mother."

Father's eyes widened slowly.

Feeling remorseful and also a bit trapped, I tried again. "I will obey Mother."

Father gave me a half smile, and his hand slid from my shoulder. "You are a good girl."

Knowing that I really wasn't such a good girl but desperately wanting to be, I held my tongue, threw my arms around him as if I were a young girl, and complained into his rough woolen tunic. "If I'd been a boy I could go with you," I said, voicing a source of pain. Even though Father never mentioned it, I always wondered if he wished I had been a boy to follow in his footsteps and those of my grandfathers. Was I a grave disappointment?

His head bent to my ear, he whispered, "But I am glad that you are a girl."

Wanting to believe him, but fearing that he was simply sparing me from grief, I felt even more strongly a reluctance to let him depart. "I wish you didn't have to go."

Father patted my back. "And I am sorry to leave you."

I pushed back, my hands still on the sides just above his belt, and sniffed. "But you have to."

The warmth of morning sunlight enveloped me, cutting the morning chill as he touched his forehead to the top of my head. "We must be who we are meant to be, even if it is hard. And for me, it is my duty—and my honor—to be of service. The land and people depend on it."

I inhaled sharply, dropped my hands, and straightened. "Yes, but you will be careful."

Father nodded. "As should you."

We both knew that the curtailment of my morning ritual and the care Father took in his work with the fairies prevented the same type of peril.

Though unsatisfied, I knew the subject was closed, so I shifted my attention. My gaze fell on the lumpy parcel that Father held. It had a soft luminescence. I widened my eyes inquiringly.

"Ah, yes," Father said. Then he paused and looked down Hart Cottage Lane toward Fairian Castle, its turrets piercing the sparsely clouded sunrise, colorful banners trembling in the chilly breeze. His hesitancy caused my interest to pique. And then even more so when the local fairy queen, Arianna, winged her six-inch, petal-pink-frocked self in from the adjacent fields and settled on Father's shoulder. She grinned at me and glanced expectantly at the glowing package. A flurry of smaller fairies, about one to two inches in size, followed her and hovered over Father's head creating a multicolored, fluttering halo at which he huffed out a chuckle.

Holding the bundle with both hands, Father pressed his lips together into a grimace. He glanced down at me, and his face colored just a touch. This uncharacteristic behavior puzzled me greatly to the point that I grew wary.

"What's in the wrapping?"

Still he delayed, which sent my imagination into a gallop. Was it some requirement from Mother? Some restriction on my activities? How could such a thing be wrapped? The robin, now vocalizing from the kitchen roof, seemed to boast of its liberty while I feared for my independence.

Finally, Father said, "Uh, you are now sixteen, and I have noticed that you and Prince Charmain have grown quite fond of one another."

My face flamed like a lightning strike. This was the very last thing I expected to hear, and I hardly wished to discuss my friendship with our prince with my father. I shrugged.

A sideways glance from Father to Arianna told me that they were communicating wordlessly together, another skill that I had not mastered.

With arms folded across my chest, I scowled. "Uh-hum, telling secrets?"

Arianna looked mischievous and giggled, which sent the haloing sprites spiraling upward in merriment. "Of course. But you could understand if you practiced."

I rolled my eyes at both the playful queen and my parent.

Father, however, did not share Arianna's mirth. He nodded and straightened. "Very well. Griselda, this will surprise you, but I ask for your forbearance."

Arianna, with fluttering cohorts circling overhead, now beamed so happily that the news couldn't be as ominous as it sounded, so I mumbled, "As you wish," and gave him my guarded attention.

"I wish to find a means to eliminate the law against fairy sight, and I have a quiet, rather long-term, plan to do so."

"Oh," I said with relief, "that's welcome news." So far this sounded great, but I couldn't imagine how a tax collector, my friendship with the prince, and a lumpy bundle would accomplish this. I raised my eyebrows in question. "How?"

My father's eyes fell. He actually looked at the ground and shuffled his feet. I don't remember ever seeing him do that before, not when he cautiously stood his ground advising the king, and certainly not before me. This reticence on my father's part made me very uncomfortable.

When he looked at me again, it was with an apologetic expression. "I don't know what else to do but to come out and say it." He inhaled deeply, exhaled, and steeled himself to continue. "If you and Prince Charmain were to wed, you could encourage him to change the law when he became king. Or in any case, your child would have fairy sight, and then eventually, as ruler, he would naturally abolish the law."

Startled, I took a step back, pressing into the rhododendrons and crushing a hyacinth that exuded its floral sweetness, my eyes bugging open and my jaw dropping.

Father looked both embarrassed and winded after presenting this implausible plan, his eyes on me with both uneasiness and hope.

To delay my response, I glanced to the side at our soon-to-be-planted vegetable and kitchen gardens, scanned farther to the animal sheds with attached pens for pigs, cows, chickens, and sheep, and finally gazed at the orchard trees beyond, all the while pondering how to answer. In truth, the prince frequently threatened to marry me, but I knew it was only in jest. My heart skipped a beat. Wasn't it?

Hitching my jaw back up, I declared the obvious. "But Prince Charmain must make a political marriage. The king will demand this."

"That…" Father held the glowing packet out to me. "That is where these will be of service."

I grasped the lightweight, linen-wrapped item and peered up at Father.

He nodded. "Open it—carefully."

With a touch of trepidation mixed with curiosity, I unwound the rough fabric and exposed a pair of white linen slipper-like shoes that shone like moonlight. Arianna launched herself from Father's shoulder, hovered next to the shoes, and stroked the shiny fabric uppers, her fingers leaving a trail of sparkles. The other fairies, now tightly orbiting Father's head like a colorful, moving crown, similarly sparkled with excitement.

"Oh," I said, laughing at the circling sprites. "What makes them shine so?"

Father grinned and tilted his head toward a beaming Arianna. "Fairy blessing."

Holding the slippers gave me a hint of the giddy feeling experienced during the fairies' morning ritual. Clearly, they had some special virtue, but I still didn't understand how they would facilitate Father's plan.

I frowned with confusion. "So how do they help?"

Arianna fluttered back to Father's shoulder. She looked quite smug while he gave a little smirk and a tiny snort of amusement—wordless communication. I felt left out—again.

"A fairy-blessed item grants the wearer increased influence over others, influence that varies with the willpower of those involved. You already have natural influence over the prince." He stopped, looking embarrassed once more, and hastened to add. "An influence that is just and honest."

My embarrassment spiking, my face pulsed once again with warmth.

Father pointed at the shoes. "The true use for the slippers is to give a nudge to the king, who likes you very much, to allow the prince to follow his natural inclinations." He paused. "That is—if you are interested."

Bewildered by this awkward conversation and extraordinary plan, I wondered if my solid, dependable father, the backbone of the entire kingdom—at least in my opinion—was still in his right mind. I stood speechless, holding the shiny footwear. Father took them, gently wrapped them in the fabric, and returned them to me.

As if acknowledging that a ceremony had been completed, Arianna took off from Father's shoulder, performed a little air curtsy, gave the package a sparkly little finger tap, and flew off with a grin, the other fairies following.

Father watched them depart. "I know this is unexpected—and seemingly overreaching," he said, "but I am trying to contrive a way to protect you and anyone with fairy sight in the future—permanently."

I took a deep breath. "I don't know what to say. I'd never considered any such thing."

He cupped his hand gently on the side of my head. "Regardless of your decision, these useful little shoes are my gift for you. Now, I beg you to ponder the plan while I am gone, and when I return, you may let me know your thoughts. This will also involve our overdue talk about fairy sight."

At the comment about fairy sight, questions multiplied in my mind, but before I could reply, the clop, clop of horses on Hart Cottage Lane caused us to turn. Two red-and-black-clad, sword-bearing guards—only two, I noted—approached, ready to escort my father on his journey. Father's friend Captain Branner was not with them.

He bent and kissed the top of my head, his hands resting on my shoulders. Then he straightened, dropping his hands. "Well, I'm off."

I stepped back as he moved to the side of his mare, Lady, making ready to mount. "What is your route?"

Father inclined his head in the direction of the King's Forest, the vast woodland area south of the castle where nobles hunted for game. "Head south on King's Way, then southwest on the Great Road past Lookout Mountain, visit the southwestern castles and manors, loop south around the Dead Castle."

We both cringed at the mention of the infamous site.

"And then back up to Rella Manor to find out why Lord Rella is behind on his taxes."

I recalled my image of the portly, jovial noble, who had recently lost his reclusive wife. "Isn't he very rich?"

"Yes, quite, which is why it is all so puzzling." And then with a command to Rags to "Stay with

Griselda" and a nod toward the gate, he mounted his horse.

I sprinted across the yard, opened the gate, let him through, and quickly shut the gate so that none of the chickens would get out.

As Father joined his companions, Mother, a robe now over her nightclothes, crossed the yard and joined Rags and me, her arm sliding around my waist, her annoyance with me forgotten—for now. Mother and I exchanged a companionable look; missing Father when he was gone was one thing we shared with certainty. We raised our hands in farewell. Father returned the gesture and turned his face to the road.

We watched him as he moved farther and farther away. Then Mother glanced down at my glowing gift with a frown. "Griselda, I want you to keep those securely in your bedchamber until your father returns."

"He told you his plan?" It felt awkward to ask, because Father and I did not have secrets from Mother. However, she did not like to discuss the matter of fairy sight. In fact, she usually pretended that it didn't exist at all. So I wondered if this might be one of those times when Mother kept her distance from the uncomfortable truth.

Returning her gaze to Father's diminishing figure, she sighed. "Of course, he informed me, though I am not certain that I agree."

This did not surprise me, but it did surprise me that she was voicing her disagreement to me. She and Father occasionally had lively discussions about me in private but always presented a unified front when dealing with me or my sister, Isabella, who rarely caused concern, being more cooperative and without fairy sight.

So fearing to be a cause of future arguments, I gave a noncommittal "Hmm."

As we stood there side by side, more clouds crept in, blocking the sun and dropping the temperature. The riders became smaller and smaller. My heart felt like a hand reaching for my father as I watched until he disappeared around a bend in the road. There was finality to it. Father was gone.

Mother tightened her arm around my waist. "I will not be worry-free until your father returns."

I squeezed back. But though I shared Mother's concern, I didn't want to succumb to her tendency to worry too much—about everything. After all, Father always came home. A number of weeks and he would return. He always did.

All would be well.

Chapter 2

Tell No One

After offering to put the new slippers in my bedchamber and reminding me of embroidery to be done, Mother retreated to the cottage, leaving me with a confused mixture of excitement and uneasiness. I mulled over Father's practical but overreaching scheme to protect me from a deadly fate and shivered. From the threat of execution or the threat of wedlock, I wasn't sure. Of course, I did like the prince. But marriage?

Hmmm. Father wanted me to consider his plan, so perhaps one of my unannounced morning visits to Prince Charmain at Fairian Castle was in order. I took a few steps in that direction, paused, and decided I needed more time to mull over how I felt before interacting with my friend. Besides, His Highness would probably still be abed. Not that I minded the entertainment of rousting him from sleep, which his servants enjoyed, too, but today I'd pass on the merriment. Besides my belly was beginning to growl.

More clouds formed in the south as I headed across the yard to the rambling assortment of buildings I called home. I barged through the door of the stone kitchen and workroom structure and was welcomed by the scent of freshly baked bread. Several fresh loaves were cooling on a trestle table. My mouth watered as I scanned the familiar scene. Barrels, sacks, and bins filled with fresh, salted, smoked, and dried foodstuffs lined the walls and rested under the tables. A basket with eggs from the chicken coop and a pail of milk sat on the table, compliments of my before-sunrise efforts. Herbs hung from the rafters, and metal utensils hung from a row of hooks near the fireplace, which heated the room. Our servants, Sarah and Abigail, wearing white aprons over ankle-length gray tunics, plucked a chicken and minded a cauldron of pottage respectively.

As my hand darted out, pulled off a hunk of bread warm from the oven, and shoved it in my mouth, Sarah planted her sturdy self in my path, one hand on her hip, the half-plucked fowl hanging from the other. "Miss Griselda, jus' where've you been since gatherin' those eggs?"

I lifted my open palms, the picture of innocence. "Nowhere," I said, the bread garbling my words, "just said 'Goodbye' to Father."

Abigail smiled, shook her sweet, gray-haired head, and went back to tending the pottage. Sarah, on the other hand, plopped her limp bird on the trestle table with a thump and pointed her thick finger at me. "Now, you listen here, young lady. What I want from you is fer you to give heed to yer mother, or there'll be no peace in this house until yer father returns."

Part of me—sadly a very tiny part—wanted to follow Sarah's advice to walk demurely into the parlor, pick up my embroidery, and cooperate like Father had requested. Part of me yearned to race after Father and beg his secrets now. I could easily catch him. I was fast. And part of me—a worried like Mother part—longed to run up the Lookout Mountain to glimpse Father en route. I settled on the open air. After all, I rationalized; there was plenty of time to imprison myself in the house later.

My eyes strayed longingly to the fragrant loaf I'd gouged. I placed my hands together beseechingly. Abigail chuckled, and Sarah scowled, but she grabbed a knife, sliced off a huge chunk, and handed it to me. I accepted the bread with a grin and took a bite.

"Sarah," I mumbled, my mouth still full, "you could sell this. It's better than anything at the market."

"Don't think you can butter me up with praise, young wildling," Sarah said as she dropped the knife, grabbed a wooden spoon, and took a swipe at me. I dodged her swat and scampered to the door with a laugh.

Outside, Rags joined me. As we trekked west past our fields, I noticed Abel Garner, Abigail's husband and our man-of-all-work, and our neighbor Farmer Hugh Heaten, hard at work planting our field, along with fourteen-year-old Gilly, an orphan boy, who hired on from time to time. Abel sowed the wheat, Farmer Hugh followed with a horse drawn harrow to cover the seeds, and Gilly chased off the crows that wanted to feed. I gave them a wave, received greetings in return, and continued on my mission.

When we reached the foothills, I munched on my bread as we hiked through sword ferns, around blackberry brambles, between fir and alder trees, and up steep grassy slopes. The woods hummed with the sounds of fairies, preparing the nascent spring growth for full bloom. Finally, we crossed a small meadow and reached my destination, the cliffs partway up Lookout Mountain, a south-jutting spur of the Morelann Range in the north. I climbed near the edge of the south-facing bluff, perched myself overlooking the sheer drop, and gazed at the vast forested stretch through which Father now traveled. The Great Road, visible only in spots, snaked through the trees. I trained my eyes on the brief, visible sections of road and watched for several minutes, but no horses and riders came into view.

Disappointed, I stepped back away from the precipice, sat on a boulder, and watched as Rags plopped himself at my feet and dropped a slobbery stick in front of his paws.

As the sun played hide and seek behind breeze-arranged clouds, I reached down to rub the dog's floppy ears, kept part of my attention on the road, and gazed at the territorial view before me. To the east, Fairian Castle, colorful flags flapping in the breeze, stood overlooking the great Green River on its eastern side. The ship-going river connected LaFairia to distant Soltar City, the seat of the High King, a place so far away it didn't seem real.

The adjacent walled Fairian Village and surrounding patchwork farmland completed my eastern view. Behind me to the north, the Morelann Mountains filled the skyline, and the smaller Lassen River ran from them to the Green River below. The Great Forest, through which Father now journeyed, spread to the southwest as far as I could see and far beyond. Hidden in its vastness were the estates of the lords that Father would visit. Then he would loop back to the southeast, travel past the Dead Castle to reach Lord Rella's manor, and finally come home by way of the much smaller King's Forest, the final leg of Father's spring tour.

I shifted my entire attention to the glimpses of the

Great Road and sighed. The route had not blessed me with a sight of my father and his two companions.

Rags, as if in sympathy with my plight, lifted his head, gazed soulfully at me, and drooled on my leather shoe. I grabbed the stick and threw it for my furry companion. He raced across fresh grasses, scattering swarms of two-inch field fairies, green-garbed with flecks of yellow and brown in their wings. They circled Rags with momentary interest and then returned to humming to the grasses.

Rags brought the stick back to me, dropped it at my feet, and eyed me expectantly. When I reached down to throw the stick again, the mid-morning bells chimed from the village below. With a twinge of guilt, I realized that more time had passed than I had planned—much more. Though I had done my early morning chores, I hadn't really done my best to cooperate with Mother or to honor Father's request.

Chastened by my own criticism, I resigned myself to accepting the parlor jail and doing embroidery with Mother and Isabella. I threw the stick as far across the meadow as I could, raced with Rags to retrieve it, and repeated the sequence time and time again as we sprinted around trees, crashed through the brush, and skidded down inclines on the way down Lookout Mountain. It took me longer to get down the mountain than it had to go up.

It was late morning when I looked over my ankle-length tunic, plucked off bits of clinging grass, and brushed off patches of dirt before leaving Rags outside and entering the cottage. I found Mother and my younger sister, fourteen-year-old Isabella, seated on sturdy, cushioned, wood chairs in the parlor doing the queen's embroidery. Sun streaming through the south facing windows illuminated their work, along with firelight from the hearth and candles. A Soltarian forest tapestry, an acquisition of Father's from an earlier journey, hung from the wall behind them. Our fluffy, striped, gray cat, Mr. Tatters, snoozed near the fire.

Mother looked up and her gaze rested on the top of my head. "Griselda, you have leaves in your hair."

I reached up, patted my head, and found the offending ornaments. Isabella glanced up with interest. I stifled a grin as I removed the debris, and she ducked her head to hide her smile.

Mother returned to her stitches. "Your father has just departed, and it appears that you have been defying my wishes and roving through the woods already, Griselda."

She was right. Contrition assailed me as I settled into a chair in front of Father's locked document chest. Determined to be more cooperative, I reached into my own embroidery basket, picked up my neglected sample, and apologized. "I beg your forgiveness, Mother, but I wished to glimpse Father on the Great Road."

Mother pursed her lips. "While I approve of your affection for your father, I object to your disappearing whenever it suits your caprice." Here she glanced at Isabella, and I knew that her next words would be filtered for Isabella's ears. "Especially to the mountains, to do whatever it is that you do. While your father is gone, this must cease."

My determination wavered as Mother's reins pulled me in. "But—"

Mother threw her needlework onto her lap. "Do not

quarrel with me, Griselda. I will have no more of your sneaking here and there, engaging in unusual activities, and appearing like a wild creature with leaves in your hair. It is not normal, and it is not ladylike."

Instead of reminding Mother that I was not a lady but a commoner, I focused on Father's command, nodded reluctantly, and busied myself about my needlework. I bit back an, "Ouch," as I impaled myself with a needle. My fingers and fabric soon wore the bloodied marks of my ineptitude.

Not wanting the stitchery to be ruined, Mother soon dismissed me to the kitchen. Throughout the remainder of the day, I stayed about Hart Cottage in deference to Mother. I helped Sarah with cheese making, Abigail with churning the butter, and Gilly with scaring the crows from the freshly sown field. That evening, I tumbled into the bed I shared with Isabella. The image of my father disappearing around that bend in the road came again and again as I tossed about and sank into uneasy slumber.

I woke with a gasp and sat up, sweat dripping from my brow. My eyes darted around the moonlit bedchamber in search of something amiss that would explain my spiking unease but found nothing.

Everything appeared in order: the fire banked for the night in the hearth, the candles snuffed out, Mr. Tatters curled up asleep at the foot of the bed, the basin and pitcher on the washstand, the tapestry hanging in shadow against the wall, and a few one-inch fairies hovering sleepily above daffodils in a vase. Isabella, asleep beside me, turned over and whimpered in her sleep but did not wake.

In spite of the restful room, my terror remained.

Details of a nightmare tugged at my memory, fragmenting and dissipating even as I strained to recall the foggy impressions: a horse's head bobbing in front of me as if I sat astride, a sense of alarm, something moving in the trees lining the road, a red-garbed man with a sword drawn falling from his horse with an arrow stuck in his throat. The vague images dispersed, but the terror increased. A gripping sense of loss overwhelmed me.

Father.

A stabbing pain pierced my side. I quickly checked for a wound but found nothing. Inexplicably, I had trouble breathing, gasping for air. My vision blurred. In my waking dream, I tipped sideways, fell from my horse, and thudded to the ground, my eyes locked on an indistinct figure in the trees.

Through all the agony and then spreading numbness, a regretful thought filled my mind.

Griselda, I never told you.

Slowly, the pain disappeared, and I knew. I was certain. Something had happened to my father.

For a moment, I sat in bed shaking. Sweat drenched my nightgown. My breath came in gulps.

The fairies, no longer sleepy, whizzed about the room. Others flew in through the partly opened window and joined the chaos. They circled my head like a crown. I almost swatted at them until I guessed at their wordless communication, grieving with me, sharing my loss.

"No," I whispered into the night.

It wasn't true. My father was fine. He would return safely home in due course. Isabella, still asleep, quivered and gave a little cry, which I followed with a sob.

"No, no, no…"

My heart galloping like a horse, I stared past the circling fairies at the lifeless fireplace and threw back the quilt. With a plan forming in my mind, I leaped from the bed and hastened from the bedchamber, hearing Isabella wake behind me. "Grizzy, wha…?"

I heard no more. I knew whom I needed. Captain Branner.

Stumbling my way down the dark, narrow staircase and into the parlor, I heard Sarah and Abigail starting the cooking fires, chatting, and clattering about in the adjacent kitchen. Sarah peered in to check on my disturbance.

When I yanked open the cottage door, she exclaimed, "Miss Griselda, yer only wearing a…"

I slammed the door and sped into the chill, pre-dawn air. The moon gave the landscape a dim outline, and dozens of softly glowing fairies gave the garden touches of illumination. Grateful for the fluttering dots of light, which only the fairy sighted could see, I brushed past sprays of shadowy grasses, dodged a startled rabbit, passed the towering rhododendron shrubs, and exited the rosebush-framed gate to reach Hart Cottage Lane where I lengthened my stride.

As I pounded down our short, hard-packed stretch of lane and angled onto stone-paved Castle Road, my heart beat louder than the slap of my bare feet against the road. I prayed that my sprint for Captain Branner's aid would change the outcome of my nightmare. Never before had I experienced such a dream, and I didn't know what to make of it. All I knew—and I felt it deep in my core—was that something was wrong. And I honestly didn't know what the captain could do, but I was counting on him to do something.

Feet slapping on the cold stones, the impact jarring my joints, I sped on gradually rising ground past the Heaten's acreage and other farms along the road, furlough by furlough. The nightglow from the fairies tending the fields lent a dappled light to my footsteps as the eastern horizon dimly brightened. The West Gate of Fairian Village loomed in the distance. I strained to see if the watchmen had opened it for the coming day. Finding it just opening, I initiated a new burst of speed when… Splat. I tripped on a broken paver, landed on all fours, and skidded against the hard, rough surface.

"Oww."

The sting from my hands and knees made me gasp, but I sprang to my feet and galloped to the West Gate. The guards stationed there, Fritz and Gammon, leaned into the doors, pushing the gate open, but straightened, grabbing torches and swords as I neared. Recognizing me, they sheathed their weapons.

Fritz lifted a hand in greeting. "Grizzy, what the…?"

"No time," I called, speeding past him.

"Blazes, she's fast…" Gammon exclaimed in my wake, but I wondered if I would be fast enough.

I sprinted through the waking village, passing the many shops fronting on Castle Road, dodging a scattering of workers with baskets, wheelbarrows, horse drawn carts, and garden hoes, and ignoring exclamations of surprise. I dashed past the village green to the torch-lit King's Gate, the entry to Fairian Castle, pounded across the drawbridge, and demanded of the open-mouthed guards, "Where's the captain?"

A couple of guards in red tunics, swords sheathed at their sides, drew near, staring at my knees. "Miss Griselda, you're hurt."

I followed their eyes and discovered my blood covered feet and the reddened fabric around two holes at knee level.

With impatience, I waved my hands before my face, warding off their concern. "No, no, where is Captain Branner?"

One guard pointed to the upper level of the gatehouse. I shot off like an arrow, barreled up the spiral stone staircase, tripped on my nightclothes at the final step, and tumbled with a thud against the heavy wooden door.

The door opened. Captain Branner looked down, open-mouthed and startled. "Griselda?"

From my crumpled position, I looked up at him. His brow furrowed, and his mouth snapped shut, forming a rigid line. Reaching down, he grasped my arms and lifted me up.

I choked out the words. "Father's been hurt."

Captain Branner's grip tightened, and he pulled me into his oil-lamp-illuminated quarters, kicking the door shut. His narrow, arched windows disclosed a hint of early dawn. The shadows cast from the lamps flickered against the stone wall behind his head. He said nothing at first; the severity of his look cowed me into silence.

It finally occurred to me how childish I must seem, a fully-grown young woman of sixteen reacting so rashly to a nightmare. And in truth, part of me hoped he would, in fact, think me only a silly a girl with bad dream. Perhaps then it would be so. But my gut told me, "No."

He stared at me over his beaky nose like he wanted to climb into my mind. "What do you mean?"

That's when I identified the look on the captain's face—fear.

With his fear now magnifying the terror roiling in my innards, I recounted my experience, leaving out any mention of the fairies. His hands tightened until they hurt, but I didn't complain. When I finished, he lifted his eyes to the heavens as if seeking help, released my arms, and strode from the room with a parting command.

"Remain here."

Dismayed by his abrupt dismissal, I disobeyed and followed, concerned that he was sending someone for my mother. I started down the stairs and heard the captain shouting to the men. "Make ready. We ride at once."

At the sound of footsteps on the stairs, I stumbled back to the captain's quarters. Captain Branner strode purposefully into the room, grabbed his scabbard-sheathed sword, fastened the belt, and spoke with his back to me. "We ride."

Wanting to be of use, I offered, "I'm a good rider."

He spun about, not the familiar friend of my father, but Captain Branner, Captain of the King's Guards. He pinioned me with his eyes. "Go home, Griselda. Speak of this to no one."

I recoiled from the fierceness of his expression but still wanted to help. "But I could…"

He stepped closer and lowered his voice. "There is no time for debate. Tell no one of your dream. If you are forced to speak of this, you must say that an unknown messenger came. You heard him before he knocked, so no one else at Hart Cottage heard. He gave you a note from your father saying that he needed help. You ran straightaway to give it to me. You may tell your mother. No one else."

I nodded mutely, my body feeling numb, the captain's response underscoring the gravity of my news.

He walked right up to me and leaned down, his face three inches from my own. "This experience of yours is—unusual, Griselda. Your father would not wish to draw to attention to you in this way."

"Oh," I said, my heart cowering before his grim expression and my mind wondering just how much Captain Branner knew.

With fierce gravity, he stated, "Tell no one."

He turned toward the door, and the captain was gone.

I left the gatehouse tower in a daze, Captain Branner's words, "Tell no one," echoing in my mind. The guards cast curious glances my way as they hastened to assemble. As I stumbled back through the village, a company of guards galloped from the castle, turned south on King's Way, and headed to the South Gate on their way to Father's route onto the Great Road and into the Great Forest. The commotion, as well as my appearance, excited questions and exclamations from villagers, but they slipped off me with scarce notice. Nothing mattered but that Captain Branner reach my father in time.

Now, wishing that Captain Branner had laughed off my concerns as an overactive imagination, I felt cold spreading inside me. He had taken me seriously. It was almost as if he knew more than I did. What had

Father confided to his friend?

The sunrise had brightened the horizon, coloring the eastern stripes of clouds an orangey-red, by the time I finally trudged through the gate and limped toward Hart Cottage. Mother met me at the door. Her angry face softened as she looked at my bloodied knees. She sighed, shook her head, and yelled back into the house. Yes, my proper mother actually yelled. "Sarah, Abigail. I need wine and linen for bandages."

I leaned back from Mother's uncharacteristic loudness as Sarah's muffled acknowledgement came from the kitchen. When my parent turned back to me, her familiar, quiet tone of thinly concealed exasperation ruled once again.

"Griselda, did my words of yesterday mean nothing to you? You should be safely abed." She bent to examine my knees. "What have you done?"

With heaviness in my gut, I folded my arms around my middle and glanced around before speaking to the top of her head. "I had to see Captain Branner."

Mother stood, slid her fingers against the sides of her head, grasped her hair, and exhaled slowly. "Griselda, I thought we had an understanding. With your father gone, I will not endure your making a spectacle of yourself. Why in the names of all the gods would you need to talk to the captain at this hour?"

Dreading more of Mother's displeasure if she did not believe my report, but dreading even more that she would believe, and therefore, like Captain Branner, confirm my fears, I answered, "Father has been hurt."

I braced myself for a rebuttal, but it never came. The colored drained from Mother's face and bled straight down through her body.

She trembled. "How do you know?"

As I looked at my parent's strained face, I placed a hand over my heart, regretting that my revelation would disclose yet another odd characteristic, the kind that always made her nervous.

I whispered, "I had a nightmare, but now I don't remember much." Then I glanced about for listeners. "Fairies believe it."

The eyes in her white face grew large and filled with tears. "What did you do? Who knows?"

"I told Captain Branner."

Mother glanced beyond the yard's post and wattle fence, down Hart Cottage Lane, and toward the Castle Road in the distance. "And he has gone?"

I followed her gaze, nodded, and relayed Captain Branner's instructions to me, wondering how long it would take the guards to reach my father and fearing what they would find.

Mother grabbed my arms. Her grip hurt my already bruised muscles. She gave me a slight shake and repeated the captain's words. "Tell no one."

Heart tightening at Mother's unquestioning acceptance of my claims, I agreed, pulled out of her grasp, and limped inside. Mother directed me to a chair in the parlor as Sarah entered with a basket of clean linen and a small jug of wine. The two women proceeded to clean and bind my wounds in silence, Sarah with an occasional "tsk" or glance from Mother to me.

As they finished, Mother addressed Sarah. "You are to keep this among ourselves."

"Yes, ma'am," Sarah replied with a gravity that belied a couple of skinned knees.

As I climbed the stairs, I wondered how much Sarah had heard.

Fairies drifted here and there in the bedchamber. Isabella, still abed under our patchwork quilt but sitting up, glanced around our room as if she'd never seen it before. If I hadn't known better, I would have thought her eyes followed the flights of the winged visitors that hovered near a vase with daffodils on the washstand, but I knew that was not possible. Isabella did not have fairy sight, and our parents shielded her from the problem. And Isabella, for her part, avoided the topic as assiduously—and fearfully—as Mother.

She greeted my entry with a confused expression. "What's happening?"

Isabella did not need to be worried until Father was rescued, so I muttered, "Tripped and fell."

Isabella glanced at my knees. "Oh, I'm so sorry, Grizzy."

Leaving Isabella in ignorance, I threw open the armoire door, grabbed accessories and an ankle-length tunic, and pulled the garment over my bloodied night chemise. After pulling on and securing hose and shoes, I faced Isabella, who still wore that befuddled, wandering look. Annoyance tested my patience. I'd had the nightmare, not Isabella. She had no current cause for perplexity.

She would be able to settle into her usual daily tasks, but I, now pacing the bedchamber as Isabella watched wide-eyed, planned to wait for word from the captain and mentally debated the best location. Since Father, and therefore Captain Branner, had traveled south on the King's Way before turning west onto the Great Road toward the Great Forest, I decided that the wall walk adjacent to the South Gate of Fairian Village, held the best vantage point to observe the captain's return.

I chose a belt. "Tell Mother I am going to the South Gate."

Her gaze floated around the bedchamber again before settling on me. "You will get in trouble."

My mind waged a brief battle between going about my duties and watching for the captain. The victory was decisive. How could I pretend to work when Father was in danger?

I secured the belt around my hips and grabbed my cloak. "So be it."

After I snuck from the cottage—yes, I admit, I did sneak—I darted across the yard, out the gate, and to the lane. Rags loped up to join me, and I ruffled his ears, appreciating his solidarity in missing Father.

When we reached Castle Road, Rags and I turned left and trotted the same route I had taken such a short time ago. Not wanting to engage in village chatter, I turned right onto the Harbor Connecter, a road that circled most of the outer walls around the village and the castle, ending only at the sheer cliff face that dropped to the Green River Harbor east of the castle.

Familiar guards stood at their South Gate posts when I arrived outside the gate. With my finger pointing up at a side tower, I said, "I'm going on top."

The corners of one guard's eyes drew in as he asked, "What is happening?"

I looked at the ground and shook my head.

The other guard, his face mirroring the first's concern, waved me through.

I nodded silently to them, marched up the spiral

staircase of the South Gate with Rags following, ignored comments as I passed the guardroom, and stepped onto the wall walk. With my cloak pulled tight, I positioned myself between the gap-teeth crenellations and focused on the point in the road where King's Way exited the King's Forest. I half expected Mother to send Sarah to drag me back home. But she did not.

When questioned from time to time by guards passing on the wall walk, I kept my thoughts to myself out of respect for the orders, "Tell no one," from Mother and Captain Branner and only dignified the inquiries with a single word.

"Waiting."

My response did not invite further conversation, so at length they left me alone.

And I waited.

I waited as the sunrise filled the sky with color and the morning bells greeted the day. The cheerful, predictable chimes gave me hope that soon Captain Branner would return with word of Father's safety.

I waited as the sun reached its zenith in the sky with the midday bells accompanying. The sound held a knell of desperation in its vibration. I pushed the feeling back as a guard silently left food and drink, which I ignored but gave to Rags who remained stolidly beside me.

I waited as my muscles cramped into painful knots in my feet, legs, and shoulders, but I discountenanced the discomfort and steeled my focus on that distant point in the road where riders would appear.

I waited as the sun approached the western horizon and the evening bells tolled the darkening of the day.

Then in the distance, I saw horses.

They emerged from the forested south, and eventually, I made out the shapes of riders mounted on their backs. The red livery of the King's Guard became clear as they snaked their way toward the walled village.

My muscles tightened, my breath quickened, and I fixed my sight on the distant group, willing myself to recognize the form of my father astride his horse, his posture, his bearing, his presence.

Eventually, the forms became clearer. Captain Branner led the group, leading a riderless horse. The horse, a bay with black mane and tail, carried what looked like a roll of fabric draped limply across its back. Two similarly burdened horses followed other guards.

From the gatehouse, a guard joined me on the wall walk. He pointed at the tower. "Miss Griselda, I think you should come inside."

I didn't answer. Cold spread from my heart to my shoulders, my throat, and my extremities. Resisting the nightmare, I walked unsteadily to the tower, stumbled down the steps to the gate, and fell to my knees, choking on the salty wetness covering my face and dripping from my nose. As Captain Branner and his charge neared, I pushed myself up, took unsteady steps forward, and broke into a wobbly run. Captain Branner dropped his lead rope, kneed his horse, and cantered to me. Then he flung himself from his mount and into my path. I dodged but could hardly see through the flood covering my face. He caught me, and I writhed in his arms.

"No, no, no."

"I'm sorry, Griselda, by the gods above, I'm

sorry."

Then I pummeled him with every ounce of strength I had. He just took it but did not let me go. When my strength was spent, and I couldn't strike another blow, I stopped and pushed back from the captain. He still held my arms. My eyes strayed to the roll of red fabric draped over the horse—Lady, Father's horse. Hanging from the roll were brown leather boots, their surfaces marred with spatters of dried blood.

By now other guards, two leading horses bearing similar burdens, encircled Captain Branner and me. I yanked my arm from his grasp.

He let me go and repeated with a voice that cracked. "I'm sorry, Grizzy."

We stood mutely for a moment of shared grief with Rags whining at my side. Then I stepped away from Captain Branner and walked tremblingly toward the draped form of my father.

Chapter 3

Stupid Bandits

I strode across the dandelion-dotted yard scattering chickens, robins, and fairies in my haste, an open-ended basket swinging from one hand, a pair of clippers clenched in the other, my mind whirling like a storm. No one could replace my father, not for me, not for my family, not for the kingdom.

Reaching the flowers bordering the yard, I threw the basket and clippers on the dirt near the dried-up hyacinths and daffodils. "Stupid bandits," I sobbed, snot dripping from my nose. "Stupid, stupid bandits."

The sun, now one-quarter of its journey through the sky, warmed my face but not my heart. I brushed past the flowering red azaleas and pink rhododendrons, skirted around Isabella's arbor-covered garden bench, angled through the freshly sprouting vegetable and herb gardens, and stumbled my way past the sheds to the fallow field about an arrow's shot from the cottage.

I threw my black-clothed self to the ground and glared back at the cottage. How could my mother marry this man, Lord Rella, not yet two months after my father's death? He was wealthy to be sure, but the man had very little sense—I was sure of it. And he would never be a father to me.

Eyes clouded with tears, I gazed at the blurry shape

of my home: the stone and wood family dwelling built by my grandfather Willem, the sturdy stone kitchen built by my great-grandfather Neilen, and the wattle and daub Hart Cottage built by my great-great-grandfather Jamis, which now housed the servants. Though the rambling estate, along with its outbuildings, was substantial now, I was proud that the grounds retained the humble name—Hart Cottage. I felt connected to the name, the buildings, and the land, but now my father would never add his signature to the place. It was too late. I wiped my nose and eyes on my sleeve, leaving streaks of wet and slime and despairing that the roots of my life had been destroyed.

As if to interrupt my morbid thoughts, Rags loped up to me, churning clods of soil in his wake. He dropped a stick at my side and shoved his wet nose in my hand. A wave of isolation washed over me, and fresh tears burned behind my nose. I threw my arms around my dog's neck, buried my face in his warm fur, and wept. When the tears stilled to sniffles, I released him, and he lay before me with his head flopped in my lap, eyes staring up at me sadly.

I lowered my hand to my furry friend's head and rubbed. "I think you are the only one who misses Father as much as I do."

Rags put a paw on my shoe, thumped his tail once, and nosed the stick at my side. I sighed, tossed the piece of wood, and watched as Rags galloped away, leaving me to my sorrow.

As I sat mourning, several winged field caretakers, about an inch in height and flecked with the greens, browns, and yellows of dried grass, approached and flew slow, oval patterns around me, seemingly sympathetic to my grief. As I listlessly watched them, a whisper of air passed my cheek and a flutter of pink gossamer heralded Arianna's arrival. Without a word, she slowly lowered to the ground about an arm's length away.

My eyes leaked afresh. "I don't want to talk to you, Arianna."

Arianna, who normally didn't take that tone from me, remained silent. With the radiance of her body subdued, her wings fluttered, reflecting the late-morning sunlight. Her pink frock trembled in the soft breeze; she bowed her head, toed the dirt, and glanced off the ground every few seconds. "I lost your father, too, Griselda."

I wanted to grab her, shake her, make her understand. "It is not the same. I will never have another father. You can find another fairy kin."

She stopped her sad movements, winged her pink-garbed frame slowly and warily onto my knee, and seated herself with legs crossed. In a voice as soft as mist, the soothing effect of which I mightily withstood, she said, "And I have. As I have told you, you are the fairy kin now."

Frustrated at her persistence on this topic, I pounded the dirt with a fist. "No, not me. I can't; I won't."

The temptation to tip her off my knee into the dirt was strong, but I resisted. "Besides, Mother won't allow it."

While Arianna still balanced on my knee, I recollected how Mother had given me a stern warning. "No more talk of fairies. No more interactions with fairies. Not now. Not ever."

Though the exchange had happened many weeks ago, I remembered it with painful clarity and ruminated over it daily. I had come in after a cathartic run with Rags, and Sarah had informed me that Mother wished to speak with me. I found Mother in the parlor seated with her back to the Soltarian forest tapestry. She motioned to Isabella's chair next to her, put her embroidery in her lap, and scanned my dirt-and-dog-slobber-covered dress but made no comment.

After I seated myself, she took a deep breath and said, "Griselda, I have lost my husband." A tear escaped from the corner of her eye. She caught it with a finger. "You and Isabella have lost your father, a sorrow we will always share."

The now familiar pressure behind my nose returned, and my eyes filled. I nodded but said nothing.

Dim shadows created by the windows, candles, and fire in the hearth cast Mother's outline against the forest tapestry as she continued. "There are things concerning which you and I must have an understanding."

With my elbows pulled tightly to my sides, I braced myself, mystified about what she might have to say. After all, I had followed the order to "Tell no one" about my nightmare, the messenger story fabricated by Captain Branner seemingly accepted throughout the village, though some thought the messenger stupid to have delivered the message to Hart Cottage rather than Captain Branner himself. And for weeks, I had faithfully followed her strictures about fairies. Why wouldn't I? Father had told me to obey Mother; I did love and respect her, even though we didn't always get along; and fairy sight was punishable by death—all good reasons to comply.

So what issues were on her mind: my absentmindedness about the state of my attire, my penchant for long hikes to the cliffs with Rags, my inattentiveness to my embroidery. So much about me disturbed Mother. I did not intend to be disturbing; I simply didn't enjoy sticking a needle in and out of fabric for hours on end like Mother and Isabella.

Mother picked up the embroidered trim almost completed for the queen and began to work, seeming reluctant to begin. With nothing to do but wait, I reached for my own needlework.

"And now," Mother finally said, her needle flying in and out of her fabric, "I must speak to you of a serious matter." She looked furtively around the parlor. Clatter and conversation drifted from the adjoining stone kitchen structure. Isabella, I knew, was moping in our bedchamber. Mother and I were quite alone. A sensation fluttered in my stomach like fairy wings. Ah, secrets.

Mother lowered her voice. "I do not like to speak of this." She paused. "In the past I thought it best to leave this topic to your father."

I sat as still as a rabbit hiding from a fox.

Mother glanced toward the kitchen and whispered, "But now that your father is gone, we must have an understanding. In honor of your father's wishes—and mine—you shall not talk of fairy sight at any time—ever. Indeed, I deem it best that you never speak of fairies at all."

"I keep my secret, Mother, as you well know," I whispered, judging her demand to be unreasonable, "but everyone speaks of fairies."

"And you can allow them to do so, but I have good

reason to forbid your participation."

I opened my mouth to object, but Mother held up her hand. "This has always been a great worry for me. I will help as I can, but I regret that you are burdened with this—gift." Clearly, she did not consider it a gift at all, but sympathy colored her voice. "I am sorry. Without your father, it is yours alone."

My chin drooped to my chest. Alone. Mother was right. A sense of isolation squeezed around me. Then I remembered Father's promise, lifted my head, and looked at Mother, buoyed by her offer to help. "Father said he would tell me why we have fairy sight when he returned. Can you tell me?"

Mother's face tightened and aged before my eyes. "Griselda, such inquiries can only lead to trouble. You know the laws."

"Yes, but I have been faithfully cautious, and I am sure that King Beaumain would not…"

Mother threw down her stitchery. Her eyes flashed. "Never speak of this to the king—or the prince. Never. You are to obey me in this, Griselda. You must acknowledge the risk of this perilous fairy sight."

At a noise near the staircase, Mother craned her neck, looked past my shoulder, and widened her eyes, a hand coming to her mouth. I turned to see Isabella staring at Mother as if she'd seen a ghost.

Mother rose, walked to Isabella, and addressed her in a gentle tone. "Isabella, pray do not concern yourself." She pointed to a basket by the door. "A few tulip buds are still in bloom. Could you gather some to arrange for the dinner table?"

Isabella stood motionless. Her mouth moved, but no sound came out. I exchanged a glance with Mother.

Her eyes narrowed with concern. "Isabella dear, what are you trying to say?"

Isabella remained stationary.

Worried that my sister had been a statue for long enough, I stood, crossed the floor, wrapped my arm around her shoulders, and squeezed. "Izzy, speak!"

Isabella's mouth finally produced words. "Execution is the penalty for fairy sight."

Mother took in a deep breath; the intake lasted so long I feared she would burst like an overfilled wineskin. Finally, she exhaled. "That is so, but it has not been enforced for decades."

How Isabella turned even whiter I do not know, but she did. "B-b-but it sh-should not be wrong to see fairies; fairies are good."

"Of course, they are good, my dear," Mother said, taking Isabella's hand. "It is those who can see them that the law questions." Here she looked at me meaningfully. "So pay no mind to your sister's fancy, and do not trouble yourself."

As always, I felt uncomfortable about deceiving Isabella, but looking at Isabella's blanched face, I followed Mother's lead. "Yes, Izzy, you know what a wild creature I am."

Though my comment earned a glare from Mother, she agreed with me. "Yes, please leave Griselda's vivid imagination to herself."

I patted Isabella on the back as if in agreement and dropped my arm.

Isabella remained quiet for a second. Then showing that she was not as ignorant as Mother and I thought, as well as the first defiance I had ever seen from her, she said, "It is not Grizzy's imagination, Mother. I think you are scared."

Speechlessly, Mother and I stared at Isabella, marveling at her spark of forthrightness. Though Isabella and I had shared rare whispered words about fairy sight in the dark in bed when we were younger, for years she had appeared to believe it was all my imagination. After all, she couldn't see them, and Mother used to say that I had mistaken butterflies for fairies. So it was a topic we avoided: me because of parental mandate, Isabella because she was a good, cooperative daughter. So her bold declaration was all the more out of character.

Then with slumping posture our parent replied, "Yes, you are right. I am afraid."

Though I had always known this to be true, the starkness of her admission gave me more sympathy for her position, and I resolved to be more cooperative.

Recovering, she straightened and looked sternly at both of us. "Afraid with very good reason. So there is to be no more talk of fairies. No more interactions with fairies. Not now. Not ever."

Her momentary boldness past, Isabella looked horrified by her impudence. She nodded meekly to Mother, collected the flower basket, and opened the door. Then she dropped the basket, spun around, and scampered upstairs.

Mother raised one eyebrow. I, who couldn't master mother's trick, raised two, but we did not comment on Isabella's abrupt change of plans. Mother turned a worried face to me. "Griselda, though Isabella unfortunately knows your secret, there must be no talk of it. Every word brings the risk of exposure."

Feeling the door of discussion closing, I made one

more desperate attempt. "But Father planned to explain our secret. Surely, you could honor his dying wishes."

Mother stared at me for a minute, a debate raging behind her eyes. Finally, with reluctance and gentleness, she answered, "My daughter, that is what concerns me. Some secrets are better left buried."

Despite my recent resolve to cooperate, I had argued, but to no avail. And oh, how it rankled. What was Mother hiding from me?

And further, since Father's death, Isabella seemed to be avoiding me, perhaps because of her recently expressed fears. But she had clearly kept her belief in fairy sight to herself for some time, so avoiding me now didn't make sense and hurt my feelings.

With Father gone, everything was amiss.

Excited barking interrupted my musings about the past and brought me back to the present moment. I turned my head to see Rags, tail wagging furiously, face to face with Mr. Tatters. The stout gray feline, having none of Rag's playfulness, sat on his haunches, attempting to ignore Rags and maintain his unruffled dignity. The familiar exchange made me huff out a brief chuckle.

Then I looked back at Arianna, who regarded at me with understanding, a few tiny fairies hovering behind her.

I knew that she had followed my thoughts as I remembered my confrontation with Mother. "You see what I mean. Mother won't allow it. And Father told me to obey her when he left."

Arianna spread her wings, rose in the air, and hovered before my eyes, her gaze piercing, her mouth still. "Your father did not know he would not return."

I jerked back. "Did you just mind speak to me?"

Arianna nodded, her face strained. "Yes, but it is quite draining to do so. Nevertheless, just as you can hear me now, in time, you should be able to pull fairies from the light. Your father would wish it."

While I appreciated hearing Arianna's unspoken voice for the first time, I regretted the strain the effort obviously caused her and doubted that I would ever grow into the role expected of me. I wasn't even sure that I wanted to.

The whine in my voice made me cringe, but I couldn't help it. "But I have never been able to do it— even with arm movements and breathing."

Arianna's face relaxed and her mouth moved. "You need to practice, to concentrate, but most important is to relax and let it happen naturally."

Mother's recently stated worries, Father's parting directive, and my own fear of beheading quaked through my heart. "But even if I can, it's too dangerous. I won't be able to do it mentally. I could get caught."

Arianna drifted a bit in the rose-scented breeze before she replied, "I cannot—and would not—force you to shoulder this burden. Ultimately, you alone must choose. Nevertheless, you are now the fairy kin for this kingdom. Nothing will change that."

Great. What a way to make me feel guilty regardless of what I chose to do. If I tried to learn to pull fairies, I would be disobeying Mother—and Father—and putting myself at risk. If I chose not to learn, I would be letting down Arianna and the entire kingdom. What an unfair decision to dump on a sixteen-year-old. Any choice seemed wrong.

Arianna watched my mental debate with alertness,

and annoyance surfaced in me that I couldn't keep anything private.

Finally, she spread her arms, palms up. "Remember, I, too, feel the loss of your father."

My emotions churned. *Of course, you miss him. He did what you wanted. Now you only have me. And I am not enough.*

My mood plummeted further, but then an obvious question occurred to me, giving me a fresh hope. "Arianna, Father promised to explain my gift when he returned. Now he can't. Mother knows but refuses to tell me. Can you?"

Arianna's expression mirrored the shuttered look that Father had worn when the topic had come up. "You know all you need to know. You are the fairy kin. That is enough—more than enough of a burden."

Then she did an aerial bow and flew toward Lookout Mountain, followed by her cohort, leaving me in the dark about what further burden was hidden from me.

At that moment, a round-faced head poked around the corner of the kitchen structure. Sarah yelled, "Miss Griselda, Isabella is waitin' on the flowers."

With Rags at my side, I sighed and rose from the dirt, trudged through the field, and passed the sheds and animal pens, scooping up an escaped chicken and depositing her into the enclosure attached to the coop. Upon passing the gardens and finally reaching the yard, I retrieved the clippers and basket and scanned the floral perimeter of the space. The once-colorful daffodils and tulips were past use, the tight-fisted peony buds—Mother's favorites—needed another week or so, and the giant rhododendron blooms were not right for

Isabella's vases. Rosebushes stretching along both sides of the gate had begun to bloom and looked promising, and tall irises, some purple, some yellow, looked healthy and well formed. Roses and irises it would be.

Though the turmoil inside tempted me to lash out at everything, I curbed my frustration, snipped the stems, and laid them carefully in the basket, all out of respect for the effort the fairies made to bring the delicate flowers to maturity.

With my basket laden with choice blooms, I strode to Hart Cottage, leaving Rags and Mr. Tatters outside, entered the stone kitchen that smelled of roasting meat and baking bread, and banged my basket on the wooden trestle table. This startled Isabella, also clad in black, and made her drop the greenery she was arranging in an earthenware vase for the evening's dinner with our future stepfather, Lord Robert Rella.

Our servants Sarah and Abigail, clad in ankle-length gray tunics and ample aprons, glanced at me, exchanged a look, and then recommenced chopping potatoes and carrots. Mother, dressed like Isabella in black garb, looked up from inspecting the sizzling meat turning on a spit in the fireplace.

She gave me her familiar look of fondness tinged with exasperation. "Griselda, the decorum of a young lady would be desirable, if you please."

The retort that I was not a lady, young or otherwise, strained to get out, but I swallowed the words, nodded, and gave her a tiny curtsy.

Her eyes raked my appearance and rested on the skirt of my black dress. "And you have a smudge of dirt on your mourning clothes."

I glanced down. She was right. I did have a

smudge, several in fact, and I wondered which spot in particular had excited Mother's displeasure this time. Immaculately tidy, as always, Isabella reached out a hand and tried to brush some of the soil off my garment with her fingers. She failed, shrugged her shoulders apologetically, and began to insert irises among her waxy, green salal leaves and fern fronds.

With a shake of her perfectly coifed head, Mother left me stewing in my thoughts like the cauldron simmering over the fire and returned to supervision of dinner preparations. Everything had to be just right for the early evening arrival of Lord Robert and his daughter, who was sixteen like me. After tomorrow's marriage ceremony, in which Mother would become Lady Constance Rella, they were to embark on a journey to visit Lord Robert's friends while a separate carriage would take Isabella and me, along with our new stepsister, away to Rella Manor, and I didn't want to go.

Soon Sarah would collar me, march me upstairs, and do her best to make me presentable for dinner. I didn't want to do that either.

Sarah, now mincing parsley on the kitchen's central wooden table, glanced up, spied me chafing where I stood, and froze in mid-chop. She put her knife on the table, swooped over, and steered me to a corner.

With her muscular hands resting on my shoulders, she spoke softly. "Miss Griselda, be of good cheer. This is a suitable match for yer mother. Lord Robert Rella is a gentleman and a man of means."

I crossed my arms, both hands squeezed into fists, and looked at the floor. "He's a fool, Sarah, nothing but money and manners."

She shook my shoulders gently and glanced around the kitchen to see if I'd been overheard. "Now jus' you bite yer tongue, young lady."

I leaned my face closer to Sarah's so I could whisper. "But it's true, Sarah. I know Mother has affection for Lord Robert, and that he is a very good sort of man, but I fear he has no sense at all."

Sarah rolled her eyes heavenward. "Fairies preserve us, child. What's to be done with you?"

Even though I was forbidden to talk of fairies, people around me had no such strictures. Their references to fairies usually amused me, because most people no longer believed in them. But today little amused me.

"You don't believe in fairies, Sarah."

With a quick sideways glance at Mother, Sarah hissed, "We're not speakin' of fairies, young lady—not ever. We're speakin' of you bein' grateful for yer mother's good fortune—and yers as well."

I turned my head away from Sarah. She sighed, gently cupped my chin in her hands, and turned my head to face her.

"I'm not sayin' that he's all the man yer father was, but put on a glad countenance for yer mother's sake. It's what yer father would want."

I observed Mother as she tested the soup, added a handful of parsley and a few pinches of spice, and gave some directions to Abigail. Of course, Sarah was right. Father would support Mother's decision to marry and to provide a father for her daughters. But in spite of this logic, I couldn't accept tomorrow's nuptials. I felt a queasy twist of guilt about my attitude, but how could any man replace my father?

Turning back to Sarah, I found myself to be no match for her furrowed brow and pleading face. So I ground out my acquiescence. "I will try."

Sarah's face softened into a smile, and she patted my shoulder. "That's a good girl."

But I wasn't a good girl. Nothing Sarah said would change the aversion I had to the coming wedding.

Chapter 4

A Royal Summons

With an admittedly sullen face, I took turns minding the spit, stirring the soup pot, and chopping herbs for Abigail's green sauce. Isabella finished filling her vases. Mother hovered over all preparations, sampling each recipe. Sarah, with an eye on me, guarded her golden loaves, cooling after removal from the bread oven. A comforting, yeasty fragrance filled the room, along with the smell of sizzling meat, but I did not find it bolstering. My nose tingled, and a wet pressure built behind my eyes. I sniffed a couple of times and twitched my nose.

Mother raised one eyebrow and glanced at Sarah before crossing the space, reaching out, and giving me a hug. I returned the gesture but tightened my face to keep from loosing a sodden display of grief.

Mother released our embrace, held my shoulders at arms' length, and searched my face, settling on my eyes. "I am grateful for your help, my dear."

Given my hostile attitude about the upcoming events, I'm sure a look of surprise registered on my face. Mother smiled, a hint of forbearance in the expression, but it was a smile. "I know that this is most difficult for you, Griselda, but all will be well. You will see."

Unable to agree with Mother, I remained silent, imagining countless ways that things would not be well. It would not be well for me. It would not be well for my family. And it would not be well for the kingdom. But Mother refused to acknowledge this, thinking that an alliance with Lord Robert would solve our problems— as if moving to Rella Manor would eliminate my danger.

She squeezed my shoulders and leveled her gaze at me. "Now, when we are all dressed, we will spend the rest of the afternoon in the parlor with our needlework as we await our guests, whom we will welcome graciously."

I grimaced, eliciting a brief frown from Mother, which was quickly replaced with a forced smile. "The green gown will look well with your lovely eyes, and I beg you not to fuss as Sarah tightens your laces. Henceforth, you will always be fit to be seen amongst our acquaintances."

Behind Mother, Sarah's eyes filled with amusement, but my mouth dropped open with incredulity. This must be a consequence of connection to a noble family, because Father had never fussed about my attire. Nevertheless, noting Mother's determined expression, I nodded my compliance, exited the stone kitchen, entered the brick and timber family section of the cottage, and climbed the stairs. Sarah followed me with a look of determination that mirrored Mother's but with an added hint of laughter, and I knew what it meant. One way or another, I was going to be painfully clean, spotless, and impeccably presentable before she was finished with me, my promise to obey Mother binding me like chains—or at least like suffocating laces.

And so I submitted to the tedious process. After what felt like days of standing in front of my washbasin and mirror, Sarah slid one last pin into the netting that held my wild, wavy brown hair in a bunch at the nape of my neck.

"It is too soon to cast aside mourning clothes, Sarah," I grumbled, glancing at the discarded black garb tossed on my quilt-covered bed.

"Who ever heard of wearin' black to a wedding?" she said, the long skirt of my green dress swirling as she spun me around, inspected me from head to toe, and gave a satisfied nod. "Now, the slippers from your father will add the final touch, miss."

I glanced at my luminescent slippers nestled in fabric in a small open trunk next to a lovely embroidered pair—without glow—that Father had given Isabella. A wave of pain pulsed through my chest and lodged itself in my throat. I shook my head.

Sarah frowned. "Whyever not? I'd think ya'd want to wear such a pretty gift to honor his memory, not just keep them hidden away."

Though part of me longed to wear Father's final gift to me, I'd be cursed before I wore them to greet his replacement. Not a chance. And furthermore, now that he was gone, what about marriage to the prince? Should I pursue it? He had explained that the shoes were to be worn to influence people. Did I want that? It sounded like too much responsibility. So to be realistic, it was probably best to lay Father's matrimonial plans for me to rest.

Still conflicted, I shook my head again and earned a deep sigh from Sarah. She reached forward to fuss with wisps of hair framing my face and to wipe at imaginary smudges on my crisply pressed dress.

I jumped back from her ministrations and leaned against the bed that Isabella and I shared. "Enough, Sarah."

"Very well then." She shook a brush at me, which lightened my mood. "Down to the parlor with you."

I rolled my eyes, hopped from the bed, and laughingly dodged Sarah's playful swipe at me with the brush.

Brush shaking, she said, "Now scat, and see that you keep yerself tidy, young lady."

I grinned. And I scatted.

Mother and Isabella, who had outfitted themselves in Mother's bedchamber while Sarah labored with me, were elegantly attired, Mother in dark blue and Isabella in light blue, colors that enhanced their eyes, and settled near the parlor windows with their baskets of embroidery. Mother worked on some decorative gown trim commissioned by the queen, Isabella on a small pillow covering. Watching them at their tasks, I quietly blew out a long exhalation. I just didn't have the patience for it that they did, and today less so than ever. This waiting for Lord Robert and his daughter, Cynthia, would be unendurable.

I entered, slouched into a chair in front of the forest tapestry, and picked up my own neglected sample, my gloomy mood contrasting with the bright sunlight coming through the windows. Mother kept glancing at me with pursed lips. Though acknowledging the grief that we all shared, she clearly wanted me to welcome our new prospect. I simply would not—could not—concur.

As I stifled any comments and curled absentmindedly over my needlework, three metallic raps sounded against the front door.

"Oh my," Mother said. "They are quite early." She dropped her work into her basket, rose, and smoothed her dress. Isabella copied her behavior while I dragged myself to my feet and glared toward the entry.

Momentarily, Abel Garner appeared with a rolled parchment in his hand. He gave it to Mother with a slight bow. "Twas a messenger from the castle, ma'am."

Mother nodded that he could withdraw, broke the seal, and unfurled the letter. Her eyes scanned the words, widened with interest, and then shifted to me. "It is for you, Griselda—from the prince."

My heart gave a little leap. Isabella giggled, raising one eyebrow. Mother, too, raised that one eyebrow of hers, and her mouth battled between a smile and a frown. She presented the paper to me. My mind swirled with curiosity as I read the prince's hastily composed note.

Dear Grizzy,

I greet you and wish you well. And I offer my sincerest good wishes regarding your mother's upcoming nuptials.

Now, you must come to me at once, for I am imprisoned in endless council meetings on taxation with Lord Uriah Ursa. I want to do my duty but am aggravated that Lord Ursa is hammering us with his opinions about policies. Sometimes I wonder who is the king here. I depend upon your expedience for I need a means of escape.

Make haste.

HRH Prince Charmain

A tumbling series of emotions: annoyance, anger, unease, and eager anticipation, accompanied my reading. First, I didn't want good wishes about the marriage. I would have preferred interference. Second, how dare Lord Ursa propose changes? My father's methods were fair and in no need of modification. Third, the comment, "I wonder who is the king here," disturbed me. Finally, and this was the most pressing issue at the moment, he wanted me to visit him at the castle. This would provide both of us with a means of escape.

Sarah, who had come down the stairs after straightening the washstand, craned her neck over my shoulders and then turned to Mother. "Oh, no, ma'am. You can't be thinking of lettin' her go. Not after I fixed her up so tidy."

Eager to seize the chance to flee from an afternoon of tedious waiting and pretending to do embroidery, I stretched the parchment open to Mother. "Surely, I must be permitted to obey the prince's summons."

Mother glanced from my carefully coifed hair to my spotless dress and frowned. I saw her struggle between respect for the crown and her need to keep me neat and clean, which meant inside.

Finally, she impaled me with a look. "Very well, Griselda, out of deference to His Highness, I will permit you to go. But see that you mind your hair and clothes."

Sarah twapped my shoulder with a rag. "Oh, you scamp. I hate to let you outa the house." She shook a finger at my ear. "You keep tidy now."

With a grin, I straightened my shoulders, lifted my

chin, and gave my best impersonation of a well-behaved lady. "Of course, but you know that I must obey the royal summons."

Sarah harrumphed from behind me. "Obey? Fairies preserve us; you only want to get out of the house, young lady. Don't think I don't know yer ways.

I grinned and strutted away in my most stately manner. Mother scowled at my performance. Isabella snickered.

Sarah slapped her thigh and hooted. "What a sight."

On my way out the door, I rolled up the parchment and made a firm resolve to maintain my appearance. Truly.

With a spring in my steps, I escaped from an afternoon of imprisonment in the parlor doing embroidery. That was for Mother and Isabella; outdoors and sunshine were for me. The blue sky boasted patches of billowy clouds, and the breeze still held a hint of rose scent. I inhaled the delicate fragrance as I looked around for Rags, who usually bounded out to greet me. Not seeing him anywhere, I shrugged, assuming he was off harassing Abel Garner. Though I missed the company of my canine friend, this was for the best since he wouldn't jump on my dress.

The sun warmed my face as I walked through our yard, being careful not to stain the hem of my wrinkle-free dress against the cheerful dandelions that stood proudly in the grass, attended by yellow-frocked, winged caretakers. I even refrained from breaking into a jog and maintained the dignified stride of a young lady in case Mother and Sarah were watching. They would be pleased.

At my slower pace, I observed the garden fairies tending the bordering flowers and shrubs like busy insects. The closest pixies wore short, petal-like dresses that matched the red, yellow, and pink rhododendrons, the purple irises, and the multicolored roses, above which they hovered, their butterfly delicate wings whirring as quickly as a hummingbird's. I wished forlornly that everyone could see fairies and share my lonely secret. But I was alone. Father was gone.

A pain-filled space swelled in my chest. Against all reason, I still expected him to meet me in the garden, on the road, or at the castle. The pain worked its way to my throat and pressed against my nose. A stepfather would never be the same.

I walked between rosebushes framing the yard's exit, closed the gate tight to protect any loose critters, and turned on to the dirt lane. A smooth, throwing stone at the side caught my attention. I picked it up and squeezed, missing my father something fierce.

Father and I occasionally threw stones for target practice as I accompanied him to the fields or walked with him to the village or the castle. As I grew older, he sometimes let me stand on the side when he advised the king. I loved to listen as he settled differences, recommended policies, and ensured that everyone was treated fairly, whether king, noble, commoner, or peasant. I supposed it was odd to have a commoner with such influence, but Father's service-oriented leadership made everything go more smoothly. The king, whether he realized it or not, had depended on it.

Once I had absentmindedly mused to my father that he would make a good king. The sternness of his response, "Never speak of such things," made that the only time I had ever mentioned it—though not the only time I'd thought it. Father did not aspire to greatness. He believed that selfless service was the highest calling. And he had lived that way every day.

With memories of my father saddening my heart, I flung the stone sharply from hand to hand a couple of times, then swung back my arm and gave it a heave that sent it streaking into a grain field. I didn't want to think about stones anymore.

Troubled with my own thoughts, I looked down at my shoes scuffing along the lane, kicking stones, sticks, and a sturdy piece of branch to the side, until a pain-filled yelp followed by a series of barks drew my attention. I looked ahead and noticed a group of young men gathered at the location where Hart Cottage Lane joined Castle Road.

There, pushed up again the signpost, was poor fourteen-year-old Gilly. Rags, who had been tormented by these same three bullies, growled at the side. He lunged at one of Gilly's assailants, a troublemaker named Jason Gutcher, and yelped as a heavy booted kick connected with his furry side.

Fury rose in my chest, my muscles tightened, and my hand dropped the prince's letter. They hadn't seen me yet, but that was about to change.

I reached down, palmed one of the roadside stones, took aim, and hurled it, accurately beaning Jason across the top of his head.

He exclaimed, "Ow," jumped back, looked around, and saw me.

I spotted more stones and the sturdy piece of branch, grabbed them, and started to run toward the ruffians. My foot caught on the hem of my dress, and I heard a quick rip. A flash of concern scythed through me, but I had other issues to address now. Rags, who thankfully appeared unhurt, at least not as bad as possible considering that brutal kick, galloped to me and leaped, putting his paws on my dress.

With Rags at my side, I advanced toward the group, stopped ten feet away, and brandished my stick at the leader. "Jason Gutcher, you just leave him be."

Jason, a strapping young man of eighteen, who to my disgust was somewhat sweet on me, released Gilly and swaggered to the front of the group. His hulking partners Deke and Dirk continued to press Gilly against the post.

Jason scrutinized my hair and clothes, eyed my stick, and sneered. "Get lost, Grizzy. We're just having a bit of fun with the motherless whelp."

Annoyed that he always used my family name but horrified that he used a slur for an orphan, I maneuvered my position to catch the eyes of the two bulky boys holding Gilly, flourished a stone, and drew back my arm.

"Well, the fun's over. Now let him be, or you'll think you've been struck by lightning."

Deke and Dirk exchanged glances and looked from my rock to Jason, whose temple now sported a thread of blood.

Deke, the larger of the two oversized toughs, spoke up. "Uh, Jason."

Jason, ignoring his accomplice, stared so lingeringly at me that my gut grew queasy. Then he shrugged. "Aw, let him go. It's no use arguing with a girl, 'specially when she's all dressed up."

Deke and Dirk released the struggling orphan and

stepped back. Gilly pushed away from the two, stepped a safe distance away, and glared.

Annoyed with Jason's continued appraisal, I wielded my rock at him. "Good choice. Now be off with you."

The two partners looked down the road and back at Jason, but Jason didn't budge. He actually puffed out his chest as though I should be impressed for some reason.

His mouth curled to a smirk. "You should show me more respect, Grizzy. Lord Ursa's letting me join the guard."

The image of Jason Gutcher becoming one of Lord Ursa's toadies sent alarm through my chest. I flung the stick to the side, tossed my rock from hand to hand, and growled, "Then I suggest you keep your helmet on, so your head won't grow more lumps."

Jason's hand reached quickly to the mound on his pate that I'd raised moments ago. The thin trickle of blood inched down his cheek toward his jawline. Embarrassment flashed across his face as he noted a spot of blood on his hand and quickly wiped it on his breeches.

Jason's eyes slowly roamed over me from head to toe, taking in all of Sarah's recent effort. "I don't know why I listen to you, Grizzy."

The way he was looking at me made my nose crinkle into a sneer and my fist want to connect with his nose, but I said nothing, just snapped my rock firmly from palm to palm.

Jason started to join his buddies but turned for one last shot. "You'll soon learn you can't walk around like you own the kingdom anymore. Your father is dead."

Only the image of my invoked father—and the fact that I'd already drawn blood once—stayed the eager rock in my hand.

The three assailants loped down the road as I approached Gilly, who glared after the retreating trio.

With concern, I noted a bruise on his face. "You all right, Gilly?"

He nodded, his disheveled black hair flopping in his brown eyes, his fists clenched at his sides. Humiliation colored his tan cheeks, his narrowed eyes still tracking the threesome vengefully.

Gilly, though small for fourteen, had a tough, wiry build. He could have taken Jason on his own—but not with the addition of the two hulking toughs. Still, Gilly was embarrassed.

Not wanting to further mortify the victimized boy with discussion, I said, "Why don't you go to my house. Tell Sarah I sent you. She'll give you something to eat, but then stay out of her way. She's really busy today."

Gilly's stormy face perked up inquiringly at the mention of Sarah's cooking.

I chuckled with understanding. "Yes, there is fresh bread."

As if to rid himself of his recent encounter, Gilly took a deep breath in and out, gave me a grin, and with a salute from his forehead by way of thanks, ambled in the direction of Hart Cottage, leaving me with Rags.

"Rags, go with Gilly," I said.

Rags, undeterred, planted his paws against my waist. I quickly placed his feet on the ground, rubbed his ears, and pointed after at Gilly, who turned to wait.

"Rags, go home."

He cocked his head at me. I dropped to my knees, gave him a vigorous neck rub, and pointed again. "With Gilly."

With a bark, Rags scampered to the orphan's side, and the two to them trotted companionably down the lane past the curled document that I'd dropped moments ago. I retrieved the missive, dusted it with my hands, and watched as the figures of Jason and his cronies got smaller and smaller.

For a moment, the satisfaction of curbing Jason's troublemaking—again—left me feeling upbeat. Then I remembered the tearing sound. With trepidation, I lifted the skirt of my dress and found that the hemstitching had ripped just slightly. Relieved, I judged myself still in good condition. After all, the damage could not be seen. I let the fabric drop and noted that the hemline drooped just a bit at the rip, but surely no one would notice. I vigorously slapped off the paw prints left by Rags and the dust on my knees and felt confident that I was making good on my promise to Sarah. I'd head to the castle, rescue the prince, and be back in presentable condition for the unwelcome family gathering.

In the distance, the flags flying above the Fairian Castle towers flapped lazily in the gentle breeze. It also ruffled the wisps of stray hair framing my face, making me want to shake off the constraints of ladylike behavior. Nevertheless, with longsuffering patience, I padded along Castle Road, passed Heaton's acreage and other neighboring farms, and headed so slowly toward Fairian Village that I wanted to scream. Finally, unable to take it any longer, I concluded that walking took far too long. So I picked up the edges of my skirt and broke into a trot. Surely, Sarah wouldn't mind a gentle trot. It wouldn't muss my dress at all. I'd return home a close to perfect lady—or at least the appearance of one.

A light traffic of villagers entered and exited the West Gate pushing carts, shouldering farming tools, or carrying baskets of goods. I approached the gate, unobserved by the two guards clad in red tunics, who seemed engaged in anything but guard duty. One guard, Fritz, leaned against the entrance stones attempting to play music with a blade of grass. The other guard, Gammon, was bent forward slightly to listen to Farmer Hugh Heaten, my old neighbor, who wore a tan knee length tunic and baggy hose. I caught a bit of Farmer Hugh's comment, "...my best cow..."

I approached the trio. "Greetings."

Fritz looked up, dropped his grass, and gaped. I had meant to breeze right through the gate as usual, but he kept staring.

So I stopped, stood in front of him, and peered into his open-mouthed face. "What?"

He shut his mouth and swallowed. "Miss Griselda."

Now, I knew something was wrong, since he usually called me Grizzy, which from him was fine with me. So I echoed my name with a question in my tone. "Miss Griselda?"

Fritz shuffled his feet and found his coin pouch to be very interesting. "You, you look different."

I felt the pins sticking into my scalp and glanced down at my dress. Yes, I was turned out all fancy, but I was still the same old Grizzy. I noticed the other guard, Gammon, and Farmer Hugh staring at me, too.

Their conversation forgotten, they both nodded. "Good day, Miss Griselda."

I laughed, gave them a theatrical curtsy, and promenaded in a circle under the stone archway with a theatrical show of elegance. That earned me a laugh from the three men. So I saluted the group, picked up the edges of my skirt once more, and jogged off into the village, recalling Farmer Hugh's mention of his best cow. I hoped it wasn't sick. I would need to inquire about it later.

The aroma of stews and meat pies wafted through the air as I hurried through the village. The stone, wood, and plaster homes with their backyard gardens lined the streets, many with ground floor shops. Townsfolk bustled about making purchases, exchanging the latest gossip, and corralling their young. Shopkeepers displayed their goods from their open-shuttered, street-front businesses. There was plenty of time before the shutters would close for the evening, but I needed to be home well before then, which reminded me to make haste. I picked up my pace to an easy canter.

I waved as I passed the baker, the greengrocer, the cooper, the chandler, the innkeeper, and the goldsmith and silversmith, both from the far south like Gilly. I received many good wishes regarding the morrow's wedding—good wishes that soured in my gut. Finally, I passed the butcher, Mr. Carver, a giant of a man with a great girth and a large meat cleaver.

He shook the blade in my direction. "And what manner of trouble have you stirred up today, Grizzy dear?"

I stopped to chat with my friend. "Sarah has forbidden me to get in trouble today, sir."

Then his face scrunched up in puzzlement. "Well,

I'll be. You can't get into trouble in a fancy dress like that, now can you. You look the proper lady, indeed."

Tired of observations about my appearance, I refrained from reminding him that I was not a lady, took my leave, and headed across the village green. The green, site of markets, tournaments, and my favorite climbing tree, was presently dotted with children laughing, shrieking, and racing through its length.

A young girl streaked past me, her long tunic flapping around below her knees. "Look at me, Grizzy. I'm as fast as you."

I clapped and cheered for the young sprinter as I approached the King's Gate. Above the arched opening hung a freshly painted coat of arms: a crown above two crossed swords. Under that was a chiseled inscription, faded with time.

Peace and prosperity fill the land when governed by the true king's hand.

The entrance welcomed, its drawbridge down, the portcullis up, and guards standing at relaxed attention. They looked impressive with their shiny leather boots, black breeches, and red tunics emblazoned with a gold crown placed above crossed swords.

After exchanging waves with the guards, jogging under the portcullis, and passing into the courtyard, I set about my mission. It was time to rescue Prince Charmain from the evil clutches of a tedious meeting.

Chapter 5

Dueling Authorities

The courtyard of Fairian Castle churned with activity: the strikes of a blacksmith's hammer, the barking of dogs in the kennels, the scrape of cartwheels against stones, the grind of a carpenter's saw, the screech of a falcon in the mews, and the gossip of laundresses, scullery workers, and stable boys. The aroma wafting from the castle kitchen contrasted with the smell of animals and hay. I dodged a horse and groom exiting the stables, returned a wave from Sarah's cousin Nell, who worked in the kitchen, and loped past the royal apartments, fairy-tended gardens, one for the kitchen and one for the queen's leisure, and chapel, finally reaching the stairs of the giant stone keep.

Constructed with three main levels, the building had a basement level for storage, a guardroom on the second level, where off duty soldiers ate and assembled, and a cavernous great hall on the top level. Round towers anchored each corner of the edifice. The structure boasted ornate stained-glass windows, which illuminated the great hall inside, and huge oak doors with ironwork fixtures guarded the entrance.

Bounding to the top step, I stopped and inquired— just as a formality—of the red-and-black-clad guards at the door. "Greetings to you, and where might I find

Prince Charmain?"

They looked at each other before one replied. "The prince is in the great hall with the king and Lord Ursa, but I regret…"

He paused, looked at his feet, and shifted his weight.

This puzzled me, so I bent down and turned my face to look up into his downcast eyes. "Regret what?"

He straightened; I did too.

He cleared his throat. "Lord Ursa doesn't want to be interrupted."

I raised my eyebrows.

He flushed, bowed, pushed open the doors, and gestured to the entrance, clearly not inclined to talk further.

Perplexed by the embarrassed guards, I shrugged, passed through the arched doorway onto the guardroom level, and wound my way up the stone staircase. In the antechamber at the top, two more guards stood like statues in front of the great hall's elaborately carved double doors.

One of the guards, Hammond, held up his hand, a pained expression drawing his eyes in. "Greetings, Grizzy. I regret to inform you that there is to be no admittance at present."

Taken aback, I froze, my mouth dropping open with surprise in spite of the awkward warning from the downstairs guards. All of my life I had moved freely about the castle. When my father had been in service to the king, I had spent hours in the great hall, listening as he and the king had conducted the business of the kingdom. And it was rare that the great hall was not open to its subjects. Things were certainly different today, and I did not like it.

Though Hammond was simply doing his job, and I felt no ill will toward him, I still had a summons to obey—even though I only obeyed because it matched my own inclination.

I hitched my jaw back up, curtsied, and nodded at the paneled doors. "Hammond, please send word to the prince that I am here at his command and await his pleasure."

Hammond hesitated, and his eyes shifted from me to the closed door. "Lord Ursa said—"

I raised my rolled summons like a sword. "Oh, yes, I am quite sure that Lord Ursa has said a great many things, but His Royal Highness requested my presence at once, and here I am." I spread out my arms to prove my point.

Hammond reached for the parchment, unfurled its length, and frowned at Prince Charmain's scrawl. He pursed his lips, shared the letter with his fellow, and shifted his weight, making a scraping sound against the tiled floor.

"The prince is defying Lord Ursa's will."

Not amused by the dueling authorities, I hid my annoyance at Lord Ursa's control tactics, smiled at the conflicted guard, and gestured to the prince's letter. "Perhaps, but surely neither you nor I wish to defy the expressly written desire of our prince."

He hesitated for a second, then nodded, turned to the door, and pushed open the ornate panels.

The great hall boasted colorful tapestries hanging from the walls, coats of arms affixed in a row above, and arched stained-glass windows on all sides, permitting abundant sunlight to stream in. Painted columns supported galleries on both sides, and full suits of heirloom armor stood on display in niches. Built into the middle of each side wall, giant carved stone fireplaces faced each other, flames crackling from their depths leaving a smoky tang in the air. Iron chandeliers set with wax candles hung from heavy chains overhead.

At the far end of the hall, the largest tapestry in the room portrayed the crowning of King Benedict with two slightly smaller tapestries on either side honoring his son and grandson. The current monarch, Benedict's great-great-grandson King Beaumain, sat enthroned on a dais in front of the images of his ancestors and the coat of arms of the House of Fairian, a crown over two crossed swords on a red background, centered above the historic scenes. He wore a royal purple robe, a bejeweled crown, and a medallion bearing his family emblem. His scepter tilted loosely in his grip.

With the ruler stood his brown-robed steward, the village reeve in a brown tunic and breeches, and Lord Uriah Ursa, wearing a black robe edged with white ermine. A heavy medallion embossed with a mink hung from a chain around his neck. The king's clerk watched from the side, sitting at a small desk with quills, ink, and parchments at the ready.

No other nobles were present, which I found odd. My father had encouraged other representatives of the kingdom to take turns being available to advise the monarch before he rendered his decisions. He said it provided balance. It made me uneasy to see Lord Ursa as the sole counselor to the crown and reminded me of the comment in the prince's letter, "I wonder who is the king here?"

Prince Charmain, tall, muscular, and golden haired,

lounged on a smaller throne next to his father. Dressed in perfectly fitted hose, breeches, and a mid-length indigo tunic, the prince attended to anything but the discussion at hand. His eyes wandered toward an errant dog sniffing around his chair, a servant carrying a ceramic ewer, the stained-glass windows illuminating the hall, and finally to the reeve, who leaned forward, hands on his hips, frowning at Lord Ursa. My fists tightened from a familiar sense of frustration. Why couldn't our prince, our future king, take more interest in the affairs of the kingdom? I'd have to remind him—again.

King Beaumain gestured from the angry reeve to Ursa. "Perhaps we should be guided by the reeve. Farmer Hugh's cow…I'm not sure that was necessary."

Lord Ursa, stiff as a statue, replied, "Your subjects can afford heavier taxation, Your Majesty. Past policies have been too lenient, too lenient indeed."

As the attendants cast worried glances between the king and Lord Ursa, my indignation flared. How dare he question my father's practices? They were fair and just. Now, I realized that Farmer Hugh's recent comment at the West Gate referred to his cow being taken for taxes—probably to benefit the ermine adorned lord somehow. I could only hope that, in spite of the greedy lord's wishes, surely there was some mistake. And I would cajole the indolent prince into rectifying it.

At this point Lord Ursa noticed me, and the look he shot across the room made me catch my breath. Hammond must have caught it too, because he tried to shut the door.

I positioned myself centrally in the doorway in full view of the throne, so that the door couldn't be closed without making a scene.

Hammond bent and whispered near my ear. "I beg you to return later, Grizzy. Lord Ursa is incensed."

As I considered whether to comply with the request from the frightened guard, King Beaumain looked up and broke into a grin as though relieved to have a distraction.

He beckoned with his hand. "Miss Griselda, my dear girl. Why do you stand there on such ceremony? Approach us at once."

The prince looked up from scratching the dog's head, left the dais at once, and walked across the patterned tile floor to meet me.

"Grizzy, you are late. I was afraid that you would not come, and I'm..." He paused, glanced at my attire from head to toe, and stared.

I poked his shoulder. "You're what?"

He blinked and found his voice. "I, uh, you look different...uh, nice."

For the first time I felt the glow of pleasure in someone's reaction to my appearance. I wouldn't, however, give such evidence to Prince Charmain, so I opened my eyes wide at him and shook my head. He grabbed my arm and led me before the king, to whom I curtsied deeply.

He spread his arms in welcome. "Miss Griselda, you may rise. We are most pleased to see you. And now tell us." At this he leaned forward and lowered his voice conspiratorially. "What sorry knights have you vanquished today?"

Lord Ursa sneered, but the attendants chuckled with one of them muttering, "That suit of armor still has dents."

The prince and I glanced to King Benedict's antique armor displayed in a wall niche near the dais. We both grinned sheepishly, remembering how childishly we had behaved—and only a few months ago. The prince had been futilely chasing me around the castle, up and down winding staircases and behind tapestries, when we had collided with the valuable heirloom. What a loud, crashing, damaging commotion had ensued.

In truth, the worst part of the incident was that I had disappointed my father, which I never wanted to do. However, all he had said was, "Perhaps running outside…" Then he had grinned and patted my shoulder. But that was more than enough correction when coming from him. And shortly thereafter, he'd died. A fresh dart of pain for my loss pierced my heart, along with regret for my childishly disruptive past.

With a forced smile, I curtsied again. "I have been quite well behaved of late, Your Majesty."

He took a moment to stare at my hair and gown. "Yes, so we see, all dressed in your finery today, Miss Griselda."

Here he grinned broadly at the prince, who ducked his head. The king chuckled and returned his gaze to me.

I bent my knee deeply once more. "If it please, Your Majesty, Lord Robert Rella and his daughter arrive this evening."

The king nodded and beamed in response. "Yes, oh yes, may we offer our best wishes regarding your mother's upcoming nuptials?"

The men echoed his sentiments with the exception of Lord Ursa, who remained silent, his mouth puckering in disapproval. He stood beside the king, the light from a window glinting off the mink embossed silver medallion that he wore. I always thought of that mink as a weasel when I saw it hanging from his neck. He gazed upon me with the same sour expression he had always reserved for my father, who had thwarted many of his proposals. Apparently, his dislike now extended to me. I felt it.

The sour one spoke. "Ah, Miss Griselda, though we all no doubt wish your family well on this joyous occasion, you must forgive us. We are engaged in important matters and must continue our council in private. Good day to you."

He looked severely at the prince. "Your Royal Highness, if you would join us."

The prince and I exchanged glances, his a look of uncertainty, mine a puppy-faced look of pleading.

He stifled a laugh and directed his request to his father. "Father, if I might have a moment."

The king grinned and waved us off. "Yes, yes, off with the two of you."

Lord Ursa stiffened, which surprised me because I didn't think he could get any stiffer.

"Your Majesty, if I may, this is ill timing. Your son must be privy to our proceedings."

The king brushed him off with a good-natured gesture. "Oh, yes, yes, yes, do return promptly, my son. And Miss Griselda, allow me once again to wish you and your family good fortune."

I curtsied and backed away from the throne, realizing that the prince's ploy had been well conceived. I had indeed been an effective means of deliverance.

Prince Charmain, clearly eager for escape, jerked his head toward the door, which Hammond held open anxiously. As we quitted the throne room, I glanced back to see Ursa's eyes following us reproachfully. With his ill-will at our backs, we departed the great hall and headed to a favorite vantage point, the largest maple tree on the village green.

As I sat in the tree, a sense of impending loss washed over me. I looked toward the castle's crenellated walls looming to the east. Flags flapped atop the towers, banners emblazoned with family crests against backgrounds of green, yellow, and blue hung from the walls and the King's Gate. From the highest tower, the king's standard, a crown over crossed swords on a red background, snapped in the breeze.

The streets and buildings of the walled Fairian Village stretched to the West, North, and South Gates. But the new maple leaves surrounding me obscured my outlook somewhat. Oh, how I wished that the concealing foliage could hide me from my fate.

Though recoiling from my perceived familial doom, I had still managed to honor my need to return spotless, at least reasonably so. After climbing the trunk with special care, I now sat gingerly in the branches of the large maple tree on the green, taking care not to snag or stain my dress. Thankfully, the paw prints from Rags hardly showed, and only the most acute observer would notice the torn hem. So I would be presentable. I was sure of it—almost sure.

From my perch, I watched the clouds' growing presence in the sky, casting shade on the village green in which lingering children still played, avoiding their chores. I listened to their game.

"Catch a fairy, make a wish, make a wish, make a wish. Catch a fairy, make a wish, fa, la, la, la."

The youngsters chanted the words of the familiar rhyme as a pair of them made a bridge with their arms. The others crept under one by one, trying to avoid capture.

Finally, a child was caught between lowered arms, and the laughing pair of captors shouted out their wishes.

"I wish for a fine carriage."

"I wish for a beautiful gown."

Others chimed in with ideas that I couldn't make out.

It occurred to me that if I captured a fairy, maybe I could wish my new stepfamily away. But Father had firmly told me from a very young age that it was wicked to capture a fairy. Legend had it that the Dead Castle in the south was created that way. That was warning enough that catching fairies was wrong, especially since now I was the only person I knew who could. Besides, Arianna would be horrified that I would even think of such a crime.

I supposed it would also be wicked to destroy Mother's opportunity for matrimonial happiness, but I couldn't bring myself to feel as bad about that though guilt pricked at my conscience.

The "Catch a Fairy" song recommenced after the singers released the imprisoned playmate and began the game again. Near the children in the grasses and around me in the freshly sprouted leaves, the fairies, about which they sang, kept busily about their task of tending to the growing plants. I leaned closer to watch a nearby two-inch fairy with leaf green clothes and gossamer wings streaked with yellow and brown, when below me, the prince slapped at my leather shoe.

"Are you listening to me, Grizzy?"

I ignored him.

After he had promised, following much persuading from me, to use his influence to return Farmer Hugh's cow, he hadn't been sufficiently sympathetic to my familial plight, so I was annoyed. And I wondered how I could have considered Father's now-buried plan to marry myself to His Heartless Highness. Sure he was my friend, but sometimes I wanted to shake him. He needed so much prodding to step up to his responsibilities and to pay attention to the needs around him. And right now, the needs were mine.

Positioned up high in the branches of the maple that grew on a rise in the village green, I peered over the village wall to view the surrounding countryside and saw two carriages, followed by two wagons, traveling up King's Way from the south, coming closer, closer. The conveyances turned toward the west on the Harbor Connector, bypassing the village, and headed in the direction of Hart Cottage. My stomach churned. At this distance, I couldn't see the family crest on the sides, but I was certain that they carried my future stepfamily, the Rellas, and I wasn't ready to greet them. I never wanted to greet them.

"Grizzy, why are you so distracted?" The prince grabbed the hem of my dress and yanked, nearly unseating me from my branch. "Did you hear that I will be representing the crown on summer tour with Lord Ursa?"

I pulled the fabric free from his grasp, hoping the hem was still reasonably intact, and a touch of resentment wormed its way into my chest. The prince would be journeying with a full complement of guards and attendants, rendering him safe. While on that same route, my father had lost his life. Also, I dejectedly pondered the reason for his journey. Apart from launching the prince on his royal responsibilities, it was rumored, but not confirmed, that the king wanted his son to meet some of the eligible young ladies of the realm, titled young ladies. Not that I cared—I told myself. I had always known that, in spite of the prince's teasing about marriage, I was a commoner, not good enough for the prince. My father's plan seemed futile, and even though I loved the shiny slippers, and I loved my father for wanting to protect me, I wasn't sure about using them to gain influence. And the king, though he liked me, clearly had other ideas.

In response to the scion's question, I finally sighed, stretched out my toes, and tapped him on his golden curls with my shoe. "Yes, yes, I heard every word, but I don't see why you have to go on tour and pretend to be an adult?"

He knocked my foot away from his head. "I am an adult; I'm older than you."

An unladylike guffaw escaped me. "Don't act it. You should pay more attention in court, so I don't always need to tell you what's going on." Then a sobering consideration struck me. "And you shouldn't let Lord Ursa make changes to systems that already work. Stand up to him. He's just greedy."

"You are overreacting. And I do pay attention and act my age."

"Oh, really?" I needled. "I recall it was you that crashed into King Benedict's armor and left all those dents."

"Me? That was your fault."

I sighed with false humility. "Yes, it probably was."

He pointed a finger up at me. "You should start being more respectful. I'm your future king."

"Very well, my future king." I whacked him on the head with a sprouting twig and pointed to the King's Gate. "Earn my respect."

In response to my challenge, he began to maneuver himself out of the tree. "I'll beat you today, Grizzy."

I laughed, swung down from my branch, being mindful not to snag my dress, and beat him to the ground. I hit the field running and heard him breaking branches and cursing as he clambered out of the tree, followed by the heavy thuds of his pounding feet. I had to admit; he was getting faster. Lately, he'd been putting more heart into physical skills, but he'd never beat me in a race.

I looked back and taunted. "Make haste, Prince Charming. The enemy is getting away."

The prince gasped out, "Don't call me that, Grizzy."

I laughed, picked up the sides of my skirts out of respect for my mother, and sprinted beside the dry moat toward the King's Gate. The coarse field grass slapped against my ankles, leaving green streaks and snags on my hose, but the gown would cover those spots, so I didn't worry. Of course, running in a nice dress wasn't ladylike, but that never bothered me, at least not until I got in trouble or somehow embarrassed myself. And besides, I was fast, no one faster.

With the village on my left and the King's Gate on

my right, I turned right, cantered across the drawbridge and loped under the rusted portcullis, waving at the guards stationed at their posts.

I heard them laughing and commenting behind me. "He'll never catch her, and she's not even trying."

And it made me smile, because they were right.

When I breezed through the King's Gate and entered the courtyard, I turned right, sprinted across the dusty ground into the stable, and dodged a groom leading a sweaty horse.

"Oh, I'm so sorry," I said in passing and tagged the tack room door, the customary end of our races.

Prince Charmain came pounding into the stable, collided with the groom, and barked, "Watch where you're going!"

The groom stepped back and bowed. "I beg your pardon, Your Highness," and then continued leading the horse toward the stalls in the far end of the stable.

The prince collapsed on a dusty trunk inside the tack room, breathing heavily, mots of dust floating above his head in the light from the doorway. Stable smells of hay, leather, and horses filled the air.

I stood over him with one hand on my hip and the other wagging a finger in his face. "You shouldn't yell at the servants like that. Besides, it was your fault."

He waved off my comment and said breathlessly, "Always my conscience, aye, Grizzy."

I waited as he puffed away, trying to catch his breath. I wasn't even breathing hard.

He clutched his chest, still panting. "I almost caught you this time."

In your dreams, I thought and wondered, not for the first time, why such a tall, muscular young man presented so limited a challenge?

As his heaving breath slowed, it gradually sank in that I would not see him again for who knew how long. Even though he irritated me, our friendship worked well with me prodding him and him reluctantly acknowledging the justice of my positions—really they had been my father's positions.

When he could breathe normally again, I asked, "So how long will you be gone?"

He slouched back on the trunk, resting his loose curls against the tack room wall that was covered with hanging bridles, and heaved a theatrical sigh. "Years probably."

I smacked his shoulder. I really did want better information about the rumors. "Stop it. How long really?"

The prince stood up and gazed down at me with an expression that made me want to move closer or back away. I wasn't sure which. "Will you miss me?" he asked.

I settled for shoving him as hard as I could.

He fell back onto the trunk, laughing. "Looks like it's getting harder to push me around."

He made a grab for my hand, but I was, of course, too quick for him and hopped out of his reach. Annoyed, I said, "Be serious." And then curiosity took control of my tongue. "What exactly does the king want you to do on the tour?" There, I'd said it. And I couldn't take it back.

A flash of impatience crossed his face. "Look, Grizzy, you can't always butt into everything like your father."

I stepped farther away from him and said nothing.

Sure I was being nosy, but he was my friend, and it felt like a fist had just punched my chest. As we stared at each other across several feet of empty space, I watched the realization of how cruel he'd just been register on his face.

His shoulders sank. "I'm sorry. I know your father gave the best advice."

I still said nothing.

He leaned forward and assumed a beaten puppy expression. "So will you miss me even though I'm a jackass sometimes?"

What I wanted was to slap him soundly on the arm and walk away furious. But this being the last time I'd see him before leaving for Rella Manor, I stifled my fury. "Just don't be a jackass during your travels."

Okay, so most subjects wouldn't have called their prince a jackass, even if he deserved it, but at least I hadn't slapped him—yet. He leaned back on the trunk again and fingered the reins from a bridle hanging next to his head.

"Ursa and I can handle this…"

I sprang forward, kicked the trunk with my foot, and watched in satisfaction as the prince jerked his leg farther from my strike point and eyed me warily.

I leaned toward him. "Don't let that man lead you by the nose, Charmain. You're the prince. You've got to stand up to him."

With our faces only inches apart now, I watched that unsettling expression creep back into his eyes. Given our current topic, it made me want to reach out and strangle him.

"Grizzy, when I get back, Father will hold a feast to celebrate my return."

I threw up my hands in frustration. That wasn't even on the subject. I'd had enough, even if it was the last time I'd see him for weeks, probably months.

"Well, have a happy feast." And I turned to leave.

He rose from the trunk, grabbed my left arm, and spun me back around. "Guess what else."

I shrugged, weary of trying to say good-bye amicably. "I don't know, but I need to go. I've stayed too long, and my family's waiting."

He continued to hold my left arm and now grasped my right arm as well. "I asked Father for his consent to announce our betrothal at the feast. He said he'd give it due consideration."

Before I could react, he grabbed my head and smashed a hard, sloppy kiss on my mouth.

I jerked my head back. "You what?"

He dropped his hands and smirked at me like he'd just gotten away with something, which he certainly had. "See you when I return."

And he spun on his heel and swaggered from the tack room like he'd just won a prize.

Chapter 6

The Stepfamily

Betrothed?

I stood there stunned, staring at the prince-free space. Yes, he'd been threatening to marry me since we were children, but in spite of Father's hopeful scheme, I'd always known he'd make a political match. Apparently, I'd been wrong, and my observant parent had analyzed the prince's intentions correctly. And it appeared that perhaps the king was more agreeable to the match than Father had anticipated. After all, he hadn't rejected the idea outright.

Now, with my flaming face and beating heart, a troubling thought occurred to me. He had asked for his father's consent. Had it ever occurred to him to ask for mine?

My father had done me the courtesy of asking if I was interested; Prince Charmain had simply assumed as much.

With my emotions battling between pleasure and annoyance, with annoyance prevailing, questions tumbled in my mind. Could it be that Father's plan to change the fairy sight law would work out? Would Mother, though scared of the plan, eventually be pleased? Would I be able to learn to manifest fairies without fear? Could I help my neighbors and their fields with my new position? It felt like my entire world was shifting.

In a daze I turned to leave the stables, when—

"Caught yourself a prince, have you?"

Startled out of my skin, I spun about to discover the speaker. The groom, with whom the prince had collided earlier, strode toward me through the dusty light of the horse-scented stable, cradling a dirty saddle. His clothes, boots, and face were equally soiled. While I respected someone who looked like they worked hard, I didn't like to be startled, and my face warmed once again with embarrassment.

I planted both feet firmly on the ground, put my hands on my hips, and barred his way to the tack room. "I beg your pardon."

He halted a few feet from me, shifted the saddle to one hip, and smirked. "You're quite right, m'lady. You'd have to catch him, because he'd never catch you."

Though I knew that was true and felt no small amount of pride in it, I didn't like people to make fun of the prince, my prince, especially smirking, cocky, lanky-looking strangers.

I leaned forward from the waist, pointed a finger at the groom, and took him to task. "That's not how to speak about your prince."

"Suit yourself, m'lady, but I saw you beat him fair and square. So he must be a sluggard, that prince."

My embarrassment shifting to anger, I took a step closer to him, almost touching the saddle, while the grinning interloper held his ground.

I wanted to wipe that smug grin right off his face. "Take that back."

He shrugged. "Or what?"

Then he sidled around me into the tack room.

As he brushed by, I followed his progress and noted that he smelled of a confusing combination of soap and sweat. He was tall but a touch shorter than Prince Charmain, skinnier too, in that tight, wiry fashion of those accustomed to hard work. And he hoisted the saddle onto a rack with an ease I knew Charmain would never match.

He turned, caught me watching him, and smirked again. My stomach jumped like something was inside trying to get out, like I was going to be sick, but not really.

He leaned that wiry body of his back against the saddle, crossed his arms, raised his eyebrows, and asked again, "Or what?"

"Or…"

I paced the short space in front of the tack room door once, twice, casting my mind about for a punishment suitable for calling my prince a sluggard and also severe enough for irritating me so thoroughly.

"Or…" With confidence, I chose my old standby. "I'll challenge you myself, and we'll see who's the sluggard."

His grin widened, which got my ire up even more. I was determined to remove that arrogant smile from his face at any cost. I'd show him.

He straightened and bowed with a sweep of his hand. "Where to, m'lady?"

Oh, his sarcastic tone riled me, and I really didn't have time for this. I was due at home to greet my new stepfamily. I'd have to make this quick. "The tall maple near the wall on the green."

He paused, looked up and to one side considering, and then nodded. "Ah, yes, I know the one. And when should we engage in our little contest?"

Self-confidence twinkled in his eyes, like this was all a big joke to him, so I decided this was no time to be polite, or even fair.

"Hmmm, let me see." I clasped my hands behind myself and strolled casually away from the tack room door, keeping my head turned and my eyes on his.

He frowned, suspicion lighting his eyes, which gratified me greatly.

When I had a straight shot at the stable exit, I yelled, "Now."

The look of shock that crossed his face filled me with immense enjoyment as I sprinted away from the tack room. He recovered quickly. After hearing a few oaths and a bit of crashing about behind me, I heard the firm pounding of his running stride on the stable floor. I dashed from the stable into the warm sunlight with my arms pumping, my skirt flapping against my legs, and my heart glowing with confidence.

Even though this young man was smaller and thinner than Charmain, I sensed that this would be a real race, and I couldn't have been happier. I was going to bury this smug what's his name. So what if I cheated just a little at the start. He deserved it.

I left the stable yard in a cloud of dust and galloped through the gatehouse like lightning, if I do say so myself, under the portcullis, and across the drawbridge. Oh, I just love to run.

"Run, Grizzy, run," I heard from the guards as I pounded across the drawbridge toward the village green, followed by, "Faster, Grizzy, he's gaining on you."

Gaining? Nobody gains on me. And I even gave myself a touch of a head start. I felt a twinge of guilt and also an unfamiliar moment of doubt. I didn't like it.

I grabbed the sides of my skirt and lifted to give my legs more room to run. I turned on more speed as I ran an arcing left turn on the green, which fortunately was now clear of children who were probably home for dinner—where I should be. I dashed for the maple tree a long stone's throw away. The grass and weeds slapped at my hose and the hem of my dress, and I felt the pulling and snagging of fabric. I hadn't been mussed up after racing Prince Charmain. I simply hadn't run fast enough. But now I realized with dismay that at this speed I would be snagged, torn, and streaked with filth. Now, I'd arrive both late and messy to my family gathering, and Mother would be ashamed of me. I'd have to face that later. For now, I needed to finish vindicating my friend.

Confident that at this speed my opponent was lagging behind me, I glanced back. What I saw felt like a blow to my heart. He was right behind me. Expecting to hear heavy pounding like Charmain and other boys, I hadn't realized how close the groom was, his footfalls light and quick on the grass.

I called on my reserves once again for a new burst of speed. My legs obeyed, but now I was at full tilt and breathing hard. I never breathed hard. Rats.

The sound of springy footfalls and panting breath drew closer behind me. I had never been so spent. My sides ached; my breath stabbed; my feet throbbed, but I kept them pounding toward the maple tree.

Only a few more yards, my opponent was at my

90

heels, by my side. I could feel his heat, his breath. I reached out for the tree just as another hand reached as well. We both crashed into the trunk and tumbled to the grass on opposite sides, I on my hands and knees, my opponent splayed face down on the green, both of us gasping for air.

I didn't want to look at him, didn't want to look at anyone ever again. I didn't want to face it. It wasn't by more than a hand length, but I had just lost.

Neither one of us said anything for a couple minutes. The field grass prickled under my hands, and the shade of the maple tree cooled my shaking frame.

I felt sick, light-headed. On hands and knees, I hung my head down from my shoulders and tried to steady my breathing to clear the dizziness. It was slow to pass.

Finally, I pushed back, sat with my legs folded under myself, and noticed the dirt- and grass-stained knee areas of my skirt from where I'd hit the ground. An avalanche of remorse assailed me. Even though I was not in favor of my mother's upcoming marriage, greeting my new stepfather again and meeting my new stepsister for the first time were important to my family and to me. Now, my appearance was beyond redemption.

The groom rolled over and sat up, leaning back on his elbows, his legs stretched out on the green. Bits of grass dotted his clothes. He looked at me and grinned. How dare he mock me when he'd just bested me in a race?

"I beg forgiveness for what I said about your prince. No wonder he can't beat you. You're fast."

I wasn't even slightly mollified. "Not fast enough it

seems."

He laughed and stood up, reaching a hand down to me. "Oh, you're fast enough, m'lady. I'm the fastest runner in my company, and I barely caught you."

I frowned at his offered hand and didn't move.

He raised his eyebrows with entreaty and stretched his hand to me again.

Realizing that I was being both a poor sport and impolite, I reluctantly took his hand, and he raised me to stand next to him. I dropped his hand quickly and busied myself with brushing off some of the damage to my dress with my hands, but it was no use.

Unable to keep the sullenness from my voice, I said, "Company? I thought you were a groom."

He plucked a long blade of grass from my hair. "And so I am for my exhausted horse, but I'm Courier Jon, new to the King's Guard."

I stepped back from him, crossed my arms, and scanned him from top to bottom: his soiled clothes, his worn boots, and his lack of uniform. I also noticed how the clothes draped on his muscular body.

"You don't look like you're with the guard."

He glanced down at his dirty clothes and slapped at them with his hands, creating clouds of dust.

"Travel wear." He raised his eyebrows. "I can't always wear my uniform. It's covered with scores of medals for honor and bravery. I can hardly stand up under the weight."

I rolled my eyes at him, earning myself another of his all too frequent grins. Great, he beats me in a race and then turns into a jester.

I'd had enough. "Please pardon me. I must take my leave."

He pretended to remove a non-existent hat from his disheveled brown hair and bowed. "As you wish m'lady, but for whom should I ask if I wish for a rematch?"

For the first time in my life, I was uncertain about a race. Nevertheless, I'd be hanged before I'd back down from his challenge, so I snapped back at him as I started to walk away.

"You're on."

I took several strides through the dandelion speckled grass away from him and noted with dismay that the sun was now sinking toward the trees. It was later than I realized.

"Hold it."

I spun around, vexed at being stopped. "What?"

He stood with his weight on one leg looking amused. "Do you have a name?"

Now, on top of humiliation, I felt foolish. I wanted to get away from this young man, well, not really young, as quickly as possible.

"Oh, yeah, Griselda. Griselda Hart."

Amusement drained from his face. "Hart? Matthew Hart?"

The dramatic change in Courier Jon's manner caused me to grow very quiet inside. "My father."

He tipped his head back, raised his eyes to the heavens, and exhaled. He shook his head. "I'm sorry about your father, Miss Griselda."

Not as sorry as me, I thought, as the hole in my chest expanded sending pulses throughout my body. They threatened to pour out through my nose and eyes. But I did not wish to be vulnerable to someone who had just humiliated me so completely, even if he did know of my father.

So I grasped for a distraction. "You are not from here."

Apparently not deterred by my change of subject, Courier Jon ignored my statement, narrowed his eyes, and looked at me as if trying to figure something out. "Your father had a good reputation."

As much as I appreciated his good words about my father, I had the feeling that this courier was keeping something to himself, and I did not like it.

Now, it was my turn to look at him, trying to figure him out. "Yes, I thank you."

He nodded but continued to scrutinize me like he was trying to read my thoughts. He glanced up at the tree. "Miss Griselda, out of curiosity, what do you see in the maple?"

I looked up. The fairies fluttered about with their usual busy abandon, a hint of their luminescence glowing as nighttime fell, but I knew better than to reveal that to anyone. I looked back at the groom or courier or whatever he was only to be impaled by his intense, visual probe. I stepped back from his gaze and raised my hands and eyebrows, partly to show how obvious the answer was and partly in self-defense.

I coughed out a disdainful exhalation and gestured upward sharply. "Leaves."

And I turned and strode away across the green.

I didn't like this Courier Jon. He was too fast and too arrogant and too nosy. When I reached Castle Road, I glanced back. The courier hadn't moved. He was still watching me.

I broke into a weary jog and headed for home.

As clouds accumulated overhead, I trotted west

along Castle Road, my focus alternating between my humiliating loss to Courier Jon and Prince Charmain's potential proposal. Even though His Highness's proposal—really more of an announcement than a proposal—was presumptuous, it pleased me that he wanted to marry me in spite of the king's reticence. Maybe I should consider Father's plan and try wearing the slippers around the king. His Majesty seemed bent on a match with a titled female, but perhaps that could be unobtrusively changed—nudged as Father had said.

It surprised me that Father's plan might be so easily implemented, that eventually our fears about fairy sight could be alleviated. Nevertheless, due to the uncertainty, I decided not to mention it to Mother. The king could make his wishes known to her should the event become a reality. This way I wouldn't be heaping embarrassment upon embarrassment if Charmain had spoken carelessly, which was entirely possible. With that matter resolved for the moment, I fell into thinking about that nosy messenger.

I approached my home, still fuming about my loss to that courier. Fortunately, the sight of the old cottage, the stone kitchen, my stone and wood family house, the outbuildings for animals and storage, and our rambling gardens with their glowing attendants lifted my spirits as always. The tension drained from my muscles for a couple of seconds, and then I saw them.

Parked past the house were the carriages I'd seen traveling up the King's Way earlier. The Rella family crest, two red roses crossed at the stems, graced the carriage doors. My breath quickened and the briefly alleviated stress returned. I was late and dirty and had to face not only my mother but my future stepsister and stepfather as well. And I didn't want a stepfather.

I slowed to a walk, trudged between the rose bushes framing the gate, and plodded into the yard. The sun, now lower, gave the increasing clouds peachy highlights and cast an orange glow through the apple and pear trees in our small orchard located past the herb and vegetable gardens. The softened light also touched across the roses, rhododendrons, irises, and wildflowers edging the fenced yard. Glowing fairies adorned in petal colors fluttered about the colorful blooms. Their radiance, always more apparent at nighttime, brightened as I approached, and in spite of my doldrums, my insides warmed with pleasure. Fairies.

It puzzled me that some people no longer believed in fairies, even though temple services were replete with references to them. I guessed that folks felt themselves too sophisticated for such old-fashioned ideas. But it didn't make sense. How else could flowers bloom, crops grow, rains fall, and birds sing?

When I was very young, Father had told me that I could see fairies because they felt a kinship with me. He had said that it was a secret that he would explain when I was older. Now, he was gone, and I didn't care about the stupid secret. I wanted my father—not some poor substitute.

Continuing toward the cottage, I passed the arbor-covered garden bench where Isabella used to sit, sometimes doing embroidery, before Father's passing. Since his death, and since her confrontation with Mother about fear several weeks ago, she had avoided going outside, complained of headaches, and acted silent and withdrawn much of the time, even from me, which made me sad. As a matter of fact, Isabella had begun to behave so oddly that it worried Mother. I, while sharing the concern, guessed it was her way of coping with grief, which I understood all too well.

As I neared the cottage entrance, I heard a door slam and the rustle of fabric. I tried to dodge behind a rhododendron, but no luck. Sarah, in her ankle-length gray tunic and white apron, spied me and bustled out to corral me.

"Miss Griselda, Miss Griselda. Oh, yer so late, and..." She gasped and looked at the knees of my gown.

I shrank before her gaze, filling with remorse for my failure to keep my promise.

Sarah shook her head and bent to brush at my soiled fabric. "You are such a sight. What'll yer mother say, and with Lord Robert here..."

I reached down to assist Sarah in her attempt to make me presentable. "Sarah, I'm sorry. I truly am, but I had to race this courier, and I fell."

Sarah straightened and faced me. "Race some courier? You had to do nothin' of the kind."

"But he called the prince a sluggard."

Sarah sighed and placed her hands on my shoulders. "Child, child, I know ya mean well, but how do these things always happen to you?"

I shrugged as she wrapped an arm around my waist.

"There's nothing to be done about you now. Yer mother and Lord Robert are waitin' on you."

She tried to inch me forward, but I resisted and my eyes welled. "He will never be my father."

Sarah patted my shoulder. "I know, I know, but put on a good countenance for yer mother. Come now."

She reached out, tried to re-pin the hair falling from my netting, and gave two final slaps at the dirt and debris on my clothes before giving up.

"Well, there's no help for you now. Make haste…"

As Sarah ushered me into the cottage, my nose crinkled in response to the tang of fireplace smoke and the faint scent of beeswax candles used specially for this occasion.

Mother's strained voice came from the parlor. "I am sure that Griselda will be here soon."

Sarah gave me a shove. "Go on, child, don' keep them waitin'."

I didn't want to go in. Though not usually prissy about my attire, two large dirt-brown knee stains were beyond even my tolerance.

I peeked into the parlor. Lord Robert, wearing black boots and breeches, a shirt with voluminous sleeves, and a knee length brown tunic edged with jeweled embroidery, sat in a carved oak ladder-back chair next to the fireplace. He was coughing phlegm into a handkerchief.

A girl about my age, whom I assumed would be my new stepsister, stood in the center of the room like a princess wearing an embroidered silk dress of sapphire blue. My mother and younger sister, Isabella, stood on either side of her, attired in crisp linen dresses, dark blue and light blue respectively, a trio of blonde beauties in complementary colors. I looked down at my soil-spotted, grass-streaked dress and cringed.

Though it was the last thing I wanted to do, I entered the fire-and-candle-illuminated parlor with its whitewashed walls and hanging tapestries, my favorite being the one with a forest scene. All the homey features increased in importance to me with the thought of leaving tomorrow. The exposed wood beams in the ceiling created a white and brown pattern overhead. The fireplace boasted a crackling fire that cut the beginning of evening chill.

My footsteps squeaked against the wooden plank floor and then muffled as I stepped onto the wool carpet. Conversation ceased. All eyes raked my soiled clothes and then rested on me.

Mother gasped and stared at me for a moment. Then she hitched a smile onto her face, walked to Lord Robert, and put her hand on his shoulder.

"My lord, you remember my daughter, Griselda."

Lord Robert coughed, wiped his mouth with his handkerchief, and arose, leaning on a carved mahogany cane.

"Miss Griselda." He took my hand and bowed. "The fresh air brings such a pretty glow to your cheeks. You take after Constance, your beautiful mother."

In response to Lord Robert's graciousness, a fleeting thought scampered across my mind that maybe he wouldn't be too bad.

I curtsied. "Thank you, sir. I am pleased to see you again."

He grinned like a retriever and gestured to the silent girl. "And this, Miss Griselda, is my little princess, Cynthia."

The "princess" stood stiffly in the center of the room as though afraid of defilement. Her expression looked like she smelled a skunk.

I glanced around our parlor, so spotlessly cleaned by Sarah and Abigail, and wanted to grab that "princess" by the shoulders and give her a good shake.

But I did as courtesy demanded; I curtsied and held out my hand.

The "princess" stepped forward, scanned my dirty clothes and race-blown hair with a sniff, nodded curtly, and kept her hands plastered to her side.

I dropped my hand and an awkward silence hung in the room as Lord Robert, Isabella, and Mother glanced between Cynthia and me.

Mother broke it. "Griselda, did you have a chance to say good-bye to the prince?"

"Yes, Mother. He soon leaves for the royal tour, and I don't know when—"

"Oh yes, the prince." Cynthia interrupted as if she suddenly remembered something. "You have been with Prince Charmain?"

I nodded at the melting ice "princess," her obvious interest in His Royal Highness outweighing her equally obvious revulsion of me.

Mother came and put her arm around me. "Grizzy, I mean Griselda, and Prince Charmain have been playmates since childhood."

Now, the "princess" stepped forward with a smile that stretched from ear to perfect ear.

She slipped her arm through mine like a best friend and said, "I am so looking forward to having sisters."

I wanted to run.

Later that evening, Lord Robert left with his attendants to stay with a wealthy merchant in the village, leaving his "princess" to get to know her new sisters. The steps creaked as I led the way up the narrow, candle lit staircase. I glanced behind myself at Isabella and Cynthia, who had linked arms in an exploration of familial closeness. I cringed inside and struggled to keep my lips from curling in disgust. Isabella, I knew, sincerely wished to be Cynthia's friend. However, of Cynthia's motivation, I had my doubts.

I listened to Cynthia's prattle. "Dear Isabella, you must permit me to style your hair. I have some old combs that will suit you splendidly."

As Isabella glowed in anticipation of Cynthia's cast-off combs, I gagged silently in response, thinking that Isabella's hair looked fine—better than Cynthia's bejeweled coif in fact.

My gut grew queasy as Cynthia praised Isabella's simple gown, patted her head, and stroked her arm as if she were a new pet that I feared would be discarded when no longer entertaining. How was I to endure all of this? Not only was Mother marrying the pleasant but entirely silly lord, but also my sister was being played like a puppet.

At the top of the stairs, I reached for the door and swung it open to the bedchamber that Isabella and I shared. I glanced at the basin and pitcher on the washstand, the hanging tapestry adorning the far wall, the sturdy clothing armoire to the right of the door, and a few one-inch fairies hovering sleepily above fragrant roses in a vase on the chest of drawers.

Finally, my eyes rested on the feline-occupied bed that the three of us would share—far too closely in my opinion—for the night. The thought of sleeping next to Cynthia made my stomach churn, but there was no help for it. I entered, wondering what my new stepsister would make of the room. Isabella followed.

Cynthia stopped in the doorway. Her eyes surveyed the room slowly, and I'm certain that I heard her sniffing as if for some foul odor. My gut roiled. My home might not be fancy, but it was spotlessly clean and as fresh as the spring flowers decorating the room.

Isabella stood breathlessly gazing up at tall, slender Cynthia as if awaiting some pronouncement regarding the suitability of the chamber. I waited for her to reject its simplicity, which would have been fine with me. I'd suggest that she join her father at the merchant's or go sleep by the hearth for all I cared.

Cynthia, however, stepped inside. "What a charming bedchamber." She made a sweeping gesture with her hand to include the whole of our humble room.

Isabella clasped her palms together. "Oh, I'm so pleased that you like it."

They walked around the room with Cynthia inspecting every beloved item: the comfy bed with its homemade quilt, the carved oak washstand with a basin and pitcher, the special occasion beeswax candles resting in wall sconces and candleholders, and the chest of drawers topped with a vase filled with pink roses.

The only things that Cynthia couldn't examine hovered near the flowers. A few petal-clothed fairies, about an inch in height, fluttered half-heartedly around the cut blooms. Fairies often followed their flowers into the house, but they never had the same enthusiasm for cut plants. When they finally wilted, their fairies would abandon them for the new growth outdoors.

Cynthia and Isabella passed by the fairies without seeing them—although Isabella glanced at the flowers rather nervously—and approached our large trunks stacked against the tapestry covered wall, the evidence of our departure tomorrow. Most were secured with straps, but one smaller trunk atop the others remained open, revealing a few items of particular value to Isabella and me that we had chosen to pack separately, including Father's final gift to me.

My slippers lay nestled in soft fabric and peeked out with their fairy-blessed glow. Cynthia, whose eyes roved the room with critical appraisal, zeroed in on the slippers at once. I immediately wished I had closed the trunk.

Cynthia crossed the space swiftly, pulled the slippers from the trunk, and examined them with an eye practiced in evaluating items of value.

"These are most unusual." She turned them over in her hands. "Made of linen yet with the sparkle of diamonds."

It was the first time I'd heard awe in Cynthia's voice. She cradled the shoes possessively.

I had an urge to rip them from her hands, an impulse that I curbed. "Thank you, Cynthia. I'm glad that you like them. They are special to me."

I held out my hands in silent demand for my property. Cynthia didn't move. So I gently tried to lift them from her grasp, but she held them like a vise. The moment threatened to become a tug-of-war before Cynthia released her grip, her covetousness regarding my slippers a palpable presence in the room. Our eyes fenced for a second, and then we both stretched our lips across our teeth in thin, forced smiles.

Cynthia lifted her chin, walked to the bed, and turned to Isabella and me.

She spoke like a lady addressing her servants. "I believe that this room will be tolerable for one night. Where will you sleep?"

And with those words, she dismissed Isabella and

me from our own room.

Isabella startled beside me, her jaw dropped and her eyes widened, and I, too, was momentarily shocked into speechlessness.

Cynthia observed us both, and a look of smug satisfaction played in her eyes.

I considered telling Cynthia that Isabella and I planned to sleep in our own bed and that Cynthia would be most welcome to make a little nest of blankets on the floor or curl up near the cinders by the fire, but I remembered that I was a hostess and Cynthia was my guest.

I nodded to her graciously but could see that she was not deceived by my courtesy. "Isabella and I will sleep with Mother. Good night to you."

I picked up our small trunk with personal valuables, placed my slippers in their nest once again, and headed to the door with Isabella following mutely. Cynthia shooed an indignant Mr. Tatters off the bed as her eyes roved about the room clearly curious about other unique items that she might find.

As I opened the door, I envisioned sneaking back into my room in the middle of the night and dumping Cynthia, attitude and all, out of the bed and onto the floor. With that image in my mind, I turned back, caught Cynthia's eye, and gave her a malicious grin, which netted a delicious reward: her smug, superior expression wavered and confusion flickered in her eyes.

The expression didn't last, of course, but I was happy to discover a means of entertaining myself when the demands of courtesy tried my patience.

Chapter 7

My Mother's Marriage

The next day, I dropped several coins into the alms box as I entered the village temple for the marriage of my mother, Constance Hart, to Lord Robert Rella. In spite of my mother's weekly prodding, this was the first time I'd graced the house of worship with my presence since my father's funeral. I figured that if the gods had abandoned him, then they had abandoned me, too, and I vowed to return the favor. I scowled at the figures of the four great gods, their images carved in stone behind the altar. Preeminent Soltar, the sun god, glowered down on me as if aware of my rebellious thoughts, but I didn't care. I wanted nothing to do with any of them.

The likenesses of fairies carved or painted throughout the arched structure and represented in the stained-glass windows tempered my displeasure a bit, as did the many sprites hovering above the arranged altar flowers, but every time I tried to force a smile for my mother's sake, I'm sure it came out a grimace.

Finally, in order to endure the unwelcome, intimate ceremony, I resigned myself to standing stone-faced throughout the entire ritual. After a time, I noticed one other person whose expression mirrored my own: Cynthia's. We both glared at the newlyweds, Lord Robert and the new Lady Constance, as they kissed at the end of the ceremony, and then we glared at each other. What an inauspicious start to our happy family.

Later in the day, my newly formed family gathered outside Hart Cottage under an overcast sky to send the couple off on their wedding trip. As Lord Robert handed my mother into the carriage, he broke into a gargling cough.

She put her hand on her new husband's shoulder. "Perhaps we should postpone our trip, my dear, until your cough has abated?"

My stepfather—oh, how I loathed to think that word. He shivered, though wrapped in a heavy traveling cloak, and shuddered as his body convulsed with yet another ghastly cough. Congestion rattled in his chest, sounding deeper than the previous night. In light of the worsening cough, I thought my mother's offer was sensible, but Stepfather wouldn't hear of it.

"By Great Soltar, no, I want to show off my beautiful bride, Lady Constance."

Cynthia, standing at her father's side, lowered her eyelids and rolled her eyes, imperceptibly to the others, but I caught the rudeness and wished to slap her face for her disrespect to my mother.

Mother was unaware of Cynthia's slight, and her face glowed with pleasure. But with another bout of hacking from Lord Robert, a worried frown clouded her countenance. Nevertheless, in spite of Stepfather's illness, he and Mother departed. We watched as their carriage, followed by a wagon with supplies, rumbled down Hart Cottage Lane, turned on Castle Road, and rolled off to start the two-day journey, with stops at prosperous inns, to finally reach Norlan Castle, the vast estate of one of Lord Rella's noble friends.

As the clouds began to drizzle, I turned to the second carriage waiting on Hart Cottage Lane, the Rella crest of two crossed roses on its door. Cynthia climbed in, assisted by a footman.

She turned, peered out the window, using her hand to shield her face from the light sprinkle, and glanced at Hart Cottage with a look of disgust.

With forced pleasantry, she called, "Isabella, Griselda, I beg you to make haste. I do so wish to acquaint you with your new home."

Interpreting her words to mean, let's get away from this hovel as soon as possible, I turned from Cynthia and looked at Isabella with wide rolling eyes, hoping that she had picked up on Cynthia's double meaning.

Isabella, however, frowned at me, appeared confused, and responded promptly to Cynthia's request. She gave a quick wave to Abigail and Abel Garner, our servants who would stay to maintain Hart Cottage and its acreage, and joined Cynthia in the carriage. They both stared expectantly at me.

I looked from Abigail and Abel standing at the kitchen door to Cynthia and Isabella in the carriage and back again. With a ripping sense of loss inside me, I ran back to the cottage to give the old couple hugs but found myself bumped out of the way by Sarah, who excused her way between us, carrying a lidded basket that rocked, hissed, and yowled in her arms.

"Miss Griselda, must we take this beast?"

I reached out to steady the basket that nearly tumbled from her arms. "I can't leave Mr. Tatters, Sarah. He'd be so lonely without me."

Sarah shook her head. "You and your critters, miss." She sighed. "Well, you'd better call that terror of a dog of yers and tie him up somewhere, or he'll follow us all the way there."

My insides fell and my shoulders slumped. This was news to me—terrible news. "But—"

A loud yowl cut off my protest.

Sarah, arms still wrapped around the lurching basket, lifted a hand. "No buts, young miss. Yer mother wants you to start behaving like a lady, and it's to start with leaving behind that ragged dog of yers."

As if to prove Sarah's point, floppy-eared Rags came racing around the corner of the cottage and leaped up, giving me his version of a hug. I pushed him down, leaving muddy paw prints on my ankle-length, travel tunic, and rubbed his ears.

Sarah scowled and tossed a length of rope at my feet. "Yer mother said, miss."

As I stood speechless in the misty rain, Sarah, still carrying the caterwauling carrier, trundled to the wagon to join two servants from Lord Robert's manor. I ignored the rope and mournfully called Rags into the kitchen. And then with a heavy heart, I pulled the door shut. As my furry friend began to bark, moisture filled my eyes.

Abigail patted my shoulder. "We'll take good care of him for you, miss."

Abel agreed with a nod and a look of sympathy. "An' Gilly will keep a watch out, too, miss."

With the assurance that the trio of friends would care for my canine friend, I nodded and turned quickly toward the carriage, tossing my head to shake back the threatening tears. As the precipitation increased, I crossed the yard, climbed into the boxy, wooden conveyance, and sat on a leather covered, cushioned bench seat with the background noise of Mr. Tatters yowling his displeasure to the world and Rags barking his confusion from the house. I couldn't agree with them more. I wanted to howl.

The footman closed the door behind me, the coachman shook the reins, and our journey began, bumping down the lane away from Hart Cottage. I sat facing my sisters, the back of the carriage, and the rain shrouded sight of my home—a friend whom I was abandoning. As we pulled away, I felt a cord stretching between my heart and my home. The place looked forlorn, the trees drooping, the windows cheerless, like a loved one with sad eyes. I wanted to leap from the carriage, run back to the house, and refuse to leave. Isabella and Cynthia could live with Mother in Lord Robert's manor, and I'd stay here with Abel and Abigail Garner to care for Hart Cottage.

With dread, I anticipated reaching Rella Manor, where we would settle in before the newlyweds' return, but it would never be a home to me.

Now early afternoon, the sky weighed heavier and heavier with gray clouds and increasing rain when we turned on Castle Road. Thistles, white and purple clover, buttercups, and dandelion puffs dotted the sides of the road, but their usual winged attendants were absent. Though fairies enjoy cavorting in a misty rain, they take shelter from more determined precipitation, allowing the goddess of water to grace their work with her liquid blessing.

Moisture from the air filtered into the carriage. I glanced up from a sneeze and found Isabella and Cynthia engaged in whispered conversation. They glanced at my lap and giggled. Giggling did not suit

Cynthia. It captured my attention for the sheer novelty of the expression. It appeared forced, calculated.

The two girls glanced at each other and giggled again. They seemed to be broaching the beginnings of friendship, and I felt left out.

I raised my eyebrows in question.

Isabella patted my knee. Her face flushed with embarrassment. "Forgive me, Grizzy, you have a paw print on your dress."

I glanced down, and sure enough, I did have a paw print, several in fact, and I wondered which spot in particular had excited their disapprobation. Isabella tried to brush off the offending dirt with her hand. She only succeeded in spreading the stain farther and so stopped with a sigh. I used to think that I could stay tidy if I made the effort. Unfortunately, the last two days had proven otherwise. It was beginning to bother me, but I shrugged to show that I didn't care.

Cynthia smoothed her blue silk gown with its floral embroidered bodice, lifted her chin, and looked down her nose at me. "Please forgive us, Griselda. We did not wish to embarrass you."

Isabella echoed her words.

I looked across at the pair of them, blonde beauties dressed in blues that complemented their eyes, forming a prim, ladylike alliance that left me out. This particularly stung because Isabella had been so non-communicative since our father's death. I shrugged, stretched my lips across my teeth, and turned to look out the window where I strained to make out Hart Cottage as it receded in the blurry distance.

Cynthia spoke again. "Are you enjoying your ride in a carriage, Griselda?" Here she paused. "Or perhaps you are accustomed to riding in carriages with your good friend Prince Charmain."

Isabella burst out laughing. "Oh, no, Grizzy has never ridden in a carriage. All she and the prince ever do is run around the castle and cause trouble."

My mouth tightened. Among village acquaintances, such knowledge was known and enjoyed, but with Cynthia I wished Isabella would practice some discretion.

"Izzy, that was when we were children."

Isabella looked doubtful, opened her mouth to object, but was cut off.

"What sort of trouble did you cause, Griselda?" Cynthia asked, looking hungry with interest.

"Oh, we played Hide and Seek, Catch a Fairy, the usual children's games."

Isabella, not following my lead at all, wiggled in her seat and couldn't keep quiet.

She turned to Cynthia. "Grizzy and Prince Charmain ruined King Benedict's armor with one of their games."

Cynthia's eyes glittered. "Oh, an heirloom like that must be four or five generations old."

I could see that she didn't care about the royal heirloom, just the gossip, and I wished Isabella would be quiet. But wishing to ingratiate herself to our new stepsister, she babbled on.

"Grizzy can shoot arrows, wield a sword—well, only a wooden one—hit targets with rocks, ride horses, and climb trees. She is the fastest runner in the village, maybe even the kingdom. And she always defends the prince if anyone teases him."

Cynthia's eyebrows raised, her eyes danced with

controlled amusement, and her mouth puckered as if struggling not to laugh. "Well now, that is remarkable. I would hear more of this."

I sighed, wanting to silence Isabella, but I decided that I'd rather explain things in my own way rather than leave it to my chattering sister.

I remembered how I used to—and still did at times—tease the prince, calling him Prince Charming. Then I'd race off as he tried futilely to catch me, which had led to the damage to King Benedict's armor. Father had cautioned me about the name-calling, telling me with uncharacteristic sternness that my place was to support the prince, just like Father's was to support the king. Now, with Father's plan to remove the threat to those of us—well, actually only me—with fairy sight, I had a better understanding of the reason for his insistence that I both befriend and support the prince. I had listened to my father. I always did. Although sometimes I did slip up, like I did yesterday, and hiss a quiet, "Prince Charming," in private. It never ceased to annoy my friend, which I found most gratifying.

But I didn't want to tell Cynthia that confidence, so I ground out a brief version of what Isabella would expect.

"When we were children, the prince and I would run around the castle green playing tag and other games. Since everyone saw that I was faster than the prince, the village boys taunted him for being beaten by a girl. So I challenged them one by one, left them all choking in the dust, and then they left him in peace. It's all pretty dull."

Cynthia grinned as if she'd just received a surprise gift. "Not at all. I see you are a knight in shining armor defending the honor of your prince."

Isabella nodded, her face glowing with pride. "That's right. Grizzy always defends the prince."

I knew that Isabella was sincerely proud of me, but I was annoyed that, because of her guileless heart, she couldn't see that Cynthia was making fun of me.

Cynthia shook her head. "Grizzy, Grizzy, Grizzy."

I usually liked the sound of my nickname when said by friends and family but didn't like Cynthia's mocking tone.

My evil stepsister continued. "What boyish behavior. You know, someday the prince will want to meet a girl."

The fact of my possible engagement to the prince caused a corner of my mouth to twitch up.

Isabella's brow furrowed, and she looked puzzled. "But Grizzy is a girl."

Cynthia snaked her arm through Isabella's. "Of course, dear Isabella, I only meant someone who behaved like a girl."

"Oh." Isabella's eyes widened with comprehension. "She's right, you know, Grizzy. You should listen to Mother and act more ladylike."

Cynthia put her arm around Isabella's shoulders and gave her a little squeeze. "Now, do not be concerned, Isabella, I will make it my mission to teach your sister how to behave like a lady."

Then Cynthia looked at me, sweeping her eyes appraisingly over the contours of my face.

"Please forgive my boldness, Griselda, but since we are now sisters, I believe I may say that I'm sure you could be quite pretty—if you made the effort. Honestly, you could."

Both sisters smiled widely, Isabella with the sincere hope that I would benefit from Cynthia's sisterly offerings, Cynthia with the awareness that her comments were like dagger cuts.

In response, I imagined stopping the carriage, dragging Cynthia out by her golden hair, and decorating her arrogant face with roadside mud. This pleasant thought produced a smile from me that mirrored Cynthia's own, and my pleasure increased at seeing a shadow of confusion flicker in Cynthia's eyes. It was a small victory, but it would do for now.

With Hart Cottage no longer in view, the sight from the carriage windows filled with the nearby village wall and farther castle turrets. We connected to the King's Way going south and, after passing rain-soaked fields and farmers' cottages, entered the great swath of forest, King's Forest, that separated all that was familiar to me from our destination, Rella Manor. The air soon cooled, the overhanging branches reduced the rainfall, and the trees quickly obscured the castle and village, making them only memories.

We soon passed the turn off onto the Great Road that wended its way through the endless reaches of the Great Forest, which made me think of another memory, my father's death. I sank further into a sad, silent mood.

The rain lessened and occasional beams of sunlight filtered through the trees' canopy as we rolled and bumped our way through the forest. Cynthia and Isabella chatted about dresses, fabrics, and furnishings while I gazed out the windows, catching glimpses of squirrels darting up trees, rabbits scampering across the road, and green-hued forest fairies glowing in the dappled forest light. In time we passed out of the forest, into less dense woodlands, and finally, with the clouds breaking and sun shining through, into farmlands with an occasional small cluster of buildings, all subjects of the crown. We were much farther from home than I had ever been.

Our journey through the King's Forest, made mostly at a trot with occasional walking breaks to rest the horses, had consumed perhaps an hour and a half or two. Throughout the time, Isabella had sent looks informing me that my limited effort at conversation was impolite. After cooling off from Cynthia's barbed comments and rallying a bit from my sadness, I felt guilty about my attitude toward my stepsister. Though I did not like her, this perfumed, bejeweled creature was, after all, my new sister. Then an inner chuckle occurred to me. If my father could work with that sour Lord Ursa during all his years of service to the king, then I could endure this floral-scented Cynthia.

I decided to make an effort. "Cynthia."

Both girls stopped speaking and turned to me.

Chagrinned, I realized I'd been rude. "I beg your forgiveness for interrupting, but when will we reach your lands?"

Cynthia tipped her nose toward a well-to-do looking farmhouse with surrounding fields. "We already have. These are our tenant farmers."

As Isabella peered out the window, I marveled at the prosperous appearance of the dwelling. "That's a tenant home?"

Cynthia glanced sidelong at me. "Yes, quite a hovel, is it not?"

Isabella and I exchanged a look. The "hovel" was on the scale of Hart Cottage.

Something didn't make sense. Usually, tenant farmers in the kingdom had small but comfortable one-story timber and plaster, thatched-roof houses with three rooms and a loft, but many of the tenant homes we'd passed were built with stone or brick and included a full second story and attic. They had extensive outbuildings, more like a small estate—more like Hart Cottage. Perhaps Lord Robert was generous to his tenants. He rose a bit in my estimation.

With so much to see in my new surroundings, I hung out the window to drink in the sun-drenched scene. My eyes roamed the landscape: fields with rows of green shoots, workers hoeing in the furrows, and odd tiny dots of shadowy gray sprinkled as if randomly. I puzzled over the unfamiliar gray spots for a moment and then was distracted by three playful children neglecting the cows they were driving to new pasture.

Suddenly, a distant structure resting on a hill caught my eye. At the sight, my chest tightened and my breathing faltered. The carriage hit a rut in the road, jolted, and knocked my head on the window frame. Rubbing my head, I gazed at the far away formation, a crumbling shell of a castle. A chill formed within me and shivered out to my extremities. I had forgotten.

The Dead Castle.

Here.

I pulled my head back into the carriage, settled into the seat to ponder this new shock, and found Cynthia scrutinizing me.

She tilted her head toward the window. "You noticed the old castle."

I nodded and said in a somber tone, "The Dead Castle."

With a huff of derision, she replied, "Do not be melodramatic, Griselda. It is of no concern. We give it no thought."

Still with a cold feeling in my core from the sight of that mythological portent, the sensation increased with my stepsister's dismissiveness. "How can you be so nonchalant? Something bad happened to fairies in that place."

Cynthia shrugged. "Only if you believe in fables."

Her mocking expression tried my sisterly resolve, but I tightened my jaw and answered carefully. "That does not look like a fable."

Cynthia looked affronted for a second, but then her eyes narrowed and her expression shifted into a look of intense scrutiny. She pointed a finger to her chin and looked at me steadily. "You are right. The castle and whatever happened there are quite real."

Isabella glanced between Cynthia and me and then hesitantly craned her neck to see the ominous castle.

Cynthia slowly stroked her chin, gazed past me in the direction of the Dead Castle, and then leaned toward the window.

"Oh, look, Catch a Fairy," Cynthia said, pointing at the trio of youngsters.

I glanced out the window again at the neglectful cowherds, two now capturing one in the game.

"If I caught a fairy," Cynthia said, "I would wish for diamonds."

This talk of fairies made me uncomfortable. I had not considered that my family secret now had to be kept from two new family members, especially someone who would come up with a greedy wish like that.

I relaxed back into my padded leather seat,

deciding it would be best to ignore Cynthia's comment. However, Isabella, who well knew to keep the secret, looked like a cornered hare.

I gave her what I hoped was an imperceptible shake of my head, but she burst out. "It's just a game, Cynthia. Besides it would be wicked."

Cynthia must have caught my headshake, because she studied me before patting my sister's arm.

"There is no need to be melodramatic, Isabella." Then she shrugged and coughed out a laugh. "Unless you believe in fables."

Isabella looked guiltily at me and forced a giggle. "Most certainly, no."

Isabella was not a good liar.

Cynthia giggled back, which still didn't sound natural to me. Then a look of calculated calm settled on her face. She stroked the perfect curve of her chin with her thumb and index finger as her eyes shifted between Isabella and me. She leaned to look out the window at the children, now back to herding their cows. As she watched the threesome, I could see questions forming in Cynthia's mind. I realized that, while my stepsister might be vain, she clearly wasn't stupid.

Isabella leaned back, her eyes pinched in pain, the sign of one of the headaches she'd become prone to since our father's passing. And me, the cold spot in my gut that had formed at the sight of the Dead Castle grew large and icy and made an uneasy home inside me. We all remained silent for the remainder of our ride.

Chapter 8

A Queen's Demand

As we neared Rella Manor, the carriage rattled past a small village cluster of homes, pens, gardens, and shops, including an apothecary and a land agent— whatever that was. This seemed to be the center of business for all the prosperous tenant farmers in the area. A few miles past the settlement, Rella Manor came into view. The manor and grounds before us boasted plentiful outbuildings and a substantial stone house with short barrel towers anchoring its four corners. We arrived at the manor's gatehouse and rolled through the unattended entrance, a structure that seemed superfluous since the walls that should have extended from it to surround the entire property remained unfinished after only a few yards in either direction. Our journey had taken slightly over two hours, and now we were home. But to me, this was anything but home.

The driver of Sarah's conveyance pulled over to the side of the manor where I assumed the kitchen entrance to be. Thankfully, Mr. Tatters had given up on his yowling early during the passage through the King's Forest. I hoped that he would be happier here than I was.

Our coachman pulled the horses to a stop in front

of the wide, stone, entry stairs, and the footman opened the doors, solemnly handing Cynthia and Isabella down from the carriage onto the gravelly drive. I hoped out on my own and gave him a grin, which he returned. We ascended the entry stairs, passed through the double doors held open by two female servants, and entered the manor's great hall, its black and white marble tile floor spread before us like a chessboard. Marble statues stood in niches throughout the expanse with tapestries displayed between them. Gold and silver chalices and jewel-encrusted vessels rested on pedestals and small tables. The contrast between this grandiose interior and the substantial but understated exterior struck me as odd.

My stepsister appeared very much Lady Cynthia as she stood with a satisfied air in the midst of her domain.

Then she glanced at one of the curtsying servant girls. "Hannah, what are you doing here? Where is Hobson?"

Hannah curtsied again so deeply that her knees almost touched the floor. "I beg your pardon, Lady, but Rebecca and me…" She gestured at the other servant girl, who cringed. "We dunno."

Our lady sister looked momentarily taken aback and then collected herself. She waved off the servant. "Very well, prepare my peach gown."

Hannah scurried away, while Rebecca inched back, anxiously waiting for instructions and clearly wishing to flee.

With a gesture dismissing the frightened Rebecca, Cynthia turned imperiously to us and lifted her arms slightly. "Griselda, Isabella, allow me to welcome you both to your new home. I hope that you will find it to your liking."

I caught her implication; her house was better than our house.

It tempted me to retort that I preferred my homey Hart Cottage to this over-decorated cavern any time, but that would be unkind—not to mention antagonistic. And even though she did not deserve it, I was determined to overcome my dislike for Cynthia—as much as possible—and start our co-habitation cordially.

I smiled and nodded. "Thank you, Cynthia."

Cynthia, not content with my response, returned my nod stiffly and looked at Isabella.

My sister's neck swiveled around, her eyes taking in the opulence. "Oh, it is more grand than the castle. What an unexpected delight."

I agreed with "unexpected." This respectable country manor was like a good linen tunic trying to look like a silk gown embroidered with jewels. I knew, however, that such thoughts must be kept to myself. This was, after all, Cynthia's home, as dear to her as mine was to me.

I tried to generate a more enthusiastic response. "This is grand, Cynthia. Your father has elegant taste."

To my surprise, Cynthia's face clouded and her shoulders dropped slightly. She gestured dismissively at the finery surrounding us. "Not my father. This is my mother's taste, and my father wished to please her. He did his best."

This made sense to me. Lord Robert seemed like a country gentleman, more given to pursuing genial, if trivial, conversation rather than gaudy displays of wealth. So it appeared that, though her father may have spoiled her, Cynthia was very much her mother's daughter.

Making an effort to be appreciative, I took several steps across the tiles and pointed at a faded and chipped fresco, the only one in the room. Centered in the picture were a king, queen, and infant enjoying a family moment in a solar—the solar that was familiar to me in the castle.

"That is remarkable. The characters look so lifelike."

Cynthia appeared slightly nonplussed. "It is King Nicholas and his son, the ones who died suddenly before Benedict became king." She waved her hand indifferently toward the artwork. "Mother always had it covered with a tapestry, but my father likes it."

Something about the fresco drew my attention. It was almost as if the scene moved. I shook my head, realizing how silly that was. Maybe there was something to Mother's comments about my imagination after all.

Cynthia redirected our attention by gesturing to the largest tapestry. "This is our masterpiece. The crowning of King Benedict."

She led Isabella and me to stand before the representation of an ancient king, kneeling to receive his crown.

Isabella gaped at the expansive needlework. "The one who was king during the famine?"

Cynthia, gazing at the monarch, nodded absently. "Hmm, I believe so. Our reigning monarch descends from his line."

Isabella, not much for history, frowned, her growing headache apparent in her eyes. "Are there two royal lines?"

Cynthia soon amazed me as she launched into a detailed explanation of the old tales about the death of King Nicholas, the death of King Nicholas's son and heir, and the ascension of King Benedict to the throne one hundred fifty years ago. Isabella hung on her every word, and though I knew this information, I was reluctantly impressed.

"One might say," Cynthia said, "that King Beaumain and Prince Charmain are not truly of royal blood, because they come from the line of the stepbrother, King Benedict."

Isabella frowned. "But even though they had different mothers, King Benedict was still the king's son."

Cynthia shook her head, looking smug with her superior knowledge. "No, he was an adopted son, adopted when the king married his mother. So he was no blood relation to the royal line."

Though clearly a great reader and student of history, Cynthia's conversation could be construed as treasonous, or at least disrespectful, to the reigning king. I wished to put an end to the subject, and as if in answer to my wish, my eyes rested on the inscription stitched on the tapestry.

Peace and prosperity fill the land, when governed by the true king's hand.

In order to refocus the dialogue, I pulled from our underlying mythology. "King Beaumain is clearly the legitimate ruler." I pointed to the familiar words. "Because we would not have peace and prosperity without the true king."

Cynthia gave a single, considered nod before speaking. "True, but during the reign of King Benedict,

LaFairia experienced famine and no small amount of civil unrest. Pray, how could such things be described as peace and prosperity?"

I had to admit that Cynthia had a point. I also had to admit to some respect for her interpretive abilities, but her conclusions were wrong. "But we have peace and prosperity now. That can only mean that the true king is on the throne and has been for generations."

Isabella bobbed her head in agreement, but Cynthia smiled indulgently. "Well done, Griselda. And with this, you put to rest the mysterious legends of the past and gallantly defend your prince once again."

Though I knew I was right about the king, Cynthia's comments left me annoyed, and it showed in my retort. "You should not speak with disloyalty to the crown, Cynthia."

"Of course not, my dear sister. Though I have a great interest in analyzing the inconsistencies of history, I am the most loyal subject of the king. Now, if you will excuse me, I will retire to change before dinner. May I show you to your own chambers?"

Isabella, now looking worn out and in pain like her head was in a vise, accepted the offer, but I declined. The two blondes disappeared up the wide, principal staircase on the right of the grand room, its handrails, balusters, and newels carved with roses as though they grew from the wood. Relieved to be on my own for the moment, I set off to explore.

As I poked my head into the rooms off the great hall, the library, the parlor, the music room, and the dining room, servants scurried in and out of doorways, their footsteps making soft, scuffling sounds. They gave me curtsies and shy smiles as they set about their tasks carrying linens, pitchers of water, and scrub brushes. I grinned broadly in return, which seemed to confuse them. Their confusion puzzled me, because I was accustomed to getting on well with servants. I looked forward to becoming better acquainted, but for now I continued my exploration.

I reached the back door, exited, and found a broad staircase with steps widening as they reached the garden level. My first thought was that it would be fun to have a furry friend barking up the stairs to greet me. I missed Rags. So not in the very best of moods, I scanned the grounds.

The garden, bathed in sun and slightly steaming from recent showers, smelled of fresh, rain-washed air. It spread out before me in a symmetrical design with shrubs cut in sharp angles and curves, so unlike the asymmetrical abandon surrounding my Hart Cottage. The manor garden reminded me of a woman laced so tightly for the sake of some silly fashion that she couldn't breathe, something I avoided if possible. How could one run in such a garment?

Positioned at measured intervals throughout the garden were statues of the four great gods, as well as several kings, including King Francis, his son King Nicholas, and his stepson King Benedict. One unexpected statue was of a monk, whom I soon realized was a likeness of King Francis after he had turned his crown over to his son. I recalled that King Francis was the last monarch to practice the long-held tradition of turning the crown over to his heir, leaving for a monastery in Soltar City, and living the remainder of his life as a renunciant. Father had approved of this practice. He said it showed that, in the past, the

LaFairian kings were able to serve their subjects as long as they deemed it to be right and then were able to walk away from the position of power without clinging. However, he never criticized our recent rulers for failing to follow this tradition; he simply stated a fact.

Talks such as these had always left me wondering why some people, like Lord Ursa, were so inclined to grasp at power, while others, like my father, seemed willing to share that same power and release it in due course. And, of course, there were others, like the king, who were heavily influenced by strong personalities, whether for good or for woe.

Taking my leave of the statuary monarchs and the thoughts they generated, I trotted farther down the path, listening to white-crowned sparrows that flitted among the greenery. In the center of all this geometry was a circular garden, planted with evenly spaced shrubs that could only be rosebushes. Spirits lifting, I jogged down the main path to see if these rose fairies were like those at home. As I trotted along, fairies for grasses, shrubs, and flowers in a rainbow of different colors whizzed by, circling my head by way of greeting, before flying off to attend to their plants. I laughed at their antics, as always wondering whether a fairy was working or playing. Perhaps the two were one and the same to them.

When I reached the circle of rose bushes, fairies flew everywhere nurturing the many tight buds and the few open blooms. I bent and breathed in the fragrance of a yellow blossom. This wasn't home, but at least there were flowers and fairies in profusion.

The Rella Manor fairies were like the two-to-four-inch fairies from home, but with individuality of color, clothing, and wing design. Once I asked Father if fairies made their own clothes or if they just were part of them like petals on a flower. This was one of the few times that he had looked at me quite perplexed.

"I don't know," he had said. "I have never considered that."

And since fairies were inclined to giggle and fly away without divulging information, that remained one of the many mysteries to me about my busy companions. I spent several quiet minutes comparing the roses and their corresponding winged caretakers when a radiant, rainbow-hued fairy, about six inches tall, caught my attention. In contrast to the whirring chaos of other fairies, she sat, wings fluttering, on a large bloom graced with cream, yellow, and pink pastels. She stared fixedly at me. I thought about Arianna at home and knew—this fairy was the local boss, the fairy queen.

Eager, and a little apprehensive, to become acquainted with this imperious-looking queen, whose presence reminded me of Arianna but whose scrutinizing attitude did not, I bowed, wondering if I should speak first.

She saved me the trouble, speaking to my mind. "You must get to work."

Startled, I straightened and stepped back. "What do you mean?" I said aloud, unaccustomed to mind speaking.

Her expression grew stern. "You know very well. You are the fairy kin. This garden needs more fairies—with haste."

A trembling confusion swept through my frame. My past failures to manifest fairies, the constraints imposed by my mother, and the threat to me if I was suspected all crashed in on me.

With a full whine, I replied. "That's not fair. I can't, I'm not allowed, and I could get executed."

The monarch launched from her throne of petals, winged into the air, and impaled me with a fierce glare. "These things do not matter. For my realm to thrive, it needs the fairy kin to manifest more fairies. That is you. That is all."

"Arianna is nicer than you," I said sullenly.

Not daunted by my comparison, she hovered a few inches from my face, slightly moving in the breeze. "That may be, but she, too, needs you to fulfill your role."

With the weight of my failure pressing on my heart, I said, "Didn't you hear me say, 'I don't know how'?"

She paused, still bobbing in the air, really examined me for a second, and then fluttered back a couple of inches. "Oh, I see now. You are not the same one."

My whole body went slack. "No, that was my father. He's dead."

The rainbow fairy's face softened. Now, she looked more like Arianna, only with different coloring. "Ah, yes, I see that is so, and I am grieved," she finally said, "but it does not change the fact that you are the fairy kin."

While miserably considering what a lonely, helpless, inept, incompetent failure I was, the queen considered me with a kinder expression. "I am Rosanna. And I will help you, but you must make the effort and practice. It will come to you."

I took in a deep breath and threw it out with an exasperated sigh.

Rosanna actually chuckled, finally looking the part of a mentor to me. "So you think it is so hard? Have you noticed? You momentarily switched to mind speaking when we conversed."

Startled, I blurted aloud. "I did?" Then I recalled. "Oh, yes, I did."

The sovereign flew in a circle, laughed, and nodded. "See it comes naturally." Then her countenance grew solemn. "We will begin by destroying the imps."

Alarmed, I gasped. "Imps?"

Thankfully, I'd never seen one before, because imps couldn't infest any locale where my father lived. They wouldn't dare. And when he traveled, he'd pull fairies into manifestation to ensure that cultivated areas were properly attended.

The little winged monarch gestured toward several bushes. "The gray marks of disease are in my roses. Come."

As I followed Rosanna, I spied the same smoky gray dots that I'd seen earlier in the tenant fields. Unlike the gray specks that I'd seen earlier from the carriage, these were deeply embedded in the rosebushes, hard to see, as if hiding. One shadowy spot dissipated upon my approach, but not before I saw the hint of a little impish face—a highly annoyed impish face—in the grayness.

"See," the rainbow fairy said. "You can do this."

I leaned toward the location of the vanished imp. "But I did nothing."

The queen settled herself onto a large pink rose,

looking much more pleased with me than she had earlier. "You are the fairy kin. Your presence alone is something. Now let us destroy…"

She stared past my shoulder, and to my dismay, her multi-colored radiance faded to dull. "Beware," reverberated in my mind.

The sound of gravel crunched behind me. "Oh, there you are."

With a jerk, I straightened and turned to see Cynthia, wearing a fresh peach silk dress, approaching and eyeing me with a calculating expression.

Feeling cornered like a stag surrounded by hounds, I didn't reply.

Cynthia lifted her arm and swept it before herself to include the expanse. "Do you find the gardens to your liking?"

Worried about the fairy, now flickering between dull and bright, I wanted to bend down to see if she was all right but couldn't with my stepsister watching so closely.

I attempted to act nonchalant. "I like the gardens very much. The rosebushes remind me of home. Of course, you have more and a greater variety."

As a cloud moved to obscure the sun, casting a little chill in the air, Cynthia stepped forward and snaked her arm through mine. "Of course, you mean *we* have more, dear sister Griselda."

My insides recoiled at her touch, but I allowed the intimacy for it would be rude to pull back. "Of course, Cynthia, you are very kind."

Cynthia squeezed my arm. "Not at all."

My stepsister's eyes roved near the pink rose where the fairy queen sat enthroned, her weight making the flower dip slightly.

I scanned the surrounding fairies with unease. The nearby fairy activity had ceased. The winged creatures all hovered at a distance watching the seated queen. The monarch watched me. For some reason, my new family member made them apprehensive.

Impatient to put distance between the watchful sprites and my stepsister, I gestured to the massive house. "I am eager to see my bedchamber. Shall we return to the manor?"

I tried to walk away, pulling Cynthia with me, but she resisted. "What do you find so fascinating about this particular rose?"

With a gasp, I reflexively tried to deflect her hand but failed. She thrust a pointed finger right into the pink, rosy throne, just missing the fairy queen, who had taken flight. A thin, chill wind whistled between Cynthia and me, making my skin prickle, and the cloud overhead thickened.

I pulled my hand back and realized that my mouth was hanging open. Snapping it shut, I glanced at Cynthia who said nothing. She just looked at me, making me feel like a mouse just spied by a hawk.

"Shall we go?" I asked. "The air has developed a chill."

Cynthia gazed evenly at me, questions forming in her eyes. She, however, asked nothing, but gripped my arm and led me back to the manor, her eyes lingering on the large pink rose.

"Yes, let us return to the manor. You will find that your trunks have been delivered to your bedchamber and are being unpacked."

As we promenaded away from the rose garden and

through the geometric shrubs, the patch of clouds overhead dispersed into nothing, the surrounding fairies returned to their work, and Cynthia chatted as if we were on the most familiar of terms. I only half listened for worrying about Rosanna, until I realized from her conversation that Cynthia had been in my chamber coveting my slippers again.

"They are such a rarity. Where did you get them?"

The impulse to yank my arm from her grip, shove her away, and demand that she keep her greedy hands off my slippers tempted me greatly, but sisterly restraint prevailed.

My reply triggered the familiar sadness that expanded and contracted inside my chest. "They were a gift from my father, the last gift before he died."

Cynthia, with theatrical concern, reached an arm around my shoulder. "Oh, then they must be very dear to you. Does Isabella have a similar pair?"

Fighting my revulsion to her touch, I replied, "Yes, she wore them to the wedding."

Cynthia paused in her stride, glanced thoughtfully up to one side, and searched her memory for Isabella's wedding attire.

She breathed in, snaked her arm back through mine, and nodded. "Ah, yes, Isabella has a charming pair of embroidered slippers, but there is something unique about yours that I cannot identify. Do you know what it is?"

I felt both angry and concerned about Cynthia's persistence. I would tell her nothing, but I'd stop her in her tracks. "Yes, I do."

Cynthia turned to me, a greedy hunger alight in her eyes. "Pray tell me."

"They are unique because they are from my father, whom I loved and will always love."

The greedy anticipation drained from Cynthia's face to be replaced with blankness. "That is a uniqueness beyond compare, dear Griselda. We have both lost a parent."

Chapter 9

An Unwelcome Caller

Cynthia and I walked, that is I walked and Cynthia paraded, up the back stairs, through the grandiose great hall, and up the principal staircase that led to the second level. Cynthia lifted her skirt slightly and floated up the steps. I followed, tilting up my nose and imitating her bearing for my own entertainment. We entered a long gallery with portraits hung on the walls, separated at intervals by carved bedchamber doors.

My stepsister led me down the carpeted hall, illuminated by large mullioned windows at the far ends and candles held in wall sconces. Framed portraits of family ancestors looked down their noses at me from the walls.

With a gesture at the paintings, Cynthia said, "My ancestors. Father said that soon my portrait would be added to the collection."

I glanced up and down the hall, looking for vacant wall space. "Where will it go?"

Cynthia's posture sagged momentarily and then straightened. She led me farther down the hallway almost to the mullioned windows, stopped, and scowled. "Next to my mother."

An exquisite painting of Cynthia looked imperiously down upon us, causing me confusion.

"Perhaps I misunderstood. I thought you said your portrait would be added soon."

Cynthia glared. "That is not my likeness. It is my mother's."

I didn't understand why my mistake should make her angry. The portrait was beautiful. But clearly, I had stumbled upon a sensitive topic. "I beg your pardon."

With a lift of her chin, she scrutinized the picture, patterned sunlight from the window crossing its features. "Did you know that my mother should have been queen?" A hint of disdain colored her voice.

With difficulty I contained a guffaw. Though the woman in the artwork held a queenly bearing, surely my stepsister's claim was overreaching. "No, I was not aware."

Cynthia shook her head. "Laugh if you must, Griselda, for I see you restraining your amusement. But I assure you it is quite true. The king courted my mother perhaps eighteen years ago but then made a political union. Soon after, my mother married my father. He did his best to make her happy."

Uncertainty replaced my inner laughter, and the idea of a partial similarity to my relationship with the prince occurred to me. But I shoved my comparison aside, since it had nothing to do with me. Perhaps Cynthia's story was true, or perhaps Cynthia's mother wished it to be true. In either case, I now guessed the reason for the manor's palatial décor. Cynthia's mother wanted this country manor to be the royal residence that she never had—better in fact. It was a good thing that Lord Robert's resources had been able to afford his wife's expensive taste, and now apparently his daughter's as well.

A touch of sympathy for my stepfather flickered in my heart. "Your father is a good man."

She exhaled a deep sigh. "Yes, he is, and so instead of Queen Katherine, Mother became Lady Katherine Rella."

With a glance between Cynthia and her mother's rendering, I commented cautiously, "You are aware that your appearance favors your mother."

Her jaw tightened. "I am, but I am not my mother."

I nodded and kept my disagreement to myself. Cynthia not only looked like her mother and apparently acted like her mother, but seemed to be in competition with her, too. Cynthia gazed at her mother's portrait, her nose now high in the air. Fortunately, we were inside, because with her nostrils at that tilt, rain would have been a problem.

The "princess" gave a haughty sniff. "Have you not wondered why I have not been at the castle?"

I hadn't. But now that she mentioned it, it not only appeared odd, but also quite insulting to the king. "Why?"

"My mother refused to set foot in the castle after being treated so dishonorably. She did it as a deliberate insult to the king. And he, spineless beast, just let the matter pass. That was the measure of my mother's hold on him."

While recoiling from Cynthia's low opinion of our monarch, I searched my memory and found no recollection of Lady Katherine ever paying her respects to the king. I did, of course, remember Lord Robert's attendance from time to time, which is why I had been slightly acquainted with him. "But your father paid his respects."

"Yes, and he now deems it fitting to present me at court for the first time. He will do so at the feast when the prince returns from the summer tour."

With the possibility that my betrothal to the prince would be announced at that very feast, I wondered if my stepsister would welcome the news.

Then I cringed at the thought of attending the feast with Lord Robert as our head of the family, but I hid my aversion from Cynthia. "Then I imagine we will attend as a family."

"Yes, I believe so," she said, and then looked me over from head to toe. "And I would be pleased to help you prepare to see your prince again. Like I mentioned earlier, if you exerted some effort—especially with your hair—you could be quite pretty."

Irked, once again, with Cynthia's insulting comments about my appearance, my simmering dislike of her rose to a boil.

Before I could formulate a sisterly reply to forcibly grind from my lips, she stifled a yawn and pointed to two nearby doors. "My chambers." Then she gestured to a single door down the gallery, closer to the stairs. "Your bedchamber. I hope you will find it to your liking."

She turned, walked a few steps, turned back, and tapped her fingers against her cheek. "And did you know, you have dirt on your face?"

I bit my tongue as I glowered after Cynthia's departing figure. She disappeared behind one of her two chamber doors, and I wondered how I was going to endure this new stepsister of mine. Shaking my head, I reminded myself that Cynthia had endured a lifetime of Mother-imposed isolation, and it should be my pleasure to share my world with her. After all, for better or worse—and I feared it might be worse—we were family now.

My own bedchamber door now drew my attention. I approached, thumbed the latch under the curved handle, and pushed it open. A large room, tastefully decorated, met my sight. The manor's palatial excess did not extend to my room, and I was glad.

The chamber smelled of roses due to several vases of the flowers, along with their tiny winged attendants, placed about the room, and the early evening sunlight spilled through the west-facing windows spreading patterns of rectangles on the carpeted floor. Carved-oak pieces furnished the room: oak chairs near the fireplace, the writing table by a window, and the tall posters of the bed. With a running leap I landed on the damask spread that draped over the mattress and looked up at the canopy. I bounced a couple of times, tossed an embroidered pillow in the air and caught it, and then rolled off to investigate the armoire. I found my clothes and personal items folded on the shelves. My wardrobe, though by no means meager, didn't fill the available space.

My special slippers, the ones Cynthia admired, sat displayed on the chest located on the side. I picked them up, gazed at them for a minute, imagined Cynthia's covetous hands fondling them, and then knelt down to hide them in the bottom of the armoire beneath some undergarments, not wanting to display temptation to Cynthia's avaricious eyes.

I stood, stretched, and decided it was time to check on Isabella, even though she seemed so distant of late. Though excited about living in the manor, I predicted that she'd be homesick and probably in need of a cool cloth for her headache. I headed toward the door, passed the washstand mirror on my way, and noticed the dirt on my face. Sigh.

I grabbed a cloth, dipped it in the basin, and wiped my cheek. As I finished and walked to the door, I made myself a promise, I'd really try not to be such a mess.

Later that evening, after an awkward supper in the large dining room with Hannah and Rebecca serving Cynthia, a revived Isabella, and me, I left the manor hoping to find Rosanna in the garden, but she, probably off overseeing another area of her domain, was nowhere to be seen. Concerned about my mother's mandate that I not engage with the fairies, I wondered how I could satisfy both Mother's requirements and the fairy queen's demands. I decided that simply walking around could not be disobedient to Mother and would help with Rosanna's current directive. After all, I was the fairy kin like my father before me.

Resolute, I wended my way across the chilly, dusk-darkened grounds to the rose garden and guardedly approached the nearest gray spot. Harder to see with night falling, the grayness pulsed with something that I could only describe as the opposite of the glimmering glow of a fairy. It seemed that where fairies were designed to bring health to plants, these little imps, being their opposites, were designed to bring disease. No wonder Father had traveled the kingdom to keep these at bay.

The ash-colored speck writhed like smoke as I neared, the impish face in its midst contorting in anger and then dissipating like a mist before sunlight. With an exhalation of relief at my success, I crept around the rose garden, cautiously closing in on each shadowy area one by one. As the sky darkened, it grew harder to see the gray-cloaked imps, but the movement of their shadows gave them away. In addition, fairies would target and illuminate a hidden urchin, showing me where to focus. Finally, all the imp locations were cleared, and as I scanned the shadow-free, fairy-illuminated area, a touch of happiness flickered in my heart, the first such feeling since Father's passing. However, the moment was soon tempered as I noticed dry, crackly rosebuds left where the shadows had been. Again, I could see first-hand why Father had traveled the kingdom.

After that, sleep eluded me. Worrying about the local fairy monarch's demands as opposed to my mother's, sleeping in a strange bed, and churning about my snobbish stepsister's overtures to Isabella contributed to my fretful night.

Also, I wondered when Prince Charmain would leave for the summer tour, for I wouldn't be easy until I heard how he fared on the journey, both for his safety and for news of titled marriage prospects.

It did not feel like I had slept at all; nevertheless, the morning after our arrival at Rella Manor, I woke at dawn, hopped out of bed, and pattered to the washstand to splash water in my face. Remembering my vow to be tidier, I took care with my cleaning routine and chose a crisp, clean chemise and ankle-length tunic from the armoire for my attire. Next, I brushed my wavy brown hair several strokes more than usual, tied it back in a knot, and secured a piece of netting over the back of my head. It didn't look quite right, so I'd need Isabella or Sarah to fix it for me, but for now it would do. I hastened down to the kitchen, located on the lower or basement level, to see how my beloved Sarah was settling in. I hadn't teased her for almost a full day.

The smells of porridge and yeast greeted me before I reached the kitchen. Upon arrival, I entered a scene of clanks, clatters, and thuds, with Sarah, who had just arrived yesterday, already presiding as queen of the kitchen. She stood in the room's center next to one of the two long wooden tables, kneading bread dough and shouting orders to the kitchen maids. One maid stirred the porridge in a cauldron that hung over the fire. Another plucked a chicken at the second table, while still a third worked at chopping vegetables.

Sarah turned from her floury dough and noticed me. "Miss Griselda, why can't you stay abed and rise at a proper time like the other young ladies of the house?"

I walked to Sarah's table, grabbed a mound of dough, and started to knead, earning openmouthed shock from the manor staff. I grinned at them. They giggled and returned to their tasks.

I pushed and folded my dough as I replied to Sarah. "The sun's rising, and I want to scout out the grounds."

Sarah slapped my hands and grabbed my dough. "This is no work for a young lady. Now, off with you and stay out of trouble."

She dropped the dough, grabbed a wooden spoon, and whacked playfully at my backside. I hopped out of her reach and made a taunting face.

She shook her spoon at me. "You're not too big for me to paddle your backside, missy. You just see if I don't."

I assumed an innocent expression. "I'll behave. I promise."

"See that you do. And come like a deer chased by hounds when you hear the bell."

I waved at her. "Fast as the wind."

And I ducked out the door, but not before Sarah snuck up behind me and caught me with a quick shot to the rear.

"Hah, one for me." She stood triumphantly with her hands on her hips, wooden spoon sticking out at an angle.

I taunted. "Just tickled."

And hearing more giggling from the kitchen maids, I sped from the kitchen before Sarah could land another parting blow.

The sun cast an orange glow above the eastern horizon, and the air still had its morning dampness as I worked my way around the side of the manor house and toward the rose garden to search for the rainbow fairy, Rosanna. After all, I hadn't seen her last night.

There wasn't as much activity as I had expected around the outbuildings. Abandonment or rare usage marked many of the structures: the blacksmith, the brew house, the carpenter's workshop, and the kennel. In the stables, the horses attended to their mangers, and near the coop, the chickens clucked and scurried about loose on the grounds. Milk cows, fresh from morning milking, ambled toward the pasture to feed. A maid exited the dairy, struggling with two buckets of milk.

I ran up to her and held out a hand. "May I help you?"

She looked startled. "Oh, no, miss. I jus' couldn't."

I fell into step beside her. "But I would be happy to help. Hannah, isn't it?"

"Yes, miss, if it please you, but I couldn't have you

doin' servants' work. It jus' wouldn't be right. Not right at all, miss."

She headed to the kitchen, and realizing there was nothing more that I could do, I forayed on, made my way past the silent buildings, and discovered an unkempt vegetable garden. A few vegetables and kitchen herbs were planted at one end while most of the garden was going to weeds. In one corner grew some seedlings that would produce pumpkins in due time. Their caretakers, three-inch fairies with light green wings streaked with orange, flew up and circled my head before returning to their dance around the green shoots. I laughed and wondered again if they considered their tasks to be work or play, or if there was no difference between the two.

Deciding that this pace was taking too long, I broke into a jog, wove through an adjacent orchard with apple, pear, and cherry trees, noted the extensive fields further south, and soon angled toward the formal garden with the circle of rose bushes. Glistening drops of morning dew graced the colorful petals. I headed toward the creamy pastel blooms, against which the rainbow fairy had initially looked so beautiful yesterday. And she was there, looking as radiant as the morning.

She fluttered among the plants, supervising the smaller fairies at their work. As I approached, she turned to me, hovered to my face level, and scrutinized me just like yesterday. "Arianna has told me of you, Griselda."

Wondering if Arianna and Rosanna were capable of long-distance mind speak, I felt chagrined by her tone, which implied that she thought I was capable of all manner of mischief.

I blurted out, "I'll do my best, and I did clear imps last night, but my father told me to obey my mother, and…" A sudden question came to mind. "Do you know the secrets everyone is keeping from me?" I asked, breathless.

The rainbow fairy inched back from me, her head tilted in analysis. "I concur with Arianna; you have enough of a burden for now."

Dismayed at yet another refusal to reveal the truth, I started to protest when enthusiastic yapping sounded in the distance, drawing my attention. The familiar barking came closer and closer. I turned to see a brown dog with flopping ears bounding toward me. He leaped at me, licked my face, and raced back and forth in front of me.

Delighted, I reached down and gave his head and ears a good a good rubbing of welcome. "Rags, you got away."

When I straightened, Rosanna was gone and Sarah's bell rang for breakfast. I listened again. A cowbell. Sarah was calling me like a cow. Well, this required an appropriate response. So as I trotted back to the manor with Rags at my heels, I imagined mooing in reply to everything Sarah said to me, and I chuckled at how it would likely earn me a bit more attention from her long wooden spoon.

I broke into a run, raced Rags around the corner of the manor house, and swerved sharply to avoid colliding with Sarah, who stood there in her flour-dusted, ankle-length gray tunic and whitish linen apron, one hand raised in self-defense, the cowbell in the other.

"Fairies preserve us, child. Where did that mongrel come from?"

I petted Rags's head, grinning like a fool. "He found me."

Sarah reached down and ruffled his ears absently. "He's a good cur, he is."

Then she looked at the weedy ground. "Miss, I beg yer pardon, but may I take the liberty of asking a question?"

I gaped at her, shoulders bent, eyes not meeting mine. Her uncharacteristic reticence made me uneasy. "What's wrong? Why are you acting like this?"

She shifted her weight from foot to foot. "Well, miss, I don' like to be telling tales about yer stepfather, but somethin's amiss, you can take my word for it."

I threw my hands up. "Just tell me, Sarah."

She squeezed her hands together nervously. "The servants here have not had their full wages for months now. Some of 'em just gave up and left Lord Robert's service, and more are leavin'."

I glanced with new understanding at the vacant outbuildings and stood silently for a second as a sliver of dismay worked its way into my chest. "This can't be."

"It's not for me to say, miss. I thought Lord Robert was a man of means with this fancy manor and all, but he don' appear to have a copper to his name."

I shook my head. "There must be some mistake. Lord Robert and Mother will be home in a fortnight. It will all be straightened out."

But as I spoke, I looked at the unused blacksmith shop, the silent kennel, and the poorly tended vegetable garden.

Sarah's eyes followed my gaze. "I hope yer right, miss."

Sarah turned to leave. Her shoulders sagged as though she was carrying bricks, but her mouth was set like she could shake those bricks off as easily as water. She took a few steps away, then stopped and turned her head. "I dunno if you'd be interested, but Lord Robert's land agent has jus' come. He's asking for his lordship."

Puzzled at this unacceptably early visit, I asked, "Did you explain that he is away?"

"Yes, miss, but he refused to leave and asked for Lady Cynthia instead." Here Sarah sighed deeply and rolled her eyes. "The household servants say that the little princess won't be disturbed so early. Perhaps you should come."

Deciding that it was my duty as a family member to extend some form of courtesy to the land agent, I made my way with Sarah through the servants' entrance on the side of the manor, into the basement level kitchen, up the service stairs, and into the great hall. Through the library door, I viewed bookcases filled with parchments, scrolls, and books and a nervous-looking gentleman dressed in a knee-length, russet tunic, breeches, black cap, and black riding boots. He strode between the carved mahogany desk and a marble bust of King Benedict that rested on a pedestal. The man's footsteps barely made a sound on the thick carpet. He held rolled parchments in one hand and slapped them sharply into the other hand as he paced.

As we entered, Sarah made an awkward curtsy. "I beg yer pardon, Mr. Dankman. I dunno when Lady Cynthia will available. This is Miss Griselda."

Mr. Dankman spun toward me, considered me for a

few seconds, and seemed to reach a decision.

He bowed and removed his hat, an eager glimmer in his eyes. "Ah, you are Lord Rella's stepdaughter."

The muscles in my nose and upper lip curled involuntarily. I didn't like this man. And I definitely didn't like to be referred to as Lord Rella's stepdaughter, even if it was true.

However, the demands of courtesy prevailed, and I curbed my distaste. "I am, sir."

The west-facing windows cast dim light in the room as he briefly resumed his pacing and parchment slapping routine before facing me again. "I don't like to speak to anyone but Lord Robert, but something must be done."

I feared that this man hoped to take advantage of us during Lord Robert's absence. I wanted him to leave. "Mr. Dankman, I'm sure that anything you have to say can wait for my stepfather's return."

Dankman shook his head, an expression of regret momentarily shadowing his face. "Ah, but there you are mistaken, Miss Griselda. There is no good time to say something like this. Your stepfather is ruined."

As I stepped back, recoiling from this shocking pronouncement, he unrolled the parchments and displayed them to me. "These are legal documents written on behalf of former servants for services rendered but not remunerated, as well as from merchants yet to be paid and other creditors."

My earlier sliver of dismay grew to a log of fear in my stomach, because Sarah's recent words lent credibility to his claims.

My voice quavered as I replied, "There must be some mistake."

"There most certainly is, and the mistake is Lord Robert's. He is broke."

The earlier hint of regret now absent, he leaned into my face and spelled the word b-r-o-k-e slowly as if this would give weight to his assertion. Then he straightened and continued. "He has no money. He has debts for servants' wages, debts at all the nearby shops, and debts abroad."

I recalled passing Lord Robert's extensive land holdings on our way here and grew defensive and angry. This had to be a deception. It had to be.

"Mr. Dankman, I saw several tenant farms as we traveled here only yesterday. I saw nothing but prosperity."

Mr. Dankman threw his head back and laughed. "They are prosperous all right. Prosperous for their owners."

I took a step forward to emphasize my declaration. "Lord Robert is the owner."

Mr. Dankman rolled up his documents and shook his head. "I deeply regret giving this news to such a comely young lady, especially one newly arrived here, but Lord Robert has been selling his property, field by field, to his tenants ever since he married eighteen years ago. He now owns very little of his former holdings."

Anxiety growing, I didn't know what to believe. My breathing quickened, and the log of fear in my stomach twisted and rolled. If this was true, no wonder the servants were leaving. Much to my dismay, my instincts about Lord Robert were coming true, a genial gentleman with no sense. Mother would be so disappointed, since I knew part of her motivation for marrying the man was to provide for her family—and to protect me.

In my frustration, I couldn't keep from blurting out. "Why would Lord Robert do such a thing?"

Mr. Dankman slid his hands on the rolled parchments and shook his head. "Lord Robert has been living beyond his means for many years. Selling his property helped him appear to keep up."

"But why?" My voice grew shrill. "Why not live within his means?"

Mr. Dankman almost spat. He swept an arm expansively to include the voluminous contents of the library and then spread both arms to encompass the whole of the manor. "How could he possibly, formerly with his extravagant wife to please, and now a similarly extravagant daughter?"

I pointed a finger at him accusingly. "You should have explained the matter to him."

Mr. Dankman mirrored my pointing finger. "Don't accuse me, miss. I cannot be held accountable for Lord Robert's lack of judgment. I only did as directed."

I glared at Mr. Dankman, who shifted his weight from foot to foot and slapped the parchments against his leg.

He bowed to me. "You appear to grasp the situation, Miss Griselda. I leave it to you to acquaint your stepfather and your mother with this matter. However, I will return."

He bowed again, placed his hat on his head, and strode from the library. I turned to find Sarah wringing her apron as she watched Mr. Dankman's departure. Mr. Dankman glanced back at her and quickened his pace. I didn't blame him. The look on Sarah's face indicated that it wasn't the apron that she wanted to wring.

When Mr. Dankman closed the front door behind himself with a bang, Sarah turned to me. "This is a fine mess, Miss Griselda. What will we do?"

I didn't know what to say. Here we lived in an elegant old manor with apparently no money, tremendous debt, and a fool for a stepfather.

The communication from Mr. Dankman left my stomach unsettled throughout the morning. I disliked being expected to divulge such troubling news and considered simply waiting until my stepfather returned, but I thought that Cynthia's assistance might be needed to convince her father of the seriousness of the matter. So despite my misgivings, I had to act.

My opportunity came in the afternoon when I found Cynthia alone perusing books in the library. The windows faced west and gave slanted illumination to the room. Candles now lit in the evenly spaced wall sconces between bookcases and low flames from the fireplace provided the light available for reading. My stepsister stood near the carved mantel holding an open book, apparently enrapt by the manuscript's contents. I knocked sharply on the open door as I entered.

Cynthia looked up. "Good afternoon, Griselda."

She gestured around the room, her face filled with pride. "As you can observe, our family has one of the most extensive collections of ancient writings in the kingdom." Her expression grew secretive, and she lifted the book in her hands slightly. "Even some banned books."

I remembered my father telling me that there had been a vast book burning a few generations ago. My curiosity piqued, I looked at the rows of shelves crammed with books, bound and rolled parchments, and stacks of vellum. Though the room was clean, the smell of dust and a hint of mold emanated from the books.

Cynthia held up the ancient tome in her hands, turned a stiff, crackly page, and coughed out a laugh. "Griselda, do believe in these stories?"

I glanced at the faint gold title etched across the aged leather cover, *Legends of the Fairy Kingdom*, very likely a banned book. The breath within me grew still and guarded. Though daily life and religion in LaFairia were filled with references to our fairies, belief in fairies had been discouraged since King Benedict's proclamation condemning those with fairy sight.

So avoiding the subject as I'd been taught, I tried evasion. "There are fantastical claims in some tales."

The corners of Cynthia's mouth tipped up and her eyes narrowed. "True, but could there be some truth behind the fables? Do you believe them?"

I felt cornered like a sheep corralled for shearing. Father had warned me never to reveal my fairy sight. And Mother, Mother had threatened to lock me in my room if I couldn't control what she preferred to describe as my embarrassing imagination. Though Mother and Father had different outlooks, their messages were the same. Tell no one.

I walked past the bust of King Benedict, stopped in front of the mahogany desk, and leaned against it to appear calm.

Forcing a laugh, I tried a variation of one of Mother's frequent concerns. "Are you asking if I am stark, raving mad? Surely, you jest, Cynthia."

Cynthia stared at me silently for a couple of heartbeats while rubbing her thumb over the book's rough spine.

Then she smiled. "Of course, I jest. After all, during The Purge following King Benedict's coronation, those who believed in these stories were often jailed, and those who could see fairies were put to death."

A cold wave spread through my chest. It was common knowledge that King Benedict put those suspected of fairy sight, and even their families, to death during The Purge. But that was ancient history, and those laws, though still gathering dust in the castle, had not been used in my lifetime.

My father's ancestors with fairy sight had immigrated to LaFairia and had fortunately slipped through the cracks somehow, but I did not know the truth of it. That information had died with my father, unless Mother hoarded some of this knowledge in the secrets she was unwilling to tell.

Now, with nosy Cynthia staring so probingly, I began to see why Father and Mother had both been so insistent about secrecy.

Choosing to make light of the matter, I joked. "Cynthia, if you see a fairy, I promise not to tell."

Cynthia's face assumed the appearance of a pleased feline. "And I make you the same promise, Griselda."

The memory of Cynthia walking up on me in conversation with Rosanna and now her silent perusal of me shivered through my thoughts. I wasn't tempted to trust Cynthia with my secret. Even Isabella and I avoided the topic, me because of parental commands, Isabella because she was scared—like Mother. So Cynthia could speculate all she wanted, but it would

Griselda Rella

avail her nothing.

At present, there was nothing to fear, except our current financial problems. And I still needed to acquaint Cynthia with Mr. Dankman's claims. Thankfully, this gave me a good excuse to redirect our conversation. I rubbed my hand across the smooth desktop on which Mr. Dankman had placed the disturbing documents earlier in the day. A stack of old books, that hadn't been there this morning, rested on its surface topped by a large, moldy tome titled *History of the Realm*.

With my finger sliding up the side of the stacked volumes, I broached the uncomfortable topic. "I came to ask if your father has a land agent who manages his affairs."

Cynthia looked amused at my change of subject, but also curious. "Yes, but Father also depends on me."

I felt a morsel of hope. "And are you acquainted with your father's bookkeeping practices?"

I watched Cynthia's eyes. Her curiosity flickered with wariness. "No, my father and his agent, Mr. Dankman, are responsible for such matters. However, I choose many of our purchases."

She lifted her hand and gestured to the pedestal table on which rested the bust of King Benedict. My heart sank. Clearly, Cynthia had no idea of the ruin we faced.

Tentatively, I inquired, "And do you see Mr. Dankman frequently?"

Cynthia paused, gripped her book in both hands, and appraised me with heightened alertness. "Why do you ask?"

The tightness in my stomach twisted, and I took a

deep breath. I didn't look forward to bringing pain to Cynthia. Even though we didn't have the makings of friends, we were still family. Cynthia, her posture rigid, awaited my response.

"Mr. Dankman was here this morning when you were—unavailable. He chose to speak to me."

Cynthia's eyes sharpened. She thumped her book on top of the history book with a thud. "To what purpose?"

"He claims that your father no longer owns the tenant farms on the surrounding land and that he is unable to pay his debts."

Cynthia stared without response for several seconds. I waited for her to cry, to fume, or to deny.

But she coughed out a laugh.

And I felt my eyes stretch to saucers.

She laughed again, a haughty laugh, the laugh of someone who considered the subject beneath her consideration. She grabbed the stack of books, including *History of the Realm* and *Legends of the Fairy Kingdom*, hefted them with her slender, steely arms, and swanned from the room, chuckling as though I had told a good joke. I stared after her in disbelief until tingling in my feet told me it was time to move. Now what was to be done? I guessed there was nothing to do but to hope in my stepfather. And I had no faith in him.

Chapter 10

An Infuriating Letter

Several mornings later, Cynthia, Isabella, and I sat in the parlor sipping tea and working on embroidery. That is Isabella worked on embroidery, Cynthia dabbled at embroidery when not exclaiming over her jeweled bracelet and large pendant necklace, and I— dreadfully bored—dangled threads for Mr. Tatters to chase and then scratched his ears when he claimed a seat on my lap.

The room, furnished with carved wooden chairs and settees covered with embroidered cushions, had a thick carpet, an ornate stone fireplace mantel, and north- and west-facing windows, which provided indirect light, inconvenient for Isabella's intricate stitchery. Fragrant roses of many colors, picked by me, arranged by Isabella, and not even appreciated by our stepsister, graced vases resting on a sideboard and ornamental tables positioned against the walls.

In the aftermath of our conversation about the land agent, Cynthia and I had made a strained effort to be polite to each other, and neither one of us had broached the topic of Mr. Dankman again. I felt torn between never wanting to see him again and wanting Cynthia to hear his news for herself.

When finished with her tea, Cynthia rang a jeweled

bell. No response was forthcoming, further evidence that many servants—especially the men—had quit the manor. My stepsister, her face tensed with annoyance, rang the bell again, this time more vigorously.

Eventually, Sarah trudged into the room carrying a silver tray, collected Cynthia's cup, and cast a mutinous expression at the back of her head. As Sarah and I exchanged glances of amused longsuffering, we heard sharp rapping on the front door. Sarah placed the tray on the sideboard and left to answer it. We heard a man's voice and then Sarah's returning footsteps.

She quickly padded into the parlor, her eyes twinkling. "Miss Griselda, a messenger from the prince is here for ya."

Isabella gave a little chirp of excitement. Cynthia popped up like a weasel from a hole, her neglected needlework falling to the carpet.

Sarah glared her down. "The message is for Miss Griselda."

I stood up, forcing Mr. Tatters into a startled retreat, and swiped at the cat hairs covering my lap. Eager to hear from Prince Charmain, I hastened out, only to stop in my tracks.

Courier Jon.

My racing nemesis stood carelessly inside the door in his dusty travel clothes, appearing quite at home in the palatial great hall. He shot a half grin across the space between us, bowed, and held out a rolled parchment closed in wax and impressed with the royal seal.

"Miss Griselda." Even his tone mocked me.

I blew a breath through my nose, crossed the last few yards between us, and took the paper with a nod and a shallow—very shallow—curtsy.

To my embarrassment, his eyes drifted to the cat hairs still clinging to my garment. He smirked as if remembering the grass-stained knees from my defeat.

He leaned back on his heels. "You moved quite a distance to avoid a rematch."

I reached for the coin pouch hanging from my belt. "Don't flatter yourself."

He saw me fishing for a copper, held up his hand, and shook his head.

So I folded my arms and nodded curtly, clearly indicating that he could leave. "Thank you for the message, Courier."

He copied my folded arms, raised his eyebrows, and settled his weight. "I am to wait for your response."

I shrugged to let him know that it was no concern of mine. "Then if you will excuse me…"

I turned away, ignored the expectant faces of Isabella, Sarah, and Cynthia peering from the parlor, and strode to the main stairs, wondering if Courier Jon was watching me leave—not that I cared.

When I reached the landing halfway up the stairs and turned safely out of that courier's view, my focus shifted to Prince Charmain's letter. Tightness tied up my gut and my heartbeat quickened as I anticipated reading about the prince's first summer tour representing the monarchy and about the titled young ladies with whom he would be spending so much time. I still had a thin hope that Father's plan might be possible. Even though it was admittedly overreaching, the concept was sound, strategic, and quietly revolutionary. But with the prince and I being separated, so many things could go wrong.

I stepped into my bedchamber, leaned my back against the closed door, and ran my fingers over the rough parchment and the bumpy wax seal. Taking a moment to savor the tingly hope of a message from my best friend or potential betrothed or whatever he was, I glanced around determined to locate a ladylike reading spot: the canopied bed draped with damask fabric and needlework pillows, the carved oak chairs positioned near the fireplace with its welcoming blaze, or the carved oak writing table with its matching chair. Oh, bother, I broke the seal right where I stood, unrolled the parchment, and began to read.

Dear Griselda.

I took note of his use of my formal name and my enjoyment faltered. He rarely called me Griselda. I began again.

Dear Griselda,

As I promised, I greet you from Norlan Castle, the first stop on the summer tour. I wish you and your family well, and I had the opportunity to give my regards to Lord and Lady Rella only yesterday. I hope his cough will improve.

Now, I feel compelled to inform you that, as we journeyed, Lord Ursa spoke to me at length. He made a most convincing case that we should allow our nobles to exercise more authority regarding tax collection. He wants to close the almshouse, a boon for the lazy, bind peasants who can't pay their taxes to their overlords, and allow overlords to sell their laborers in order to pay off their debts. I have come to believe that he is right, and I am sure that you and other subjects of the realm will eventually come to see the wisdom of Lord Ursa's proposal.

I dropped the letter from eye level to my thighs, hearing the parchment crackle against my dress, my initial happiness at the letter now gone. This was troubling news. Any further tax burdens would certainly not be welcomed anywhere, especially if they curtailed charitable services and basic freedom. I feared that the greedy noble was misleading the prince, and probably the king as well. I crossed the carpeted floor, dropped onto the bed, sank into the quilt and pillows, and raised the letter again. Now, feeling somber and wishing that I could be there to knock some sense into that prince's head, I began to read again.

With all due respect to your father and his memory, it is time for a change in our tax structure. Lord Ursa says that your father's death was a sign that we need to change.

With breath stopped as though punched in the gut, I stared unbelieving at the letter. That perfect fool. If he'd been in the room, I'd have clobbered him. How could he consider such injustice? How could he turn his back on a lifetime of work, my father's work?

Our king was a good and easily guided man, an elegant head of state, but I had grown up watching as my father—a mere tax collector—had stabilized the kingdom from behind the throne. Always he deferred to the king, or at least appeared to, but always the king depended on my father. I knew this.

Now, there was Lord Ursa, the same easily guided king, and an impressionable prince. Surely, there were other advisors with voices of reason to guide the king and his heir. Unfortunately, because the kingdom had been peaceful and prosperous for so long, the nobles had become complacent. I looked back at the letter and braced myself to read the rest.

Lord Ursa says that we should take advantage of LaFairia's present abundance and welcome changes that will increase our prosperity and royal oversight over all aspects of community life. I wish that you would join me in the furtherance of our kingdom's fortunes. Indeed, I am sure that you will when we return from our triumphant summer tour.

Please allow me to caution you against any comments in opposition to our fair will. Lord Ursa has spoken most insistently on this point.

I look forward to greeting you upon my return and to making our important announcement.

His Royal Highness...

He added a postscript:

I know that my words will make you angry, Grizzy. But please put your mind at rest and remember that this is men's work, and you are just a girl.

All ladylike aspirations gone, I threw the parchment across the room and followed it with a series of poorly aimed pillows.

"Just a girl?"

Just a girl who can whip your tail, you buffoon. I sent another pillow after the letter. Misdirected, it knocked a candlestick from the washstand, which clattered to the ground, the candle dripping wax and singeing the carpet. I darted from the bed, grabbed the candlestick, and stomped on the charred carpet. The smell of burned wool rose from my shoes.

I glanced at the offensive parchment lying among pillows on the floor.

Just a girl?

I might be young and I might be a girl, but I knew

my father's tax system was fairer than anything Lord Ursa would establish, as evidenced by his greedy seizure of Farmer Hugh's cow. Perhaps some people might think it a small, isolated incident, but my father always said that small injustices tended to grow to larger injustices. And I agreed.

After dropping the candle in the ceramic washbasin, I looked around my room with futility, feeling the need to do something but not knowing what. I reached my hand toward the letter and grabbed it once more, not sure whether I wanted to rip it to shreds or endure its closing words. Then I clenched my teeth and forced myself to finish the remainder.

Remember that this is men's work and you are just a girl.

You can be confident that Lord Ursa and I are working in the best interests of king and kingdom. And I covet your good will in this matter.

We wish you and your family good health.

HRH

I rolled up the parchment, crushing it in my grip. Oh, I wanted to shake that weak-minded dupe, and I tried to remember why we were friends. And why would I even consider marrying such a fool?

How could he fall so easily under Lord Ursa's sway? Hadn't he been listening to my father all these years—to me?

He needed to stand up to Lord Ursa, to say, "No." How could he dishonor the king, the people of LaFairia, and my father—and me?

And now he wanted my approval?

Approval of policies that would destroy all my father's work and cruelly burden ordinary subjects?

I stood stationary in the center of my chamber, hands trembling. My chest tightened and pressure built behind my eyes and nose. I squeezed my face tightly, but the tears leaked out anyway. I shook my head savagely. This wouldn't solve anything. Wiping the back of my hand across my face, I took a deep breath and racked my brain to come up with a plan. My eyes lit upon my small trunk against the wall near the window, and I knew what I had to do.

If the prince wanted a response to that infuriating letter, then I would give him one.

With fury roiling inside, I stormed across the room, grabbed a handle on my trunk, and pulled it away from the wall, flipping open the lid. Next, I stomped to my armoire and gathered a couple of dresses, tunics, chemises, hose, extra shoes, and an assortment of undergarments. These I tossed into the trunk as I fumed, he "covets my goodwill in this matter." So when I catch up with him, I'll give him a piece of my "goodwill," several pieces in fact.

Stripping off my dress, I clawed into a chemise, hip-length tunic, and wide skirt suitable for riding attire and stumbled over a couple of pillows strewn on the floor from my earlier tirade, as Mother would call it. I lifted a box of powder, accidentally dousing myself as I did so, and flung it into the trunk where it spilled all over my clothes. Oh well, it would save me the trouble of putting it on later. I threw in some combs, a brooch, and a belt and slammed the lid shut. I didn't think I'd packed properly, probably not, but I wanted to get started right away. And that irritating Courier Jon was downstairs in the great hall waiting for my response. At that remembrance, my stomach did an odd little roll.

With my hand gripping the chest's handle, I dragged the container across the chamber floor. It kept creating folds in the carpets and getting stuck. I didn't have time for this. After a series of brutish yanks, I had the trunk through the door, down the gallery hall, and to the top of the stairs. Then thump, thump, thump, I began my descent, silent curses gusting in my mind.

Sarah appeared at the foot of the stairs. "Miss Griselda, what a racket yer makin'. Are ya tryin' to bring the house down?"

In no mood to explain myself, I made no reply. So she lumbered up the steps and grabbed the other end of the trunk, saving the stairs from further damage. I continued down the staircase now with Sarah in tow.

She persisted. "What are ya doin' with the trunk, miss?"

I dropped my end of the trunk on the marble tiled floor at the foot of the stairs. The great hall was empty, but heads peeked in from the parlor. Isabella surveyed me with wide-eyed curiosity but no alarm. She was used to my ways. Cynthia, now framed by the parlor entrance, evaluated me with perplexed amusement on her face as if she watched the performance of a troop of players engaged in some foolery. I didn't care. This had to be done.

Courier Jon, who had apparently been outside, reentered the hall. My stomach did that annoying flip again.

He looked at my trunk and crossed his arms. "No, Miss Griselda, you're not coming."

I heard two gasps: one from Sarah behind me, one from Isabella in the parlor.

I ignored them. This courier wasn't going to tell

me what to do even if he had beaten me in a race, and then again, maybe because he had beaten me. I'd come if I wanted to.

My fists now rested on my hips. "The prince wants a reply, and I'm going to give him it to him."

Courier Jon grinned and tried to rein it in by dropping his head, but his shaking shoulders gave his feelings away. Tired of being thwarted, first by the prince, now by this courier, I wanted to punch something, and Courier Jon was closest.

He seemed to sense my mood, because he stepped back with his hands up in mock fear. "I'm sure it needn't be said that a written reply was expected."

"Well, he's going to get a lot more than he expected. Do you realize what they're planning?"

Amusement vanished from his face. "Forgive me, miss. It is not my place to comment. I would be pleased to carry your response to His Highness; however, I cannot carry you."

With a scowl at the courier for implying that I needed his assistance in any way whatsoever, I reached down for my trunk and pulled. "No one is asking you to."

I got my trunk outside with grudging help from Sarah, who muttered constantly, "What will your mother think?"

Courier Jon assisted, supporting the side in silence, but his disapproval was deafening.

Blue sky dotted with scattered clouds and warm weather greeted us as we exited the manor, where Sarah and I dropped our ends of the trunk at the top of the stairs. When we looked down at Courier Jon's horse being led from the barn after being watered and fed, the problem with my plan became ridiculously apparent. Courier Jon stood at his ease and watched me as the realization of my folly settled in.

I couldn't travel on horseback with a trunk.

My cheeks flushed, but I lifted my chin and looked undaunted into his amused eyes. "This is but a brief hindrance."

And I set off to the barn before he could break into outright laughter. I marched, scattering chickens in my haste, ignoring Rags who came bounding to my side, and slapping at the voluminous fabric of my riding garments. I strode faster when Courier Jon joined me, matching me stride for stride.

At first, he said nothing, so I took the opportunity to make things perfectly clear. "I can manage by myself, thank you."

Doing very little to hide his amusement, he replied, "Of that I have no doubt."

Nevertheless, he followed me to the barn, helped to saddle a mare, secured the saddlebags, and led the horse to the front of the manor, completely ignoring the fact that I neither needed nor wanted his assistance.

He backed off, patting Rags on the head, when I began to stuff the contents of my trunk into the saddlebags. He looked away when I shoved some personal items into the bags, but that didn't soften my embarrassment. My face warmed from something quite other than the sun overhead. When I finished, the saddlebags on my mount bulged with the contents formerly stuffed in my trunk. Spilled powder dusted the flaps, and I realized that I certainly wouldn't arrive with a well-maintained wardrobe, but I'd surely arrive. And that was the point.

My preparations—such as they were—finished, I noticed Isabella and Cynthia standing in the manor doorway. I climbed the stairs to take my leave and heard a hissing sound behind me. I turned to look and found Sarah, nose to nose with Courier Jon.

Her finger pushed into his chest. "The prince must have left Norlan by now."

The messenger held his ground. "It is likely."

"So what, in the name of all the gods above, do ya' think yer doing agreeing to take Miss Griselda on the road to who knows where?"

He looked at Sarah steadily and did not give an inch to her anger. "I have not agreed to escort Miss Griselda anywhere. You know as well as I that she is determined to go whether escorted or not. I am simply not abandoning her to attempt the journey alone."

Sarah harrumphed and appeared reluctantly mollified by his statement. I, however, was not. It frustrated me to hear them talking about me as if I were a child. They didn't understand. The prince was intent on ruining my father's legacy, all because Prince Charmain, and for that matter the king, had allowed themselves to be manipulated by that sour old Lord Ursa.

Finishing my ascent of the front stairs, I gave Isabella an affectionate squeeze, which she returned enthusiastically, and gave Cynthia an I'm-trying-to-be-a-good-stepsister hug, which felt like hugging a statue. Turning, I left them at the door and strode down the steps, my riding skirt tangling around my ankles. I freed my legs with a couple tugs and reached the hard packed drive. My shoes kicked up dust as I approached the horses. Courier Jon led the horses to the shade the manor provided from the late morning sun. Neither he nor Sarah smiled upon my arrival.

Sarah reached out her hands pleadingly. "Miss Griselda, what will your mother say?"

I knew Sarah was right, and I felt a touch of remorse that she'd have to explain it to her, but someone had to knock some sense into that prince. He would listen to me. I'd make him stand up to Lord Ursa—and then the prince could advise the king. Surely, that would work.

Courier Jon shifted his weight to one leg, dangled the reins in his hands, and eyed me with resignation. "I advise you to give heed to your servant, Miss Griselda. Clearly, your mother will disapprove of this journey, and there is no certainty of safety."

I realized that I was holding my breath, and so let it out fast and strong. How dare he speak to me as if I, of all people, was unaware of the perils of travel, especially for small parties? My emotions teetered for a moment between grief and anger.

Not wanting to deal with the sadness, I landed firmly on rage and replied through gritted teeth. "You need not instruct me concerning such risks."

His chin down, he looked at me. "You are right." He paused. "Very well, I travel with haste."

I grabbed my reins from him. "I can move just as fast as you can."

He exhaled a breath of exasperation and cupped his hands, creating a step for me to mount. "This is still an ill-conceived plan."

I spun away from his proffered assistance, slipped my foot into my stirrup, threw my leg over the saddle, and tried to settle confidently in the seat. The problem was that I'd mounted too energetically, and so my momentum and weight continued over to the other side. I saw the ground closing in on my head, and I yelped as I clawed for saddle, stirrups, and girth to stop my fall. A vice grip clamped around my ankle, my descent halted with a jolt, and my skirt went flying over the horse like a banner. Now, red in the face from more reasons than just being upside down, I righted myself, shook free from Courier Jon's grip, and glared at both him and Sarah, daring them to laugh. They, however, wore twin, straight-faced expressions of complete innocence. I nodded curtly to Courier Jon by way of thanks. He returned my nod, kept his mouth in a tight, straight line, and walked to his horse.

I leaned down to Sarah, who was now shaking her head, gave her a pat on the shoulder, straightened, and waved to Isabella and Cynthia at the top of the stairs. Isabella waved back readily. Cynthia just stared.

Next to me, Courier Jon mounted with one easy movement and looked at me, eyebrows raised. "Try to keep up."

I nudged my mount to get started ahead of him, looked up the hard packed drive at the unmanned gatehouse, and pulled back on the reins, bewildered by what I saw.

Confusion filled my mind as Lord Robert's carriage, pulled by two matching bays, entered through the gatehouse and rattled down the drive, the horses at a trot. They were a fortnight early. I watched the horses pull the carriage closer and closer, the wheels crackling against the drive, stones shooting from the rims. The pace was hurried, not leisurely like it should be on a wedding trip, the horses lathered and breathing hard. A wave of fear curled in my stomach and spread to my extremities. Something was wrong.

The carriage jerked to a stop and out leapt my mother, Lady Constance, in an obvious panic. She looked up at me, the blue of her eyes encircled with white.

"Whatever you are up to, Griselda, it must stop. Send for the apothecary at once. My husband is ill."

She burst into tears.

Courier Jon tapped my shoulder. "I will go for the apothecary."

I nodded. He kneed his horse and galloped away, and I watched him grow smaller as he raced through the gatehouse toward the nearby village. My thoughts battled over my conflicting demands: the need to ride to the aid of the kingdom, for that's what I deemed this flight to Prince Charmain to be, and the need to remain here to assist at home.

I remembered my stepfather's congested cough and the hesitation with which Mother had gone on their trip, and I watched as Mother frantically spoke to Sarah, who, along with the ever-accommodating Hannah, was already assisting my stepfather from the carriage, a quilt wrapped about his shoulders. His frail appearance alarmed me. His cane wobbled in his hand, and it took both Sarah and Hannah on either side to keep him on his feet.

Cynthia, having made her way down the stairs, came to a stop in front of her father, blocking the trio from further movement. Lord Rella held a delicate jeweled tiara in his shaking, second hand and held it out to Cynthia. I marveled, that man is too ill to stand on his own, and yet he thinks only of his little princess.

Her eyes gleamed as she took the gift, but then narrowed to knifepoints as she looked at my mother. "What did you do to him? He was in perfect health before now."

Though I knew this to be untrue and resented Cynthia's accusation of my mother, it wasn't the time to argue. It was time to act. I dismounted and hurried to the carriage. I was needed here. Affairs of LaFairia would have to wait.

Chapter 11

The Passing of Lord Rella

While anxiously waiting for Courier Jon to return with the apothecary, I returned to my bedchamber, sat at the oak writing desk by the window, and penned a short letter to Prince Charmain. My anger at the prince and my fear for my stepfather combined to make the quill shake in my hand, resulting in a much-blotted parchment, hardly fit to send.

Your Royal Highness,

I thank you for your remembrance of me, and I beg you to forgive the brevity of this response. My stepfather has just returned and is gravely ill.

Regarding your business, I must say that the course on which you are currently set will prove injurious to the Crown's loyal subjects, and I strongly advise against it. More than that, in meddling with my father's work, you dishonor my father, your father, the subjects of the realm, and me.

Please forgive my bluntness, but I must attend to my family.

I wish you good health and a speedy return.

Your humble servant...

I knew that my letter was not as deferential as it should be, but I didn't have time for niceties. Though I was furious with the prince and longed to confront him, my stepfather, a good man in spite of his failings, was gravely ill and needed attention. What more could I do?

The missive sealed, I left my chamber, made my way downstairs, and heard the approach of galloping horses, followed by the sound of boots stomping quickly up the front steps. Hannah opened the door for Courier Jon and the apothecary, and Sarah hurried the healer upstairs to Lord Rella's bedchamber. Courier Jon remained downstairs.

I approached the messenger, handing him my written reply. "Thank you for your help in both of these matters."

He bowed, his usual casually mocking bearing absent. "I hope for the best for your stepfather."

And he spun on his heel, left the manor, and rode away without a backward glance, leaving me with an unexpected sense of gratitude for his ability to be efficiently helpful when needed.

As the messenger exited the unattended gatehouse and reached the road, he paused briefly to exchange words with a couple of passing riders, who looked a bit like Fritz and Gammon, but I knew they could not possibly be here. The threesome glanced toward the manor. Then the courier urged his horse to a gallop, and he was gone.

What followed was a night of waiting, pacing, crying, and praying. I rescinded my abandonment of all the gods and beseeched them fervently for my stepfather's life. I had already lost my father; I didn't want to lose my stepfather, too. My mother, Lady Constance, alternated between time spent at her husband's side and time pacing in the parlor with Isabella and me. Cynthia disappeared into her own bedchamber and refused all attempts at communication, which worried me greatly.

Sarah, Hannah, and Rebecca, with help from me when available, scurried upstairs and down with towels, water, and herbs as demanded by the apothecary. The healer tried desperately to cool Lord Robert's feverish head and relieve his congestion but to no avail. By morning my stepfather was dead.

The funeral that followed was well attended by nearby nobles and neighbors. In spite of his financial ineptitude, Lord Robert was apparently well liked by the greater community, and though this was a tragedy for all of us, I felt especially bad for Cynthia. I knew how hard it was to lose a parent, and now my stepsister had lost both. We were her only family now, and she hardly knew us. I decided to make an extra effort to be kind to her.

After the funeral, I was surprised to find Cynthia out of her bedchamber and in the library. Cold ashes filled the fireplace, and candles remained unlit, due to the abandonment of the manor by most of its former servants. The only light came from west-facing windows, which only dimly illuminated the area.

My stepsister wore a black silk gown with embroidery on the bodice and the sleeve edges. Her blotchy face and puffy eyes were the only evidence of distress. Otherwise, she sat with cool composure at the mahogany desk; the banned book *Legends of the Fairy Kingdom* and a journal lay open on its surface, a pile of very old books and parchments to the side.

Knocking on the doorframe, I peered in, hoping that we could talk. "May I disturb you, Cynthia?"

She looked up, nodded, and closed both book and

journal. Curiosity flamed inside me, but I extinguished it out of concern for my stepsister.

"Cynthia, is there anything that I can do for you? Or would you like to take a walk in the garden? I'm sure that Isabella could be persuaded to join us."

Cynthia stroked the book of legends with a finger. "Thank you for your kindness, Griselda, but if you will forgive me, I would prefer to be alone for now."

Though disappointed, I honored her request and left her alone. But curiosity—and a touch of concern—rose in me regarding the object of her studies—fairies.

Throughout all this, I carried an extra burden, the knowledge of Lord Robert's financial status. Cynthia had refused to entertain the idea, Mother appeared outwardly more distraught than her stepdaughter, so confronting her with our financial woes seemed ill timed. And Isabella was not the one to burden with this. As a result, I was the only family member who shouldered Mr. Dankman's claim to our poverty. So the next day when the land agent gathered Mother, Isabella, Cynthia, and me in the library to deal with Lord Robert's affairs, I braced myself for unpleasantness.

The cloudy mid-afternoon light entering the library's windows provided little illumination to the gloomy room. Candle-filled sconces that Sarah and I had lit at intervals along the bookcases proved miserly with their glow as well. Mother, Isabella, Cynthia, and I sat in the library on stiff chairs brought in for this occasion. Filling the bookshelves around us were books, stacks of vellum, rolled parchments, and loose papers. I noted some empty spaces and wondered how many books, and concerning what topics, Cynthia now had collected in her bedchamber, but with the meeting about to begin, I pushed the mystery aside and focused on Lord Robert's land agent.

Mr. Dankman leaned against the mahogany desk on which he had spread a collection of legal documents. He stood and paced in front of the desk, rubbing his hands together as though washing them. He stopped, centered himself before us, and clapped his hands together.

"Now, to get on with it. Ladies, though I deeply regret the loss of your husband and father, it is my unhappy duty to fulfill my charge as Lord Robert's land agent."

I appreciated the reluctance with which Dankman began. I shared his reluctance. His information would not be welcome, at all.

He brought his hands together again and rubbed vigorously. "I regret to say that, for many years, Lord Robert spent beyond his means."

Cynthia inhaled sharply, sat forward in her chair, and looked as though she would flay Mr. Dankman with her eyes.

He glanced nervously at her and paused, but since she said nothing, he cleared his throat and continued. "To meet his expenses, he resorted to selling most of his property to his tenants. Lord Robert's estate now consists of nothing but these manor grounds, and his income consists of some small payments from farmers who do not yet own their farms outright. This income is insufficient to run this household. It is also insufficient to pay Lord Robert's outstanding debts. It will be necessary—"

Cynthia stood. The gloom of the room now lit with her anger. "Mr. Dankman, how could you engage in such a vicious falsehood? My father is but newly in the grave, and you come here circling like a vulture. This is not to be endured."

Mr. Dankman leaned back as though blasted by the heat of a smith's furnace, recovered, and became all business. No pacing and hand washing now.

He pointed at the document-laden desk. "Lady Cynthia, my claims are here documented. I am not culpable for Lord Robert's refusal to recognize the financial hole he was digging for himself and his family or for his failure to curb his spending. You may appeal to the king, but I can assure you that he will find no differently than I have."

Cynthia, standing tense with fury, didn't immediately reply.

Mr. Dankman reached out to the group. "Surely, this news comes not as a complete surprise. Miss Griselda must have acquainted you with my earlier visit."

Mother, Isabella, and Cynthia all turned to me, Mother and Isabella with looks of surprise, Cynthia with a look of accusation. Mr. Dankman looked at me questioningly.

I knew that I'd done nothing wrong but felt profoundly uncomfortable nevertheless. "I beg your pardon, sir, but when Lord Robert arrived so ill, it was not timely to acquaint Mother with your words. I did, however, mention your visit to Cynthia."

Cynthia looked daggers at me. "I recollect no such mention, Griselda."

In spite of my resolve to be kind to Cynthia, I wanted to spring from my chair, tackle her, and wrap that long golden hair around her throat until she coughed up a confession about the truth. But current circumstances robbed me of any satisfaction from the image.

Mother leaned forward and stretched her hands out between Cynthia and Mr. Dankman. "You must understand, sir, that this comes as quite a shock to the family, especially upon the loss of my husband."

Here Mother's voice broke, and she lifted a handkerchief to her nose. Mr. Dankman bowed his head, leaned back on the desk, and folded his arms across his waist. He waited for Mother to regain her composure.

She dropped her hands to her lap. "We will need to acquaint ourselves with all the particulars of my husband's estate and work with you to deal with the matter at hand. Perhaps, until everything is settled, we could relocate ourselves to Hart Cottage. After all, we remain tenants of His Majesty, though the Garners work the land."

Mr. Dankman nodded at my mother. "Lady Constance, perhaps that would be most prudent."

Cynthia broke her silence. "No, this is my home, and I will not leave."

I felt sympathy for Cynthia's attachment to her home; I felt the same connection to Hart Cottage.

But then she turned on Mother. "This is all your doing, yours and your daughters. You have brought nothing but ruin. My father is dead; my home is threatened. I will not leave so that vultures like Mr. Dankman can vandalize my valuables."

Cynthia turned and strode from the room with her back as straight as a sword.

Chapter 12

Plundering Rella Manor

Unfortunately, after consulting with other advisors, it was clear that Mr. Dankman was right, and Cynthia's furious lack of acceptance could not change the sad facts. So with the certainty that the finery of Rella Manor would need to be sold to pay off Lord Robert's debts, Mother shook off her grief, at least outwardly, and shouldered the burden of household manager. With promises of payment as soon as possible, the remaining manor staff members were dismissed. Two Rella servants, Hannah and Rebecca, chose to stay in spite of the uncertainty of payment. Sarah, really more family than servant, stayed, too, though she grumbled about maintaining the vast manor, a sentiment I shared.

We faced doing chores ourselves or going without them being done. In addition, we were tasked with cataloging the valuables throughout the manor for Mr. Dankman's perusal. While Cynthia remained cloistered in her bedchamber, which was understandable, but worried us all, Isabella and I, carrying ink, quills, and writing paper, followed Mother outside to list all the animals, carriages, and equipment in the outbuildings. Then we returned to the manor and paraded from room to room on the main floor listing the books, furniture, musical instruments, artwork, fancy rugs, and tableware. Finally, we trooped across the white and black marble tiled floor in the chilly great hall, its ashy fireplaces unlit, as Mother inspected each statue, tapestry, and finally the fresco.

Mother scrutinized the faded artwork. "Griselda, I suppose for the record we should list the fresco. It is of great value even though there is no way to remove it from the wall."

I scratched away with a quill on a paper supported by a book resting on my arm. The quill became dry, and I reached out to Isabella, who held the inkbottle, and noticed her squinting at the fresco, her eyes moving as if she followed some activity.

I cleared my throat. "Izzy."

Isabella blinked, noticed my dry quill, and held out the inkbottle. I raised my eyebrows with concern, wondering if she was feeling ill, dipped my quill in the ink, and finished recording the fresco.

Mother looked at my list and sighed. "At least we have finished cataloging the valuables on this floor. Next, we will begin upstairs where gowns and other clothing items must be added as well."

Isabella now mirrored our mother's sigh and rubbed her temples, confirming my suspicion about a headache.

Mother looked up from the parchment. "Isabella, dear, perhaps this is too much for you. Would you care to retire for a time before dinner?"

Isabella had been keeping pace as well as she could, but I knew how hard it was for her to prevent the headaches that had started soon after Father's death— along with her emotional distance from me.

Though her eyes were glazed with pain, she still

looked determined. "I wish to be of assistance to you and Grizzy."

Mother gave me a conspiratorial glance. "You have been a great help, my dear, but Griselda and I can continue for now."

I joined in with Mother's plan. "Yes, please give the ink to Mother, and we will see you again for dinner."

Isabella, looking both disappointed and relieved, handed the inkbottle to Mother, nodded, and with a quick glance at the fresco again, went upstairs for a nap.

Mother stared at the stairs after Isabella's departure. "It would be helpful if Cynthia would lend assistance. She could provide information about many of these pieces that you and I lack."

I agreed with Mother. But even though I still bristled at the injustice of Cynthia's recent accusations, I felt too sorry for her to ask her to face this after just losing her father. After all, I remembered how shattered I had been—and still was—regarding my father's death, and so I tried to judge her with leniency.

Since the devastating meeting with Mr. Dankman, my stepsister had hidden herself away in her bedchamber with only Rebecca permitted to enter and serve her. And even though it was inconvenient, I could hardly blame her.

So not wanting to distress my stepsister, I thought we should pass by her room and delay the recording of any of the mystery items behind her closed door. "Perhaps we should allow Cynthia as much mourning time as we can. She could look over our list of items later and make any additions and corrections at that time. I cannot ask her to face this."

Mother, still staring at the vacant stairs, replied, "You are right; it would be too much to ask." She turned to look me full in the face, her expression softer than usual. "You are a thoughtful young lady, Griselda."

The inner glow that filled me was reminiscent of how I'd felt with Father. Compliments from him had been frequent, but a compliment from Mother was rare. My face split into a smile, the pleasure of which reached my fingertips.

She returned the smile. "And now, upstairs."

As we headed to the staircase, I glanced back at the fresco like Isabella had done earlier. And I blinked. Did the royal trio move? I shook my head, looked again, and saw nothing but a motionless painting.

Our day of financial reckoning dawned. That morning, Cynthia, who now left her bedchamber for food, Mother, Isabella, and I finished our breakfast of porridge and retired to the parlor to await Mr. Dankman. The windows, which faced north and west, allowed only dim light, and the fire, built by Sarah and me, did little to cut the chill in the room or in my mood. Even though my heart wasn't attached to Rella Manor or its palatial contents, it annoyed me to think that the settee on which Isabella and I now sat would soon be pulled out from under us, as well as the matching chairs on which Mother and Cynthia sat facing us. The three pieces were really quite nice with carving and inlaid wood patterns and embroidered cushions. At that moment, I found myself quickly becoming attached to the furniture as I anticipated its departure.

We had all dressed somberly, even me, for the occasion of having the comforts of our home removed from us. Mother, Isabella, and I were dressed in the same clothes we'd worn to Father's funeral, except that mine had been vigorously scrubbed, cleaned, and pressed by Sarah, who somehow managed to remove all the dirt, dog slobber, and grass stains from the fabric. Cynthia, in another of her endless array of outfits, wore a lace-trimmed black gown embroidered with gold threads and precious stones and her jeweled tiara. It crowned her yellow-gold hair like a proclamation. I thought that last touch was too much for a soon-to-be-paupered family, but it was her father's last gift to her before he died, so given my similar attachment to my slippers, I had to have sympathy for her choice. She really did look like a princess.

Sarah and Hannah, in ankle-length gray tunics and white aprons, fluttered. That is, Hannah fluttered while Sarah trundled, in and out of the room dusting and tidying the sideboard and ornamental tables, a useless task since everything from carpets to furniture to vases would soon be gone. As we waited, the sound of an army of horse-drawn wagons rolling and creaking up the long drive to Rella Manor heralded Mr. Dankman's arrival. The muscles in my shoulders tensed. Glancing at Isabella seated next to me, I saw in her gray-cast face, a mirror of my feelings.

I put my hand on her shoulder. "Izzy, you should go lie down. We'll manage this."

She rose, burst into tears, and stumbled from the parlor. Cynthia stared straight ahead, mute, stone-faced. Mother's eyes followed Isabella's exit.

She stood and nodded to Cynthia and me. "I will tend to Isabella, but I will not be long. I believe that you stronger girls can welcome Mr. Dankman."

My idea of welcoming Mr. Dankman included introducing his backside to several swift swats with a broom. The mental picture lightened my spirits a bit. A smile tugged at the corners of my mouth.

Mother responded promptly. "Griselda."

My parent had her hands on her hips and a "do I need to scold you?" look on her face. "Politely, Griselda. We do not need any more trouble. Greet him politely."

I wondered what more trouble we could possibly create, but I organized my face into the appearance of humility and nodded.

Mother pursed her lips. "I will return as soon as I am able." She departed.

My stepsister remained motionless, still staring, and I wondered if she'd stopped breathing.

A sharp *knock, knock, knock* cracked against the main door. Cynthia's eyes shifted in a first demonstration of life. She and I exchanged apprehensive glances while Sarah hurried to open the door. The muscles between my shoulder blades tightened like the twist of an awl. And in strode Mr. Dankman, wearing black boots and breeches, billowing shirt sleeves, a knee-length tunic, and a smile ill-suited to the events at hand.

He doffed his hat with a bow. "A sad day, ladies, a sad day, but let's be on with it, and we will leave you in peace."

You mean in poverty, I thought, feeling my lip curl in its learned response to Mr. Dankman. Across from me, Cynthia arose, her back straight, her hands rigid at her sides, and her nose tilted so high that I marveled that she could still balance. I stood, too, eager to support whatever Cynthia would say.

"Mr. Dankman."

He scowled at Cynthia in a way that lacked any of his previous deference. "Yes, Cynthia."

Cynthia must have noticed. She appeared momentarily bewildered and actually took a step away from him. I didn't blame her. Nevertheless, true to the steely nature that I believed her to have, she held her new position and rallied.

"Mr. Dankman, surely this officious action is premature. With proper land management, I am certain that we will be able to settle our debts and continue to live in the manner to which we are accustomed."

I admired my stepsister's desperate attempt to save her possessions from Mr. Greedy Dankman's clutches and wished indeed that she could succeed, but sadly, I knew it was futile.

Mr. Dankman curbed his visible dislike, struggled to replace it with a more professional bearing, but only succeeded in grimacing awkwardly. "I'm afraid that your late, beloved father was given that very choice countless times, but now it is too late. Everything of value must be sold."

Cynthia stood like a statue for a minute, then another, staring icily at Mr. Dankman. His stupid grin faltered, his feet shuffled, and his hands fidgeted. Finally, after reducing him to a squirming mute, Cynthia moved, and without a word, she turned her back on slack-mouthed Mr. Dankman and swept from the parlor.

In spite of the gravity of our circumstances, I had quite enjoyed Mr. Dankman's discomfiture. When he wrenched his eyes from the doorway through which

Cynthia had departed, he turned to me. I stood as tall as I could and gave him a big grin. He scowled. I grinned wider, the broom against his backside image playing vividly in my mind.

He shook a finger at me. "See here, Miss Griselda. You've seen the accounts. This here is all above board. I can't be held responsible for Lord Rella's incompetence."

I walked behind a chair to emphasize my disapproval of his presence and faced him. "Perhaps not, but you appear to have done quite well for yourself throughout it all, and I will expect a thorough accounting of every item sold, every item, sir."

"But of course, Miss Griselda. I am at your service." He tipped his hat, replacing his scowl with a condescending smile.

My breakfast churned. "You may go about your business, sir."

The sunlight slanted through the great hall's south windows, casting geometric patterns across the tiled floor. I stood at the main door and checked off item after item being lugged out of the manor and onto the waiting wagons. Marble statues, mahogany chairs, oak tables, and silver candelabras all passed through the door. Huge tapestries were pulled down from the paneled walls, rolled up, and carried off by laborers. The clomp, clomp of boots scattered dirt on the black and white chessboard floor tiles. I felt like newly made friends were deserting me, leaving me hollow inside just like our emptying rooms that echoed their losses.

Mother directed that all our belongings be removed through the front door so that each piece could be carefully counted. We stationed servants at other exits to ensure that no item escaped unaccounted for. Sarah bustled about keeping watch for infractions, and I heard her shouts as she gave a piece of her mind to several laborers when they tried to escape with family portraits through a side door. They scurried back to the front door for my inspection like spanked puppies. Even Mr. Dankman seemed to shrink when Sarah came into the room, and he waddled away as quickly as possible.

Isabella remained abed, and Cynthia hadn't been seen since her departure from the parlor earlier. In late morning, I heard Sarah shouting from the great hall. I hurried to discover the problem.

Sarah held a hammer in one hand and a chisel in the other. "Fairies preserve us. Do ya' mean to knock the house down?"

A dumbfounded laborer stood empty-handed and speechless before her. Mr. Dankman arrived through the opposite door and crossed the floor, eyeing the hammer and chisel in Sarah's hands.

He stopped a safe distance away from her. "See here, woman. Enough of your interference."

Sarah waved the tools at him. "Interference, is it? Ya can't get that paintin' down without knocking the house down."

He spread his arms wide and looked at me. "Miss Griselda, this painting of King Nicholas has great historical value. The sale of it will do much to settle your family debt."

I couldn't believe that I needed to explain this to him. I stepped between him and Sarah and pointed to the wall.

"Sir, it is not a painting. It is a fresco."

He looked at the wall, the tools in Sarah's hands,

and the laborer, who still hadn't uttered a sound. Then he turned back to me, his mouth rounded. "Oh."

I glowered at him. "Do your documents give you the right to destroy the house?"

He shifted from side to side for a couple of seconds. "I will need to make further inquiry."

With a shake of my head, I realized that, no matter its value, we'd been foolish to add the fresco to the list of valuables. "You do that. I think that for now you have plenty of other spoils to plunder."

He looked like he had a rejoinder for my comment, but a glance past me to Sarah seemed to change his mind. He left to oversee the continuing pillage.

In mid-afternoon, Mother went outside to the dust churned drive to inspect the loaded wagons and to make sure that Mr. Dankman was only taking the items to which he was entitled. The workers had been removing selected fine furniture pieces from upstairs, when I heard pounding on the walls, then, "Open up in there," followed by more pounding.

Not knowing what to expect, I hastened across the great hall's black and white tiles and reached the bottom of the stairs at the same time that Mr. Dankman marched down.

He threw his arms up. "Miss Griselda, your stepsister has barricaded herself in her chambers."

Though weary from standing and marking off our possessions as they passed from the manor all day long, my insides tickled with pleasure to witness Mr. Dankman's sputtering exasperation. And even though I knew it was a hopeless gesture, I appreciated Cynthia's refusal to give up without a fight. Eyebrows raised, I smirked at the land agent.

He sputtered, sending spittle in every direction. "Look here, young lady, I'm within my rights. You don't want me to call the law."

I knew he was right but decided to make him sweat just a bit. "But you are the local law, Mr. Dankman. Whatever are you going to do about Cynthia?"

"Me?" He shuffled and rubbed his hands. "What can anyone do with that creature?"

I performed a theatrical sigh solely for his benefit. "What indeed?"

He crossed his arms, planted his feet firmly in one spot, and leaned back on his heels. "What are you going to do, Miss Griselda, since your mother is occupied elsewhere?"

He cast a nervous look at Sarah, who had just tromped up next to me, placed her hands on her hips, and settled in to listen. I knew we'd have to deal with it eventually, and I wanted to be done with this business and wash Mr. Dankman from our lives.

My heart heavy, I conceded. "Very well, sir."

He nodded and moved aside, so I could ascend the stairs. My shoulders sank as I started up the stairs. The last thing I wanted to do was tell Cynthia that now the finest items in her wardrobe, bedchamber, and sitting room had to be looted by our debt collector.

I had enjoyed the recent partnership that Cynthia and I had formed in defense against the assault on our newly formed family, and now I had to violate that nascent camaraderie. My shoes felt like stones as I lifted them step by step up the staircase and then willed them down the gallery, now lacking carpets, decorative tables, and family portraits, toward Cynthia's door where the workers still knocked, apparently overlooking her second door. They stepped back as I approached with Sarah and Mr. Dankman following.

I stopped in front of the door and sensed Cynthia's defiant presence behind it, but also something else: Loss. A feeling I knew. I remembered how I felt when I lost my father. A wave of grief washed over me, and I imagined how Cynthia must feel losing her father, the comforts of her home, her way of life, and how in many ways she was alone, an outsider in a stepfamily.

Mr. Dankman gestured at the door. "Go ahead. Make her open it."

I just stared at the door, frozen.

Mr. Dankman swung his arms back and forward and clapped his hands. "The day is fading, Miss Griselda."

I looked down at the floor. I knew that Cynthia might no more open the door for me than for Mr. Dankman, but that wasn't the point. I simply didn't want to make the awful request. I couldn't. I wouldn't. But I didn't know how to avoid it.

As I hesitated, a solution, a plan to make money to pay off our debt, formed in my mind. With the concept taking shape, I turned to Mr. Dankman, determined to project a confidence that I did not feel.

"Enough, sir. You have despoiled every other room in the house, leaving Isabella ill in her room and my stepsister in terror behind a locked door. It is time for you to leave."

Mr. Dankman puffed out his chest. "It is my duty to satisfy these debts."

"I do not dispute that. When you have sold the items you have, bring me an accounting. Then we can evaluate our debts further."

"This is not to be born, Miss Griselda."

I glared at the weasel, trying to squeeze every last copper out of my impoverished family.

Stepping back, I spread my arms to include all the workers. "Gentlemen, I bid you all good day."

I heard Sarah step closer behind me. The workers glanced at Sarah, nodded to me, and clomped out of the gallery.

Mr. Dankman opened his mouth like he wanted to order them back, but instead he turned to me. "You haven't seen the last of me."

I dreaded the next encounter, but I didn't want him to know that. "I certainly hope not. You must account for every item to the last copper."

"I shall do so; I'm an honest businessman."

I gestured to the stairwell. "Sarah will see you out, sir."

Sarah moved his direction like a wrestler spoiling for a fight.

As Sarah advanced, he stepped backwards quickly. "Until later, Miss Griselda."

I felt a hollow triumph as he turned and practically ran from the gallery and down the stairs with Sarah in trundling pursuit.

This left me waiting at Cynthia's door. I heard the shouts of workers, the cracks of whips urging the horses forward, and the sound of wagons leaving the grounds. Finally, it was silent, and I heard the creak of a floorboard in the room. I put my ear to the chamber door.

"Cynthia?"

"Are they gone?"

"Yes."

"Swear to me, Griselda, on your father's memory, that they are gone."

"I so swear. They are gone."

When I heard the sound of heavy furniture being dragged away from the door, I realized that Cynthia, though slender, was as strong as an ox. Then the handle clicked, the door opened slightly, and Cynthia emerged. Chin high, eyes defiant, and face streaked with recently dried tears, she closed the door quickly as if not wanting me to see into her chambers.

She tossed her head. "I am most grateful to you, Griselda."

I reached out my hand to her. "Let's get some tea."

Chapter 13

Isabella's Confession

A hand on my shoulder shook me gently. "Miss Griselda."

I rolled away from the voice and moaned, pulling the old quilt over my head.

The shaking stopped. "I'm sorry, miss, but ya' did threaten me with a lifetime's annoyance if I didn't wake ya' this mornin'."

I curled my body into a ball and pulled the bedding more tightly around myself.

Sarah, already smelling of flour, sighed and patted my quilt-covered head. "Why don't ya' just sleep until sunrise after all, miss? The maids and I can manage."

That got me moving. I groaned, threw back the covers, and swung my legs over the bedside, my bed now a wood and rope frame with a thin mattress, and the chamber now furnished with equally rustic furniture, leftovers from the quarters of departed servants, items that Mr. Dankman had not seen fit to despoil. It surprised me how much I missed the absent carved oak pieces, which had become comfortably familiar in such a short time, missing them more due to the circumstances of their disposal.

The darkness of the room was lit with one candle on the plain washstand and another held by Sarah, who peered at me through the dim light.

I rubbed my eyes with the heels of my hands and stretched. "No, Sarah, this was my idea, and with all you have to do, I won't add to it without helping out. I'll be right down."

Sarah shrugged, her flame flickering with the movement. "As you say, miss. I'll get back to the kitchen."

Sarah trundled from my bedchamber, and I heard the sound of her heavy, uneven tread recede as she clomped through the now carpet-less hallway and down the flights of stairs.

I hopped off the bed and my bare feet landed on the chill wood plank floor. Shivering, I walked to my washstand and poured water into the basin. After a brisk splash that sent goose bumps all over my body, I managed a quick dry with a thin towel and a few yanks of the brush through my hair. I tossed off my blue linen nightgown, a lovely embroidered vestige brought from Hart Cottage, and pulled a long-sleeved, ankle-length chemise over my head followed by a long tunic, a dirty one suitable for chores. Next, I tied an equally dirty apron around my waist and a scarf around my untamed hair.

A quick glance in the mirror made me pause. I looked just like a scruffy-haired servant. Well, no, the scruffy hair was my own signature, but the ensemble bespoke of servant attire. Now, I liked our servants very much and spent more time than Mother felt was proper working with them, but only days ago I had vowed to look more presentable. I shook off any feeling of discouragement and assured myself that this was surely a temporary state of affairs. Soon my family would re-establish its financial footing, and if I had my way, we'd move back to Hart Cottage, where we could once again live comfortably, even if not as elegantly as my new stepsister desired. But for now I had a plan to solve our family financial problems, and today I'd begin. I gave myself the luxury of a deep yawn and a final stretch, then left my bedchamber and headed to the kitchen.

I passed through the vacant gallery, down the stairs, and into the great hall, my footsteps echoing in the hollow room. Empty spaces where tapestries, tables, and marble statues had been displayed just yesterday drew my attention. Dirt left by the booted feet of laborers was scattered over the cold tiles.

The warmth emanating from the kitchen embraced me as I entered. A fire, the only one lit in the entire manor, already blazed in the hearth, and tallow candles on the walls lit the room. Herbs hung from the rafters. Half empty baskets and barrels of foodstuffs were under the tables and stacked against the walls.

Sarah, clothes white with flour, stood in the center of the room between the two long wooden tables, lording it over the remaining household staff. Hannah, who had originally been a dairymaid, stood next to the hearth and scalded some milk over the flames. Rebecca, the scullery maid, who was now often conscripted to serve Cynthia, glanced sideways at me with shy curiosity as she carried ingredients to the tables.

Soon milk, sugar, salt, butter, yeast, and flour, ingredients we could ill-afford now, were flying around the kitchen. I measured sugar, salt, and butter into a large trough, then stepped back as Sarah poured Hannah's scalded milk, just brought from the fire, into my mixture. When it cooled, I added yeast and flour to form stiff dough that I began to knead in troughs. Soon Sarah, Hannah, Rebecca, and I were kneading in rhythm, our softening dough smelling of yeast and flour. The purposeful activity was fun, and I looked forward to the aroma of loaves fresh from the oven.

After working through this process several times, we had a table full of bread dough rising like a field of ripe grain in the heat of the kitchen. I imagined how customers would eagerly purchase our bread when an unwelcome thought made my stomach drop. The truth was that, as perfect as Sarah's breads were, they might not stand out at the market. And it was essential that we make a profit to pay off our debts. I needed a way to make our breads special, or all our hard work would be in vain.

I frowned and helplessly scanned the kitchen as if it could provide me with some source of inspiration: a butter churn, the fireplace with cauldrons hung on chains, the bread oven, hot and ready for baking, nothing to spark the imagination.

Sarah, sensing my mood like she always did, stopped her kneading and followed me suspiciously with her eyes. "What's gotten into yer head, young lady?"

After all this extra effort, I didn't want to discourage Sarah by voicing my worries, so I ignored her and looked around the kitchen some more. That's when I noted a basket of old, dried apples shoved under the table near which I was standing. I pulled a couple of red ones from the bunch. Then I began to traverse the kitchen, poking into barrels, bins, and bags. As I grabbed raisins here, cinnamon there, an idea took shape.

The scant kitchen staff now ceased their kneading and stirring and watched me with amused curiosity that burst into giggles from time to time. It didn't bother me. I was used to being called crazy. I gathered sugar, dried blueberries, cheese, sun-dried tomatoes, nuts, and handfuls of herbs. And was in pursuit of more when Sarah couldn't contain herself any longer.

She crossed the kitchen and planted herself in my path with her floury fists firmly on her hips. "Fairies preserve us, child. What are ya goin' on about?"

Without responding to Sarah, I quickly surveyed my collection and chose sugar, nuts, and blueberries. To Sarah's dismay, I gently kneaded the berries and nuts into a small mound of dough, worked in a generous amount of sugar, and patted more sugar on top.

Floury hands pressed against her cheeks, she exclaimed, "Yer ruining my perfect bread."

Reaching for another mound of dough, along with tomatoes, cheese, and herbs, I said, "Everyone knows of your celebrated bread, Sarah, but it still ordinary baked bread. We need something unique that will draw customers."

With a shake of her head, Sarah dropped her white dusted hands from her face and muttered something I couldn't hear. From the scowling set of her mouth, I knew her thoughts were not complimentary.

As I concocted other flavor blends from our supply of ingredients, I hoped that in fact I was not ruining all of our hard work, changing Sarah's excellent breads into something new and potentially not salable. On the other hand, it was possible that the novelty could generate more sales. But I couldn't be sure.

Later that morning I went outside to take a break from bread making, the hint of coolness a relief from the kitchen. Patchy, feathery, white clouds dotted the sky as I breathed in the fresh air, wound around the side of the manor, and wandered my way to the rose garden. A group of fairies flew circles around my head as if in greeting. Then they flew off doing what I'd have to describe as a dancing game of chase but probably counted as work for them. I hoped to catch another glimpse of the rainbow fairy and began to look around when...

"Oh, there you are."

I turned to see Cynthia swishing toward me, carrying a parasol, pinning a butterfly net under the same arm, and wearing a cinnamon-colored silk dress that we'd saved from Mr. Dankman. With dismay, I noticed that my own dirty tunic and apron were covered with flour and dotted with blueberry stains.

Cynthia's eyes swept over my clothes. "Dear Griselda, you have flour on your nose? You are so delightfully charming."

I didn't appreciate her condescension, especially since I was baking out of compassion for her and to save her precious possessions.

I wiped my hand across my powdery nose and shrugged. "Sarah and I made bread this morning. We will sell it at the market to pay off some of the family debt."

My stepsister looked down her nose at me, a slight upward tug at one corner of her mouth. "You are a most industrious worker. I feel so fortunate to have you here."

I wanted to say, "Well, you could help, too," but still feeling compassion for Cynthia's recent losses, I didn't think that now was the time for such a suggestion.

I resorted to common courtesy. "Thank you, Cynthia."

She acknowledged my reply with a nod, lifted her hand, and swept it before herself to include the entire garden expanse. "It is the one thing they did not plunder."

Remembering that I'd also saved Cynthia's own bedchamber from plunder, I disagreed, but wanting to continue the sisterly moment, I agreed with her. "I'm glad Mr. Dankman left them."

Near us, a few fairies were leading ladybugs to the plants and then pointing to the leaves on which the insects were to work.

The "princess's" eyes flitted from bush to bush as she twirled her parasol over her head. "You appear to be quite taken with the out of doors, Griselda. Is there some special attraction for you?"

Noting the butterfly net pinned under her parasol arm, I quickly scanned the fairies, heard them humming the ladybugs through their tasks, and felt relief that my stepsister could not see them. Her interest made me uneasy, but happily there was nothing she could do to them.

In any case, I would feel more at ease if my observant new family member left the garden. So I decided to answer her question with a distraction. "Fresh air, the fragrance of the flowers, but the sun is becoming hot. Would you care to return indoors?"

Cynthia closed the space between us, entwined her

arm with mine, and ensnared me at her side. "As you wish."

We left the rose garden and walked in silence for a moment, the butterfly net trapped between us. I tussled with my conflicting feelings about her. On one hand, I truly felt deep compassion concerning her recent losses. On the other hand, I felt as if a snake had seized my arm.

As we reached the path lined with poorly maintained shrubbery and dotted with busy winged caretakers, Cynthia broke the silence. "Griselda." She paused. "Please forgive my asking, but is your sister entirely competent?"

A chill spread through my insides from my stomach to my extremities. "What do you mean?"

With a lift of her hand, she gestured toward the manor. "I saw her standing in the great hall talking to the fresco."

I remembered Isabella's curious attention to the fresco the previous day, as well as my own brief, but obviously mistaken, imagining. "The one that Mr. Dankman wanted to chisel from the wall?"

"The very one."

I didn't know what to say, because I didn't know why Isabella had taken such a turn since Father's passing, including her polite but painful distance from me. She seemed determined to keep her idiosyncrasies, headaches, skittishness, and fears to herself, but it was a cause for concern, as well as embarrassing.

Eager to deflect Cynthia's inquisitiveness, I said, "It's just a way she amuses herself. Isabella has a great imagination."

I couldn't believe I'd just said that. After all, I was

the one accused of an overactive imagination in order to cover up any odd behavior of mine due to fairy sight.

Cynthia stopped our walk and faced me. Her eyes narrowed and she searched my face. "Perhaps." She paused. "Or could it be something else?"

My gut turned to ice. "Something else?"

"A secret—an uneasy secret—perhaps one that causes headaches."

The tone of Cynthia's voice held concern, but the ice in my gut shouted otherwise. Her probing was too close, almost threatening. Cynthia might be my stepsister, but she would never be privy to our family secret. Never.

As if raising a shield, I replied, "Isabella is fine, Cynthia. She has whimsical ways, but apart from needing occasional rest because of her headaches, she's fine."

"You're probably right. She's such a sweet girl." Cynthia smiled at me, but the expression did not ease my chill. In fact, it increased.

I stretched my lips across my teeth. "Yes, she is a sweet and very kind girl."

I didn't add that my sweet sister was too eager to please Cynthia, and that our ice princess of a stepsister would have to deal with me if she took advantage of Isabella's goodness and vulnerability.

I endured our companionable walk back to the manor all the while fuming over her nosiness regarding Isabella and wishing to wrench Cynthia's parasol from her hands and use it to administer a sound whack to her backside as a warning, the image lightening my worried heart.

Late that afternoon, Sarah and I had our last batch

of loaves cooling on the tables, so once more I escaped the heat of the kitchen and took to the outdoors, the chill of the morning gone, the temperature pleasantly warm, and the soft clouds still thin and scattered, the exception being an odd gray cloud behind the manor. Deciding to avoid the rose garden because of Cynthia's penchant for finding me there, I walked around the unkempt vegetable garden, noting the small green pumpkins and their yellow-orange flowers thriving amid the chaos. Orange and green striped fairies hovered over the blooms, and white crowned sparrows darted among the greenery. I aimed my steps toward a nearby field for a refreshing run when I heard a whimpering that came from in the garden, like the sound of a wounded animal. Crouching down with my muscles tensed to react, I crept forward following the noise. As I reached the rose garden the sound became clearer—crying—Isabella's crying.

I grabbed the sides of my skirt and ran, dodging between bushes, scattering fairies as I passed. Where was Isabella? I stopped, listened for her cries again, and noticed a swirl of fairies circling to one side under the odd gray cloud that I'd noticed moments earlier. I raced toward them and found Isabella sitting crumpled on the ground next to the bush with creamy pastel roses, her legs folded to one side, her dress in disarray. Her face was buried in her hands, and her shoulders shook as she sobbed.

Heart exploding with worry, I called out as I approached, "Isabella."

She looked up at me, silent for a second, then anguish spread across her features, and she burst into fresh sobs, louder this time. I froze. Had I caused this?

Now, torn between comforting Isabella and keeping my distance, I searched my mind to discover if I'd unwittingly been the cause of her distress. Perhaps this was why Isabella had been avoiding me.

I slowly hunkered beside her, uncertain of my welcome. "Izzy, what's wrong?"

"It's all my fault," she wailed.

Completely puzzled, I stated with confidence, "Nothing is your fault, Izzy dear. Please, what's troubling you?"

She stopped crying long enough to snuffle and say, "I'm sorry. I shouldn't have done it."

She buried her face in her hands once again and continued to weep, so I stroked her head. I couldn't imagine Isabella doing anything to warrant such distress.

"Done what, Izzy?"

Isabella lowered her hands, took a gulping breath, and blurted out, "I told Cynthia about the fairies."

Confused, I reached for her shoulders, held her at arms' length, and stared into her stricken eyes. "Why is this a cause for tears? Everyone knows about fairies, at least in mythology."

Her face crumpled again and her body trembled, but she didn't cry. She sniffed and said, "Cynthia and I were having such a lovely walk in the garden this afternoon. She said she was so happy to have sisters to share special secrets with."

As Isabella paused and pulled in a shaky breath, the icy foreboding from the morning returned to my gut.

"Go on."

"Then she asked me if I could see fairies, and I said

'yes.' "

I wondered why Isabella would lie to Cynthia and if guilt from her lie was why she was crying, when a startling thought dawned…

"Izzy, can you see fairies?"

She kept her eyes on the ground and nodded. "Ever since Father died."

Already crouching, I lost my balance, fell the last few inches to the ground, and landed on my bottom. I gaped at her. "Why didn't you tell me?"

Isabella looked up at me, her eyes glistening with tears. "I didn't want to get in trouble. I didn't want to be killed."

Finally, Isabella's recent reticence made sense. "Is that why you've hardly spoken to me since Father died?"

Isabella snuffled and nodded, wiping her eyes with the back of her hand.

Confused and feeling a hollow sense of betrayal that she had told Cynthia and not me, I leaned forward to Isabella. "But then why tell Cynthia?"

"Just to be nice to her. She seemed so interested."

I thought back to the book, *Legends of the Fairy Kingdom*, that I'd seen Cynthia reading and wondered if it was the source of her interest.

"So what happened after you told her?"

"She asked me to point to a fairy, so I did. Then all of a sudden she pulled out a little net she had under her arm and trapped the fairy."

I thought about the old children's rhyme of "Catch a Fairy" and asked with alarm. "Could she see it?"

"Yes, I guess if you trap a fairy, you can see it. I didn't know that would happen."

The anguish that had spread across Isabella's face earlier now took root in my icy innards and slowly began to grow. "What did she do next?"

"She wished for the fairy to turn a flower into a diamond. The fairy did as requested, and the nearest rose dried up and died. I started crying and told her to let the fairy go."

"Did she?"

Isabella nodded. "She let the fairy go and said she just wanted to see if the legends were true. But then she made me point out four more fairies, so that she could have more diamonds."

I glanced around the poorly maintained but still flourishing garden and spotted the violated blooms, dried up brown roses, brittle, decaying, dead.

Isabella shrugged her shoulders helplessly.

The frigid shock in my stomach now worked its way down my legs and arms. "Why did you keep pointing, Isabella?"

"Because Cynthia said a few dried roses were of no consequence."

"No consequence?" I threw up my hands, my concern for Isabella now replaced with anger. I wanted to shake the girl. "Fairies are supposed to create growth. With your help, she could have destroyed the whole garden."

At my tone, Isabella drew back, and rivulets of tears streaked down her face once again. "I cried and cried and said I wouldn't show her any more. So she promised never to do it again."

I felt half furious and half humbled about Isabella. Humbled that I'd been blind to Isabella's gift, and furious since Isabella, even with her innocent nature, should have known better than to divulge such a secret.

With an effort, I reined in my frustration with my gullible sister. "Did you believe her promise?"

"Yes, but I know I never should have told her. I never dreamed she would do something like this."

As I envisioned Cynthia netting fairy after fairy, demanding diamonds, and then gleefully clutching the gems, I noticed a spreading of the shadow cast by the gray cloud overhead, an uptake of a thin, chill breeze, and a change in the fairies circling above our heads. They slowed and settled on nearby blooms. Soon I saw why and felt as if I'd shrunk to three inches tall.

Rosanna, with a face like a thundercloud, hovered before my face. She jabbed a finger at a withered rose. "That is unnatural."

I recoiled as she pronounced the word "unnatural," making it sound vile, obscene. She hovered in place, letting me absorb her wrath and leaving me speechless. Even though I hadn't caused the violation, I felt caught, responsible, and culpable.

Rosanna clearly agreed with my conclusion. She cast a quick, accusatory glance at Isabella and then speared me with her attention. "You are the eldest; you are the fairy kin. You must learn to help, not hinder, our work."

Weighed down with guilt, I stared at the rainbow queen while Isabella shrank next to me.

After one more quelling glance at Isabella, Rosanna pinioned me with her eyes. "You are to ensure that this never happens again." Then she took flight, followed by the attending fairies that buzzed among the rosebushes with whirring concern.

In contrast to the generally sunny day with patchy

white clouds in the surrounding kingdom, the small anomalous gray cloud roiled and grew overhead, casting jagged shadows as the chill breeze sliced through the garden. The caretakers fluttered about the destroyed roses like swarms of insects with a worried hum.

I gathered up Isabella and brushed dirt and foliage from her dress with my hands. It looked like she'd hugged a rosebush. Thorns had snagged the skirt and bodice of her dress. Leaves and twigs clung randomly.

A few raindrops landed on my face and then several more, so I became concerned to get Isabella out of the unusual cold and wet as nature itself seemed to be reacting to this violation. I hurried her back to the manor, up the staircase, and into her bedchamber. I covered her with an old quilt and made sure that she was resting, albeit fretfully after what she'd done. I hated to fault Isabella, but to be honest she was partly to blame.

But mostly I blamed Cynthia.

I marched from Isabella's bedchamber.

"Cynthia."

I strode through the echoing gallery to my stepsister's rooms, banged open one of her doors, and entered for the very first time into her private chambers, a two-room-sized open space with a sitting area and adjacent bedroom.

Upon my entrance, the glare of gilded furniture, mirrors, and fabrics embroidered with precious metals and jewels confronted my eyes. I meant to yell but froze, stunned by what I saw. Gold, gold, gold, everywhere was gold: bed frame, chairs, and tables. Everything gilded. Even the designs in the ceiling were edged with gold. The light from the tall south and west windows made the room glisten. The royal chambers in the castle weren't even so grand. I was appalled by the opulence I'd unwittingly saved for her. The only contrast to the lavishness was stacks of old books and parchments, resting on plush chairs, her bedside table, and the floor near her writing desk.

Cynthia, still gowned in cinnamon, stood next to her gilded cabinet. She pushed in a small drawer and "click" locked it with a key.

Pulling the key from the lock, she turned to me. "Manners, Griselda, I see why you are such a frightful trial to your mother."

I wanted to storm across the room, pin her against her paneled walls, and make her swallow all the precious, fairy-made diamonds that I guessed she'd just hidden in that drawer. I so itched to take her on.

My fingers tightened and flexed. "Stay away from my sister."

Cynthia slipped her key into a little velvet purse that hung from her wrist and clasped her hands demurely in front of her waist.

"She is my sister, too. It is no fault of mine that you are too busy for her."

The comment hit its mark, and I cringed inwardly from the pain even though it was not fair. After all, I had conscientiously attended to Isabella time and time again. How could I have known that she was avoiding me out of fear of her new gift of fairy sight and consequently of execution?

Cynthia closed the doors of her cabinet, covering the many small drawers and displaying the ornate, gilded carvings on the cabinet's front.

I crossed the room and stood two feet from Cynthia, keeping my hands firmly at my sides and away from her neck. My words came out like a growl. "Isabella is a sweet, innocent girl, and you're taking advantage of her."

Cynthia's mouth slowly lifted on one side into a half smile. "And you, by contrast I take it, are neither sweet nor innocent." She paused, smiled fully, and extended her hand. "But come, we are sisters. We should be privy to one another's secrets."

I refused the proffered hand. "But if secrets are shared, you shouldn't exploit that information to your own advantage. Even if fairies can grant wishes, it is unnatural."

Cynthia's hand dropped, and her nose tilted up. "It appeared harmless enough to me."

"Harmless? The Dead Castle exists because of such 'harmless' choices, not to mention the potential of famine."

Cynthia's superior smile vanished and her eyes narrowed at me with diamond sharpness. "You exaggerate, Griselda. That is nothing but a tall tale."

With a finger pointing toward the south-facing windows, I exclaimed, "Tall tale? Roses shriveled and died with every diamond you demanded, and reports say that not so much as a blade of grass can live near the Dead Castle. Is that not an extreme example of famine?"

"You are overreacting."

For just a second, I wondered if perhaps Cynthia was right, and I was overreacting.

Then I recalled Rosanna's reaction, and I saw the connection with clarity. "The cost of every diamond is death."

Cynthia blinked at my pronouncement, turned away from me, and walked to a window. She stood framed between pink and gold embroidered drapes. Through the now rain-filled view, the edge of the rose garden could be glimpsed to the south, a reminder of Cynthia's recent foolishness. And beyond that, the faint shape of the Dead Castle could be seen looming on its distant hill, a dark monument to past foolishness. She grasped the gold tassels on one drape as if for support. Her posture not so straight, her regal bearing uncertain. She said nothing.

I hoped I was getting through to her. "I'm dead serious, Cynthia. It's wrong to catch fairies. I beg you. Promise you won't do it again."

Her shoulders straightened, her chin went up, and her hand released the tassels. With a decision apparently reached, she became the confident "princess" once again.

She turned from the window and faced me. "Griselda, I thank you for your wisdom. I was simply curious to see if the legends about fairies were true."

My eyes tightened. "It seems that you were curious several times."

Cynthia sighed, spread her hands palms out, and tilted her head slightly to one side. Rain pelted the window behind her.

"It is as you say. I beg your forgiveness, sister. I can now see how serious the matter is."

"Cynthia." I took a step toward her.

"Yes, Griselda."

"I asked you to promise never to catch a fairy again."

"And I did, dear sister." She clasped her hands once again in front of her waist, the velvet bag dangling.

I took another step forward. "No, you asked forgiveness. Promise me that you will never catch a fairy again."

She hesitated, but only for a heartbeat. "Oh, of course, Griselda dear, I promise. Now, do not concern yourself any further. Why don't you go to the kitchen and help prepare dinner?"

My insides churned and I wanted to say, "Why don't you come and help?" but I didn't want to damage the shaky possibility that Cynthia's promise was good. I turned to leave.

"Griselda."

I looked back to see Cynthia wearing a look of concern, that now familiar mock concern that masked her cunning.

"You were unaware that Isabella could see fairies, were you not?"

I fled before she could see my eyes fill with tears.

Chapter 14

Pardon My Appearance

Our odd, isolated rain shower passed, the clouds parted, and the sun streamed through, making it possible to get outside for a quick run with Rags before dinner to settle my turbulent emotions. I really did want to throttle Cynthia for her manipulation of Isabella, her careless abuse of the fairies, and her meanness to me—in spite of my determined kindness to her. It made me wonder how on earth my father had managed to be civil to Lord Ursa for all of those years. Because, like Cynthia, everything Lord Ursa did was designed to favor himself while oppressing everyone he thought beneath him.

Yet Father had steadily persevered in his attempts—some successful, some not—to get along with Lord Ursa in order to serve the people of the kingdom. His words, repeated to me often, that "faithful service in doing good to all is the highest calling" reverberated in my memory. And to my admiration, he always stubbornly included his adversaries, even Lord Ursa, in the "all." I tried to embrace my father's ideals, but right now they seemed inadequate to address the many things that were amiss, most particularly the behavior of my stepsister.

Out past all the rain-drenched gardens and even

beyond the small orchard, I found a sturdy stick, heaved it as far as I could, and raced after it. With a bark, Rags sprinted before me across the wet, grassy field and retrieved the short branch. Our game reminded me of my former life of just a few weeks ago. I missed it.

Rags, stick hanging from his mouth, dodged the grazing cows and trotted back to me with his tail wagging, clearly hoping for another toss. I patted him on the head, retrieved the slobbery gift, and drew my arm back for another throw, but paused when movement caught my attention. There, on the periphery of Rella Manor grounds, a lone horseman sat astride his mount. At a quick glance, the rider appeared to have the stance of a guard and a red or maybe russet tunic. He was too far away to be sure. I considered heading that direction to investigate, when...

A familiar hum informed me that a fairy queen was nearby. Indeed, Rosanna, in all her rainbow glory, fluttered into view and then hovered in front of my face, a vexed expression on her countenance. I let my arm drop, still clutching the stick, and eyed the monarch warily, wondering what was amiss now.

"I thought you understood. There is work to be done," she said with a touch of impatience.

"Yes, and I have looked for you," I replied, panic about my ineptitude—about everything—rising. "But I don't know how to pull fairies, and I promised my mother..."

"I know," she said with a softer tone. "But there are imps to clear. You can do that with little effort and without betraying your promise."

The gray spotted fields that we had seen en route to Rella Manor came to mind. "But they are everywhere.

How can I handle it all?"

If Rosanna had been human, her next expression would have been a deep, longsuffering sigh, but as a fairy queen, she just paused, looking regal and certain, before answering. "That is why, in time, you must learn to pull more fairies. Then we will have sufficient fairies to keep the imps at bay. But for now, any imps that you can disperse will be helpful. Come. We can work in the nearest field."

Rosanna flew off, clearly expecting me to follow. Rags and I ran after her, my unusual gift for speed being essential to keep up with the fast-moving monarch.

The nearest planted field, one now owned by a former tenant of Lord Rella's, looked like those I had seen from the carriage. The grain was dotted with little shadowy spots, in the centers of which could be seen little, angry-faced images. Rosanna and the local fairies led me to the small gray patches, and like in the rose garden earlier, at my approach the imps dissipated with hissing grimaces back into the unseen realm, where I hoped they would stay and not damage our coming harvest.

Though the work we were doing was serious, I enjoyed the exercise, running with Rags and working with the gathered fairies, Rosanna having departed for other duties. It felt good to be active in the fresh air after being cooped up in the manor so much. It was easy to see why I had often wondered if fairies were working or playing at their tasks. I was enjoying myself so much, it would be hard to tell the difference, if indeed there was a difference. Perhaps there was not.

As I jogged after a group of one-to-two-inch

winged searchers, heading to another hazy, gray mass, the sound of Sarah's cowbell ringing vigorously caused me to freeze in mid-motion, alarmed at the insistence of the noise.

Reluctant to leave my task unfinished, I closed the distance between myself and the closest imp, watched it dissolve with a thin whine, and noted the next direction of my tiny fairy leaders.

The cowbell rang again, more clamorously.

My attention swiveled a few times between the manor and the fairies. Then I called to the hovering sprites, not knowing if these little ones would understand, "I'll return when I can."

They swarmed as though indecisive for a second and then scattered in several directions.

Finding I still had a stick in my fist, I leaned down and gave Rags a final tap on the head. "Sarah needs me, boy."

I flung the small branch, jogged through the sodden field, orchard, and gardens to the kitchen, shoved the door open, and entered, leaving my disappointed canine companion outside with his retrieved prize. Sarah stood there, cowbell still in one hand, chopping knife in the other, gesturing wildly with her arms. Hannah and Rebecca, wide eyed, moved out of striking distance.

Sarah shouted, "Oh, Miss Griselda, he's here again. He's here."

I threw my head back and groaned. "Not Mr. Dankman again."

If he was here to collect Cynthia's stuff, I'd be more than happy to stay out of his way this time.

Sarah tossed both bell and knife onto the trestle table with a clatter and threw her hands in the air. "No, the courier. That handsome, young courier."

My insides rolled over, and I glared at Sarah. "First of all, he isn't handsome, and second, he isn't young."

Hannah and Rebecca giggled, and Sarah raised her eyebrows so high they threatened to disappear into her hairline. "If you say so, miss."

I could feel my cheeks flushing, so I backed up, crossed my arms, and lifted my chin. "I do not see what this has to do with me."

Sarah crossed her arms, leaned back, and imitated my stance. "Ya don' see that perchance he has a letter from the prince? And ya don' see that perchance Lady Cynthia is tryin' to weasel it from him even as we dither about here."

My mouth dropped open. Of course, Courier Jon was a simply a messenger. There would be no other reason for him to be here. I dodged my way around a very self-satisfied looking Sarah, through the kitchen, and up the servants' stairs to intercept my letter before my scheming stepsister could secure it.

As I walked through the parlor on my approach to the great hall, I heard Cynthia's voice. "May I assure you, I will give the letter to my dear sister with haste."

I cringed at her reference to me as "dear sister" and was about to march into the great hall when I noticed muddy paw prints, grass stains, and flour covering the skirt of my tunic. I brushed at the fabric with my hands. Not that I cared, but I was always covered with something messy when Courier Jon showed up.

As I picked off a blade of grass from my sleeve, I overheard his reply. "Lady Cynthia, I thank you for your assurances, however, it is my duty to personally present this to Miss Griselda."

I caught the courteous but uncompromising resolve in his tone and realized that Cynthia would never sway him, so I crept closer and tilted an ear in their direction for further entertainment.

Cynthia made another attempt. "My sister is at present off on one of her wild rambles. It is difficult to say when she will abandon her roaming."

My stepsister's comment presented the perfect opportunity for an entrance, so I strode in, head held high.

"My dear sister Cynthia, Courier Jon." I gave him a nod as he looked my way. "I have completed my wild rambles for the day. And now, if you will pardon my appearance, how may I help you?"

They both stared at me as I approached across the dusty black and white tiles. Courier Jon glanced at the various stains decorating my garments and grinned, which stoked my ire. Cynthia had the good grace to color slightly about the cheeks at the realization that she'd been overheard.

She recovered quickly. "So there you are. I am delighted. Please let me know if I may assist in any way."

I smiled at Cynthia. "Thank you, Cynthia. I cannot tell you how much that means to me."

Cynthia's eyes hardened, and she stretched a brittle smile across her face.

I returned her expression in kind, turned, and gave my attention to the messenger.

He held out a rolled parchment with a bow. "For you, Miss Griselda, from His Royal Highness Prince Charmain."

I reached out, received it from him, and in spite of

a visceral reluctance, gave him the slight curtsy demanded by propriety. I could tell that he was amused by my discomfort, because the corners of his mouth twitched. It always goaded me that my running rival found me so amusing.

Before I could come up with a biting remark, he mastered his facial features and spoke again. "I am to wait, Miss Griselda, for your reply—your written reply."

He emphasized the word written.

I raised my eyebrows to let him know that I'd do as I pleased, but in truth, no matter the contents of the letter, I could do nothing more than provide a written reply. Tomorrow was market day, and I had to help Sarah sell our unique breads.

Nevertheless, I couldn't help but torment my tormentor. "After I read the letter, I will inform you of my plans."

He opened his mouth to say something, then frowned, folded his arms, and settled back on his heels with a look of restrained impatience. Satisfied with his response, I looked down at the scrolled parchment, and my old concerns about Prince Charmain's spinelessness in relation to Lord Ursa, recently buried by all the events at the manor, came rising to the surface. Pressed for time, I broke off the wax seal and strode away from the other two. They left me in peace, but I could feel both of their eyes on me as I unrolled the prince's letter. I read quickly.

Dear Griselda,

I greet you again from Norlan Castle, and I thank you for your reply. We will soon be departing for Sothwern Castle, the next stop on our tour.

It grieves me to learn that your stepfather continues in ill health, and I hope that he will recover with good speed.

I lowered the letter. Prince Charmain had missed the news about Lord Robert's death and our family troubles. I looked around the vast barren hall, and noted that Courier Jon was doing the same thing, a puzzled expression across his face. Momentarily, his gaze rested on the chipped fresco still gracing the great hall. His head tilted with interest and his eyes narrowed. Then he caught me watching.

Before he could give me one of his impudent grins, I quickly looked down at the letter, hurried from the hall into the plundered library, and feeling oddly flustered, returned to the prince's words.

Now, to the business at hand, please forgive me, but I am compelled to say that you are as stubborn as a mule. Lord Ursa says that you should keep your opinions to yourself and that you should express confidence in our efforts.

The young ladies I have encountered on this tour are of one mind with Lord Ursa and me, especially Lord Norlan's daughter Nareen. I confess to finding their support most agreeable, and you would do well to follow their examples.

With fury rising in my throat, I crushed the sides of the parchment with my hands, feeling it crinkle in my grasp. First, in spite of my warning, this weak-willed prince was still being led by the scheming lord. Second, he was trying to manipulate me with comments about the ladies. And finally, he was trying to tell me what to do. If Father hadn't told me his plan to secure safety for those with fairy sight, I would have abandoned any interest in marrying the prince right then and there—and was still tempted to do so.

I paced back and forth in the nearly empty room. Fear and a bit of self-interest crept into my thoughts. I no longer had my father. The kingdom no longer had my father. I needed to learn—if I could learn—to pull fairies from the light to ensure abundant harvests each year, as well as to stave off those disease and famine-producing imps. And I needed to be safe doing it—and somehow obedient to my mother. It was too much to bear.

I tried to rationalize. To be fair—and it was hard to be fair at the moment—the prince was under the influence of a very strong personality—Lord Ursa. So he wasn't completely himself. Also, it was never realistic that he would be allowed to marry me when a political alliance made more sense.

Fearful that his words illustrated my waning influence on him, I felt helpless to intervene and dreaded the conclusion of the letter.

Lord Ursa has encouraged me to become engaged to one of the noble ladies that we are meeting on our tour.

There it was. Even though I had just thought to abandon this marriage prospect, my heart sank. Both the king and Lord Ursa wanted the prince to marry a lady. Is that what he wanted? I read on.

It is most important that Lord Ursa view you favorably, especially in light of the announcement that I hope to convince my father to make when I return.

Remember there will be a feast when I return. I depend upon your attendance.

HRH Prince Charmain

I blew out a breath, whether in relief or in disgust, I couldn't easily say. Unbidden, Cynthia's past use of the word spineless—and sadly mine, too—slipped into my mind. She had called the king a "spineless beast" regarding his relationship with her mother. I dreaded to think that it could be applied not only to the king but to my prince as well. He needed a backbone. He needed me.

I stared at the paper. The reference to our important announcement should have left me hopeful, but it left me numb. I read the letter again and stared at it some more. It was the prince's hand, but I felt like I didn't know the pompous person who had written this letter. Even though the writer still had betrothal in mind, this wasn't my friend.

In any case, I wasn't going to beg for his hand. I just couldn't, even if my father wanted it.

I glanced around the room for the supplies needed to respond. A small rustic table and chair left in the library had no writing implements, so I scavenged an inkbottle, quill, and parchment from the debris on the mostly vacant shelves. Then in the late afternoon light from the west-facing windows, I settled to write my reply.

Dear Prince Charmain,

Sadly, I must inform you that Lord Robert passed away soon after my last letter. We are grieving his loss and learning to adjust to our lives without him.

I am sorry that you do not find my opinions to be helpful. My only wish, like my father's before me, is for that which will ensure peace and prosperity for LaFairia and all its subjects. My father's example was a guide to the king as long as I can remember, and I think that his policies should not be discarded.

I am confident that you, too, wish all your efforts to ensure the peace and prosperity of the kingdom and its subjects.

I wish you good health and a successful completion of your tour.

Your humble servant...

I did not deign to comment on the noble ladies or his implications about an announcement. Let him make up his own mind. If the gods wanted me to marry him, so be it. It could solve all manner of difficulty. But I wouldn't grovel for the privilege.

Chapter 15

Hungry Ruffians

The next morning, I thought the chill pre-dawn air would rouse me, but it did not. Feeling like a sleepwalker, I straightened my scarf, rubbed my eyes, and stretched to no avail. Returning to the kitchen for a brief warm moment, I picked up another basket, yawned loudly, and carried it outside. I stumbled on the driveway gravel, nearly dumping all the bread, and loaded the container onto the wagon. Oh, I wanted to be back in bed.

Normally, the morning chorus of robins cheered me, but today their vocalizing reminded me of work to do, and the rooster's shrill cawing punctuated that theme. A couple of escapees from the chicken coop clucked and scurried around the wagon, pecking at crumbs falling from the baskets. Rebecca held tallow candles for light while Sarah and I loaded the wagon with basket after basket of our precious cargo. Sarah loaded the final basket and gazed upon the fruits of our labor. I saw the question in her eyes. Would the unusual breads sell? I wondered, too.

I glanced at the baskets filled with loaves laced with cheese, herbs, and spices, topped with tomatoes, zucchini, and cheese, baked with blueberries, or bursting with apples, raisins, and cinnamon. I breathed in the fragrant aromas. Not the usual fare for our plain brown and white bread markets, but I planned to spark interest by offering small samples, hoping that they would be tasty enough to create customers.

Off to the side, Hannah, carrying a bucket of fresh milk, emerged from the cow barn, waved, and headed for the kitchen. Sarah called to her, "Hannah, bring Lady Constance's bundle of stitchery for the queen and that bag I prepared."

"Yes'm," she called over her shoulder as she headed for the kitchen.

With worries about our success roiling in my insides, I helped Sarah harness the manor's one remaining horse, an old brown mare with a black mane and tail, to the wagon. She looked as tired as I felt, so I decided to walk.

The hint of morning light in the east signaled our time to be off. Sarah settled onto the wagon seat, arranged her shawl over her shoulders and her apron over her knees, and looked down at me expectantly.

"I'll walk a bit, Sarah. The mare looks too tired."

"But, miss, you can't walk all the way to the castle. You'll be all worn out before we even start sellin'."

At that moment, I was afraid that Sarah might be right, but I grabbed my shawl from the wagon, wrapped it around my shoulders, and began to walk. "Let's get started."

From behind us a voice called out, "Griselda, Sarah."

We turned to see Cynthia descending the front stairs and approaching the wagon. Dressed as if to greet the queen in an ostentatious emerald gown with an embroidered bodice, she carried a blanket and a parasol.

To my astonishment, Cynthia climbed nimbly onto the wagon next to Sarah, spread a blanket on the seat, and sat down.

Turning to Rebecca, she ordered, "Fetch my trunk."

Rebecca mutely handed me the candles, which we no longer needed, and left to comply.

Cynthia continued in a cheerful voice. "I have decided to forgive your harsh words to me from yesterday and to join you on your outing to the castle."

Sarah and I remained silent. Sarah's mouth hung agape, and I found that mine was, too.

I snapped it shut and asked, "Are you planning to help us sell bread?"

Cynthia giggled and my insides recoiled. Giggling didn't suit Cynthia.

"Oh, Griselda," she said. "You can be so droll."

Sincerely puzzled, I twirled the reins in my hands. "Well, then, what are you planning to do?"

"I wish to become acquainted with the village."

The look of sincere innocence that my stepsister wore on her smiling face only made me wonder about her underlying scheme. Then I felt guilty. Wasn't it possible that she was simply bored? After all, she had lived in relative isolation all of her life because of her mother's resentment of the king. I should feel happy to share Fairian Village with Cynthia. But I did not.

While I wrestled with my thoughts, Sarah sighed, climbed down from the wagon, and bunched up the reins. "I'll just lead the mare, Miss Griselda."

Cynthia positioned her parasol as the dawn's light crept across the country-scape. She settled into her place like a queen surrounded by attendants. "Oh, how good of you, Sarah."

Sarah and I exchanged hidden eye rolls and then looked at Rebecca, who had returned with Hannah. As they struggled the trunk to the wagon, I dropped the extinguished candles to the ground, made room among the baskets for this unplanned baggage, and assisted with hoisting Cynthia's belongings into the space. When everything was secure in the wagon, Hannah held out a bag to Sarah with several sturdy sticks, a couple of metal cauldron skimmers, and a kitchen knife visible from the top.

"Here's what you asked fer, Sarah."

Sarah grabbed the bag, pulled out three sturdy sticks, and dropped the rest into the wagon. She took one stick for herself, handed one stick to me, and reached a stick up to Cynthia.

My stepsister threw her hands up in front of herself. "I beg your pardon."

Sarah looked exasperated. "Forgive me, Lady Cynthia. Trouble's not likely, but we must be prepared."

Cynthia shook her head, turned away from Sarah, and ignored her. Sarah looked at me and spread her arms.

Knowing all too painfully that trouble passing through the forests, even the smaller King's Forest, was not unheard of, I took a stick from Sarah, reached it toward Cynthia, and waved it near her knees.

"Please, Cynthia."

She looked down at me, disdain spreading over her features. "This is entirely excessive."

I extended the stick farther, touching her leg. "Excessive or not. Take it or you're not coming."

The "princess" and I locked eyes for a moment. My insides didn't squirm at all. They felt hard. I imagined dousing that emerald-gowned Cynthia and her finery with driveway dust.

Perhaps she sensed my ill intent for she reached out, grasped the stick, and smiled thinly. "As you wish, dear sister, if this will please you."

I scowled at my stepsister, thanked Rebecca and Hannah, and along with Sarah started the mare down the drive. My attitude, however, was buoyed by the satisfying image of Cynthia wearing dust-covered emerald.

After leaving Rella Manor, we passed ripening grain fields and small farms once owned by Lord Robert. Sarah and I exchanged waves with neighbors and laborers on the road, otherwise, we journeyed in silence: Cynthia taking on the air of a lady attended by servants, and Sarah and I conserving our energy for the market to come. The sun gradually warmed the day and I no longer needed my shawl, so I tossed it into the wagon with the breads. Cynthia kept her parasol tilted toward the sun to shadow her face.

Eventually, we reached the forest and welcomed a respite from the growing heat. The surrounding hemlock, fir, and maple trees provided shade and reduced our visibility. Tiny forest fairies, elegant like their trees, darted among the foliage. And the thick, summer underbrush provided hiding places for the occasional squirrels and rabbits that could be heard scurrying nearby. Several miles into the trees I heard crackling noises in the dense woods. Sarah jerked her head in the direction of each sound, her hand gripped Rebecca's stick, and she picked up her pace. I followed

Sarah's example and urged the plodding mare to walk faster. Cynthia simply rode like a queen with attendants and not a care in the world.

Soon the snapping branches became too regular. Someone or something hidden by the trees was pacing us. I clutched my stick and dropped back from the horse to the wagon, planning to reach the knife, and even Cynthia glanced around for the source of the noise.

The source of the noise emerged ahead of us on the road, blocking our route. A man stood before us dressed in a short, ragged gray-brown tunic and hose with holes in the knees. I had never seen such poverty and wondered why he was so hungry when the almshouse—which I hoped was still open—would give him food and even mend his clothes. I brought food, old clothes, and offerings there at times myself. Though unnerved by his sudden appearance, I felt concern for his obvious plight.

That quickly changed.

Branches snapped behind us, and I whipped around to see that two more men, similarly dressed, had closed off the road behind us. My muscles tensed, my hand tightened on my stick, and my eyes darted between the groups of men.

The man in front, apparently the leader, stepped forward. "Well, what 'ave we here, a grand lady, and a couple wenches, and not a man in sight for protection."

Not liking the way he looked at us, I reached into a basket and pulled out a loaf, "Here. Let me offer you some bread. Now be on your way."

All the men laughed. Their spokesman stepped closer. "Oh, you'll give us a loaf, pretty wench, and much more besides."

The men cackled and advanced. I tossed the loaf back in the wagon and brandished my stick. They guffawed but slowed their approach.

Sarah raised her stick as well. "Be off, you ruffians."

The laughter continued, but they no longer advanced. Instead they eyed one another nervously. Out of the corner of my eye, I saw that Cynthia had raised her stick, positioned herself as if ready to spring, and held a steely look in her eye. Taking the measure of the three of us, I pictured Cynthia as warrior queen, Sarah as angry mother bear, and me as tournament champion. These sad, hungry scoundrels were in for more than they bargained for.

But this was no time for imagination. The outlaws were real, and though they appeared indecisive at the moment, that could change.

I reached into the wagon, seized the knife, and pointed it with an outstretched arm at the leader, hoping I looked fierce. "I know how to use this."

He backed up. Sarah waved her stick at the two in the back, and Cynthia looked imperious, as if she could command the appearance of an army if she so desired.

The leader's eyes shifted from Sarah to Cynthia to me. "I bet you know how to use that in the kitchen." His earlier bravado lessened.

Laughter came from behind again but sounded forced.

I twisted the blade in the air. "I know how to use this in any way I need to."

I took a step toward the ruffian leader, thinking, "Please back off, please back off, please back off."

Thank the gods. He did.

"Sarah, toss a loaf behind us."

She did. The two in the rear caught it and tore into the thick bread, completely losing interest in us. The fellow in front dashed around us and unsuccessfully tried to grab his share.

Partly to keep them all occupied and partly because they looked so hungry, I told Sarah, "Toss him a loaf, too."

She looked pained, but soon a loaf flew through the air to be caught by the starved bandit. We left them to their meal and urged our horse to move on at a trot, and I puzzled about why these men would choose robbery over a sure meal and possible employment through the almshouse, even though Lord Ursa meant to close it down.

When we were a safe distance from the robbers, I asked Sarah and Cynthia how they each fared. Cynthia didn't answer my question but spat out what was on her mind.

"They should be horsewhipped." And she sank into angry silence.

Sarah looked sidelong at me and muttered, "Or fed."

And in those two responses, I imagined that I heard the voices of Lord Ursa and my father as they had argued the fates of villagers on trial before the king. Though wrongdoing needed to be stopped and people protected, I agreed with my father. Solve the root problem: hunger.

After leaving the assailants behind us, I insisted that Sarah ride with Cynthia for a spell, though stepsister looked put out. We continued through the forest, looking behind us at the road and startling at every snap of a twig or rustle of foliage but did not see the bandits again. Eventually, the trees thinned and the castle with its surrounding fields and occasional farmhouses came into view. Sarah, looking at the plodding mare, decided to walk again and joined me on the road.

I glanced at Cynthia, who sat rigidly with her hands clasped tightly in her lap, her eyes drinking in the sight of the castle. She wedged the handle of her parasol against one shoulder and smoothed her gown and hair with her hands. And I realized that, as a stranger to this community, Cynthia was nervous.

In all her finery, she looked rather out of place perched on the rustic wagon. I glanced down at my work clothes and tried not to feel resentful as I plodded beside the mare. After all, I started this plan to generate income out of sympathy for Cynthia and her losses. So it didn't seem fair that she was arriving like a princess, while I, the person trying to pay our debt, was arriving like her servant.

The wagon bumped along past fields of waist-high corn. The field fairies, corn stalk green during growing season and then dotted with yellow spots like kernels of corn during harvest, whizzed from stalk to stalk across the broad fields. We also rolled past ripening grain fields as we approached the crenellated village walls. The sight gave me a sense of homecoming. The flag emblazoned with a crown over crossed swords flapped high above the partly obscured King's Gate.

Two red-and-black-garbed guards stood at the South Gate entrance, one on each side of the opening. To my surprise, one of the guards was completely unknown to me, causing me to regret my long absence from the village. But that wasn't my only regret.

The other guard was all too familiar: Jason Gutcher.

The twosome watched our approach, Jason with a smug sneer directed at me while the eyes of the unknown guard lingered on Cynthia. Before we were within earshot, Jason leaned toward his senior, said something, gestured in our direction, and laughed.

When we reached the entrance, the senior guard startled me with a surly demand as Jason snickered. "Your name and purpose."

As this was my outing, I replied, "We wish to—"

The soldier darted his eyes from Cynthia to me. "No one spoke to you, wench."

While Jason chortled, his senior looked again at Cynthia, leaving me feeling like I'd been slapped in the face. Sarah bristled at my side, but I, guessing that Jason was responsible for his partner's rude welcome, placed a hand on her arm.

Cynthia, however, took it in stride. She assumed the princess role and smiled at the soldier as though she appreciated how he had put her mouthy servant in her place.

She gazed into his eyes as if he were good enough to eat. "If you will forgive my attendant, good sir, I am Lady Cynthia Rella from Rella Manor in the south. I wish to attend the market on the green and my attendants to sell their wares."

The senior guard's mouth dropped open stupidly and his knees wobbled under the force of Cynthia's charms. He and Jason stepped wordlessly aside and bowed Cynthia through the gate. As we all passed through, I ignored Jason completely, though he huffed out a derisive snort as I went by.

I barely heard his muttered comment behind my back. "Used to be friends with the prince, all high and mighty. Now look at you."

Turmoil stirred in my heart and mind, because perhaps that vengeful Jason was right. Prince Charmain was off visiting proper young noblewomen, and I was anything but noble. Furthermore, even though his intent was still marriage, his last letter had highlighted my waning influence and Lord Ursa's waxing influence on his outlook. But what else was I to do?

Perhaps when he returned, I would try out the slippers to see if I could influence both the prince and the king. But it all seemed so devious. I knew Father hadn't meant it to be so and only suggested the plan due to his understanding of the long friendship between the prince and myself. So under the circumstances, should I attempt to proceed?

When we were well through the gate, Cynthia interrupted my mental debate. "Griselda, please forgive me. I am sure you understand that I simply wished to help."

I understood exactly how helpful Cynthia had been, meaning how condescending.

With a disdainful cough, I said, "I do understand, Cynthia. After all, attendant and sister are such similar relations. Now, if you really want to be helpful, I suggest that you help us unload the bread."

Cynthia laughed at my "joke" and let the suggestion drop.

Sarah muttered under her breath in a disgruntled fashion. "High and mighty little baggage."

I chuckled silently. Sarah took Cynthia's attitude

harder than I did, and there was something uplifting in such camaraderie.

The South Gate opened onto the green, and the chaos of market day greeted us: vendors setting up and selling wares, shoppers carrying baskets and haggling with sellers, and children racing around or begging for treats. I waved at vendors from whom I'd purchased perfumes for Mother, embroidery threads for Isabella, and thick tasty pies for Father and me. I shrugged off the awkward feeling that I, as Matthew Hart's daughter, should not be hawking goods at the open market.

Happy that the weather was so clear for market day, we wended our way through the crowds on the grassy area to meet Abigail and Abel Garner, along with Gilly, at the stall they had prepared for us. It pleased me that Abel was following my father's practice of hiring the orphan for odd jobs. I greeted Gilly and passed Mother's bundle of stitchery to Abigail, who would deliver it to the queen. Mother, too, was trying to help settle our debts.

As for Cynthia, she nodded at people like she was royalty, and they gaped at her in return. Her smile broadened, her neck lengthened, and her confidence grew as she basked in the admiration.

Calls of "Greetings, Miss Griselda. Greetings, Sarah," fell on my ears. I introduced Cynthia to several shoppers and then left her to manage her curious new acquaintances. She proceeded to hold court for her gathering throng right there on the green while Sarah and I, along with Gilly, Abigail, and Abel, unloaded the wagon. The threesome departed: Abel back to Hart Cottage, Abigail to deliver the embroidery to the queen, and Gilly to help at the almshouse, which I was relieved to learn was still open. Sarah and I finished our display.

Soon a voice called my name. "Miss Griselda, oh, we've missed you so, but fairies preserve us, what are you doing selling bread?"

With sincere affection, I welcomed the butcher's wife. "Greetings, Mrs. Carver, it is good to see you again. I hope that your husband is well."

"Busy at the shop, my dear. Now that the almshouse is open again," she replied as she looked over the breads.

"What do you mean, 'open again?'" I asked, the memory of the ragged brigands in the King's Forest fresh in my mind.

She waved her hand dismissively. "Lord Ursa had it closed for a time, but my husband, along with Hugh Heaten and others, petitioned the king—jus' like your father would have done. So it's back open."

She heaved a sigh and glanced at me sympathetically. "So tragic that messenger didn't reach the captain sooner. Perhaps...all yer father's good work..." She sighed again.

The reference to my father's influence made me both proud and sad, and also angry about how Lord Ursa seemed bent on eliminating the simple supports that kept those in need fed.

But realizing that I couldn't let my frustration with Lord Ursa interfere with the task at hand, I asked, "May I tempt you with something new, Mrs. Carver?"

I pointed out breads with blueberry, apple with raisin and cinnamon, and cheese and tomato with herbs. Mrs. Carver furrowed her brow skeptically, so I offered her a slice of blueberry bread topped with crusty sugar. She fingered it gingerly and nibbled a bite. Her furrow disappeared, her eyebrows went up, and her mouth broke into a grin.

"A loaf of blueberry and a loaf of apple raisin, if you please."

I placed the loaves in her basket, received payment, and thanked her as she trundled away. Several ladies gathered about her, talking and glancing my way. Soon our stall was crowded with customers.

"Blueberry, please, miss."

"Sarah, one tomato and cheese loaf and one apple cinnamon."

"Apple and raisin for me, miss."

Sarah chuckled to herself as she stuffed more money into her belt pouch. "Miss Griselda, we're lucky folks like you, what with selling this odd bunch."

"Our breads taste good, Sarah," I said, while smiling and offering a sample to a shopper.

"That they do, miss, but all that good taste would go right back home with us if no one would risk it." Sarah patted me on the shoulder. "Yer a good girl, miss, a bit rough around the edges yet, but we'll see."

The temperature warmed as the day progressed. Even with the welcome shade of an awning, Sarah and I were hot and tired after our hours long walk and the busy market activity. Fortunately, the success of our bread sale finished off the long morning happily. In fact, I was so engaged with selling our goods and chatting with old friends that I did not see him until he was only a few strides from the stall. Courier Jon.

Before I could duck my head, our eyes met. He blinked in surprise, frowned, and walked my direction along with a companion, Fritz, the guard from the West Gate.

Fritz clapped him on the shoulder. "Now everyone will want to take you down, Jon. That's the price you pay for being the fastest."

While Courier Jon laughed at the comment, I recalled that yesterday these very grounds would have been used for the summer contest day. He had probably vanquished all opponents in running, something I'd always longed to do, but couldn't, being a girl. I didn't want that messenger rubbing my face in another of his victories.

Purposefully engaging myself with customers, I ignored him when he strolled to my stall. He waited among the shoppers, fielding comments like, "I've never seen someone pull that far in front before, Lieutenant."

Distracted by word of an unknown lieutenant, who must have beaten Courier Jon, which I was happy to hear, I missed my coin purse and dropped a couple of coppers to the ground.

As I bent down and gathered the coins, I was surprised to hear Courier Jon reply. "Actually I have found my best competition in this town."

When I rose and slipped the retrieved money into my pouch, I couldn't resist glancing up and earned myself a broad grin for my trouble.

The messenger edged his way to the front. "A loaf with tomato and cheese, if you please, Miss Griselda."

I scowled and gave him nothing. "I thought you were a courier."

Fritz gave me a look like I was crazy, but that groom or courier or lieutenant or whatever he was just grinned.

"And so I am. I'm a courier for our prince and for

you."

Still frowning, I handed him our last loaf of tomato cheese bread. He dropped a coin in my palm, and I folded my arms. "Thank you—Lieutenant—but come to think of it, shouldn't you be on your way with my letter?"

"Fresh horse, fresh rider, Miss Griselda. Your letter has been dutifully dispatched."

I tilted my head and raised my eyebrows. "So that you could run in the games?"

Fritz leaned forward and answered for the lieutenant. "Not just run, Grizzy. Jon bested the lot in everything he entered. You should challenge him to a race and take him down a notch. No one else can."

Lieutenant Jon shoved a piece of bread in his mouth and said nothing. I wasn't in the mood to talk about racing.

I wanted Fritz and this whatever-he-was Jon to go away. "I'm sorry, Fritz, but I'm busy."

"I can see that. But why are you selling bread?" Fritz pointed to our goods. "I thought you were living in Rella Manor in the south?"

Now, I felt even more the awkwardness of my position. There was nothing wrong with selling at the market, but it just wasn't what people expected of the daughter of Matthew Hart or the stepdaughter of Lord Rella.

"I am living in the south. Sarah and I, along with my stepsister, Cynthia, are up here for the day."

Fritz persisted. "But selling bread?"

Here Lieutenant Jon pulled off a chunk of his purchase and handed it to Fritz. "Try it. It's—"

A chorus of cheers interrupted his words, and we

all looked for the source—Cynthia.

My stepsister, who had been parading through the market while Sarah and I had labored in our booth, now had a growing gaggle of slack-jawed admirers encircling her. She posed this way and that so that everyone could get a good look at her. She tipped her head from side to side; she gestured and waved; she twilled and tilted her parasol; she smiled and giggled. Again, I cringed at the sound but noticed how she worked the crowd with ease.

Lieutenant Jon found his voice first. "What is Lady Cynthia doing, posing for a portrait?"

I acknowledged Lieutenant Jon's observation. "I would say posing for certain."

He stared slack-faced and open-mouthed. "Ah."

A flash of annoyance coursed through me, and I poked him in the side. "Oh, clever comment. If you lift your chin off your toes, you could move closer for a better view."

He snapped his mouth shut, and his face flushed a bit. "I'm not...I wasn't...Thank you for the bread, Miss Griselda."

It pleased me to finally see him look uncomfortable about something. Served him right for drooling over my stepsister's performance.

He nodded and turned to go when Sarah, who had been showing our remaining breads to our Hart Cottage neighbor Mrs. Heaten, demanded his attention.

"Lieutenant." She said the title with emphasis. "Are ya' aware that Miss Griselda had to journey without escort from Rella Manor to the castle this morning?"

Her tone implied that she thought he was

personally responsible for this indignity and should be deeply concerned. I didn't expect him to care one jot, but to my surprise, his countenance registered alarm.

Before he could reply, Sarah pressed further, her finger waving in front of his face. "An' are ya' further aware that we had to defend ourselves against violence?"

Perhaps I was mistaken, but it looked like the lieutenant's tan skin turned several shades lighter as Sarah dramatically described our forest encounter, and he sputteringly assured Sarah that an escort would be provided for our return. I didn't think this was necessary, but the two, Sarah and whatever-he-was Jon, seemed determined.

Finally, ready to head to Hart Cottage for a brief respite before returning to Mother, Isabella, and Rella Manor, with my belt purse heavy with coin, I looked around for Cynthia, but she was nowhere to be found. I did, however, find a handful of village women discussing her. They appeared disenchanted.

"Kept my husband from getting his work done this morning, she did."

"And my son," said another.

Other women had similar tales. I realized that the ladies had soon tired of Cynthia's display while the men had been kept long under her spell.

From the women, "Gracious, your stepsister is a self-absorbed little vixen," was the general comment.

So I left the market in a jolly mood.

Upon arrival at Hart Cottage, my happy mood was fouled. There sat Cynthia, her parasol and a book from Hart Cottage's limited selection at her side, in the dining room, nibbling Abigail's fine cooking as though it was dirt. She still looked immaculate in a fresh gown from her trunk, amber colored this time, while I was rumpled, as usual, with my hair falling from its scarf.

Sarah wanted to get started right away. We were already late due to our successful but extra-long morning, and Mother would worry if we did not return before dark. So I received a basket of travel food, hugged Abigail and Abel, and sadly left Hart Cottage. Reluctant to leave my real home, I climbed into the wagon, hitched to a fresh and spunky horse from Hart Cottage, and sat among the empty breadbaskets and Cynthia's trunk. Apart from needing to return to Mother and Isabella, I saw no reason to return to that cold cavern of a manor.

Cynthia took her position as queen of the wagon. Sarah groaned as she climbed into the conveyance and sat next to her.

Cynthia opened her borrowed book, *Children's Stories and Rhymes*, and I noted it was open to a familiar verse.

"Catch a fairy, make a wish, make a wish, make a wish. Catch a fairy, make a wish, fa, la, la, la."

With Cynthia's interest in fairies, I hoped that her recent promise to leave them alone was dependable and that her fascination with fairies would soon fade. After all, she could not see them on her own, and so could do nothing to them. She closed the book with her forehead furrowed in thought. Then she angled her parasol against the afternoon sun and looked toward the road expectantly. I did the same and waved to Abigail and Abel. They returned the goodbye.

And there we sat.

I looked up at Sarah and raised the palms of my

hands.

With a stubborn set on her face, Sarah shifted on her seat and settled, folding her arms across her chest. "That young lieutenant promised us an escort through the forest."

I thought back to the tale Sarah had told at the market and dropped my face to my hands. We did not have to wait long before the sound of approaching horses' hooves made me cringe. I looked up to glare but instead smiled.

Fritz and Gammon rode to the side of the wagon, and Fritz announced. "We are here compliments of the lieutenant."

Puzzled about just what role this groom-courier-lieutenant played in our royal guards, I asked, "Since when does he have such authority?"

Fritz and Gammon looked at each other and shrugged while Sarah shook the reins. "Time to go home."

I scowled. We were not going home.

Chapter 16

Stolen Slippers

The next morning, I got up later than usual, spent extra time at the washbasin, and dressed in a fresh long-sleeved chemise and ankle-length tunic. I even took extra time with my hair, braiding it, wrapping it at the nape of my neck, and securing it with pinned netting. I had to admit that Cynthia's constant display of couture perfection made me feel sloppy by comparison, and I didn't like it.

I pulled open the bottom drawer of my rickety dresser, uncovered my silvery slippers, and picked them up. They were the one item I owned that would outshine anything Cynthia wore—and would vex her quite nicely. I slipped them on and walked around the chamber. Even though part of me felt that the slippers should only be used to fulfill Father's plan, another part couldn't see any harm in using them for fun. I grabbed my coin purse, which jingled with coppers from our sale of breads at yesterday's market, headed for the door, and stopped, staring at the carved panels. I stood breathing in and out, arguing with my father's memory. I couldn't do it. The slippers were for a serious purpose.

With an exhalation of resignation, I removed the starry slippers, placed them on the rustic bed, and slipped my stocking-covered feet into my well-worn, everyday shoes. I trotted down to the kitchen, feeling cheerful about honoring my father's memory by not using the slippers for selfish reasons, which he most certainly would have frowned on. I entered the kitchen, eager to show Mother our earnings from market day, and my mood plummeted.

There at the table with Mother and Sarah sat Mr. Dankman. Hannah, working on cheese, and Rebecca, watching a cauldron of porridge, listened to the trio, whose faces looked grim as their bodies leaned into their conversation. I tensed, knowing that he was here to collect the remainder of our debt.

The three looked up. Mr. Dankman waved me to the table. "Miss Griselda, Miss Griselda, you are just the person we needed to see."

I walked slowly, squeezing my bulging coin purse and preparing to explain my plan to work off the debt by selling bread and maybe other things we could produce. I stood stiffly by the table bracing myself for the worst.

He continued. "Sarah has explained your difficult journey to the castle. You ladies are facing hard times…"

With my fiercest glare, I pinioned the land agent and gripped my bulging bag of coins, ready to stave off any further insults to my family.

He threw up his hands. "There is no need for that. I am here as a good neighbor."

At a nod from Mother, I relaxed a bit of my tension, but Sarah slammed her hand on the table, making all of us start. "What is the kingdom coming to when defenseless women can't travel in peace?"

The idea that Sarah was defenseless almost made

me crack a smile, but relief that Mr. Dankman wasn't here to collect, at least not today, was stronger.

Mother pushed her empty flower basket aside, put her hand on Sarah's, and patted it. "Only the chaos of recent days made me forget myself and allow you to travel alone. It was a mistake, and I certainly won't countenance another such trip."

The group sat silent for a few seconds. The sounds of Rags barking outside, porridge bubbling over the hearth, and then of Rebecca ladling the mixture into bowls punctuated the quiet.

Mother broke the silence. "Rebecca, you may serve porridge now."

Rebecca did so, and all of us sat for a time eating the simple mixture of grains, nuts, and peas and listening to Mr. Dankman comment upon the higher taxes, the weak crops, and the increase in folks out of work, like those desperate men we met in the forest. He opined that things had gotten worse in the kingdom since my father had passed away. So, of course, my opinion of him improved. At that point, I decided to take advantage of his visit.

I slid my coin purse across the table. "Mr. Dankman, I have a plan to pay off the manor's debts. Sarah and I are selling bread. We could probably make soap and other goods for sale as well."

Mr. Dankman considered my offering and pushed it back to me. "You are an industrious young lady, but I fear that the manor's remaining debt cannot be addressed by bread and soap. It must be addressed by the likes of precious metals, silks, and jewels."

I felt winded as if he had just punched me in the gut—all my effort dismissed so lightly. As I reeled from the emotional blow, Cynthia swanned into the room. An amethyst gown graced her elegant form; a matching padded circlet crowned her head. Pink flushed her cheeks as if she had been outdoors. She carried a bulky, embroidered, velvet purse, its contents weighty and bulging. Beyond all this finery, the most outstanding ornament she wore was a smug expression on her face.

Finished with breakfast and wishing to be anywhere except with Lady Haughty Face, I picked up my bag, excused myself from the group, and returned to my chamber with my hard-earned, rejected coppers.

The moment I opened my bedchamber door I missed them: my shimmery slippers. My hand reached for my heart, which tightened as if squeezed by a fist. I'd left them on the bed. And now they were gone. My fists clenched with rage.

Cynthia.

I stormed from my room and down the gallery hall, my tunic slapping against my ankles. I'd only been in Cynthia's chambers once before, and I was going in now invited or not. Well, to be honest, I'd done that the first time, too.

I fingered the bedchamber door latch and threw the door open. It slammed into an armoire with a bang.

The glare of the gilded furniture, mirrors, and accessories combined with the morning light from the tall windows overwhelmed me in a glistening assault. I fumed, "That spoiled little brat." And now, she'd stolen the most precious possession that I owned. I was sure of it.

"Cynthia."

No response.

Remembering that Cynthia was in the kitchen, I scanned the sumptuous room. If I were Cynthia, where would I hide the slippers? I rummaged around behind pink and gold embroidered curtains, in chests of drawers made from mahogany with inlaid woods, in the panel covered cabinet with locked drawers, and through armoires stuffed with floral scented silk gowns and velvety cloaks. No silvery slippers. I slapped my thighs in frustration.

Then an offset pillow, embroidered with silvery threads and resting on a chair in the center of the room, caught my eye. I lifted the pillow and there were my slippers, almost in the open, hardly hidden at all. They blended with the pillow. Leave it to my stepsister to be clever.

I picked up my slippers, checked for any evidence that she'd worn them, and found bits of dirt and grass on the soles. I wanted to drag all of Cynthia's extravagant garments outside and through the mud, but I settled for gently brushing my slippers clean against the pillow's silvery-threaded fabric. I replaced the pillow and turned to exit the room when several books piled on a small window illuminated writing table drew my attention. Among them was *Children's Stories and Rhymes*, which Cynthia had borrowed from Hart Cottage. I scanned the other titles, including *History of the Realm* and *Legends of the Fairy Kingdom*, both of which Cynthia had saved from the pillage of the library. The pair looked well used. In addition, there were stacks of old books resting on the floor on either side of her table. Hurrying across the room to peek at what Cynthia might be learning, I wondered, once again, if many of the ancient-looking volumes, particularly the legends or the history that had drawn my stepsister's attention, were among the titles banned and burned by order of King Benedict.

Taking care not to disturb the quill and inkbottle on the side, I lifted the *Legends of the Fairy Kingdom*, placed my slippers on the table, and quickly turned the pages, noting bookmarks positioned at stories that contained common but largely ignored knowledge: fairies are unseen; fairies care for plants, sometimes for animals, rarely for people; the role of fairies is to serve nature; and the abundance of fairies signifies health in a society. I flipped through the book once more with flagging interest, when some writing in a margin captured my interest.

Fairy-blessed items grant the bearer influence— sometimes possessed by the king.

Now, I knew about the first part because of my slippers, but the second part was new. Curious, I flipped through the rest of the bookmarks, found nothing of interest, and then with disappointment gently closed the book, pondering whether or not the king might have such a token. And if so, what it might be. Clearly not slippers like mine, but maybe a belt or shoes. I had no idea. It intrigued me that Prince Charmain hadn't spilled the information while trying to impress me, if indeed the king had confided in him. I placed the *Legends of the Fairy Kingdom* back on the pile and glanced at the remaining books. One had no title.

Eager to pry, I slipped the volume from the stack, turned back the cover, and found pages scripted in a feminine hand, Cynthia's hand. A smile spread across my face—a diary. I hesitated momentarily and then rationalized that this was Cynthia's punishment for stealing my slippers. I turned several pages and began to read.

Page after page described the gifts that Cynthia had wanted and received from her father or what she had worn on a given day. There was a brief mention of her mother's passing, and I found it odd that this subject was not revisited at length. Occasional pages referenced books she had read, along with a brief summary or notes of reference. This further confirmed my impression that Cynthia was an avid reader—and was very interested in legends about fairies. Well, what else could she do in such isolation? A thin thread of sympathy tickled at my heart.

With nothing more to learn from the tedious journal, I yawned, let several pages flip past my fingers, and began to close it when some familiar names caught my attention: Constance, Matthew. I slowly spread the book wide to a selection dated just days before I had met Cynthia.

My father is three times the fool to marry this lowborn woman, Constance. What a vile name. She was married to that commoner, Matthew Hart, a filthy tax collector. I am suitably sorry that bandits killed him, but now we will be saddled with this woman and her two daughters, Griselda and Isabella. I think those are their names. What useless baggage.

I must consider how to make use of this horrible connection. I have heard that the eldest, Griselda, is acquainted with the prince. How can he bear such an association? But upon reflection, this does mean that this Griselda might prove to be a suitable tool after all.

Unfortunately, Prince Charmain is just a local prince—not the son of the High King in Soltar City.

That would be so much better. But I must work with what I have.

I will succeed where my mother failed; I will snare myself a prince.

Frozen in place and feeling like I'd just been back-kicked in the gut by a horse, I stared at the hateful words: her callous disregard for my father, her unfeeling disrespect for my mother, her heartless designs on the prince—her thoughtlessness regarding all of us. As vexation rose in my chest, my own initial, vehement disapproval of her father pricked at my conscience. I had to reluctantly admit that I, like Cynthia, had disapproved of the marriage. And yet, I had come to grudgingly appreciate Lord Robert's genial graciousness before the marriage and was truly grieved at his death.

All hints of similarity cast aside, I focused on the theft of my slippers. I wanted to grab hold of that that mean, arrogant, heartless, scheming, self-absorbed, duplicitous vixen and shake her until her teeth rattled.

Now, with all-consuming interest, I turned a few drivel-filled pages and then homed in on an incriminating selection written a few days later.

I have just returned after my journey to Hart Cottage, and to my great surprise my prayers have been answered. Even though I'm appalled by my father's marriage to this lowborn woman, it may have some of the advantages for which I had hoped. The eldest daughter, Griselda, a wild, unkempt creature, is, as I had heard, a childhood friend to the prince. She is a trial to endure, but I plan to use her to my best advantage. I suspect her of having her own designs on the prince, but that is simply amusing.

I stopped reading, gripping the diary like I could crush it. It felt like steam was rising from my head. Amusing? I hope she finds it amusing if I become her queen. I returned to the journal, found several pages of princess drivel, and then a single entry on a page.

My father is dead. It is all their fault.

In spite of my roiling fury, a flash of remorse swept through me. Though I didn't like Cynthia, I did feel sympathy for her loss, a loss I understood only too well. With a touch of misgiving, I turned the page.

Isabella is unusual. I don't know if she's mad or possessed of some special gift from the gods. I do know that she is sickly and incapable of useful work, and I would be most satisfied if she were sent to an almshouse where she would no longer be a drain on my resources.

My sympathy fled as my insides went cold and hollow. I kept on reading.

Griselda is unusual, too. I cannot help but notice the way she gazes at flowers, especially roses. It makes me think that she sees things just like Isabella but simply covers her madness better. Nevertheless, she is a useful servant, so I will tolerate her for now.

Tolerate? Servant? That's it. I kicked the leg of the ornate table, rattling the inkbottle and earning myself a throbbing toe. As I cursed my self-inflicted injury, I made a decision. Cynthia could carry her own weight and do her own chores from now on. And if Mr. Dankman wanted, he could have the whole lot of her finery if I had to chop her door down myself.

I paced near the table as I held the diary and continued to devour its foul contents.

Furthermore, I suspect that both Griselda and

Isabella can see fairies. This is quite remarkable and will require further reading. If I am correct in my suspicions, perhaps I can convince Isabella to reveal the fairies to me as a sisterly gesture. She is as eager to please as a hound. If I can catch a fairy, I will be able to...

My head jerked up at the sound of footsteps stopping outside the chamber door. I grabbed my slippers, closed the journal, slapped it on the pile of books, and watched the door swing open. Cynthia stood in the doorway and stared.

Embarrassed at being caught but feeling justified in the retrieval of my property, I held my slippers up to her accusingly.

Cynthia slowly entered the room and closed the door quietly behind her. I noticed that the velvet bag she carried now hung weightless.

She crossed the room midway, clasped her hands, and looked at me expressionlessly. "Why are you in my bedchamber, Griselda?"

I copied her expression. "Why are my slippers in your bedchamber, Cynthia?"

We held our twin stares for a couple of seconds. While my stepsister's expression morphed to surliness, I imagined my hands grabbing her shoulders and shaking the arrogance from her face.

Perhaps sensing my intent, Cynthia finally tossed her head and lifted her chin high. "As a result of my actions, our family's debt has been settled in its entirety. You may have an argument with my methods, Griselda, but surely you can have no argument with my results."

I glanced at the weightless bag hanging from

Cynthia's hand and remembered Mr. Dankman's words that our debt could only be paid by precious metals, silks, and jewels. And my gut grew ice cold.

I took a step toward Cynthia. "What did you do?"

Cynthia tilted her chin. "You are not to be reasoned with, Griselda. I will not discuss the matter with you."

My mind pictured the rose garden as I spoke. "Discuss what matter? What did you—?"

She raised her hand to stop me, stepped back, clearing a direct route to the door, and pointed to the exit. "This conversation is over. You may go."

I waited a second to let her know that I wasn't in any hurry. "And you may stop stealing my things."

I made a show of situating my slippers in the crook of my arm, hugged them to my chest, and left without another word.

Back in my bedchamber, as I locked my slippers safely inside my small trunk, I heard a tap on the door.

Isabella peeked in. "Grizzy, I was just wondering…" She stopped and hesitated before continuing. "I was wondering if you want help with your hair?"

I looked at Isabella, at myself in the mirror, and then back at Isabella. "Do I need…?" Then I remembered my task. "Oh, forget that. Come with me to the garden."

Isabella followed as I made my way down the stairs, through the great hall, and outside onto the garden path. I walked so that Isabella could keep up, but she still had to trot to match my pace.

"Grizzy, what are we doing?"

We passed the untrimmed green shrubs with their resident sparrows along the path and approached the rose garden.

Reluctant to say anything until I knew for certain, I demurred. "Just a moment, Izzy."

I concentrated on our surroundings. The chaos of fairies that usually worked so busily among the shrubs and flowers was subdued, and a thin, brittle wind threaded through the garden where a warm summer breeze should have been. A scattering of gray dwarf clouds rested over the manor grounds in contrast to the clear blue sky throughout the rest of the kingdom.

With Isabella trying to catch her breath, we reached the rose garden and froze. Dead flowers dotted the bushes. Whirling around, I saw spotted damage throughout the circular garden: dried, brown, papery roses on otherwise healthy plants, evidence of Cynthia's betrayal. Sickly fairies languished near the lifeless blooms while other fairies hovered around in distress.

Isabella stood next to me, her breathing shallow. "Oh, Grizzy, I didn't. I didn't show her again."

I inhaled a long breath, feeling my shoulders rise and my muscles tense. Isabella took a step away from me, and I realized that my expression must have scared her.

Wanting to calm Isabella, I said, "I believe you, but then how did she do it?"

Isabella shrugged, and her eyes welled with tears. Then she looked past me, her dripping eyes widening with alarm. I felt it, too, a sense of fury behind me. I turned.

Rosanna.

The rainbow fairy's colors pulsed with vibrancy in her anger. She took a quick flight around the garden, gesturing to the carnage, and whipped to a stop before my face.

She pointed her finger accusingly. "This is your fault."

I jerked back in shock. Of course, I would expect Rosanna to be angry. I was angry, too. But to blame it solely on me seemed unreasonable.

"How?"

Rosanna darted back and forth a few times in front of my face, stopped, and frowned. "You do not know?"

I flung both hands out, guessing that Rosanna was too upset to read my mind. "No, I have no idea why this is my fault."

Rosanna remained hovering and her pulsing colors softened a couple of shades. "That wicked girl has something of yours that opened her eyes. She caught my fairies, made wishes, and sickened them."

My chest tightened. My slippers. I knew they were special, but that the wearer could see fairies—that was alarming. I wished, as I had so many times before, that Father had been able to have the long-promised talk with me—the talk that would have explained so many secrets.

"I'm sorry. She stole my slippers from my bedchamber."

Isabella, who had been silent during the exchange, gasped, but I continued my explanation for Rosanna. "But I retrieved them moments ago."

Rosanna's colors softened to pastels and her wings hummed softly. "This girl must never wear your slippers again. You must see to it."

My eyes slipped past Rosanna to the profusion of skeletal petals dotting the rose garden. Rosanna followed my gaze, her colors flared again with anger, and she flew away.

I watched for a minute as she flew to a sick fairy and placed her hands on her head. A swarm of fairies then circled the pair, stopped to check the rate of recovery, and then circled again. I felt terrible about the sick fairies. Now, fairy energy would be spent on healing rather than on growing. This was unnatural.

I smacked a fist into my hand. "That does it."

And I spun about and strode away, weaving around rosebushes and then straight down the shrub-lined central pathway.

Isabella scampered after me. "Grizzy, what are you going to do?"

I maintained my pace and called over my shoulder. "I'm not sure, just something, anything."

I simply had to stop Cynthia somehow, anyhow. With a plan of containment forming in my mind, I raced off to the stable, left Isabella lagging far behind, and met her on my way back.

With a long rope from the stable now in my hand, I asked, "Are you going to help?"

Isabella, still trying to catch her breath, looked at my rope with wide eyes and nodded in response.

I gestured toward the manor. "Then follow me."

Next, I stomped up the steps to the manor, banged open the heavy paneled door, tore through the great hall, and marched up the central stairs. I tried to slow down so that Isabella could keep up, but she was dragging and breathing hard. I looked behind me.

Isabella motioned for me to go on and gasped. "I'll be right behind you, Grizzy."

I strode down the gallery, swinging the rope at my

side, and headed to Cynthia's bedchamber. Somehow or other, I would make sure that she could no longer harm any fairies.

Chapter 17

A Dear Token

I stormed down the carpet-less, window-lit gallery to Cynthia's rooms and threaded a rope through the handle of her bedchamber door. Next, I tied a knot and pulled it taut. Someone on the other side tried her door, and I felt the tug on my rope. Isabella grabbed the rope and helped me pull, surprising me with her strength and giving me more time to race to the secondary door.

Cynthia shook the first door. "Griselda, I am certain that it is you, but I am uncertain what you plan to accomplish with this little game."

I slipped the rope through the handle of Cynthia's second door, pulled it as tight as I could, and secured it just before Cynthia tried the second door. She jiggled the handle but did not otherwise attempt escape.

I heard her voice through the door, sounding bored. "Griselda, this is simply childish. You are angry, because I did what your pathetic bread-making project would never do, settle our debts."

Her statement hurt with its truthfulness but angered me with its lack of appreciation. I tested the tension on the rope between the doors, and it seemed secure. Fortunately, all of the pedestals and tables with statuary had been removed from the hall, so the binding was not impeded. I could make sure that my wicked stepsister never left her rooms without an escort, one who would make sure she did no further harm. At least that was my vague plan to satisfy Rosanna's demand. We—that is Isabella, Sarah, and I—would watch Cynthia like hawks.

While tying another knot through the handle, I accused. "So you stole my slippers and decided to settle your debts by destroying the entire fairy kingdom."

My stepsister's voice replied, irritated in tone. "Don't exaggerate, Griselda. I came to your room to speak to you, found your slippers on the bed, tried them on for amusement, and to my surprise found I could see fairies. So I borrowed your slippers, made some fairy wishes, and managed the debt payment on my own. It is what you and Isabella should have done yourselves."

I replied through the carved panels. "Or you should have sold some of your excess finery. You wouldn't miss it, but now the entire rose garden is littered with the lifeless debris of your selfishness."

Cynthia rattled the door. "I am sure that you and Isabella take advantage of your fairy sight when it pleases you, so you cannot blame me for doing the same. There is no reason to refrain from taking advantage of the talents of the fairies. They exist to serve us."

Isabella's face blanched, and I couldn't believe what I was hearing. It frightened me that, after all these years, someone had discovered my secret, and this person wasn't trustworthy to keep the knowledge. Father would be so ashamed.

I tried to reason. "But they do not serve us like this. Commanding fairies to make diamonds sickens them and sucks the life from the plants that they tend. Surely, you saw this."

Cynthia was silent for a couple of seconds behind her door. Her next words held less bravado. "It can be of no consequence. A few dried roses do not destroy the land."

So Cynthia knew. She knew that she was tempting destruction.

"Well, I think it is of consequence, and I'm not going to allow you out unless you are supervised."

I heard a deep sigh from behind the door. "As you wish, Griselda, but I imagine that your mother will have something to say about my captivity when she returns from seeing Mr. Dankman off and gathering flowers— or simply hears all your commotion."

Indeed, Cynthia proved prophetic, because footsteps sounded on the stairs, and presently Mother appeared, her bloom-filled basket in hand. She took one look at the rope stretched from door to door and dropped her container. Wildflowers spilled onto the floor, and the folly of my plan became clear.

As if to reinforce my stepsister's comment, words frequently used by Sarah entered my mind, "What will your mother say?"

I was about to find out.

Mother ignored the dropped cuttings and stood stationary in the hallway, staring at the rope. Her eyes narrowed, her hands went to her waist, and her face assumed that "what-have-you-done-now" expression that she saved just for me. Isabella scampered across the floor, gathered the flowers into the basket, and offered them meekly to Mother, who didn't even glance at her when she spoke.

"Isabella dear, be so kind as to take my basket with

you and retire at once to your bedchamber."

Isabella cast a helpless glance my way, and I tilted my head toward her room to spare her from the wrath to come. She hurried off and closed her door behind herself. Throughout the exchange with Isabella, Mother's eyes had never left mine. Now, she heaved a sigh that started from her toes, worked its way up through her body, and finally released from her mouth. She settled back on her heels and spoke with the appearance of someone carrying a great weight—me.

"Griselda dear, pray explain to me why a rope is strung between Cynthia's two chamber doors."

Now, I took my own turn to sigh for I knew my goose was cooked. How could I explain this when conversation about fairies was never a safe topic between Mother and me? It always set Mother's practical nature up against what she described as my fanciful imagination when in reality I knew she was simply scared.

A knock, knock came from Cynthia's door, followed by a theatrically shaky voice. "Oh, Stepmother, are you there? I do beg your pardon, but I cannot get out."

Mother's eyes widened with alarm. "Griselda, no."

She strode toward Cynthia's door, and in desperation, I tried to explain. "Mother, I had to—"

She shot me an angry look. "You had to what, lock your grieving stepsister in her room? Really, Griselda, I thought you were becoming more responsible, but it appears I was in error."

I watched as Mother fumbled with the knot on the handle.

With my hands extended, palms upward, I pleaded,

"You do not understand. Cynthia harmed the fairies in the garden."

Mother's hand snapped up to a halt position so fast that I felt slapped in the face. She ground out her next words. "Griselda, I forbid you to speak of such nonsense—of your silly word for butterflies. I absolutely forbid it."

I knew Mother was trying to keep the secret, unaware that Cynthia had been sniffing around the truth for weeks.

"Forgive me, Mother, but Cynthia knows. She made them ill, wishing for those jewels she gave to Mr. Dankman. Even Isabella agrees. You can ask her."

Mother dropped her hand, struggled with the knot, and glared at me. Still attempting to keep our secret safe, she said, "I forbid you to involve Isabella in your fantastical world. It is difficult enough that you insist on it for yourself without corrupting your sister and your stepsister as well."

From down the gallery behind us came Isabella's timid voice. "If you please, Mother, I beg you to hear Grizzy in this matter."

Mother shot me an accusing look as she worked a section of the knot free. "Isabella, close your door. I will discuss this with you later."

Isabella's door shut with a click. Mother yanked the rope off Cynthia's door, fingered the latch, and opened the door a crack.

She faced me. "Griselda, I will have none of your foolishness. It was unseemly enough when you were a child, but now you are not a child. You are never to mention this again to anyone. Now, apologize to your sister and consider what amends you will make to

Lee Renwick Steele

compensate for your thoughtlessness."

At this point, the door opened wide, and Cynthia appeared, peerlessly performing the part of a tortured innocent.

She placed a hand against her heart. "Please do not trouble yourself, Stepmother. Though frightened, I am unharmed. I hold no grudge against my sister." She added her other hand over her heart as well and leaned toward Mother with a sorrowful countenance. "But as you suggest, perhaps a small token of our sisterly bond would put this unpleasantness to rest."

My apprehension rose, because I knew the suggested "small token" would be nothing of the kind.

Mother, her face soft and filled with gratitude, appeared touched by Cynthia's response. "How courteously spoken, Cynthia. What token would you suggest?"

"Oh, I hesitate to say, Stepmother," Cynthia simpered, "I do not wish to give offense."

Still hoodwinked by my stepsister's performance, Mother insisted. "Say what you will, dear."

My stomach clenched as Cynthia hesitated, feigning too shy to make her request. "Perhaps if you make a sincere promise…"

Now, Mother's look of appreciation wavered, and a touch of irritation crossed her face. "Very well, my dear, I so promise. Now, what is it that would put this sad event behind us all?"

Cynthia smiled. "Oh, a lovely pair of white linen slippers that Griselda kindly lent to me earlier today would be the perfect expression of our bond as sisters."

Mother blinked. I could see that she realized the request was no small thing. Indeed, it was asking for my most precious possession and the means for implementing Father's plan. Mother looked at me and hesitated. She was angry with me, yes, but Mother had always tried to be fair. I knew that she didn't want to force me to part with Father's gift.

She stammered when she spoke. "Cynthia dear, perhaps you are not aware that those slippers are from Griselda's father. A different choice might be more likely to secure sisterly affection."

Cynthia, realizing that greater theatrical effort was required, rose to the occasion.

Her eyes glistened, her lips quivered, and her voice shook. "Forgive me, Stepmother, for it grieves me if I have given offense. In my hope to be accepted, to be included, to be…" Here she gave a little sniffling sob. "To be loved as a member of this family, I did not wish to have my sister, Griselda, punished for her offense against me. I thought a dear token would seal our bond. So again, I beg your forgiveness if I have caused offense, and now I leave the choice to your kindness and"—here she paused and clasped her hands in front of her heart for emphasis—"to your promise."

Though I thought Cynthia's speech deserved applause, Mother was clearly moved. She looked at me with defeat in her eyes. "Very well, Cynthia dear. They are a precious gift, but you shall have them."

As my mouth dropped open in protest, Cynthia curtsied to Mother. "Thank you, Stepmother, and you, Griselda. It is so generous of you to extend this expression of kindness."

Cynthia's eyes glittered with triumph in my direction, and she disappeared quickly into her opulent "jail."

I faced Mother. "You know the value of those shoes, Mother. What you don't know is they give the wearer the ability to see fairies. And Cynthia is not trustworthy."

Mother's eyes widened in surprise, but then her countenance firmed. "Well, now she will share in our family secret. Perhaps that will do much to make her feel more included."

While we walked away from the "princess's" doors, I glared at Mother and whispered forcefully, not wanting Cynthia to overhear. "And ruin all hopes of Father's plan. You know the slippers were part of that."

Mother's posture sagged and she sighed, shallowly this time. "Perhaps, but there was never much hope of that. Nevertheless, I am truly sorry about the shoes. But you have brought this upon yourself. And a promise must be honored, so you are to obey me—at once."

My eyes welled, and I fought back tears. Mother's shoulders drooped even farther. She turned to walk away, stopped, and looked back, her face stricken with regret. She, too, fought with tears.

A short time later, with wet streaks running down my cheeks, I left the slippers outside Cynthia's door. I then left my chamber door open a crack and watched as Cynthia opened her door, reached down, and claimed them for her own.

I wept.

Chapter 18

Cinder Rella

After spending time running off my sorrow and clearing imps in more distant fields, I retired that evening to my scantily furnished chamber, remaining heartsick that my slippers were now in Cynthia's hands, and to my dismay, at my mother's bidding. The miserly fire I made burned low in the fireplace; the candles flickered, casting shadows on the walls, the windows dark. I flopped down onto my creaking bed in front of a snoozing Mr. Tatters, ready to say good riddance to the long day, when there was a tap on my door.

Isabella cracked the door open and peeked in. "Do I disturb you, Grizzy?"

Happy to have my sister seeking me out, I motioned for her to come in and patted the thin blanket next to me. She entered, crossed the room, and settled herself on the side of my bed.

She appeared wistful. "It is so terrible about Cynthia, your slippers, the diamonds. Rosanna will be furious."

I hung my head, imaging my shame before the imperious, diminutive monarch. "I know. Let's talk about something else."

Isabella picked up her feet, curled them onto the bed, and stroked our cat, and I decided to broach a subject that made me uncomfortable.

"Izzy, why do you look at the fresco so much?"

She looked at me, her brow furrowing. "Because the pictures move. Don't they move for you?"

Intrigued, but also wondering about my sister's sanity, I shook my head. "Tell me."

With a shrug, Isabella began. "If you look at it for long enough, the fresco shows something happening. King Francis, the queen, and their baby are together. Then a man comes into the room, and the queen leaves with the baby, but she spies on the men through a crack in the door. The man pours something into a goblet and gives it to the king. The king drinks, and the man drinks from his own goblet. All the while, the queen is watching—worried looking. That's all."

Puzzled about what Isabella had seen, I sighed. "I thought I saw it move once—just for a second."

Isabella shook her head sagely. "You have to wait a long time, Grizzy, or it doesn't work."

Tilting my head at my clever sister, I asked, "How did you learn about this?"

She looked sheepish. "It sometimes happens with the forest tapestry back at Hart Cottage—just some fairies moving in the trees on the tapestry."

"Really?" I exclaimed, realizing that moving scenes on frescos and tapestries were yet another mystery that Father had not explained to me. And I wondered how many secrets were out there that I didn't know about. But Isabella knew of, or had at least observed, this most recent mystery.

With my recent understanding of Isabella's emotional distance from me, I no longer felt hurt by her lack of disclosure. I was simply curious. "Why didn't you tell me about all of this? The tapestry, the fairies, and all?"

Shadows flickered on the walls as Isabella reached for my pillow and hugged it protectively. "Because Mother was so angry about it all, and I didn't want to make things worse. And..." Here she squeezed tighter and rocked forward and back. "And I was so scared."

I hugged Isabella. "Now, we can share the problem together."

Isabella returned the embrace but sighed. "Yes, but with Cynthia, too. And it's all my fault. I just thought it would be good to trust her as a sister. I was wrong."

I patted her back. "But your intentions were kind."

When we released, we smiled at each other, and I noticed how clear Isabella's eyes were. "You look very well, Izzy."

"Oh." She looked abashed. "The headaches went away after I told you the truth. It was too much for me to bear." Then with an embarrassed glance up at me, her mouth curved up slightly at each side. "Now, I have you again."

My heart much lighter now that Isabella and I were back to normal, I grasped both of her hands in mine and squeezed. "We have each other."

We grinned at each other until footsteps approached. The quick stomps on the bare hallway floor prepared me for Mother's entrance. It surprised me that she would still be awake. The steps reached the door, the handle clicked, and the door flew open, waking Mr. Tatters from his nap.

Cynthia stood in the doorframe, her eyes ablaze. "Where are they?"

Isabella and I looked at each other with raised

eyebrows. I had no idea what Cynthia was missing and clearly neither did Isabella. We both turned to her and waited for more information. Cynthia took a few steps into the room. I could see her trying to control her temper, to settle into her unruffled princess demeanor once again, but her eyes betrayed her. This was the first time I'd seen her this angry.

She lifted her chin. "Do not gaze upon me with those daft expressions. Answer me."

All weariness gone now, I wondered what Cynthia was missing, but that took a distant second place to my enjoyment of her shattered composure. I planned to see how wound-up Cynthia could get before bursting but then realized that Isabella was uncomfortable, even scared. I needed to redirect this runaway horse before it crashed into Isabella.

I did my best imitation of my stepsister, lifted my chin and looked down my nose. "Cynthia?"

My stepsister's hands clenched at her sides. "Do not take that condescending tone with me, Griselda. This is not to be borne."

An image of steam rising from Cynthia's golden head made it hard for me not to break into a grin. "Cynthia, perhaps if you shared what you are missing, Isabella and I could assist in your search."

"You know quite well what has been stolen from me, Griselda. I do not suspect your mother or Isabella. I do, however, suspect that you or perhaps Sarah are to blame."

I sighed, slumped my shoulders dramatically, and nodded my head. "You are probably right, Cynthia. I am most likely the guilty party. Now, if you would inform me of my crime, I will gladly confess."

I could see in my stepsister's eyes that her imagination was taking the turn that mine often did regarding her. She wanted to rip my head off. And I wanted to see her try.

Cynthia, though quivering with tension from head to toe, regained control of her countenance again. "My diamonds, Griselda. You may have some silly notion regarding fairies and their magic, but that is nothing to me. You will return the diamonds, or I assure you, you will wish you had."

I felt my eyebrows rise to my hairline. "But you gave the diamonds to Mr. Dankman."

She snorted. "Of that I am quite aware, Griselda, but I did not give him all of them."

Now, I was puzzled. I hadn't taken the diamonds—not that it wasn't a good idea now that she mentioned it. Neither Mother nor Isabella would take them. I agreed with Cynthia about that. And Sarah simply wasn't a thief. I knew that about her. And Hannah and Rebecca seemed honest as well. Besides, Cynthia kept her little diamonds in a locked drawer.

Truly puzzled about the missing gems, I said, "I am sorry, Cynthia, but I am forced to disappoint you. I did not take the diamonds and so will not be able to confess."

Cynthia, in full command of her temper now, was no longer entertaining, her voice brittle and controlled. "It must have been you, Griselda, or perhaps I'm mistaken in Isabella and it was she. Who else would have taken the diamonds and left dried rose petals in their place?"

Isabella flinched noticeably, and I wondered if indeed it had been my little sister, trying to atone for her earlier indiscretion. I'd have to talk with her, but now Cynthia needed to leave. Cynthia, intent on looking at me, apparently hadn't noticed Isabella's reaction. I took advantage of that.

"There is nothing to be done tonight, Cynthia. Please go to bed, or…" I grinned and patted the bed on my vacant side. "Do you want to spend the evening with me?"

Cynthia let out a cough of disgust and glared, clearly thinking there was a great deal more to do this evening. But realizing I wouldn't budge, she spun about and left the room without the courtesy of closing the door behind her.

I climbed off the bed, scampered across the bare floor, shut the door, and returned to the bed.

Isabella leaned forward. "Grizzy, did you take the diamonds?"

I stared at her. If she was asking me, then it couldn't have been Isabella, and I was mistaken about her jumpy reaction.

She persisted. "Grizzy?"

"But I did not. I did not take them."

Isabella scrunched her forehead. "Then what happened to them?"

"I honestly don't know."

The next morning, after a satisfying breakfast of simple mixed-grain pottage eaten in the kitchen with Mother, Isabella, Sarah, Hannah, and Rebecca, whose singular service-on-demand to my stepsister had been curtailed by Sarah, I decided to help Sarah make bread. Even though Cynthia's fairy-made diamonds had apparently settled our debt, we were still in grossly reduced circumstances, not having enough servants to do even the basic work at the manor. While Hannah and Rebecca worked on cheese making, I took a deep breath, stretched my sore shoulders, and dove into some soft dough.

Push, fold, push, and fold. My tunic, apron, and even my scarf were soon covered with flour. I didn't mind bread making. I preferred it to the stitchery that Mother and Isabella were doing, but oh, I was tired, and I never had fun anymore.

Dressed in gray with a clean, but stained, white apron, Sarah, kneading bread across the table from me, looked up from her work. "Miss Griselda, I wish ya wouldn't do this, a young lady like yerself. Leave it to me."

I pushed my scarf back on my hair and punched my fist into the dough. "Things are different now, Sarah."

Sarah tilted her head toward my two industrious family members. "Yer mother and sister are still keeping to their stations, miss. You should, too."

Mother caught my eye. Our conversations had been strained since yesterday's confrontation. "Griselda, if you will not listen to me, you should at least listen to Sarah."

Mother and Isabella sat near our worktable in sturdy chairs. They looked out of place among the trappings of the kitchen, wearing their crisp linen dresses, bending over their embroidery, and trying to hold onto a vestige of our former lives. For company they spent their time in the kitchen, rather than in the cheerless, vacant rooms of the empty, cavernous manor.

Too tired to argue, I just dug back into my dough and heard footsteps on the stairs coming down to the kitchen. Cynthia, that thieving, heartless, self-important, false, vicious, slippers-stealing stepsister of mine, appeared, looking like royalty in a rose-pink gown with a matching padded circlet crowning her head. I checked her feet—embroidered pink shoes to match her dress. A slight wave of relief washed through me, but the feeling was short lived. Even though she wasn't wearing my slippers, they no longer belonged to me. They belonged to that scheming manipulator.

With Rebecca's services denied her, I supposed that she was finally hungry enough to deign to come to the kitchen where food was now served. Rebecca, who had seemed relieved to be free of service to my stepsister, was helping Hannah squeeze the whey from the fresh cheese. The two girls glanced up at Cynthia and then quickly back down, focusing with more attention than necessary on their task.

Cynthia stopped, framed in the doorway, and scanned the room imperiously. I ignored her, because I wanted to call her every name in my thoughts and douse her spotless dress with flour. But that would further strain my relationship with my mother, so I settled for rolling my eyes at Sarah, only to be caught by Mother who gave me her "don't try anything" look.

My parent rose. "Good morning, Cynthia. Would you like this chair?"

Cynthia remained in the doorway as if reluctant to lower herself to join such company. "Thank you, no. I came to inquire about our luncheon menu."

Mother nodded to Cynthia, sat down again, and said, "Sarah?" I raised my eyebrows to Sarah and mouthed, "Luncheon menu?"

Sarah, whose back was toward Cynthia, stopped

kneading, turned, and walked across the kitchen to the fireplace. There she reached for a long-handled spoon and stirred the contents simmering in a chain-hung cauldron.

"It's stew, Lady Cynthia, a hearty meal with cabbage, onions, garlic, celery, and lots of peas. There's even a bit of chicken. Come see for yerself."

Cynthia's nose crinkled with disdain as her eyes roamed around the kitchen, taking in the herbs hanging from the rafters, the sacks, barrels, and bins with grains, fruits, and vegetables, and the floury mess at my work table. Her sneer morphed into complete disgust when a tiny mouse scurried across the floor, disappearing into a crack in a stone wall as Mr. Tatters pounced. Mastering her obvious objection to entering an area for servants' work, she crossed the room, stood in the hearth, and peered into the pot. She jerked back with a sneer. I shook my head and tried to keep my breathing calm.

Sarah placed the hand holding the spoon on her hip and raised the other palm up. "I'm sorry it doesn't please you, Lady, but you can't refuse to eat jus' because it doesn't suit yer high and mighty taste."

Mother was on her feet, her embroidery falling to the floor. "Sarah, that is enough."

Sarah threw up her hands. "Well, I beg yer pardon, ma'am, but this is the best we have."

Cynthia snorted with disgust. Oh, I wanted to tell that arrogant "princess" to go forage for herself and leave us alone, but Mother's certain displeasure held me in check. I focused on my dough—push, fold, push, and fold.

Everyone in the room remained silent for a few heartbeats as if bracing for what would happen next. I surreptitiously glanced about. Cynthia straightened to her full height, her nose tilted skyward. Sarah, spoon held aloft weapon-like, glowered at my malcontented stepsister. Mother held out a hand in a conciliatory gesture. Isabella, her embroidery needle motionless, sat like a statue. Mr. Tatters, tail twitching, zeroed in on the mouse hole. The stew bubbled in the cauldron, the fire crackling beneath it.

Cynthia stood a moment, and I could feel her eyes on me, watching me work, despising me for doing a menial task.

"Griselda," she said, her voice mocking.

I stopped kneading and looked up.

Cynthia's mouth curled on one side. "You have flour on your face."

At first, I tamped down my rage, remained motionless, and did not react. Of course, I had flour on my face. I was trying to keep us fed.

Then I scanned her gown, met her gaze, and smiled in mocking response. "Cynthia, you have cinders on your dress."

Alarm crossed her face; she quickly looked down. Sure enough, several small black cinder spots now decorated Cynthia's pink gown. She screamed, jumped away from the hearth, and brushed her skirt frantically. The spots became streaks. Mother and Isabella gave little gasps.

Sarah's shoulders shook with silent laughter as she once again stirred the stew.

I chuckled, grabbed my dough, and began to knead. "It's nothing but cinders."

Cynthia stopped attacking her dress and straightened. "Clean this off immediately. I can't have cinders on me like a common drudge."

I contrived a look of mock concern on my face. "Oh, no, or we'll have to call you Cinder Rella."

Mother glared at me, but Sarah snorted with laugher over the pot.

Isabella giggled. "Oh, Grizzy, you're so funny." Soft intakes of breath came from Hannah and Rebecca, who were motionless at their work.

"Cinder" Rella's eyes shot Isabella a look that killed her laughter on the spot. Then, trembling with fury, she gave her garment a final shake, took on her frozen statue attitude, and tilted her nose to an imposing height.

She glared daggers at me. "I beg your pardon."

"You heard me. I said 'Cinder Rella.' Come on, it's a joke. If you're afraid of the kitchen, then leave."

Isabella sat wide-eyed and open-mouthed. Mother stood and took a step toward me.

Cynthia took a step toward me, too.

"Griselda, I understand your petty attacks on me. You are jealous, because you are so far beneath me that apart from this ill-conceived marriage, I would take no notice of you. You are nothing but a drudge. You act a drudge; you look a drudge; you are a drudge."

Everyone stood paralyzed for a second while the sound of the simmering stew bubbled away in the hearth.

Mother stirred to intercede. "Now, Cynthia, I beg you to—"

A gray and white blur streaked past me. Sarah planted herself in front of Cynthia, put her hands on her hips, and shoved her face into Cynthia's. "Don' ya talk to Miss Griselda like that, ya spoiled little brat."

Mother and Isabella gasped, but I felt the edge of my mouth tug into a smirk.

Cynthia's eyes grew, her height grew, and her presence grew to fill the room with fury. "How dare you?"

But Sarah stood her ground, refusing to give an inch to my stepsister's rage. Cynthia, red-faced and shaking with anger, raised her hand, pulled back, and— slap. Her palm smacked Sarah hard across the face.

And I moved. I didn't intend to; I didn't think about it; I just moved.

Neither the disapprobation of my mother nor the disappointment of my late father could have stopped me. Cynthia had turned to leave the kitchen, leaving a gap-mouthed Sarah momentarily too startled to move, but I had other plans for the little brat. I closed the distance between us, grabbed her arm, turned her back around, and whack. I walloped her across her face, harder than she'd hit Sarah.

A red mark appeared on Cynthia's cheek, and her mouth formed a large "O" before she screamed, "You beast." She jerked her arm away and struck at my face.

I dodged her slap and pushed her away. "You started it."

The "princess" growled, lifted both hands, and shoved me hard at the shoulders. I tried to push back in kind, but Cynthia grabbed my scarf and pulled it off, scratching my neck and yanking my hair in the process.

With an, "Ow," I grappled for her hair, found the pink, fabric circlet crowning her head, and tugged, pulling fabric, pins, and hair from her head. Then I tossed the lot toward the hearth.

Crying out in pain, my stepsister reached for her

injured scalp and then watched with incredulity as sparks from the fire started to smolder on the pink cloth of her circlet. Tearing her eyes from her ruined headpiece, she curled her claws and came at my face, arms flailing. I evaded her attack, but she tackled me around the waist. We tumbled to the kitchen floor in a mass of arms, legs, fabric, dust, and flour. With a swipe of one leg and a twist of my body, I managed to end up on top of Cynthia, pinning her claws to the floor to keep from being savaged.

Mother, Sarah, and Isabella, who I hadn't even noticed with my attention so focused on "Cinder Rella," began to mill about, trying to pull us apart. Mother and Isabella pulled me from Cynthia while Sarah looped her sturdy arms under Cynthia's shoulders and raised her up. Cynthia fought Sarah's restraint, so Sarah lifted her off the floor, leaving Cynthia to flap her legs and arms in the air, a sight so undignified that I laughed.

My amusement had two effects. First, my stepsister fought against Sarah with renewed vigor. Then she seemed to realize how indecorous she appeared and abruptly became motionless, trying to appear in control and above it all even though held captive.

Mother and Isabella each held one of my arms and pulled me away from Cynthia. I offered no resistance, but I remained tensed, ready for anything. Hannah and Rebecca, work abandoned, were huddled together among the bins against the kitchen wall. Mr. Tatters, tail twitching, maintained his vigil at the mouse hole.

"Griselda." Mother held me in a grip that let me know she feared I would launch another attack at my stepsister. "Apologize at once."

Breathing heavily, I said, "She should apologize to

Sarah first."

Sarah still held my adversary though she no longer struggled against her restraint.

"Sarah, release Cynthia," Mother said.

With a face that questioned Mother's request, Sarah obeyed. Cynthia, with her garment and hair in disarray, shook off Sarah's presence.

She pinioned Mother with her eyes. "After this intolerable treatment, you will allow Rebecca to assist me with my wardrobe." She gestured to her soiled gown and her chaotic hair.

Mother, though looking like she wanted to make an attempt at reconciliation, finally nodded to Rebecca and said, "Very well, Cynthia."

The "princess" gave a slight nod, as though acknowledging a servant, turned to leave, and then looked back. She looked from Mother, to Isabella, to me.

"In the future, you may address me as Lady Cynthia."

Chapter 19

The Mouse Catcher

The following morning dawned with no respite in the emotional turmoil of the family. Cynthia retained her foul humor and walked about like a piqued princess. Isabella cast anxious glances at her; Mother bore the weight of our conflict in her tight mouth and rigid posture. And me? I followed Cynthia like a shadow. There would be no more diamonds from dead roses on my watch.

This state of affairs continued as Sarah served our midday meal of stew, bread, and fresh cheese in the hearth-warmed kitchen. Hunger had driven Cynthia to join us. The silence at the table was punctuated by the sound of spoons tapping the bowls and Rags barking outside at a distance. Mr. Tatters sat parked in front of a crack in the kitchen wall, tail switching. Cynthia looked up from her food and watched him intently. I, of course, watched her.

She noticed and rolled her eyes. "Your cat is hunting a mouse, Griselda. Is that of great importance?"

Now, suspicious of anything that interested my stepsister, I challenged. "You tell me."

Mother sighed. "Girls, please try—"

Rags's barking, just outside the kitchen now, interrupted her request, and a knock on the door followed. I guessed the caller must have tried the front door, but we hadn't heard it. Sarah opened it and revealed a messenger carrying three rolled parchments. It was not Lieutenant Jon, and I was *not* disappointed. He appeared too frequently for my taste, and it annoyed me each time he changed identities: from groom, to courier, and now to lieutenant.

To all our surprise, the messenger was Hammond, guard to the great hall, which meant there was something from the king. Mother rose, and he presented the documents.

First, he bowed to Mother. "For Lady Constance Rella."

Mother's eyes widened with curiosity as she accepted the message and tucked it under her arm.

Second, he bowed to me. "For Miss Griselda Rella."

I recoiled from that name as I rose to receive my rolled paper and muttered, "My name is Griselda Hart."

Hammond looked confused but pulled himself together to discharge his final duty.

He looked once more to Mother. "And this is for all the ladies of the house."

Mother paid Hammond a copper, Sarah gave him some bread and cheese, which he accepted with thanks, and he went on his way.

After he left, Mother, who had opened and perused the third parchment with interest, declared, "His Highness Prince Charmain is returning next week, and we are invited to a feast in his honor."

The gloom lifted from the room as Mother, Isabella, and Sarah chattered about suitable clothes and what needed mending or remaking.

Mother turned to me. "Griselda, I have remade the green silk dress for you. It will enhance your lovely eyes."

I nodded to be polite but kept my eyes on Cynthia. A look of foxlike cunning had crept onto her face, and I wondered what my clever stepsister had in mind for the feast.

Amid all the talk, I leaned over to Isabella and whispered, "Will you keep an eye on Cynthia? Don't let her go to the garden alone. Follow her."

She nodded, so I left the kitchen and carried my parchment upstairs to my bedchamber. Fearing that time and distance had eroded my influence on the prince and strengthened Lord Ursa's, my apprehension about the letter's contents increased as I sat on the creaky bed in my scantily furnished room, broke the wax seal, and unfurled the stiff sheet. I read.

Dear Griselda,

We are grieved to learn of the loss of your stepfather. Please know that our sympathies are with you and your family. I do hope that now you will return to Hart Cottage so that distance will not be an obstacle to our meetings.

When you receive this letter, we will soon be arriving at the castle, and preparations to celebrate my return are already underway.

We look forward to your approbation regarding our fair purpose.

His Royal Highness…

Confusion filled my mind. What did he mean by our fair purpose? Was it a reference to marriage? It didn't seem to be. Did he mean that he wanted me to agree with all the things Lord Ursa had talked him into?

With my father gone, there was no one willing to stand up to the greedy lord. The genial, old king never would. He was too accustomed to being led. It was up to the prince to grow a spine and exert his own authority. I had been counting on it—or at least hoping for it.

I tossed the letter to the side, rubbed my forehead with my hand, and pondered what to do. And then I recalled the obvious. If I married the prince, I would be his spine. If we were wed, surely I would have more influence over the prince than Lord Ursa. The prince was a good man; he just needed me to remind him. That is if we were indeed to marry. And his letter gave me no confidence about that.

And with my influential slippers in Cynthia's possession, I had no special leverage to further Father's overreaching plan, if there had ever been any hope of that in the first place.

While I pondered the merits of matrimony and the harm of my stepsister's scheming, there was a knock on the door, and Mother entered. Her hands held a parchment, and her face wore an expression of bewilderment.

She lifted the paper, unfurling its length. "This is from the king. It says that you are to marry the prince."

Her tone implied that she did not trust her own words. Surprised after the ambiguous message I had just received, I rose from my bed and craned my neck but could not see the writing.

Mother let the parchment drop to her hips and paced the room, muttering, "Matthew hoped for this, but I never thought…"

With hope blooming in my heart, I watched as my mother began to embrace something that she hadn't believed possible.

She turned to me again, her eyes more attentive. "The king will announce your betrothal at the feast. Did you know of this?"

I didn't answer at once because Mother's words, "Matthew hoped for this," reverberated in my mind. Was it possible, Father's plan coming to fruition? Now, over time, the threat to those with fairy sight could be eliminated. It amazed me that Prince Charmain had convinced his father to allow our union. After all, part of the reason for this summer's tour had been to throw the prince into the paths of eligible young ladies—preferred young ladies. This gave me hope that my "Prince Charming" could hold his own when he set his mind to something.

Focusing back on Mother's question, I shrugged. "I knew of the possibility but not the certainty. So I did not speak of it."

Mother nodded as if this was all some scheme concerning which she was the master planner. "Yes, that is wise. And even now we must keep this between ourselves. We wouldn't wish you to behave like Cynthia's mother. Oh, how humiliating."

Though the reference caught me off guard, I remembered Cynthia's earlier claims. "Did Cynthia's mother—"

Mother interrupted, shaking her head with disapproval. "Katherine was a commoner who pursued the king, Prince Beaumain back then, with all her considerable charms—Oh, she was the beauty of our time—and he did nothing to dissuade her. But in the end, he chose his bride from a noble family. She quite snubbed the king after that, and apart from snaring Lord

Rella, she disappeared from court altogether. It was quite a scandal some years before you were born."

I opened my mouth to comment, but Mother, now surprising me with sudden giddiness, bounded to me, grabbed my shoulders, and chattered on.

"A carriage will be sent for us. The king will announce your betrothal at the feast, and I am sure that your union will ensure your safety and will be a blessing to the entire kingdom. Your father felt as much. Oh..." She straightened and stood a moment in thought. "I will need to take greater care with your dress. It is lovely, but I could..." She turned from me, lost in her plans for my garment, opened the door, and called, "Sarah..."

And there I stood, staring after my departing, distracted mother.

Yes, I would marry the prince.

And, yes, this would be fine since we got along well enough.

But it vexed me that no one but my father had consulted with me about the event: not the prince, not the king, and not even my mother.

Several days after the arrival of the invitations, I found myself standing in my chamber surrounded by Mother, Isabella, and Sarah.

Sarah swatted me on the backside. "Stop yer fidgetin', Miss Griselda, and let yer mother finish yer gown."

I did as I was told. Mother said nothing, but she tugged at the hem of the green silk dress and fussed with the sleeves. On my feet were Mother's finest embroidered slippers. They were quite lovely, but I wished that I had my slippers from Father. Even though they were plain, their shimmery glow made them ethereal. Besides, they were a gift, a purposeful gift, but more importantly, a connection to my father.

Thinking about tomorrow's feast, I knew that the slippers had been meant to nudge the king into allowing me to wed his son, but now to my surprise and in spite of Lord Ursa's interference, the goal was already managed—and all naturally. My heart warmed with satisfaction.

I came out of my musings as Isabella circled about looking me over from head to toe, nodding approvingly. "Mother was right, Grizzy, you do look beautiful. Now, if you would permit me arrange your hair tomorrow."

Thinking to frighten them all with the threat that I'd do my own hair, I grimaced at her. "I'm getting better at it."

Sarah snorted and Isabella looked doubtful, so I relented. "Oh, very well."

Isabella smiled, and Mother stood up, surveying her handiwork.

She tugged at the fabric near my waist. "Griselda, you are too thin, but you do look lovely. I am sure that Prince Charmain will not be able to take his eyes off you."

"That he won't," Sarah agreed as Isabella giggled.

I rolled my eyes to show that I didn't care, but my cheeks warmed in betrayal. Mother, Isabella, and Sarah exchanged conspiratorial glances, showing me that Mother had shared the news with them. They stood for a moment, admiring the result of their patient efforts, when Cynthia tiptoed by the slightly open door carrying a small birdcage. We exchanged puzzled glances and moved en mass to the door, only to see Cynthia disappear into her chamber and close the door with a click.

Sarah clomped a few steps down the gallery and turned to us. "She's up to something, that one is."

I agreed with Sarah, wondering with uneasiness what scheme my stepsister was crafting.

Mother, however, intervened. "You two leave the poor girl alone. We will have peace in this family."

Sarah and I traded grim looks, not believing that peace was likely.

At Mother's insistence, I dropped the subject of my stepsister's sly behavior with the birdcage, but I renewed my lapsed efforts to shadow her and was rewarded with a perplexing sight.

Later in the day, I spied Cynthia crouched with her cage in the kitchen next to a crack in the wall, the very crack into which Mr. Tatters frequently chased mice. Cynthia, so intent on her task, did not hear me. Soon a tiny gray mouse crept from the space and—slam. Cynthia covered it with a bowl, slid a parchment beneath, and then dumped the mouse into the cage. She snapped the cage shut and stood, looking as pleased as a cat. That's when she noticed me, and a flash of annoyance crossed her face.

She quickly replaced it with a forced smile and held up the cage. "Look, Griselda, is it not charming?"

The tiny animal was cute, but I hadn't pegged Cynthia as a rodent lover. "Why are you collecting mice?"

My stepsister walked past me with her prize. "You have your pets; I have mine."

And she swept from the kitchen, up the stairs, and into her bedchamber, leaving me to puzzle over the reason for her sudden interest in small vermin.

Later that evening, with the temperature and nighttime falling, I shadowed Cynthia outside. She glanced furtively around before tromping through the rampant weeds to the fairy tended vegetable garden. Concerned that she was after fairies again, I snuck around the outskirts, hid behind a shed, and craned my neck to see what she was up to.

The mouse catcher wended her way to the pumpkins, bent down, and pulled a sizable knife from her belt.

Alarmed, I opened my mouth but before any sound came out, she sliced the knife downward cutting through a green vine. Sheathing the weapon, she reached down, embraced a dirty orange gourd with a grimace, and hoisted the muddy trophy into her arms.

My eyes widened with surprise, and I silently mouthed, "Fairies preserve us, what does she want with a pumpkin?"

As if in response, the fairies rose from their work, whizzed around the vegetable garden, and then returned to busy themselves among the plants. Cynthia, not wearing my slippers I noted, left the garden, struggled back to the manor with her unusual treasure, and disappeared inside, leaving me perplexed—and suspicious—about her odd behavior.

A further mystery unfolded a couple of hours later while I was helping in the kitchen. Rebecca was summoned to my stepsister's chambers. She soon returned with a puzzled expression, a bowl of pumpkin pulp and seeds, and a report that Cynthia had painstakingly scooped the inside of the large gourd clean. Sarah, Hannah, Rebecca, and I stared at the fibrous mess questioningly. Then Sarah shrugged, grabbed a pan, and proceeded to roast the seeds.

As the nutty fragrance of roasted pumpkin seeds and spices filled the kitchen, I pondered my stepsister's behavior. Though her inexplicable actions left me baffled, they also increased my wariness. What was she up to?

The next day dawned with a clear blue sky. In early afternoon, Fritz and Gammon arrived, at Lieutenant Jon's request, to escort us through the King's Forest. Though having an escort was advisable, the involvement of the enigmatic groom-courier-lieutenant put me in a bad mood. I was sure it was not because he had not come himself.

The two guards apologized for failing to bring a carriage, as well as a couple more guards, but apparently Lord Ursa had interfered with the king's plans at the last minute. That figured. The sour old lord had always thwarted my father; now he was thwarting my family and me.

We, however, were only slightly inconvenienced. Our wagon, hitched to our only horse, the one that we'd switched for during our market day visit to Hart Cottage, was brought to the front of the manor. Sarah placed our folded cloaks in the bed of the wagon. Mother and Isabella climbed into the conveyance, sat on blanket-covered empty trunks with their gowns spread wide to avoid creases, and opened parasols for shade from the sun. I climbed onto the blanket-covered driver's seat, spread the skirt of my gown at Mother's direction, and took the reins from Sarah, who stood to the side. Mr. Dankman, mounted on horseback, made a surprise arrival and requested to accompany us for a time.

Sarah kept glancing at the manor and fussing with the fabric of my gown to keep it from wrinkling.

She exhaled with impatience. "Where is that girl?"

As if in response, Cynthia opened the door, glided down the stairs, and swanned her way to the wagon. Her hair, done earlier by Mother, was crowned with her sparkling tiara, and her sapphire gown boasted embroidery set with jewels on the bodice and sleeve borders. Her embroidered shoes matched the dress. Even I had to grudgingly admit, my stepsister looked like a goddess.

Fritz, mouth agape, dismounted, preparing to assist the lovely vision into the wagon, but she held up her hand.

The goddess addressed Mother. "Stepmother, please forgive me, but I will be unable to attend the feast for our prince. I hope that you and my stepsisters will enjoy the event."

As she turned to leave, I caught a gleam in her eyes, which ignited my apprehension. The group of us, stunned into speechlessness by Cynthia's announcement, did not respond at once.

It was Mr. Dankman who sputtered to life first. "Lady Cynthia, surely a lovely young lady dressed as you are must be planning to attend the feast."

Mother, overcoming her speechlessness, echoed his sentiments. "Cynthia, you are the picture of an elegant lady, and we are so looking forward to introducing you at the castle. I hope that you will reconsider."

I sat silently, wondering with suspicion what we were missing. That Cynthia would skip an opportunity to meet the prince was incomprehensible.

My stepsister looked back at us. "Thank you for your kindness, Stepmother, but I am quite determined. I will now leave you to your journey. Good day to you all, my dear family."

As she turned away, I saw the glitter in her eyes. She's laughing, I thought, and I bent down to Sarah and whispered, "Will you keep an eye on her?"

Sarah followed Cynthia with her eyes and snorted. "I'll keep both eyes on her. That little vixen's up to something; you can bet on it."

With no time to investigate further, I shook the reins and our journey began. The horse plodded along, and the wagon rocked, creaked, and bumped along on the dusty road. This was no way to travel to an important event like a feast, but it was all we had.

If the king's failure to provide a carriage for his future daughter-in-law was any indication, perhaps a shift in royal intentions had occurred. Consequently, Mother's wish for secrecy about my as-yet-unannounced betrothal had been good advice.

As we rolled our way to the forest and I pondered the uncertainty of my status, Mr. Dankman chatted with the guards and with Mother, while Isabella listened and watched the fairies hovering over the recently harvested fields. I noted with dismay the gray imp spots needing attention in the harvested fields farther from Rella Manor. These I hadn't been able to reach yet in my intermittent fairy-led forays to clear the land.

Eventually, Mr. Dankman asked Fritz and Gammon if they would give him a moment to speak to Mother. They looked a bit suspicious but, with Mother's assurance, dropped back several horse lengths. At this point, I learned why he had shown up earlier.

He remained silent for several of his steed's paces, appearing reluctant to speak, but finally did. "I thought you should be told; the diamonds are missing."

Mother's brow furrowed at first, then her eyes widened with understanding. "The diamonds that Cynthia gave you in payment for the remainder of our debt, they are missing?"

"Yes, and it bears investigation," Mr. Dankman replied, "but whatever happened, it happened in my own house." Here he stopped, as if questioning his next words. "And the oddest thing is that in place of the diamonds were dried petals—roses, I think."

I glanced back and shared a puzzled glance with Isabella, who had listened, too. Neither of us said anything, but I recalled Cynthia's mention of dried rose petals when she missed her diamonds. What could it mean?

After this inexplicable disclosure, Mr. Dankman took his leave, and Fritz and Gammon rejoined the wagon.

We traveled past the rolling farmlands under blue skies and reached the forest without incident, but then the weather behind us took an odd turn. The sky swirled with thin gray clouds and a biting wind sliced at our heels. Mother tossed my cloak to me while she and Isabella hid under theirs. Our horse-mounted companions spoke softly to calm their prancing animals. I frowned back at the chaotic skies and wondered at the unseasonable change as we moved into the trees.

During our journey through the forest, I noticed Isabella casting furtive glances at the forest fairies with their green and brown streaked bodies, coverings, and wings. In time, she relaxed enough to smile at nature's caretakers, overcoming her visceral fear—at least for now—of her fairy sight, while I pondered a confusing series of images: missing diamonds, mysterious rose petals, captured mice, a collected pumpkin, and Cynthia's inexplicable refusal to attend the feast.

Our two guards, Fritz and Gammon, swords sheathed at their sides, flanked the wagon, their eyes roaming through the trees and darting at any sudden sound.

Mother, not noticing the edginess of the guards, exchanged news with them: first about Cynthia's strange absence, then about neighborhood gossip, and eventually about the rumors spreading throughout the countryside. I learned that Prince Charmain had indeed rescued Farmer Hugh Heaten's cow from Lord Ursa, as I had demanded, only to have it repossessed later by Lord Ursa. And just who had been Lord Ursa's agent? Jason Gutcher, along with his two hulking followers Deke and Dirk. Shockingly, the valuable milk cow had been slaughtered for meat. Most folks thought this was because Farmer Hugh, always a supporter of my father's programs, was not a sycophant of Lord Ursa, so the greedy lord had chosen to make an example of him. While the king had done nothing, popular and outspoken Mr. Carver, the main village butcher, had refused to participate in the matter of Farmer Hugh's cow, so he, too, was now a target of Lord Ursa's displeasure, receiving threatening visits with warnings not to interfere with the powerful lord's policies.

Fuming over this story, I was glad that soon I would have the prince's ear and would be able to talk some sense into the kingdom's proceedings the way my father had. Only I was sorely grieved for our good Hart Cottage neighbor, Farmer Hugh Heaten.

Before we reached the northern edge of the King's Forest, galloping hoof falls sounded ahead, hidden by a curve in the road. Fritz and Gammon quickly urged their mounts ahead, motioned for me to stop the wagon, and drew their swords. Soon two horses, with red-and-black-clad guards astride, appeared around the curve. The riders brought their steeds to a trot, then a walk, and Fritz and Gammon sheathed their weapons. I realized why.

Lieutenant Jon.

With many a nod among the guards, the lieutenant and his fellow joined Fritz and Gammon. They arranged themselves: Jon in front of the wagon, his partner in the rear, and Fritz and Gammon flanking the sides. And then with a forward gesture from the groom-courier-lieutenant, I shook the reins, and onward we rolled. Why we needed four guards, and why the lieutenant had been in such a hurry to join us were mysteries to me, but I guessed that maybe it was because, in spite of Lord Ursa's interference, I was soon to be betrothed to the prince. There could be no other reason for such special treatment. It did make me feel increasing warmth toward Prince Charmain for his thoughtful attention.

As we came to the forest's edge with the castle in view, I looked at the fortress and felt a swell of welcome inside. It was so good to be home, and with all that surrounded my upcoming betrothal, I hoped that, in time, we would be set free from that awful Rella

Manor. I couldn't help but smile that Father's plan was working out so seamlessly.

Chapter 20

The Feast

The sky before us was blue as we exited the forest and continued on King's Way through the fields, but the clouds and wind we had encountered prior to entering the forest seemed to have followed us and threatened to change the sunny and comfortably warm weather of Fairian Village. Two red-and-black-garbed guards stood on either side of the South Gate entrance, the same surly, unknown guard who had been stationed there for my last visit and—groan—Jason Gutcher.

The twosome exchanged words as they watched the approach of our group. I braced myself for another round of challenges from the unknown guard, but he eyed our escorts and stepped back.

With a tilt of his head toward the castle, he said, "Lord Ursa is not pleased that you left your post, Lieutenant."

In response, Jon nodded curtly and said, "Understood, Malacus." Then he led us through the gate.

Jason stepped back, too, looking very pleased with himself, and launched into a verbal attack.

"You should've been nice to me, Grizzy. Now, all your hopes after the prince are gonna be disappointed. Ursa's seen to that."

From the other side, Malacus hissed, "Lord Ursa, you fool." Then to our backs, he called, "Proceed directly to the castle. No loitering in the streets."

With trepidation about what Lord Ursa had seen to that would cause me disappointment, I shook the reins over our horse's back, urging her to increase our distance from the unfriendly guards at the gate.

Soon we passed my favorite maple tree, the village green, and a few shops along King's Way before we needed to turn right onto Castle Road to head toward the castle. I glanced near the intersection of King's Way and Castle Road, caught sight of the side-by-side goldsmith and silversmith shops, and noted Gilly sweeping out front. The orphan, who hired out to Hart Cottage and Farmer Heaten, did odd jobs for the two kindly smiths in exchange for food and a secure place to sleep at night. When Gilly noticed our wagon, he dropped the broom and sprinted over, looking agitated.

With a pull on the reins, I brought our horse and wagon to a stop. "Greetings, Gilly."

Without any preamble, Gilly blurted out, "They jus' arrested Carver."

A chorus of gasps, including mine, sung from the wagon and its escorts.

Lieutenant Jon, who had turned back when the wagon stopped, exclaimed, "On what grounds?"

"D'no," Gilly said, looking down and shuffling. "Ya know how he always says his piece."

With tension building in my throat and shoulders, I took a calming breath, thanked Gilly for his information, and formulated a quick plan. If I was going to talk Prince Charmain into releasing the butcher—and I was—I needed to learn the facts, so I hopped off the wagon and held the reins back to Mother.

She cast a worried look at passersby. "Griselda, get back in the wagon at once."

I stretched the reins closer to her. "You and Isabella go on up to the castle. I'm going to Carver's shop."

Mother rose from her blanket, nodded to a passing acquaintance that waved hesitantly, leaned toward me, and hissed, "You'll do nothing of the sort. This is no time for your mischief."

I looked pleadingly at her. "I want to ask His Highness directly to release Mr. Carver. His wife will have the necessary details to make my case." After a pause, I added, "It's what Father would have done."

Mother looked down the road toward the turn before Carver's shop and then at me. She took in a deep breath, let it out, took the reins, and whispered, "Griselda, use more caution than you are wont to use and keep away from the guards. And by all the gods above—keep your gown clean."

A poorly concealed snort at my side caused me to glance at Lieutenant Jon, who was struggling not to laugh. I glared at him, which only increased his difficulty containing his amusement.

He controlled himself enough to say to Mother, "I will escort Griselda and will endeavor to keep her from falling in the dirt or…" Here his mirth got the better of him again.

With an exaggerated eye roll at the not-amusing and not-required escort, I nodded to Mother and Isabella, both of whose brows were identically crinkled with concern, and tapped the wagon in good-bye.

As I trotted off, Jon dismounted, left his horse with Fritz, and followed in my wake. I wasn't waiting for his unnecessary company, but to my irritation, he caught up with me easily.

As if to rub it in, he said, "We are not racing, Miss Griselda. And your mother does want your gown to remain clean."

With an exhale of disdain, I left the smiths' shops behind us, noting the furtive movements of villagers and hearing whispered comments about Carver's arrest.

"Always speaks his mind."

"Have to be careful with Ursa."

The incident had clearly rattled the populace. The mood affected me, too. I padded down the cobbled street to the intersection, turned onto Castle Way, and approached the butcher's shop.

"You wait here," I ordered the lieutenant as I tiptoed to the shop's door, knocked softly, and whispered, "Mrs. Carver, it's Griselda Hart."

I, of course, used my true name, refusing to use the surname Rella.

The stairs inside creaked, a crack opened in the shutters, and an eye peeked out. The crack snapped shut. I heard shuffling against floorboards, a bolt slide from its place, and then the door opened. A hand reached out and pulled me into the gloom of the closed shop. Mrs. Carver's red-rimmed eyes met me inside the door, and the eyes of the three Carver children peered down at me from the living quarters at the top of the stairs.

Mrs. Carver looked up at the three pairs of frightened eyes and said in a hushed voice, "Now, children, come away from the stairs, and let yer mother

298

have some words with our Miss Griselda."

The Carver children disappeared, and Mrs. Carver released my arm. "Have ya heard? They've taken Dale."

I nodded, tightness growing in my chest. "Why? What happened?"

She glanced nervously around the shop with its hanging meats, as if someone could be hiding behind some salted ham.

"When Lord Ursa returned from the summer tour, he took Hugh Heaten's milk cow and straightaway wanted to butcher the poor beast, which was wrong as it had many good years of milk in it. My Dale refused—said that Hugh should protest to the king, which Hugh did. But that lord is keeping a tight rein on the king, so it made not a bit of difference. Folks objected. And you know my Dale; he was the most persistent—and the loudest. So they took him—an' him jus' wantin' to do the right thing."

Here she stopped and bowed her head. Fresh tears rolled down her grief-stricken face. "I wish your father was still with us, Grizzy."

I reached out, held her, and found a trickle escaping down my own cheek. Finally, after a bit of snuffling together, we straightened once again.

Mrs. Carver wiped her eyes with the back of her hand. "I dunno what to do, Miss Grizzy. I'm scared, and I'm not the only one."

Helplessly, I searched for a reply but was saved by a knock on the door. Mrs. Carver crept to the shutters and peered out.

She pulled back as if struck. "Oh, here's fresh trouble now."

I walked to the window, peered out the crack, and coughed out a dismissive sound. Mrs. Carver started to shake.

I put a hand on her shoulder. "It's all right. It's just Lieutenant Jon. He is most aggravating, but he's not like Lord Ursa's toadies."

I surprised myself as I said it, because I realized it was true. I never wanted to see him again, yes, but apart from his humiliating me in our race, I saw no real harm in him. I hoped my perceptions were accurate as I opened the door to his impatient face.

"Miss Griselda, your mother is depending on me to deliver you to the castle without a sartorial mishap. Please come."

I wanted to argue with him, because it galled me to accede to him in anything. But Mrs. Carver snorted a soft laugh through her tears. "Yes, you don't want to muss your nice dress."

I scowled, not at Mrs. Carver, but at Jon, struggling to maintain his composure yet again. Oh, it vexed me that no one thought I could stay tidy.

Then the butcher's wife gave me a push from behind. "Go on, Grizzy. Maybe you can talk some sense into someone—perhaps the prince." The last said with a faint hope.

Lieutenant Jon stepped back so I could exit and nodded to Mrs. Carver. "I am sorry for your troubles, ma'am."

She closed the door behind me, and I heard the bolt slide into place.

When we left Carver's shop, I marched in silence for several strides before exploding, albeit quietly, with a string of questions directed at Lieutenant Jon, even though suspecting that he could not answer them.

"What is happening here? What right does Lord Ursa have to butcher Hugh Heaten's cow—especially after His Highness returned it before the tour? And what right does Lord Ursa have to arrest Dale Carver for having an opinion?"

As a couple of unfamiliar guards approached us, Lieutenant Jon glared at me, raised a hand, and made a sharp cutting motion across his throat. "Not now."

My familiar frustration with him threatened, but noting the set of his jaw, I knew that arguing would be futile. Besides, the guards appeared to be watching for infractions, perhaps like Mr. Carver's, I surmised. As the guards passed us, I received a glare and Jon a curt nod. So we strode in silence toward the castle gates, that is Lieutenant Jon strode while I jogged to match his pace. Pairs of soldiers wove through the streets as if on patrol. They left us in peace or nodded a wordless greeting.

We continued toward the King's Gate and were halfway past the village green, debris from the most recent market day littering the grass. No one was close, so I tried again, still whispering strongly.

"Lieutenant, what is happening? This is all wrong. Lord Ursa knows the law. How can he allow it?"

We continued in silence for a moment, and I was afraid that he would refuse to answer. But then he spoke in a low voice.

"In short, sides have been taken. There are those like Jason Gutcher and Malacus, who support Lord Ursa, and those like Hugh Heaten and Dale Carver, who support your father."

I stopped in my tracks, suddenly breathless.

Then I gasped out, "But my father is dead."

Compassion filled his eyes as he spoke. "Yes, but the way he governed is remembered, and that has created tension with Lord Ursa, hence his overreaction to the butcher's dissent."

"Carver had good cause," I fumed. "Ursa's counsel is sheep's dung."

Lieutenant Jon lowered his voice even more. "Lord Ursa, Miss Griselda."

I raised my voice. "Call him what you want. He's wrong."

Lieutenant Jon looked quickly around to see if I'd been overheard, grabbed my arm, and squeezed so hard that I tried to pull away.

He drew me close and bent to my ear. "Griselda, this is no longer your father's kingdom, and you of all people must be cautious."

I jerked my arm from his grasp and noticed the guards at the King's Gate watching us. "Me of all people. Why?"

Lieutenant Jon didn't answer immediately. He just looked at me and frowned. Finally, he pursed his lips and spoke. "You are your father's daughter, and this trouble involves your father."

I raised my hands, palms up, and repeated. "But my father is dead."

Lieutenant Jon looked at me with an expression I knew all too well from my father—secrets. My face grew hard. "Lieutenant, if you are keeping something from me, tell me now, especially if it concerns my father."

His jaw muscles moved as he looked at me. Then he tilted his head toward the gate. "The feast has begun, and you are missed."

He walked toward the drawbridge. At first, I remained stationary, hoping that he would relent, return, and talk to me. But he continued to the gate.

Cursing that stubborn, secretive groom-courier-lieutenant, I caught up in a few quick jogs and grabbed his arm, forcing him to stop.

"I need answers."

He turned, opened his mouth—

And we both froze.

A shrill wail, filling the air and seeming to emanate from the ground itself, started weakly, rose in intensity, and finally shrieked through my bones, my blood, and my very breath. Lieutenant Jon's still opened mouth and his round, shocked eyes confirmed that he felt the same. Guards at the gate left their posts, swords drawn, knees buckling, and eyes glazed with terror. Lieutenant Jon's sword remained sheathed, but his head swiveled about, his eyes searching. As the howl continued, a biting wind whistled around the walls, tumbling clouds formed overhead, and icy darts of rain pierced my face. A crack of lightning split the southern sky past the King's Forest, and after a few heartbeats' wait, thunder rumbled from the south.

The lamentation continued and grew in strength until I clapped my hands over my ears and curled my head into my chest. Dust from the road swirled up into my face, making it hard to breathe. The sound screamed on and on, and I feared that it would never end. Finally, it subsided bit, by bit, by bit, and stopped. The subsequent silence was deafening. A sense of destruction hung in the air.

To my surprise—and embarrassment—I found

myself with my face buried in Lieutenant Jon's chest with his arm wrapped around my back. I pulled back, and his arm slipped off. To avoid awkwardness, I looked away only to see the guards recovering from various reactions to the tempest: two kneeling on the ground, one stirring from lying face down on the drawbridge, and one retching into the dry moat.

I forced myself to look back at Lieutenant Jon and found him staring into the distance, an expression of horror on his face. I touched his shoulder cautiously. He remained motionless.

Then his mouth moved like a talking statue. "That was the sound of land dying."

The image of the Dead Castle filled my mind, and I knew in my bones, my blood, and my breath—in all that made me who I am—that he spoke the truth.

A moment later my escort blinked and inhaled gravely, his narrowing eyes focused on the south. "This means fairies have died."

A wave a horror washed from my heart to my extremities at his declaration. But I did not doubt him.

"Can anything be done?" I asked, feeling something akin to the helplessness I'd felt about my father's death.

The lieutenant shook his head. "The deed has been done."

"Who would do such a thing?" I asked but suspected that I knew.

Lieutenant Jon's face looked grim. "Someone who will now reek to high heavens and repel the presence of fairies forever."

"How do you know all this?" I asked as the tempestuous sky roiled above.

He ignored my question, touched my elbow, and inclined his head toward the gate, and I wondered more and more about this groom-courier-lieutenant.

With reluctance, I moved forward. It seemed frivolous to attend a feast after something of such magnitude had happened—at least if my escort was correct. However, it also occurred to me that, if fairies were in danger, my betrothal to the prince was even more imperative—just like my father had envisioned—both for Isabella's and my protection and perhaps for the fairies, too.

As we reached the drawbridge, my focus landed on the arched inscription chiseled above the entrance.

Peace and prosperity fill the land when governed by the true king's hand.

With all that was happening, it seemed that the words mocked me as the recovering guards waved us over the drawbridge. We passed the King's Gate and hurried through the courtyard, where grooms tried to calm the horses, servants cleaned up the contents from spilled carts, and scullery maids ran into the great hall with piles of rags. Upon entry into the hall, we saw signs of disruption: overturned benches, spilled goblets of wine, and whole platters of roast meat broken and splattered across the floor. Everyone cast their eyes to the tall, slender windows of colored glass through which light and shadows still shifted.

Guests milled about, righting benches and chairs, brushing off garments, and looking disoriented. I glanced down at my own gown in relief—still tidy—and then realized the probable reason for my neatness. My escort had kept me upright during the shrieking wind, or I'd have had another case of ground in dirt at my knees. As I battled between appreciation and resentment, hesitant murmuring began as a hum and grew to an anxious buzz. Servants scurried about cleaning up spilled bowls and platters and resupplying food and wine.

Lieutenant Jon shook his head as he scanned the disarray, and then he looked at me, his eyes roving over my face. He lifted his hand close to the side of my head. "May I?" he asked. "You have dust."

I slapped at my cheeks, hoping not to need his help.

He grimaced dubiously, letting me know I had failed.

I huffed out a sharp exhale. "Oh, very well."

He gently wiped several spots on my face and stroked loose strands of hair into place. "I did tell your mother I'd see you delivered clean."

This earned him the most overdone eye roll I could muster.

He responded with a slight half smile, pointed to where Mother and Isabella sat on the side with some wealthy merchants, gave me a nod of good-bye, and went to stand close to the door near Hammond.

At the high table, raised on a wide dais and framed with a backdrop of tapestries, sat the king with his queen, Prince Charmain, Lord Ursa, and Lord Norlan and his wife with their daughter Nareen. The dark-eyed, dark-haired beauty sat side by side with the prince, clinging to his arm in apparent fright. They all seemed rattled by the recent event but trying to gather themselves.

The king, robed in purple, crowned with gold, and wearing a frown, sat looking down at his hands. Lord

Ursa, in his black robe trimmed with a thin border of silver fur, stood up, whispered in his ear, and gestured that the king should stand and speak. As the lord scanned the bewildered guests, he looked in my direction and scowled. Even across the room I felt the weight of his displeasure.

Near the king, the prince stood up, detaching himself from Nareen's clutches. He was garmented in purple-and-red finery, his blond curls touching his shoulders and a crown weighting his brow. I hardly recognized him in such grandeur. He bent close and listened to Lord Ursa's words. When the lord completed his communication, the king waved him off and rose. The buzz in the great hall abated.

His Majesty spread his arms wide, forced a grin onto his face, and spoke jovially. "An unsettling bit of weather to be sure, but be of good cheer for it is now past, and we may once again celebrate the victorious return of our son and heir. We most gladly embrace the homecoming of His Royal Highness Prince Charmain."

Guests gathered their wits, cheered, and raised their goblets if they could find them. And though I joined in the cheer, I wondered at how the king could refer to the prince's return as victorious. All he had done was troll the noble families for a bride.

As Prince Charmain stood enjoying the praise from his subjects, I felt a resurgence of uncertainty. In the past, I had always been able to tell the prince what to do, but he'd been under the influence of Lord Ursa for months, and his letters made it clear that my influence was dwindling. According to the king's letter, the prince and I were to be betrothed, but I wondered if he would be a stranger to me.

And furthermore, why was Nareen seated next to him? Was it a courtesy due to her father's nobility? Or was Jason right? Had Lord Ursa interfered with my friend's betrothal plans?

The king, who stood beaming next to his son, caught sight of me and grinned broadly across the hall. I curtsied in response. The king laughed and waved, causing the prince to look my direction.

His face lit up with a smile. "Grizzy."

He left the king directly, worked his way around the table, and strode across the tile floor, his arms outstretched, his grin from ear to ear. With a bear hug embrace, he discarded the customary bow and curtsy routine demanded by the situation, generating a warm feeling in my heart that stretched across my face. Here was my best friend again, not the stranger who had written those awful letters.

With an arch look, I teased. "Well, if it isn't Prince Charming."

I hoped my voice sounded casual, because my heart pounded like a blacksmith's hammer.

The prince rolled his eyes. "You're the only one who can get away with calling me that. How are you?"

It was my old friend back again, in spite of his purple-and-red finery and all those horrid missives. Once again certain I could talk him into anything, I wished to start right away—with Mr. Carver.

"I have been fine, but we need to talk."

He threw up his hands. "Yes, yes, I know I'm due for a long lecture, and I'm prepared to hear it."

This was what I wanted to hear, so I began. "First of all, it started with Heaten's cow—"

He held up his hand. "But first, we feast."

With desperate hope that I wasn't pushing too far, I grabbed his arm. "No, Your Highness."

My formal address got his attention right away, his grin replaced with surprise and then solemnity.

"Dale Carver has been arrested."

His countenance registered shock. "No."

"Yes, just because he wouldn't butcher Heaten's milk cow—and spoke out about it. So Ursa had Carver seized."

To my relief, his face now morphed to anger. "I ordered that cow returned."

I could see that while part of the prince's concern was about justice, part of it was simply about being defied. I decided not to quibble about motives at the moment.

"Yes, now pray have the butcher released."

With a glare at Lord Ursa, who watched us stonily from the dais, my friend gestured to Hammond, stationed near the door.

When the guard reached us, the prince ordered curtly, "Release Dale Carver at once. I want to see that he has been set free."

With a furtive glance toward the ermine-trimmed lord, Hammond bowed and departed to obey his liege.

His task done, the tension drained from Charmain's face, and he peered hopefully at me. "And we feast?"

As I nodded, he took my hand, started toward the king's table, and stopped with a snort of disgust. I glanced up into his scowling face.

He turned to me, looking embarrassed. "Oh, I forgot. You were meant to sit with me, Grizzy, but Lord Ursa has seated Nareen in your place."

I caught Lord Ursa's eye, and the corner of his

mouth twitched upward. Smug self-satisfaction played across his features.

To avoid showing how annoyed I was, I quickly turned to Prince Charmain, squeezed his hand, and smiled. "Pray do not concern yourself. I will find a place with Mother and Isabella."

He hung his head for a second and then brightened. "One thing is certain; after Father announces our betrothal tonight, we will never have this problem again."

A second after speaking, he looked flushed, and I felt a corresponding warming in my own cheeks. He ducked his head and wended his way through servants and performers as he returned to the high table while I found Mother and Isabella and squeezed in between them.

Mother, watching as the prince reseated himself next to Lord Norlan's daughter, hissed in my ear. "Why is that Nareen sitting next to His Highness?"

I sighed. "That is Lord Ursa's doing. I assure you, Charmain is quite annoyed."

With her eyes filling with suspicion, she leveled them at the powerful lord. "He always thwarted your father as well."

Surprised at Mother's admission, I realized that since she no longer had Father to talk to, she was choosing to divulge her concerns to me. I also realized that it must have been very hard for Mother to watch her husband stand up to such a formidable opponent year after year. Now, she was watching him antagonize me.

While jugglers performed, Isabella bumped my elbow. "Grizzy, what did you make of that frightful screaming?"

I didn't see any reason to evade the question, so I answered honestly—but in a whisper. "It was land dying."

Both Isabella and Mother gasped. Mother grabbed my arm and glanced at those seated nearby. "Griselda, keep your fanciful imaginings to yourself."

Tired of always being the odd one, I shifted the blame. "Lieutenant Jon said it, not me."

Mother harrumphed. "This has been a disagreeable day, but I trust that the evening will improve."

Mother turned to face me, grasped my hands, and pressed them between her own. She forced a determined smile onto her face and kissed each of my cheeks.

She whispered, "This will be a great moment. Your father would be so happy."

This thought settled, and I enjoyed the pleasure it would give to both my mother and somehow to my late father.

My gratification was further heightened when Hammond escorted Mr. Carver to the door, fulfilling the prince's command to release him. The butcher caught my eye, waved, and gave a little bow in my direction. After waiting a short time, His Highness noticed, and the former prisoner gave the scion a deep bow, which Prince Charmain acknowledged with a lift of his ornate goblet. At this, Mr. Carver departed, allowing me to enjoy the feast without that nagging concern.

With Mother beaming and Isabella casting happy glances my way, minstrels began to play from the gallery and the feast resumed. There was course after course: pork and cheese tart, baked shrimps, chicken and berry pie, beef and onions, eel and spinach tart, and a spectacular stuffed peacock carefully redressed with all its feathers and plumage. Wine and ale flowed freely as jugglers, minstrels, jesters, and acrobats kept us entertained. One of the younger acrobats did a somersault in the air and landed in front of me.

I clapped, but he winked. "Want to try it, Grizzy?"

I grinned, remembering the time I'd talked him into teaching me, but Mother glared at him and he tumbled away.

She bent to my ear. "Griselda, do not encourage that insolence. You are to marry the prince."

As the feasting continued with cheeses, fruits, custards, and puddings, my favorites being fig and almond, rose petal, and sweet cherry puddings, the musicians began a lively tune from the minstrels' gallery.

The prince, pulling himself away from a grasping Nareen, crossed the open floor with all the guests watching and held out his hand to me. "Grizzy, may I have this dance?"

Accompanied by lutes, horns, recorders, and drums, Prince Charmain and I began to dance, and I noticed that he wasn't as awkward as I remembered. Perhaps his time on tour had done him good. Soon ladies in colorful gowns and men in long robes joined us on the dance floor. The fires blazing in the hearths and flickering torchlight created shadows on the walls as the dancers moved.

Watching the scene, the queen sat at the high table attended by her ladies-in-waiting, like the golden center of a flower surrounded by petals. They looked like a garden of finery: the gold, the jewels, the rich fabric, and the delicately embroidered details—many stitched by my mother. When my partner and I danced near the king and queen, the scent of roses wafted from them, competing with the ever-present smell of roasted meats and savory spices.

The queen nodded and smiled. The king beckoned to us. "Miss Griselda, it pleases me to see you once again. You and your mischief are missed about the castle. That will have to change."

The king winked at his son and waved us back to the dance floor, which I was only too pleased to do. Lord Ursa, at the king's side, looked at me as if I were garbage he'd like to throw out.

The prince led me back among the dancers and leaned to my ear. "Father is most pleased about our betrothal."

I felt relief. As his betrothed, and even more so as his wife, I could give him the help that he needed to stand up to Lord Ursa, to govern more like my father would have done, and eventually to change the fairy-sight law, but in the meantime, I could enjoy the festivities. What could possibly go wrong?

Chapter 21

Fading Wishes

And so…

We chatted; we danced; we reminisced about old times. Everything was perfect.

And then…

She arrived.

My prince stopped dancing in mid-stride, landed on my foot, and froze like a statue staring at her as she stood framed in the arched doorway. Then, without another glance in my direction, he drifted toward her like a puppet on a string.

She was, of course, Cynthia.

On her head she wore her jeweled tiara. On her feet she wore *my* slippers. They sparkled like stars, and my heart burned to see my father's precious gift on that selfish little thief.

Cynthia's dress was new to me, its cloth threaded with gold and silver, all beset with jewels. As she moved, the folds of fabric shimmered. The enchanting effect reminded me of the fairy sparkles created when Arianna had touched my fairy-blessed slippers. That's when I knew. The dress was fairy made. And recalling the shrieking winds of just a short time before, I suspected that somehow Cynthia's appearance was connected with it. None of that was apparent to the assembled guests or the prince. Nor was the fact that my stepsister exuded a pungent smell like rotten eggs mixed with manure. I recalled Lieutenant Jon's recent words, "Someone who will now reek to high heavens," and questioned again how he knew.

The stench was so powerful that I crinkled my nose in offense and wondered that no one else had the same reaction.

Music stopped and the crowded room hushed as the prince approached the new arrival. He bowed, spoke, and held out his hand. Cynthia placed her hand in his and accompanied him to the dance floor. All eyes followed the couple as a general murmur of whispering spread throughout the great hall.

I overheard two women gossiping next to me. "Have you even seen such an enchanting beauty?"

As I battled resentment over my stepsister's celebrated attractiveness, Isabella came up behind me and tapped my shoulder. "Grizzy, you have to see this."

I ignored Isabella, my eyes following Cynthia and the prince. My heart quickened with concern as Cynthia glanced at me with triumph.

Isabella grabbed my arm and gave it a little shake. "You really have to see this."

Eyes still on the dancing pair, I responded to my sister. "I can see just fine, Izzy."

Isabella, her nose crinkled in distaste like mine, pulled at my arm. "No, it is outside, Cynthia's carriage."

I yanked my arm from my sister. "The manor no longer has a carriage."

Isabella, with assertiveness foreign to her, linked her arm with mine and pulled me away from the dance floor. Rather than make a scene, I gave in. We left the great hall and made our way to the courtyard, where Isabella pointed at a golden carriage.

"I had just come out for some fresh air when Cynthia arrived in this odd, round carriage. Where did she get it? And the footman, coachman, and horses?"

Mystified, I stared for a minute at the carriage and my understanding opened. With horror I realized, the carriage wasn't gold; it was orange. And it wasn't a carriage; it was the pumpkin Cynthia had gathered and hollowed out yesterday.

"It's not really a carriage, Izzy. It's a pumpkin."

Isabella screwed her face up in confusion and then opened her eyes wide with dawning realization.

Anger, but also fear roiled inside me. She had clearly caught a fairy, probably more than one, and forced them to create unnatural things: a carriage, lavish clothes, and who knew what else. And where did she get those six beautiful, mouse-colored, dapple-gray horses? And what of the coachman? Was I mistaken or did his shaggy hair look oddly like Rags' floppy ears? And the footman's face, did his beard and whiskers remind me of Mr. Tatters? I shook my head to clear my thoughts. Surely, my imagination was getting the better of me.

In my shaky judgment, Cynthia's only natural items were her tiara and my slippers. And then I caught my breath. My slippers weren't natural either. They had the power to influence people. No wonder the weak-minded prince had fallen so directly under her spell. What a disaster.

My slippers were a fairy gift with power to influence, to help the wearer to give a nudge in a helpful direction. But now Cynthia, a person with selfish intent, wore them, and she wielded their power. And based on the margin writing in one of her books— fairy-blessed items grant the bearer influence—she knew it.

Isabella squeezed my arm, interrupting my thoughts. "Grizzy, what has Cynthia done?"

I didn't answer but looked up at the cloudy sky. A chill wind blew from the south. I pulled Isabella with me as I headed back to the great hall. Everything was out of joint: the prince, the kingdom, even the heavens above.

Reentering the great hall, I watched with a sinking heart as my prince danced with my stepsister. His face held a spellbound look, not the slack-jawed manifestation of admiration that usually followed Cynthia, but a bewitched expression.

I glimpsed my slippers peeking out from under the hem of Cynthia's dress and my insides boiled. Father had entrusted me with those slippers to use to right a wrong in the kingdom, and here was Cynthia using that precious influence to ensnare the prince—my prince. I wanted to tear across the dance floor, rip the shoes from her feet, and reclaim my father's final gift. But I would only appear to be a jealous competitor for the prince's attention. And to my humiliation, I realized that, at the moment, it was true.

As they moved across the floor, Cynthia spoke and the prince leaned toward her and listened. Abruptly, he stopped dancing with a look of shock on his face. The music continued. He leaned close, continued to listen, and his brow furrowed into a frown.

When Cynthia finished speaking, they both looked

my way. The prince said something to Cynthia and then strode toward me with his face stony, his eyes angry. Cynthia wore a satisfied smirk.

Confused about what to expect when he reached me, I smiled to lighten the mood. "Greetings, Prince Charming, are you enjoying the revelry?"

But there was no answering smile from him. He stared at me coldly. "You may address me as Your Highness."

His words felt like a knife in my chest. I gave a slow curtsy to my spellbound prince. "As you wish, Your Highness."

He narrowed his eyes and spoke accusingly. "How could you, Griselda?"

My recent altercation with Cynthia came to mind. "I beg your pardon."

The prince almost spit out his next words. "Cynthia told me of your cruelty: squandering her father's wealth, forcing her to be a servant in her own home, and making sport with her name."

My chin dropped with shock as he continued.

"She said you made her sit in the fireplace cinders and taunted her saying 'Cinder Rella.' She says you refused to allow her to join you for this feast and refused to introduce her to my acquaintance."

The influence of my slippers appeared to be complete. I could see no other reason for his behavior. Cynthia had turned my prince against me, and though the king would still announce our betrothal later this evening, our relationship felt like shattered glass.

Knowing it was futile, I still sought to defend myself. "There is more to the story, Your Highness."

He shook his head. "I thought I knew you better

than that, but I guess people change."

I guess they do, I thought and watched the prince spin away and march off to rejoin Cynthia, who gazed at me with a venomous smile.

The prince and Cynthia began once again to weave among the dancers with Cynthia talking enthusiastically to the prince. My enthralled prince just stared unblinking into her eyes and nodded occasionally. Then they stopped dancing and walked toward the dais. The prince left Cynthia, approached the king, and exchanged a few words. The king rose, the music stopped, and the assembled guests turned to their monarch.

He winked at me with a grin. "Ladies and gentlemen and honored guests, I bid you now to give ear to His Royal Highness Prince Charmain, who has asked to make a special announcement himself."

The king nodded smilingly to me and gestured to his son, who stepped forward and spread his arms, lifting them slightly.

His eyes locked on Cynthia. "My father has given me the great joy of announcing my engagement to the finest of women, Lady Cynthia Rella."

He held out his hand. Cynthia walked forward, stepped up on the dais, and took his hand. She turned to face the assembled guests and beamed triumphantly.

Dizziness, nausea, and faintness enveloped my body. I couldn't breathe. The air felt thick, like water. All movement and sound around me seemed to slow.

Behind the prince and Cynthia, the king's eyes and mouth rounded with surprise. He glanced at me, looked down at the floor, and shook his head violently. He leaned toward his son, but Lord Ursa intercepted him.

The lord put one hand on the king's shoulder, grasped his hand, and shook it vigorously with an accompanying smile. The king's posture sagged; he dropped onto his throne and slumped with a visible sigh.

Lord Ursa now joined the prince and Cynthia and engaged them in conversation, all of them apparently unaware of Cynthia's putrid fragrance. As a crowd of people offering congratulations surrounded the couple, I left the dance area, moved to the edge of the room, and leaned against a wall. The people around me seemed unreal, the sounds of music and conversation muted.

The only time I'd felt worse than right now was when my father had died. That was the uncontested worst moment of my life; but this betrayal by my best friend, my fiancé, it was a bitter drink. Regarding Cynthia, I wasn't surprised. She had confirmed my opinion of her most spectacularly.

Isabella appeared at my side and pulled at my sleeve. "Grizzy, look at Cynthia."

I jerked angrily away from her. Was it possible that she didn't realize what Cynthia had just done to me? She knew that I was to have been the prince's bride.

"Isabella, what has gotten into you this evening— always grabbing me? I hardly wish to look at our stepsister."

My persistent sister bent to my ear. "Not Cynthia, her clothes. They're fading."

In response to Isabella's claim, I moved away from the wall to get a better look at Cynthia. Isabella was right. A faint outline of Cynthia's undergarments was beginning to show through her gown.

Isabella clutched my arm and rested her chin on my shoulder. "Why do you think it's happening?"

"I don't know, unless..." I thought about the disappearing diamonds, both Cynthia's and Mr. Dankman's. "Maybe wishes don't last—at least not always."

"Well, whatever Cynthia did isn't lasting." Isabella said. "So you'd better do something."

Not inclined to help Cynthia in any way, I chuckled. "You mean something other than watch and laugh?"

Isabella, my newly opinionated little sister, gave me a stern shake and whispered, "And show evidence of fairies? Then it may come out that we can see fairies."

I sighed. Isabella was right. I had to warn Cynthia. And so, though it was the last thing I wanted to do, I wove my way through the crowd to the newly engaged couple. Cynthia reeked so pungently that I held my breath, still wondering why others did not recoil from her stench. What else had Jon said? The smell would, "repel the presence of fairies forever." Perhaps those with fairy sight could also have fairy smell. That might explain it.

Finally, standing before them, I spoke with stiff formality. "Your Highness, Lady Cynthia, may I offer you my best wishes?"

They both nodded down to me as if I were nothing more than a common villager—which, of course, I was and quite proudly. I wished I could just leave Cynthia to the fate of facing the world in her undergarments but protecting the fairy knowledge came first.

I ground out my request with forced courtesy. "If I

may, I would like to speak briefly with Lady Cynthia."

Cynthia smiled to Prince Charmain, and as she moved in my direction, the prince called out, "Griselda, I command you to behave yourself."

I wanted to grab his nose and twist it right off his face, but I just curtsied and turned to Cynthia. She and I took a few steps away from the prince.

I confronted her immediately. "Cynthia, I know fairies made your clothes. They're beginning to fade."

Cynthia didn't appear to hear the important part of my message, because she replied, "You have been instructed to address me as Lady Cynthia. Do so."

Though it was like my stepsister to be conceited, it was not like her to be dense. I swallowed my annoyance, as well as my gag reflex from her stench, and tried again.

"Lady Cynthia, your dress is fading. It will soon disappear just like your diamonds."

Cynthia sniffed. "You refer to the diamonds that you stole from me."

I exhaled in exasperation. "Think whatever you want, but soon you will be on display in your undergarments."

Cynthia stretched up even taller than before. "Griselda, I understand your jealousy, but it does not become you. Please excuse me. I must return to my betrothed."

Cynthia turned. I grabbed her elbow, and she glared at me ice cold.

I dropped my hand. "Just watch your skirt, Lady Cynthia. Soon you will see that I have spoken the truth."

Cynthia rejoined the prince and, at first, appeared

determined to ignore my advice. Then I saw her glance down. She blinked. She stared. She pinched some fabric in her fingers, lifted, and spread it out very slightly. Gasping, she thrust herself away from the prince. He followed. Cynthia turned toward the door, broke into a sprint, and hurtled through the great hall, dodging guests and ignoring calls from the prince and exclamations of dancers. She stumbled and one of my slippers came off her feet. She left it and fled through the doors, leaving several dried rose petals in her wake.

The prince stared after her helplessly and then strode across the floor, stopping in front of me.

"What did you say to her, Griselda?"

"I, uh, told her that her dress was, uh—special."

The prince's expression grew befuddled. "Grizzy, what's happening. I feel like I'm coming out of a fog."

"As to that, Your Highness, I cannot say, but I suggest that you follow your betrothed. She looked rather upset."

His face looked blank. "My…Oh…"

I could see confusion spreading over his features, but I returned his original blank stare and offered no help. How could I? His fate was sealed when he made that announcement.

After staring helplessly at me for a moment, Prince Charmain ambled away, ignoring guests who peppered him with questions, picked up the slipper, and followed his fiancée.

At this point, being well after midnight, the festivities broke up. Servants scurried about removing platters of food, cleaning tables, and serving a last goblet of ale to those unwilling to depart just yet. The murmur of conversation rose and fell as attendees gossiped about their scion's betrothal to the beautiful Lady Cynthia and her inexplicable departure. The king, queen, and Lord Ursa appeared to be placating Lord Norlan, his lady, and his daughter, Nareen.

Lieutenant Jon appeared out of the crowd. He shepherded Mother, Isabella, and me from the great hall to our wagon and offered to escort us home. To my dismay, Mother readily agreed. He walked next to our conveyance with a lantern as we rolled toward Hart Cottage with me sitting up front holding the reins.

I felt numb; the prince was to marry Cynthia. Mother and Isabella kept respectfully quiet regarding my humiliation. My prince had abandoned me and taken up with my stepsister. I knew it wasn't entirely his fault, but really…If he hadn't been so completely weak-minded, it wouldn't have been so easy for Cynthia to control him.

It was possible that Lieutenant Jon also knew of my failed engagement to the prince, and I made an effort to avoid looking at him as he walked along the wagon's side, lantern swinging to light our way.

After our passage through the West Gate, Mother made a request. "Griselda, give the reins to Lieutenant Jon."

He reached a hand to me in obedience to my mother, and I reluctantly gave him the reins. He passed me the lantern and vaulted into the seat beside me. As we pulled away from the village noises, the clop, clop of the horses' hooves on the road, the crunch of the wheels rolling on the pavers, and the occasional lowing of a cow broke the silence. Lieutenant Jon remained quiet with the rest of us.

I didn't want to talk with him, but a question about

the shrieking wind compelled me to whisper, "Why would fairies die?"

He turned and looked at me searchingly. "The fulfillment of a wish—or wishes—drained the life from them—and therefore from the land."

As my eyes widened, he turned his attention to the road again.

We creaked along, and Isabella, who looked like she was falling asleep to the rock of the wagon, grunted awake when the wheels hit a bump. She sat up, straight and wide-awake.

She pointed. "What was that?"

I glanced about. I had seen it, too, a streak of something racing across the road. Lieutenant Jon pulled on the reins and stopped the wagon. Between the remains of corn stalks, two reflecting eyes shone. The eyes moved forward and a cat that looked just like Mr. Tatters appeared. He stared at us for a couple of seconds and then dashed down the road toward Hart Cottage.

Mother reached for the lantern, held it high, and stared after the animal. "Did that look like our cat, the one we left at the manor?"

I exchanged a look with Isabella and knew we were both thinking about Cynthia's carriage, horses, and attendants. And if it was Mr. Tatters, inexplicably so, I was relieved that he was unharmed. With my eyes scanning the harvested fields on either side of the road, I wondered if my stepsister was hiding in the darkness, wearing nothing but a slowly fading gown but did not see anything.

Mother returned the lantern to me, adjusted her seating, and smoothed her skirt. "There is some mischief about. We best make haste."

Lieutenant Jon looked from Isabella to me, eyes questioning, but said nothing. He shook the reins and the wagon bumped forward, following the mysterious cat.

After a few more minutes on Castle Road, we turned the wagon onto Hart Cottage Lane, and I, leaving Mother to thank Lieutenant Jon, left the lantern on the seat and leaped down. The glow from the windows of Hart Cottage filled me with warmth. I was home. The house looked merry, expecting our arrival.

As I approached my welcoming home, a happy surprise greeted me. Rags came barking and bounding out to meet us. He leaped up on his hind legs, placed his front paws on my shoulder, and licked my face.

Mother came up behind and pushed Rags down. "Griselda, when will you learn to control that beast?" Then she stopped abruptly and confusion crossed her face. "And how did he come to be here?"

Next, the door to the kitchen opened, spilling light into the evening, and Sarah's frame filled the door.

She waved a stirring spoon in her hand. "Rags, you miserable cur. Leave the family be."

Then she bustled out to greet us. As Abel and Abigail Garner peered from the doorway, I wondered, what was Sarah doing here?

Chapter 22

Sarah's Story

Sarah corralled us all, including a surprised Lieutenant Jon, carrying the lantern, and hustled us into the house.

"C'mon in, c'mon in the lot of you, out of this chill. Oh, the tale I have to tell."

She herded the puzzled group of us, along with a meowing Mr. Tatters, into the kitchen and shut the door on the night. The kitchen blazed a welcome with a cauldron of fragrant stew simmering in the fireplace and the smiles of Abel and Abigail Garner, who submitted good-naturedly to Sarah's bossiness. Hannah and Rebecca from the manor stood timidly to the side.

Mother looked at Hannah and Rebecca and then to Sarah before finding her voice. "Sarah, girls, what do you mean by abandoning your duties at the manor?"

The girls remained mute, but Sarah, who never raised her voice to Mother, put her fists on her hips and leaned forward. "I beg yer pardon, ma'am, but running for my very life, if you please."

Mother tutted. "What is this foolishness?"

I remembered the mournful wail from earlier in the evening and wondered if it was connected to Sarah's story.

She dropped her hands and stretched them out to

her sides. "Ag'in, I beg yer pardon and yer patience, ma'am, for I have seen doings the like of which ya'd never wish to see. But gather 'round and I'll tell ya the tale of how we came to be here just mere moments before yerselves."

We all pulled up benches, stools, and empty barrels and gathered around the kitchen worktable in deference to Sarah's demand for an audience. Mr. Tatters made himself comfortable near the fireplace. I pulled a barrel up to the table's side, plopped myself down, and leaned forward on the table, resting on my elbows, eager to hear Sarah's report. Seeing Isabella struggling, I dragged her stool up to the table next to me. Lieutenant Jon placed a bench across from me and handed my mother to the seat. The Garners sat at the end of the table while Hannah and Rebecca stood behind them. Sarah presided over our progress and peered at each of our faces to ensure that we were duly impressed. She remained standing and planted herself at one end of the table, canopied overhead by dried herbs hanging from the rafters.

Mother, exhausted from the disappointing turn of the evening's events and disturbed to find everything amiss, looked impatiently at Sarah. "And now, Sarah, pray acquaint us with the reason that we find you, Hannah, and Rebecca here."

She nodded to Mother. "Yes, ma'am."

Sarah placed her hands on the table, leaned forward, and took a deep breath.

"After yer departure—" Sarah gestured to Mother, Isabella, and me. "I determined to keep an eye on that sneaky lady, as promised."

Mother looked puzzled, then suspicious. "As

promised?"

Sarah looked sheepish and strayed a glance in my direction. Mother caught the look. "What trouble have you two wrought?"

The sheepish expression dropped from Sarah's face to be replaced with indignation. "What trouble have we wrought? You mean what trouble has that Cynthia conjured?"

Mother sighed and wearily motioned for Sarah to continue.

Sarah scanned all of us around the table, making sure we were attending.

"Cynthia went to her bedchamber and spent some time making lots of noises. It sounded like moving things about. Next, she went to the rose garden with a little net and cage. She carried on with swinging that net about, grabbing at nothing, and putting nothing in the cage. I thought she'd gone quite mad."

Isabella and I exchanged a look, which Lieutenant Jon caught, but we said nothing. Everyone else remained with eyes fixed on Sarah, who hadn't noticed our glances.

Mr. Tatters stretched in front of the hearth, and the herb-fragranced stew simmered in the cauldron as Sarah took up her tale again.

"Well, that conniving lady carried the empty birdcage back to her chambers and was quiet for a spell. I carried on with some of my tasks, all the while listening for sounds of activity, wondering what she was up to. Finally, I looked out the parlor window and here comes that Lady Cynthia strutting down the front stairs still wearing her tiara, but dressed in a traveling cloak under which just her undergarments peeked out."

At our incredulous expressions, she threw up her hands. "That's what I mean—no gown—just her undergarments under the cloak. And to add to the oddness, she was carrying that empty birdcage. She put it on the front drive and proceeded to go up and down the stairs bringing the strangest collection of cages, baskets, vases of fresh cut roses, and rope and placing it all on the drive in front of the manor.

"Well, I couldn't make sense of what she was doing, so I went out and addressed her. 'Lady Cynthia,' I said, 'don' ya be doin' all this work. May I assist ya?' "

I couldn't imagine Sarah having this exchange with Cynthia; so curtailing a snort, I raised my eyebrows in disbelief. Sarah caught my look, and her shoulders sagged, but only slightly.

"Oh, very well, truth be told. I said, 'What the devil are you on about—and wearing Miss Griselda's slippers, too?' Because she was, Miss Griselda, she was wearing those slippers from your father."

I sighed. "I know, Sarah. Please continue."

With a huff, Sarah slammed her hand on the table. "Well, that little vixen said the slippers were hers, and that she was simply doing some housecleaning."

My mother harrumphed, which surprised me, because Mother always tried to be nice to Cynthia.

Sarah heard Mother's expression and joined in promptly. "My thoughts exactly, ma'am. I knew Lady Cynthia wasn't inclined to do any such thing, so I grew more suspicious, and though I let her be, I made it my business to watch her, and this is what I saw."

Sarah paused for a moment and looked into our faces, clearly enjoying our enrapt attention. In the background, the stew bubbled out of the cauldron and sizzled as it spilled into the fire, but I, along with everyone else, ignored it. We waited for Sarah to resume.

"After all her to-ing and fro-ing, Lady Cynthia had the oddest collection lined up in the drive: one empty birdcage, two vases of roses, one cage with six gray mice, one large basket with a strap and lid that shook occasionally as if something were trying to escape, and a giant orange pumpkin."

Mother, face clouded with doubt, said, "A pumpkin?"

Sarah looked annoyed at the interruption. "I know, ma'am, but all I can tell ya is what I saw, and it was a pumpkin I tell ya—with the insides all hollowed out, too."

Mother, with a longsuffering sigh, gestured for Sarah to go on, which she did.

"Then I heard barking coming from the side of the manor and into view comes that schemer pulling Rags by a rope."

Now, I slammed both of my hands on the table. "What?"

Sarah looked apologetic. "Yes, I know, miss, but I felt something a might strange was a foot, and I was determined to see what that little minx was about. I didn't think no harm would come to Rags. Honestly, miss."

We heard a bark and scratching at the kitchen door. Rags must have heard his name.

I nodded to Sarah. "Rags seems fine. Please go on."

Sarah put her hand to heart, followed by the other

one. "Oh, but your precious pet was not fine, miss."

"Sarah," Mother said wearily, "your story. Please make haste, the night passes."

"Yes, ma'am. Well, like I was sayin'. She had Rags, and she tied him to the hitching post and walked to the empty cage."

At this point, Sarah stopped and looked at each one of us around the table. She colored a bit and seemed smaller, her bluster leaving her. She shifted her weight from foot to foot, looking embarrassed.

"Sarah, we are waiting," Mother said sharply.

"Beggin' yer pardon, ma'am," Sarah said with a side-glance at a contented Mr. Tatters, snoozing near the hearth. "But this next part sounds like a fairy story, and I'm the only one to see it. Save for that Lady Cynthia. And, well, I hope you won' think I've gone quite daft."

Now, Mother lost her patience and snapped. "We know you're not daft, Sarah. What in the name of all the gods happened?"

At these words, Sarah took courage and forged ahead.

"It's like I said. She walked over to the empty cage and talked to it. Next, all the roses in the vases glowed, shriveled up, and the dried petals fell to the ground. Then there was a glow about the lady, and she stepped out of her cloak wearing a gown fit for a goddess. I've never seen anything like it—gold, silver, and jewels a plenty. With her diamond tiara and Miss Griselda's slippers, well, I admit, her appearance quite took my breath away."

True to her word, Sarah appeared a bit breathless after describing the scene, so I lifted my hands in entreaty.

"What next, Sarah?"

Sarah leaned in. "Then she talked to the empty cage again, and you won' believe it but that scooped-out pumpkin began to glow and grow. It grew until I took quite a fright. It grew right into an orange carriage, sitting right there in the drive."

Sarah placed her fists on her hips and went on. "Well, that Cynthia stood staring at that orange monstrosity for a moment and then turned to the empty cages and yelled, "I want to arrive like a princess, not some object of mockery."

Several snorts of suppressed laughter, including one from me, broke out around the table, but the outbursts were quickly quelled by a look from Mother. Sarah, who appeared pleased with our response, took Mother's non-verbal hint and started again.

Our storyteller raised a hand and jabbed at the air with her index finger. "That lady pointed at the monstrous orange pumpkin and yelled, 'You have to do my wishes.' Then she stomped her feet and waved her hands at the giant pumpkin again and again, like she was going plain mad.

"Soon the pumpkin glowed again and changed to a golden carriage, still a bit too orange to my taste, but it seemed to satisfy Lady Cynthia."

Sarah glanced around to see how we were receiving her news. And when our only response was attentive silence, she recommenced.

"The lady picked up the cage containing the gray mice and placed it in front of the carriage. Then she talked to that empty cage, and those mice glowed for a moment before bursting the cage apart and sprouting into six mouse-gray horses, all fastened in harnesses."

Sarah paused, looked up as if to the heavens, and slid her eyes around the group. A fearful expression entered her face.

"That's when the wind began. It whistled like chill death. All this scared me somethin' silly, and I thought this isn't natural. The gods never meant us to make carriages out of pumpkins or horses out of mice. I have to stop that little vixen before she stirs up the very heavens in protest.

"I left my window watch and ran to the door, hollering to Hannah and Rebecca to meet me out front for I was sore afraid, and my heart warned me to fear for our lives."

We all turned to see Hannah and Rebecca standing at the other end of the table gripping one another as if for protection, their eyes round as saucers, their heads nodding in unison at Sarah's report. They offered no words, so we turned again to Sarah.

"When I opened the front door, I saw Cynthia put on her cloak and speak to that empty cage one last time. A glow engulfed the hissing basket and the barking Rags, and there before my eyes stood Mr. Tatters as a bearded footman and Rags as a coachman with shaggy hair.

"That's when the wind picked up in earnest, and Hannah and Rebecca joined me at the door. Lady Cynthia leaped into her golden carriage and took off like a fox chased by hounds. A wailing sound, like the coming of death, grew with the wind, and I knew in my bones that we had to flee or perish. So we fled, the lot of us."

Sarah glanced down the table again at Hannah and

Rebecca. They both nodded furiously, and Sarah went on.

"We ran, we hobbled, we stumbled, and got back up, but we kept moving to escape from the wailing wind. The very breath of life was being sucked out of the air around us. As we ran, we found it harder and harder to breathe. I thought we would die.

"We crossed through the manor gatehouse and I stumbled to the earth too short of breath and too pained in my sides to move any farther. Hannah and Rebecca tried to raise me, but there was no strength left in me."

Sarah looked around at all of us, clearly wanting to know if we believed the gravity of her situation. Appearing satisfied by our alarmed expressions, she picked up where she left off.

"But I did not die. I found I could breathe. The air outside the gatehouse was windy but breathable, and we lay there for several minutes catching our breath. Then I noticed that cows, sheep, goats, chickens, birds, and even swarms of insects had fled with us. The area near us teemed with life.

"The wailing wind continued for a time; I couldn't tell ya how long."

She glanced at Hannah and Rebecca who shrugged, so Sarah went on.

"Bit by bit the wind stopped, and we looked back at the manor grounds and saw a wasteland. Skeletal trees, flowers, shrubs, and grass withered like a land cursed. There were small skeletons of animals that had not escaped littering the ground, a land without life. It's just like…"

Sarah paused and whispered her conclusion to her silent listeners.

"Like the Dead Castle."

After Sarah's whispered pronouncement, no one said a word. But Abigail, with Hannah's assistance, roused herself to tend the stew. The rest of us were all pondering Sarah's tragic report when Rags began to bark in earnest. I stood, left the table, and opened the door to check on my canine friend.

As a faintest hint of light touched the eastern horizon, the object of his excitement approached the cottage—Cynthia, wearing nothing but her undergarments.

She did not look the elegant princess now with her white undergarments streaked and smudged, a sure sign that she had been hiding in the leftover crops or shrubs to conceal herself as she snuck her way to the cottage, apparently having no other alternative in her present state of dress—or more correctly state of undress.

I wanted her to myself, so I closed the door behind me.

Several fairies, with their evening illumination, acknowledged my presence by circling above my head as I walked into the yard. In contrast, all of the winged sprites in the vicinity vacated a vast circumference around my stepsister as she paraded past the rosebush canes and toward the cottage, wearing orange-smeared undergarments dotted with rose petals, a single shoe, a tiara topped with a chunk of pumpkin rind, and a regal bearing that contrasted starkly with her appearance. If I hadn't been so angry with Cynthia, her plight might have been comical, but I couldn't laugh. I saw only the woman who had taken my slippers, stolen my fiancé, destroyed healthy land, endangered lives, and killed fairies for her own selfish gain.

The urge to spring at her, take her to the ground, and paint her face with dirt like I'd been itching to do for months was strong, but her stench repelled me. Cynthia, who had wisely stopped out of arm's reach, eyed me like a combatant.

Sneering, I gestured to her attire—or lack of it. "I guess we now know what happened to those diamonds you thought I'd stolen."

My stepsister ignored my comment, lifted her chin, and delivered her opening statement like a jab to the ribs. "You are the true ruler of LaFairia, Griselda."

Shocked, I backed up, too stunned for a verbal response.

Cynthia laughed mirthlessly. "Surely *you* know this. According to the banned historical books, the rulers of LaFairia have always had fairy sight. That dull Prince Charmain clearly has no such virtue."

Nearly gagging from the stench, I replied, "You are delusional. Fairy sight was common before King Benedict's reign."

She snapped back. "No, it wasn't. Only King Nicholas had fairy sight. His stepbrother Benedict did not. So to protect his claim to the throne, Benedict started that little fiction and unjustly put those suspected of fairy sight to death. He was searching for King Nicholas's son, who allegedly died. It says so in *History of the Realm*—well, not in the book but in the margin notes. They are most illuminating." Here Cynthia sighed, as if sympathizing with me. "So it seems, my dear sister, that by some mysterious twist of fortune, you are an heir without a throne."

As my head spun with the absurdity of Cynthia's claims and with nausea from her foul smell, I remembered the second part of the margin notes I had seen in the book, *Legends of the Fairy Kingdom*: Fairy-blessed items grant the bearer influence, sometimes possessed by the king.

Even though I had to admit that the first part of the statement was true, I was disinclined to grant the margin notes unquestioned merit. Besides, I knew that my lying stepsister was just playing with me, and I wouldn't have it.

"Your words are disloyal to the prince. It is you who have created the fiction."

Cynthia didn't respond immediately but looked quizzically at me for a couple of seconds.

She blew out a short laugh. "He didn't tell you. Your father never told you before he died. "

It felt like she had kicked me in the gut. I couldn't breathe. The cruelty of speaking of my father in this manner astonished me and renewed my wish to take her to the ground. But the truth that my father had planned to inform me of things regarding our fairy sight and had been unable to do so gave some weight to my stepsister's words. A wave of pain coursed through me that brought moisture to my eyes.

To combat my feelings, I curled my fists and spat out my reply. "My father has nothing to do with this, and I refuse to be involved in your fantastical imaginings."

Cynthia smiled, her eyes following the circlet of winged attendants over my head. "Oh, but you are involved. It is within my power to tell Lord Ursa that you and your sister have fairy sight like the rulers of old. The penalty may have been forgotten, but it is still death."

Though I knew that Cynthia and I were enemies, I hoped her animosity would not reach this far.

I grasped for a negotiating point. "Then you would inform on yourself, for you, too, have fairy sight."

My stepsister leaned back slightly with a startled expression, her forehead creased. "But I do not…"

With a finger pointing toward the single, soiled, yet still shining slipper on her foot, I raised my eyebrows accusingly. "Oh, yes, you do. That very slipper accuses you. And everyone at the feast saw you wearing the pair of them. The prince has the second."

Alarm registered in her widening eyes.

I furthered my assertion. "The law states: Any person suspected of fairy sight shall be apprehended, tried, and, if found guilty, executed. It is really quite clear."

Fear settled into her eyes, like an animal in a trap. "Then…then we share a family secret…a secret that we all must be faithful to keep."

With a sense of relief that Cynthia would take the secret seriously, if only for her own sake, I nodded. Then wanting to encourage our reluctant alliance, though it pained me to include my stepsister, I replied, "Yes, we must be faithful to family."

In response, she tilted her head and eyed me appraisingly, pondering my statement, her own resistance to our familial bond as clear as mine. Finally, she exhaled and her shoulders relaxed. "Agreed."

Then her eyes glanced from the bright fairies hovering above my head to those in the surrounding garden, their movements subdued and their glows dim. She took a step toward a group of fairies. They moved away en mass. She tried again with the same result.

My one-shoed, tiara-wearing, undergarment-clothed stepsister frowned. "Why are the fairies so far away?"

With deep satisfaction, I said, "Because you stink."

Her chin raised; her nose tilted up. "I beg your pardon."

"You beg my pardon?" I said, gesturing at the withdrawn fluttering beings. "The fairies keep their distance because you killed some of them at the manor. Your wishes killed them. Now, as a result, you reek to them—and to me."

Cynthia blanched and said, "I did no such thing."

She looked around the garden, tried again to take a few steps toward some fairies, and just like before, they backed farther away.

"Oh, but you did," I said. "And now you know the Dead Castle that scowls down at Rella Manor from the distant hills. Well, now it has a Dead Manor scowling back."

Now, Cynthia really did look white, ghostly even. "How could you know of this?"

"Because Hannah, Rebecca, and Sarah are here after barely escaping with their lives. Sarah told us the whole thing."

Cynthia gulped and glanced at the cottage. "Sarah is here?"

I enjoyed her discomfort. "Yep."

For the first time in our acquaintance, Cynthia looked remorseful. "I never meant to…" Cynthia stopped and started again. "I only meant to…"

Chapter 23

Revelations

While Cynthia fumbled with her words, I reeled
from the revelation she had just dumped on me. Could
what she said be true? If even a part of it was true, I felt
like an idiot. I should have figured it out somehow. Yet,
why would I ever think that I had royal blood? It was
too far-fetched. But then hadn't I always thought that
my father would make a much better king? And instead
of brushing off my idea as amusing, Father had sternly
clamped down on the topic. Had he been trying to
maintain his secret? Even from me—until I was ready
for the burden of truth.

As I pondered this astounding possibility, the
sound of galloping horses approached on the still-dim
road, torches held aloft by their riders. Cynthia spun
about with alarm on her face and sprinted past me into
the kitchen. Several volleys of yelling ensued with
Cynthia's and Sarah's voices rising above the rest.
Cynthia re-emerged clad in an ankle-length cloak. Her
hair looked like someone had mangled it, and her tiara
was off kilter and now missing its pumpkin rind
ornament, but she took a large breath and re-established
her regal bearing. Following her, family members and
servants spilled from the kitchen with Sarah in pursuit
of Cynthia, Mother trying to maintain calm, and

everyone else observing the show. Lieutenant Jon, holding that lantern again in the faint light, hung back and displayed no inclination to become involved in family battles.

Prince Charmain and four castle guards carrying torches reined to a halt outside the gate to the yard, dismounted, tied their mounts to the fence, and marched into the garden. Sarah, with her fingers just sinking into Cynthia's tiara-crowned hair, caught sight of the prince, froze, and backed off quickly.

Cynthia, her hair and tiara awry, shook off Sarah's attack, pulled the borrowed cloak, Mother's I thought, securely about her undergarments, and paraded regally to the prince.

She curtsied. "Your Highness, how charming. To what do we owe the honor of your visit?"

The prince and guards, clearly puzzled by what they'd walked in on, exchanged glances without speaking until the silence became uncomfortable. Prince Charmain looked toward me; his eyes implored my help. I raised my eyebrows and kept my mouth shut. After all, the easily led prince had gotten himself into this predicament. It wasn't mine to solve. Finally, it occurred to the weak-minded scion that he was supposed to be in charge here.

He pulled out my slipper. "Lady Cynthia, you left your slipper at the castle. We thought to follow you south on the King's Way before realizing that you would likely be here." He held out the footwear.

Cynthia approached, took my slipper, and smiled up into his eyes. "How kind of you, my prince."

His Highness looked dumbly from Cynthia to me, no longer the accusing prince of the dance, but a confused prince caught in a web. I felt my heart, which had so recently burned with betrayal, now softened to my spineless friend. There was no real harm in him. However, the combination of an impressionable nature and Cynthia's single-minded influence through the slippers had clearly overwhelmed such a character.

I curtsied. "May I wish you every imaginable happiness, Your Highness?"

Prince Charmain reddened and moved his mouth as if to speak, but Cynthia interrupted with a smile of triumph on her face. "We thank you for your good wishes to His Highness and myself."

Here the prince looked startled, reddened even more, and stammered, "Y-yes, thank you."

With that last "thank you," I'd had enough: enough of being polite, enough of Cynthia, Prince Charmain, and his entourage, and enough of the entire, terrible evening. They all had to go. Now.

I put on my best insincere smile, reminiscent of many I'd seen from Cynthia, and pursued my goal of a Cynthia-free home.

"You are both most welcome. Perhaps Lady Cynthia would feel more comfortable staying in the castle in attendance upon the queen until your nuptials. It would be a loss to our little family, but I do so want what is best for my dear stepsister."

The prince now looked like he wanted the ground to open up and claim him, but I had painted him into a corner. Cynthia's eyes narrowed, but I knew she wouldn't object. First, she didn't want to compromise her engagement, and second, to be installed in the castle was her dearest desire. So what if this stretched the bounds of propriety. There was a lot that was indecent about all of this.

Mother, knowing that it would really be more appropriate for Cynthia to stay with us at present, interceded. "Cynthia is family and is most welcome to remain until the ceremony."

The prince turned to my stepsister. "What is your wish, Lady Cynthia?"

Cynthia, eyes glitteringly aware of what I was about, stretched a smile across her teeth. "Though I am grateful to be included in the family circle, I do not wish to be parted from you, Your Highness. I would be pleased to attend the queen."

Now, it was my turn to cast a smug smile, because I couldn't imagine Cynthia being pleased to attend anyone, not even the queen. My stepsister clearly imagined the same, because her smile looked like it might crack.

The prince looked uncomprehendingly at Cynthia for a moment and then remembered himself. "So be it." Then he turned to all of us. "We will no longer intrude on your evening. Good evening to you all."

And after a helpless look in my direction, he led Cynthia and his attendants away.

After Prince Charmain and Cynthia left, Mother rounded on the group of us and leveled a directive. "Now, about Sarah's story, there is to be no further talk of it."

Sarah lifted her hands to the heavens. "But it's the gods' truth, ma'am. And beggin' yer pardon, for I know how you feel about fairy talk…"

Sarah glanced at me before continuing.

"How she did it I can't pretend to know, but that minx of a Cynthia must've caught some fairies and made some wishes, evil wishes that cursed her land."

Mother took a deep breath and settled her shoulders. "I do not doubt you, Sarah. But neither my husband nor I permitted such talk while the girls were growing up, and that is not going to change, especially not now."

Mother finished with a severe look around the group and received nods of acquiescence from Abigail and Abel, Hannah and Rebecca, and Isabella and Sarah.

After I, too, nodded agreeably to her, she turned to Lieutenant Jon. "If I may count on your discretion, Lieutenant?"

He bowed. "That you may, ma'am. Please call on me, or perhaps on Captain Branner, if you encounter any difficulty, but now perhaps you will permit me to attend to your horse and wagon."

With Mother's acceptance, he nodded to the group, caught my eyes, lingering a moment as though wishing to say more, and then led the mare to the shed.

The rest of them trundled back into the kitchen for Abigail's hearty stew, but Mother directed me to stay outside. The moon and stars, fading as the eastern horizon cast a thin light, along with glowing fairies that Mother could not see, shone on us as we wandered near the rhododendrons and the garden seat.

Mother, who generally looked strong to me, now seemed fragile. Her hands clasped tightly in front of her heart, her breath came fast and shallow, she faced me, worry marring her face. "Sarah's story…" She couldn't bring herself to continue.

Not sure whether my words would be welcome or not, I offered, "Sarah was telling the whole truth, Mother. I'm sure of it."

Mother hugged herself and shivered. "Of course, she was. But this is a dangerous affair. And that stepdaughter of mine…"

Apparently, Mother was done with standing up for the soon-to-be real princess and now accepted that Cynthia was not whom she had pretended to be, but the thought gave me no pleasure. It was truly unsettling to realize that such an untrustworthy person now shared the family secret.

Then my recent conversation with Cynthia came to mind. Her fear of exposure seemed sincere, and her agreement to be faithful to family seemed genuine if entirely self-interested. So because she was implicated as well, I trusted that she had enough survival instinct to be true to her word.

Hoping that my words would relieve my mother's anxiety, I said, "Cynthia realizes that she, too, has fairy sight of a sort, and she agreed to be faithful to family. After all, she is in danger, too."

Mother's brow furrowed, and her eyes shifted up and to the side in thought. "Yes," she said slowly, her focus sliding to me. "Yes, she is a smart girl, and we can trust that she will protect her own neck."

I watched as Mother squared her shoulders and took a deep breath, resolution settling into her expression. "Yes, let us pray that she will realize her culpability and that there is some goodness in the girl."

Then her face fell. "I am so sorry about your ruined betrothal. Your father's plan has failed."

At that she embraced me quickly and then fled into the cottage, joining the others inside. I watched her, expecting a sense of disappointment to fill my heart, but to my surprise, it did not. A sense of relief took its place.

I realized that as much as Prince Charmain had been my friend, I hadn't really wanted to marry him, except to fulfill Father's plan. It felt like I was betraying my father with that thought, even though the failed engagement was not my fault.

As I mused over the feelings of relief versus betrayal, a door to one the sheds shut sharply, drawing my attention, and the lean, wiry form of Lieutenant Jon, finished with caring for the horse and wagon, approached.

As the groom-courier-lieutenant drew near, I wondered that he never remained who he seemed to be and felt a little on guard. After all, he had become privy to so many of my family secrets, and I wasn't sure whether he was a friend or foe, which was a little unfair, because he had been nothing but helpful to the family. I simply still nursed my grudge about losing to him in a race, as well as my irritation at his mocking little half grin. But when he reached me, no grin graced his features.

He gestured to the garden bench. "Can we talk?"

The fairies capering nearby still exuded their nighttime glow though dawn now lit the eastern sky.

Uneasy about this enigmatic man, I said, "I am too tired to hear any more surprises, Lieutenant."

"There are things you need to hear." He paused and added, "And it might ease your mind to know the truth." He pointed again to the bench.

Though I wasn't sure that I could trust him, the sense of authority behind his declaration caught my attention, steeling my resolve to hear him out.

As the lieutenant waited for me to sit, he stood

leaning against a garden seat trellis. Several tree fairies circled his head, cavorting in a way that showed more than casual interest in the man. I remembered back to his nosy question about what I saw in the maple tree when we first met and wondered, once again, who was this groom-courier-lieutenant?

No longer reluctant to hear anything he had to say, I crossed my arms over my chest, glared at him, and said, "You have kept me in the dark long enough, Lieutenant. Tell me everything."

He tightened his lips around his teeth and moved them from side to side indecisively before answering. "You know the stories about how King Nicholas and his heir died from illness and Nicholas's stepbrother Benedict then assumed the throne?"

I nodded, now uneasy with this commonly known story.

The lieutenant glanced around the yard, down the lane, and across the harvested fields before continuing in a lower voice. "What you don't know is that King Nicholas was not ill. He was poisoned by his stepbrother Benedict, but the infant son escaped a similar fate thanks to the queen and his nurse."

Isabella's description of the moving fresco came to mind, along with the realization that it showed events from the past. I no longer nodded at Jon's words, my insides became still, and my body felt unsteady like I was standing on the edge of a cliff.

"They traveled to the High King at Soltar City and found refuge while this small kingdom, LaFairia, fell into famine and internal strife, those accused of fairy sight facing execution."

I listened in silence. My father had spoken well of

the distant High King. It did not surprise me that he would give refuge to the heir to the LaFairian throne, LaFairia being a petty kingdom under the High King. I waited to hear more.

"The true heir grew up in Soltar City for more than thirty years and then returned to LaFairia to rule once again, only not directly from the throne."

My hands and feet became cold, and my breath grew faster. Though I could see where Lieutenant Jon was going, I didn't want him to say it.

He took a deep breath and said it anyway. "This royal bloodline continued through to your father, who, while he did not sit on the throne, ruled—or at least greatly influenced—LaFairia through selfless service like the generations before him."

My hands and arms shook. The memory of Cynthia's words mocked me. *He never told you.*

I felt blind, betrayed, angry. Father should have told me.

Lieutenant Jon looked at the ground, lifted a hand, and rubbed his chin. "I'm sorry. It is as I thought; he never told you."

My eyes welled at the sting of his words. They sounded like criticism of my father, and I wouldn't tolerate it.

"He died, you fool. He said he had something to tell me, but he died."

Now I wept; I cried more than I had ever cried for my father, deep gulping sobs that shook my body. It felt like a dam had burst and flooded everything in life with pain. I feared it would never stop.

My companion said nothing, just let me cry, and in time, the sobs subsided to a steady watering of tears and then to sniffing. I hadn't realized it, but Lieutenant Jon had come to sit next to me, his elbows on his knees, his head bowed to his fists, the fairies above both of us now subdued in their movements as if respecting my grief.

I shuddered a few breaths in and out. "I miss him." Fresh tears flowed, but the dam burst was over.

My bench mate looked at me. "I know, Grizzy."

He had never called me Grizzy before, and it tugged a wet smile from one corner of my mouth.

He pulled in a long breath and let it out slowly. "You are your father's heir, and by virtue of that, the throne of LaFairia is rightfully yours."

I covered my face with my hands. "But I don't want it."

"No, you don't, but that too is a mark of your heritage, for a true king or queen never desires preeminence."

I felt overwhelmed by the news, but at the same time, I knew it was true. And a question formed in my mind. I considered Lieutenant Jon.

"How do you know all this? Who are you and where do you come from?"

"We have covered this, Miss Griselda. When we met, I told you I was from the east."

I glared at him with a look that said, "insufficient explanation."

He relented. "When your father was killed, it alarmed and worried the leadership in Soltar City. I was sent by the High King to investigate and offer some token of assistance. I've worked with Captain Branner and a handful of trustworthy guards, who have been watching over you at Rella Manor." Here he grew sheepish, looking at me sideways. "Except for that morning you left unannounced and got waylaid in the forest."

I remembered how alarmed the lieutenant had appeared when Sarah had informed him of our attack en route to market day, as well as the ready provision of a returning escort, and finally the occasional guard that I had seen on the periphery of the manor grounds.

The representative of the High King continued. "It is important to work with local authorities, like Branner, because even though LaFairia is a distant vassal of the High King, this is not my kingdom. It is not my place to interfere."

But my thoughts settled on the connection between the High King and my father. "So all those leaders in the Soltar City, they knew who my father was while I did not?"

He looked caught. "Yes."

I scowled at him. "Very well, High King's Emissary, I realize my family line now, but why do we have fairy sight?"

Jon sighed. "In most of the kingdoms, this knowledge is well known, at least as legend."

I waited, impatient to finally learn what my father had never told me.

As though embarrassed to go on, Jon said, "Millennia ago, humankind was a savage, self-destructive race, so the gods sent what you might call angels..." Here he chortled. "Or really big fairies, to marry humans and give birth to the royal lines of Soltaria and its petty kingdoms: kings less inclined to war, more inclined to peace; less inclined to greed, more inclined to benevolence; and such. So that is why the royal line can see fairies, they are distantly related to fairies by birth. They are called fairy kin."

"So why isn't this in our history?" I challenged.

"It is," he said. "But King Benedict had all the old books burned and threatened anyone who talked about such things as being guilty of fairy sight. He had many honest people executed. It became necessary for this kingdom to only acknowledge fairies within the constraints of King Benedict's dictums. Or folks paid with their lives."

"So why didn't the High King do anything?"

"He did. Though LaFairia is the most distant petty kingdom, he sent settlers to mitigate the trouble when they could. The High King at the time trained the heir to the LaFairian throne, your great-great-grandfather, and sent him back to the country. With the true king's return and with his growing, though quiet, influence, the tide of famine, civil unrest, and executions turned—and continued that way through to your father.

"It was a good plan to have you marry the prince. In time, it would have solved the problems of this petty kingdom."

I sighed. "I know—and I did try to make it work." My shoulders sagged. "But I failed. So how am I supposed to fill my father's shoes? They're too big. I am all alone."

He shook his head. "First of all, there are others who can pull fairies—at least a tiny bit. They just don't know that they are doing it."

I gaped at him in disbelief.

He smiled. "Oh, yes. It's called having a green thumb. You know people who have it."

I pondered the farmers nearby and smiled. "Farmer Heaten."

"Yes," Jon said. "That farmer is probably the most powerful, but he doesn't know it. He just loves his crops, and they and the fairy kingdom respond."

Relieved, I said, "So I don't have to pull fairies."

"Yes, in the cultivated acreage, you do. The scale of work done by the fairy sighted is greater than any green thumb."

"Then I still don't know how to manage it."

"Don't worry. Your father and grandfathers worked the land for generations. The virtue of their work will last for a time. So you have time to learn."

"How much time?"

"It depends on the area, on how recently your father visited."

I nodded, pondering the difference between the pristine fields around the castle and the imp-dotted acreage near Rella Manor.

Then a dilemma occurred to me. "But even if I do learn to pull fairies, how will I get to all the places that need them?"

He smiled. "Between Captain Branner and myself, we can work something out. You are not alone."

The assurance that I was not alone brought fresh leakage to my eyes and nose. I turned my head to the side and tried to wipe the moisture with my sleeve. Trying to keep my voice steady, I replied, "Thank you."

He put a hand hesitantly on my shoulder. "You are welcome."

Part of me wanted to lean into his assurance, but part of me needed to be strong and self-assured. I pulled in a deep—rather sniffling—breath and nodded like I was fine.

He rose and, after gazing at me for a moment, said,

"I will let you return to your family." He began to walk away and then turned. "Remember, you are not alone."

I watched him leave the fairy-lit garden, turn down Hart Cottage Lane, and raise his hand in farewell. I returned the gesture, and he walked toward the brightening dawn.

Chapter 24

Finally Fairies

Instead of returning to Hart Cottage, I sat on the garden bench, wished I had my cloak to ward off the chill, and watched the glowing fairies hover about the plants in the yard: the canes of the rosebushes, dried stalks of the bulbs, and the evergreen leaves of the rhododendrons. Occasionally a group of them would swarm over to me and loop around my head several times before returning to their dawn routines.

The more I watched the luminescent beings, the more the joy of their selfless service infused my being. I didn't even feel cold anymore. It occurred to me that even though I had always been able to see fairies and had joined them in their sunrise routine, I had never simply sat with calmness for an extended time and watched them. Always being so focused on achievement, I had never simply basked at length in the feeling of their presence. That awareness washed over me and filled me. At first like a stream filling a pond and then like a river pouring into a lake.

I stood. My breathing deepened, each inhale a giddy gladness bubbling in my chest, each exhale a growing sense of lightness. Standing near the rhododendrons, I continued to breathe, increasingly intoxicated with the effervescent feeling.

Soon the fingers of the sun crept from the east across the landscape, and the busy fairies ceased their activities and rose to greet the rays. Arianna flew in from the west, graced me with a radiant smile, and proceeded to deliberately breathe along with me. As we breathed in, her glow increased. As we breathed out, her glow expanded.

As the rays of sunlight touched us both, Arianna faced the shining orb. And side by side, we breathed. To my joy and surprise, tiny points of light, representing brand new half-inch fairies began to dot the area directly in front of me. Presently, I realized, that I, too, was glowing. And the more I breathed in and out, the more tiny dots of fairy lights appeared in the sunlight before me.

In wonder, I realized, this is easy.

Arianna, reading my thoughts, nodded. "You were trying too hard before, and it blocked your potential."

Then she whizzed around me in congratulatory excitement as the sun blazed across the landscape and the fairies, both old and new, joined their queen in celebration.

I had done it.

Finally.

And I hadn't even used my hands, just my breathing and my overflowing heart.

So I would be able to serve the kingdom after all. And it didn't matter that I would not be queen. My father had served as a commoner, so I could, too. Lieutenant Jon and Captain Branner would figure out a logical reason for me to travel where I was needed. And Cynthia would keep the secret. After all, it was her secret, too.

I sought out Isabella's bench once again and settled onto it. The tiny fairies that I had manifested were already busy about the garden, humming life into the soon-to-be autumn soil and resting plants, preparing them for the time of sleepy winter rejuvenation.

Arianna hovered over my shoulder, grasped a hank of my hair, and then settled next to my neck. She, too, gazed at the new garden pixies. "Your father would be proud."

I glanced at my ancestral home, Hart Cottage, and smiled, the joy of the morning fairy ritual still fresh in my heart. "Yes, I think he would."

A word about the author...

Lee Renwick Steele lives with an orange and white kitty in a small home situated near red maples, rhododendron shrubs, and abundant avian wildlife: juncos, robins, white-crowned sparrows, towhees, and the occasional flicker pecking in the attic. She has an MFA in Creative Writing for Children and Young Adults and is a member of her local writers' association and SCBWI. She enjoys reading, writing, traveling, long walks, spending time with family and friends, and moments of quiet. *Griselda Rella* is her first novel.